Shadows
in the Night

Books by Jane Finnis

The Aurelia Marcella Roman Mysteries
Shadows in the Night (formerly *Get Out or Die*)
A Bitter Chill
Buried Too Deep
Danger in the Wind

Shadows in the Night

An Aurelia Marcella Roman Mystery

Jane Finnis

Poisoned Pen
PRESS

Sourcebooks, Poisoned Pen Press and the colophon are registered trademarks of
Sourcebooks, Inc.

Published by Poisoned Pen Press, an imprint of Sourcebooks
P.O. Box 4410, Naperville, Illinois 60567-4410
(630) 961-3900
sourcebooks.com

Library of Congress Cataloging-in-Publication data is on file with the publisher.

Printed and bound in The United States of America.
POD 10 9 8 7 6 5 4 3 2

For Richard

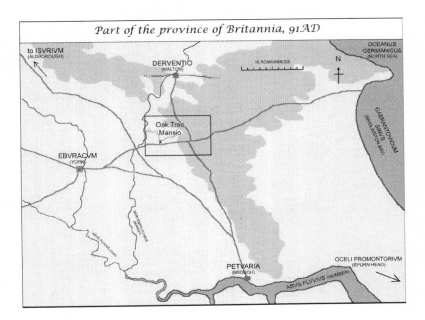

Part of the province of Britannia, 91AD

to ISVRIVM
(ALDBOROUGH)

OCEANUS
GERMANICUS
(NORTH SEA)

DERVENTIO
(MALTON)

10 ROMAN MILES

N

GABRANTOVICVM
SIN'S BAY
(BRIDLINGTON BAY)

Oak Tree
Mansio

EBVRACVM
(YORK)

DER DAVO FLVVIVS

ABVS FLVVIVS (HUMBER)

PETVARIA
(BROUGH)

OCELI PROMONTORIVM
(SPURN HEAD)

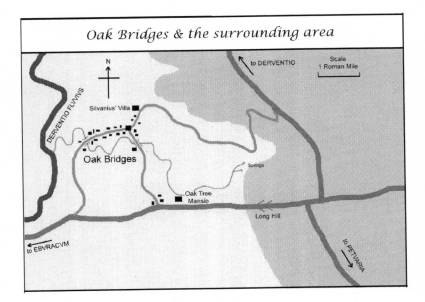

Oak Bridges & the surrounding area

N

Scale
1 Roman Mile

to DERVENTIO

DERVENTIO FLVVIVS

Silvanius' Villa

Oak Bridges

Springs

Oak Tree
Mansio

Long Hill

to EBVRACVM

to PETVARIA

Chapter I

It was a beautiful August dawn, the best sort of summer weather. The only thing that spoilt it was the body.

I didn't notice him at first. I unbolted the front door and strolled out across the forecourt, and up the short track to the main road, enjoying the fresh morning air. The market day traffic was coming down the hill, heading into town. I watched three farmers leading donkeys loaded with baskets of vegetables, then a creaking ox-cart piled with sacks, and two barefoot girls carrying a cage of chickens and driving some goats. The goats scattered as one of our neighbours trotted past in a smart Roman two-wheeled gig, calling out "'Morning, Aurelia," and I gave him a wave. A gang of native field-slaves shambled into view, driven uphill by a couple of mounted Roman overseers with whips. One of the natives turned and spat in my direction when the overseers weren't looking. The low sunlight coloured everything gold, even the scruffy slaves.

I could spend all day watching the world go by. Except of course I couldn't, because I had work to do. There's more to being an innkeeper than standing around collecting the customers' money, and getting free samples from the wine-shippers, although those are two of the pleasanter parts of the job. So I turned back to the house, surveying the wide paved area where our customers would park their animals and vehicles later. It was empty now except for the giant oak tree in the middle, and under that, in a pool of deep shadow, was the body.

I'm sorry, I know this isn't the proper way to start an official report to the Governor of the province of Britannia. But I've never done one before. Some people might say I shouldn't be doing one now, it's not woman's work. But my brother has asked me to write down the details of this whole business, so I'll do my best, and you'll just have to tidy it up before it gets to His Excellency's desk.

I should start with the date, I suppose. Right then. It was the tenth year of the reign of Domitian Caesar, on the fourth day of August, the day before the Nones. I know the date for certain, because on the first day of each month we get a delivery of wine from our wholesaler, and this was wine-day plus three. Selling wine to thirsty customers is part of what I do for a living, so that sort of thing sticks in my mind. I'm Aurelia Marcella, the innkeeper of the Oak Tree Mansio, which is about fifteen miles from Eburacum, and just up the road from the small town that we Romans call Oak Bridges. I run the best guest-house and posting-station on the road from the River Humber to the garrison at Eburacum. Well I would say that, wouldn't I?

At first I thought the man was dead, he lay so still. I saw a tall figure huddled up in a travelling cloak, with a huge lump on the back of his head and his fair hair matted with blood. He was a Roman, by the look of him; yes, definitely Roman, and well-dressed, and apparently stone dead right outside my front door. Just what I needed to start the day, and me with a hangover that wouldn't have disgraced the whole ninth legion.

Then I looked more closely, and realised he was still breathing. Just. So perhaps he might be a drunk left over from last night's party. We'd had quite a wild time—well, wild for a remote corner of northern Britannia. Two young military tribunes were staying with us, on a spot of hunting leave from their legion at Eburacum. They'd had a successful couple of days, and were celebrating by buying wine for themselves and beer for the locals as if they'd had a win at the races.

But I didn't recognise the good sheepskin travelling cloak, nor the light riding-boots sticking out beneath it; and when I gently turned his head to see what he looked like, I didn't know his face. There was blood all over it, from a cut on his cheek, and his whole face was a mass of bruises. I bent over and felt beneath the hair, touching his neck. He was still warm, but not very.

"You need to be inside, my friend," I said. "And I need some muscle to help me get you there."

I listened for the usual morning noises: horses trampling in the stable yard, chickens protesting as someone searched the hen-house for eggs, and, yes, good, the sound of hammering and whistling coming from the workshop near the stables.

"Taurus!" I yelled. Taurus is my handyman. "Come here, will you? Quick!"

Taurus came ambling round the corner. He's a big man and never seems to hurry, but he can move quickly when he wants to.

"'Morning, Mistress Aurelia. Something wrong? Oh, Saturn's balls! Is he dead?"

"Not quite. Give me a hand to get him inside, will you?"

He stood staring down at the body for a few heartbeats, then he said, "Somebody didn't like him very much."

"No, really?" Well, Taurus isn't the brightest of my slaves, and there's no law against stating the obvious. "Let's move him indoors. You pick him up gently, I'll steady his head."

He bent and lifted the limp body carefully in his arms, making it look easy, and I held the head steady, feeling the sticky blood on my fingers. We carried him through the front door into the bar-room, which was empty this early in the day, and still full of last night's wine-smells.

"He must've been there all night. There's been a mist, and a heavy dew as well. Not good for a wounded man to be out in the open." Taurus laid the stranger down with great care on one of the benches near the window. I opened the shutters, letting in the light and a draught of cold air.

I tried to remember when the party finished last night. "He wasn't here when the last of the customers went home. I locked up about midnight, I think....I don't recognise him, do you?"

He shook his shaggy head. "No. Nice cloak. Good boots, too. They look like army issue. Rather messed up though."

They certainly were; the uppers were scuffed and muddy. The front of his cloak was slimy too, and his hands were filthy. I opened the cloak out near the hem, and sure enough, his fawn wool leggings were covered in mud and grass. He'd been doing some crawling, whoever he was.

I bent closer for a look. He was around thirty, with fair wavy hair and light eyebrows, and a mouth that looked as if it could have a nice smile. I unfastened his belt and loosened his cloak. His blue wool tunic was well-made and warm, and fastened by another, thinner belt, which had a fancy bronze buckle with a dolphin on it. Carefully I felt him over and moved his arms and legs. Nothing seemed to be broken, but he was cold and pale, and lay like the dead. He'd certainly had a hard knock on the head.

I debated searching him for some sort of identification, but decided to leave it for now, or he would get even colder. First things first.

"Fetch Albia, will you, Taurus. Tell the kitchen girls to bring blankets and put some water on to heat. Then get a brazier in here to warm the place a bit. He's chilled to the bone. We'll clean him up, and see if we can wake him."

He ambled off, and almost at once Albia bustled out through the kitchen door.

Albia is my half-sister, and also my housekeeper at the mansio; I call her my chief of staff, and I freely admit I couldn't run the place without her. People don't believe we are sisters, because we each take after our respective mothers. I know that behind our backs we're known as "the pretty one" and "the tough one." Albia's certainly pretty, small, dark, and slim, with bright brown eyes; she's always cheerful and busy, and she isn't nearly as fragile as she appears. Neither is she as stupid as some men think. I don't know why there's a general assumption that women who are pretty and happy are also dim. Men don't make that assumption about me, but I can't work out whether I should be pleased or not. I'm tall and big-boned, with fair hair that waves on its own whether I want it to or not, and green eyes like my mother's. And I don't even *look* fragile.

Anyway Albia's a great person to have around in a crisis. We've been through a few of those since we came to the Oak Tree. I didn't know then that we were at the beginning of another.

"'Morning, Relia, what's…Holy Diana, who's this?" She knelt down beside the man. "He looks a bit the worse for wear! Where did you find him? I thought we'd chucked them all out."

"We did. I found him outside. I don't know how he got into such a mess, but as Taurus just said, somebody didn't like him very much."

"I've seen him before, I think." She frowned thoughtfully, pushing the hair out of her eyes as she bent closer to look into his face. Albia has a marvellous memory for faces. "I just can't place him, but I'm sure…oh well, it'll come." She stood up. "Robbed, I suppose, and beaten up, and managed to crawl here in the dark. It comes to something when a man can't travel the roads at night….ah, wait though." She stopped. She'd just caught sight of the ring he was wearing on his left hand, a gold one with a large emerald in it.

"No self-respecting robber would have left *that* behind," I agreed. "So either the robbers were interrupted, or it wasn't a robbery at all."

We heard footsteps in the hallway just then, and Junius, one of the young officers from last night's party, poked his head in through the hall door. He looked as fresh as the morning dew, which gave me a twinge of envy.

"'Morning, Albia….Aurelia. Any chance of a bite of breakfast? I could murder some bread and cheese and a cup of wine." He stopped, seeing the new arrival on the bench. "I say, who's this? Someone didn't make it home last night?"

"We think he's been attacked," Albia said. "He's got a bump on the head the size of an egg."

"Really? So that was it."

"That was what?" we both asked.

"There was a noise, a couple of hours after we turned in I think. I'd got up to find my water-flask. Bit of a thirst." He grinned. "I've still got a mouth like a sand-pit, actually! Anyhow there was this odd sort of scuffling, dragging sound, and I looked out from my window, but it was pitch dark and I couldn't see anything. I sent my servant across to the stables, to make sure nobody was trying to pinch our horses." He looked at us in turn. "You didn't hear anything?"

Albia shook her head, and I said, "No, I slept like the dead. Your man would have gone out of the door from the guest wing to get to the stable block, not the main front door from the bar-room. So if the noise was this poor fellow being beaten up, or dragging himself here, he wouldn't have found the body. Anyway, as you say, it was pretty dark."

"Oh, I told him to take a torch and patrol round all the buildings, naturally. He reported back that everything was fine."

"Well, he would," Albia chipped in. I gave her a warning look to shut her up. The officers' two servants had had a real skinful last night, and if either of them had stirred himself to patrol efficiently all round our sprawling complex of buildings in the dark, then I'm the Queen of Brigantia. But customers are always right, especially military ones.

Junius just laughed. "Quite right! My man should have seen him. Lazy slob! I'll cut down his wine ration, that'll teach him."

He came over and looked down at the motionless figure. He touched his shoulder and shook him gently, but the man didn't react at all. "Dead to the world, isn't he? I wonder if he's been robbed." I shook my head and pointed to the big emerald.

Junius pulled back the travelling-cloak further than I'd done. "It looks as though his money-belt is still there as well, under his tunic. Wait a bit though, what's this? What do you suppose...." He pointed to a small bone disc, attached by a crude bronze pin to the front of the blue tunic. Just an ordinary looking object, some kind of official medallion or pass perhaps, the sort couriers often wear. But when Junius unpinned it and began to read it, he caught his breath, and when he turned the disc over, he swore.

"What is it?" I held out my hand and took the little disc.

On one side was a rough drawing of a skull, with the words "Shadow of Death" written below it. On the other were a few crudely scratched Latin words:

ALLROMANSWILLBEKILLED

GETOUTORDIE

We stared at it blankly. It might have been in Carthaginian for all the sense it made. It sounds strange now, but at first it didn't seem frightening, just weird. Of course if I'd known what it meant, if I'd had any idea of the trouble it would bring us....

But how could I? How could any of us?

While Albia and I cleaned the stranger up as best we could, a couple of the maids came in with mops and pails, soon followed by most of the kitchen slaves, who naturally found speculating about an unconscious mystery man more fun than washing beakers or chopping vegetables. None of them recognized him, and nobody, it seemed, had heard any unusual noises in the night. Not surprising, as the slaves' quarters are set well back from the road, and anyway slaves tend to become deaf to outside noises at night, that being the nearest they can get to privacy.

"He's quite handsome," one of the girls remarked.

"The perfect Adonis," another scoffed. "If you like them with cuts and bruises. And look at that beautiful black eye!"

Actually, he was quite good-looking: fair hair, a broad forehead, eyes wide-set, prominent chin, and good skin, what you could see of it.

"Still," I commented, "as our grandmother used to say, you can't judge a scroll by looking at its case."

"Our grandmother," Albia smiled, tucking blankets round the still figure, "never read anything in her life except wine-shippers' lists. If she'd felt the need of a corny proverb, she'd have said, you can't judge the vintage by looking at the amphora."

I shooed the slaves back to work, and Albia went off to get Junius some breakfast. I'd seen them flirting last night, so I wasn't surprised when she said she'd serve him herself. He was attractive in his boyish way—early twenties, sandy curly hair, and nice grey eyes. And Albia never can resist a uniform.

I sat on a stool beside the unconscious man for a little while longer, listening to his shallow breathing, and holding the bone disc in my hand. I kept re-reading its sinister message.

ALLROMANSWILLBEKILLED

GETOUTORDIE

A threat to Romans, but why? I mean, why now?

All right, newly conquered barbarians take a while to accept Roman rule. Everybody knows that, at least everybody living in a frontier province, though the scholars sitting in Italia writing their grand histories overlook it sometimes. Fifty years ago when our legions began to conquer Britannia, only a few natives showed up with welcome banquets and carpets of rose petals. Most of them fought hard. There were battles and massacres enough, young men killed, old ones dispossessed, women and children sold as slaves. All quite justifiable, of course, but not calculated to make Rome popular. This area of northern Britannia was on the edge of the old kingdom of Brigantia, and cost our troops some bitter fighting, besides dividing the tribal aristocracy into pro- and anti-Roman factions. A generation ago, it's true, but well within living memory, and conquered people's memories are tenacious and detailed.

But Roman civilians have been settling Britannia for thirty years and more. Ex-soldiers—traders—farmers....Our own family's been in the province nearly twelve years. And the natives have gained so much from our being here. That's what we Romans are good at, bringing civilisation to barbarian lands. We make them part of the modern world, the Roman world, giving them towns and decent roads and trade and education. And as they become civilised they become our equals.

Isn't that what they want? Of course it is. It must be.

But.... "Get out or die...."

Taurus came in with the brazier. He saw the expression on my face, and asked, "What is it, Mistress Aurelia?"

I held out the little bone disc with its grisly skull drawing, and read him the message.

He thought for a while, then shook his head slowly. "It can't be meant for us. It says 'get out.' But we belong here. We've got nowhere to go to. This is where our home is. Not Rome. I've never even *been* to Rome."

"Neither have I." I regret that sometimes. Stuck in the wilds here, it feels as if I'll never get there now. Our family home was in Pompeii, and after we lost that, we left Italia. Britannia was the coming province, the place for Romans to make their fortunes, or so my father believed. Father had left the army by then, a successful centurion with a good reputation and a nice little nest-egg. First we lived in an army settlement, and then— no, you don't want the whole long story. The important point is that he got the concession to set up the mansio here seven years ago, and Albia and I gradually took over the running of it. It's in our brother Lucius' name of course, but we all knew *he'd* never settle down to being an innkeeper, and though I say it myself, Albia and I have made a pretty good job of it. All the same, I shouldn't like to think I'd never see Italia again.

"I was still a girl when we came to Britannia," I said. "And you were only a lad yourself, Taurus."

"Yes." He gave his slow grin. "Your dad bought me for a page-boy. Only I kept spilling things."

I smiled, remembering a couple of disastrous dinner parties where expensive wine ended up splashed over even more expensive gowns. "You're an outdoor man, no doubt about it. Which is more useful when your home's in a frontier province."

"So we do belong here, then. And this warning must be for new people coming over from Rome now. Don't you think so?" His dark eyes looked anxiously for reassurance.

"Yes, it must." But I felt a shiver of cold doubt inside me. The message said "All Romans," and we're Romans. Me, Albia, Taurus, and the half-dozen others we brought with us from

Italia…a handful of Romans, surrounded by countless thousands of native Britons: peasants, craftsmen, traders, and of course our locally bought slaves. We think we're at home, established and permanent. We've made Britannia part of the Empire. But this Shadow of Death, whoever he is, sees things differently and wants us out.

It came to me then, with frightening clarity: supposing other native Britons want us out? Supposing they all do?

Chapter II

I shook myself out of my gloomy pondering and went into the private dining-room where Albia had served bread and cheese and olives, and some reasonable Rhodian to go with it. Junius' friend Marius had surfaced by now, and so had our other three guests, two military contractors and a silver mine expert. The smell of the new bread reminded me I hadn't eaten yet, so I cut a crusty hunk of it, and had a drink—water, not wine, in deference to my hangover, which had started to recede. I began to feel better as I listened to the young tribunes cheerfully planning their day's hunting.

I began planning my own day. I must go outside and check on the stables. The stable-lads were short-handed, but they should cope. All the same, it did no harm to make sure they weren't cutting corners. We're an official mutatio, a posting-station where travellers on government business change horses or mules, and our operation has to be clean and efficient. There was the farm work, too; I liked to keep an eye on our farm foreman, who was competent enough, but inclined to be lazy. Then there was a delivery of olive oil due from one of the wholesalers, and his men needed supervising because they seemed to be under permanent instruction to rip us off. And this afternoon, I was expecting a visit from one of the larger fish in our small provincial pond, the Chief of the Oak Bridges Town Council, no less. He was doing his own bit of supervising, presumably, because we were supplying him with wine for an important dinner. And of course I must make time to see my beautiful black horses, my own special bit of farming enterprise.

But before all that, we'd better move our unconscious visitor to one of the guest-rooms. The first customers would be arriving soon, and it's rather demoralising, if you drop in for a reviving drink, to find yourself sitting next to what looks like a semi-corpse.

I don't suppose you, or anyone reading this report of mine, will ever have visited the Oak Tree, and you're probably picturing something poky and flea-ridden in an unfashionable street of a small provincial town. Well you're wrong. Our town, Oak Bridges, is small and provincial, certainly. I'd call it a village myself, except that the more civilized natives hereabouts have got it officially recognized as a proper town, complete with its own council, and I try not to upset them. Who they had to bribe for that, and what with, you probably know better than I do. Anyway the mansio is a mile or so out of the town, on the main road at the bottom of the Long Hill, which is a stiff climb up to the rolling wold country to the east. Our place is quite big, a farm as well as a mansio. Our main job is to look after officials on the Empire's business, but private guests stay with us from time to time, and we keep open house in the bar-room, where passing travellers, including quite a few natives, drop in for a beaker and a bite to eat.

The bar-room and kitchen and the private dining-room for important guests are in the main block at the front, and there are two wings of rooms sticking out behind, forming three sides of a courtyard. The fourth side is a bathhouse suite, with separate rooms for men and women. Oh yes, we may be in the wilds, but at least we're clean.

The left-hand wing is our private one, mine and Albia's, with windows looking onto a secluded area of garden. The other is for guests. At present there were several spare rooms, so there'd be no problem finding a warm bed for our wounded traveller.

All right, you'll probably cut all that description out on the grounds that the Governor doesn't need a guided tour of the mansio. What I'm trying to make clear is that most of the rooms are connected by corridors and there are several doors to the outside as well. So guests, or anyone, can come and go to the various parts of the house unobserved. Bear that in mind before you start blaming me for not keeping a proper eye on the stranger's room.

Taurus and one of the houseboys carefully carried the man into the cheapest guest room, the one with dull brown walls and without a glazed window. After all, I didn't know who, if anyone, would ever pick up the bill for his stay. As I tucked his blankets round him and Albia opened the shutters, he gave a groan, then a cough, another groan, and opened his eyes. He said, "Burrus! Burrus, are you there?"

Then his gaze seemed to focus properly. He looked at me for a couple of heartbeats, long enough for me to register that his eyes were a very dark blue, almost purple, and that their expression was more surprised than anxious.

"Where am I? Where's Burrus? And who in Hades are you?"

And good morning to you too, sunshine, I thought, but reflected that he was probably feeling pretty foul.

"I'm Aurelia. We're not in Hades though, I'm glad to say."

"Aurelia!" he exclaimed, and lifted his head, which was about all the movement he could manage. "Not....I mean....Aurelia who?"

"Aurelia Marcella. Innkeeper at the Oak Tree Mansio."

"But that's wonderful!" He gazed at me with a sudden dazzling smile, then his eyes closed and his head lolled back. He was unconscious again.

"Gods!" I said. "That's weird."

Albia giggled. "If this was a Greek love story, I'd say the sight of you has just driven him mad with love."

"Be careful," I warned. "It could end up as a Greek tragedy, where the long-suffering heroine beats her sister within an inch of her life for talking rubbish."

One of the maids hurried in just then, to say there was a messenger in the bar-room, and could I please come through.

"I'm busy," I said. "Can't you deal with him? Check his travel pass, get him whatever meal he's entitled to, make a note in the day book....Holy Diana, we only have about fifty couriers a day through here, you should know the drill by now."

"Yes, but he says he's got a letter for you, Mistress. From the Master, could it be?"

"Ah, that's different. I'll come."

Albia said, "We'd better not leave this poor man alone here, Relia. I'll send one of the slaves to sit with him. Baca can do it, she can bring her sewing basket. I'll tell her to fetch one of us if he wakes up."

"Good idea." Baca, aged eight, was a bit young for bar work, but a useful hand with a needle. I headed for the bar-room.

The messenger was a regular, a big tattooed German trooper who quite often changed horses at the Oak Tree on his way through with dispatches to or from the legionary base at Eburacum. He was carrying his usual bulky satchel, and in his hand was a slim papyrus scroll, tied with a cord and sealed with wax. He handed it to me with a mock salute. "I picked it up at Eburacum," he told me, "but they said it was from down south somewhere." He sat down to tuck into a breakfast of beer, bread, and sausage.

Sure enough, it was from my brother, written in his usual untidy scrawl, and dated the middle of July.

> Lucius Aurelius Marcellus to Aurelia Marcella, greetings.
>
> I'm still in the far west at Isca, Sis, spending my hard-earned pay on women and wine. But I hope to be home in time for our birthday, so make sure there's plenty of good Gaulish red in stock. Meanwhile, one of our cousins is on his way to you. He and his friend have business in Brigantia for Uncle Titus, so I told him to look you up, and I know

you'll make them welcome. Do ask him for the
story about Aunt Julia wanting an elephant for her
birthday. It's quite a laugh.

My love to you and Albia. Be good, or is that too
much to hope? Write to me when you can, and
send it to Eburacum as usual. They know where to
find me.

Keep well, and take care. There's trouble brewing
in Brigantia.

"Good news?" The trooper had been unashamedly watching
me while he ate. "Don't tell me—it's from the Emperor, asking
you to dine at the palace in a golden gown."

"No, that came yesterday. This one's from my brother, and
it's very good news. He expects to be home for our birthday."

"You have the same birthday? That's unusual."

"Not really. We're twins."

He put on an air of astonishment. "And there was I thinking
you were Lucius' kid sister! Can I come to the party? When's
the great day?"

"The Kalends of September. Or should I say, the Kalends of
Germanicus? Now that our dear Emperor has started messing
about with the names of the months, it's hard to keep up."

He laughed. "Yes, our pay clerks keep grousing about that.
Just say the first day of next month, that'll do me. And if your
party's good enough, none of us will be in a state to care what
day it is!" He finished his beer. "Well, duty calls and I must head
for the coast. See you next trip."

"Right. By the way, take care on the road. A man was attacked
near here last night."

"Another one?" He stopped in mid-stride. "I heard there was
a traveller murdered on the Eburacum road last night, the other
side of Oak Bridges somewhere. Nasty business, apparently."

"Murdered? What happened?"

"Poor feller had his head cut off."

I felt my breath catch. "How horrible!"

"I'll say! He'd been stabbed, and then his head was cut off, and taken away. Like the Britons used to do in the old days, collecting heads as trophies to hang up outside their huts. And some weird note left on the body, telling him to go home or he'd die. He could hardly go home once they'd killed him, could he?" He grinned. "Still, that's barbarians for you! You can teach them to write Latin, but not even the gods can make them think straight."

"Who was he, do you know?"

He shook his head. "Haven't a clue. A Roman civilian, that's all I heard. I always thought this was a pretty safe area, round here."

"It is. Well, it always has been."

He touched a little boar's head amulet on a cord round his neck. "There's some unrest further north, so I hear. Maybe it's spreading. Or maybe it's just a local gang of outlaws. Who looks after law and order in these parts? Do you come under the military at Eburacum?"

"No, the Town Council of Oak Bridges. There's an old aedile who's supposed to handle it. He's about a hundred, and needs both hands to lift his dagger."

"Take care yourself, then. I don't want to miss your birthday party just because some poxy native has cut your head off!" He shouldered his satchel and strode out to the stable yard.

Albia came in, and I told her about the murdered traveller. She shuddered. "Ugh! Sometimes I think we'll never get these barbarians properly civilised. What's in the letter?"

She read it and nodded. "That's cheerful news, anyway. And another cousin, too. I hope he's sexier than the dried-up old stick who stayed last winter."

Cousin meant one of Lucius' colleagues on the Governor's staff. Uncle Titus is in fact Lucius' name for his boss; my brother works on what are euphemistically called "special duties," which means doing any sort of secret dirty work that the Governor wants done. Well you know that, of course; and you know about his recent mission in the west, tracking down a native trader who was running illegal arms in from Gaul.

Whoever this *cousin* was, perhaps a spy or a political informer, Lucius knew we'd give him any help we could, and not ask questions.

I touched my belt-purse where the little bone disc was stowed away. "I hope he arrives soon," I said to Albia. "Besides helping him, we might be glad of some help ourselves, if there's really trouble coming. Hey, it's just occurred to me, you don't suppose we've already got him tucked up in bed in the small guest-room?"

She giggled. "I wondered how long it'd take you to work that one out."

"You know who he is? You've remembered where you've seen him before?"

"Yes. His name's Quintus Antonius Delfinus. And Relia, it's quite a coincidence...."

But she didn't get any further because little Baca ran in, still clutching the tunic she was mending.

"Please Mistress, the man in the bed's awake and he's very poorly. He woke up in a fright and tried to get out of bed but it made him giddy, so now he's just lying there swearing and cursing and asking for someone called Burrus."

"We'll come, Baca. You run along to the kitchen and ask Cook to make up a drink of warm wine and honey and poppy-seed to give him."

Well before we reached the sickroom, we could hear Quintus Antonius calling out.

"Burrus! Burrus, are you there? Burrus, where have you got to? *Burrus!*"

The change in him was alarming. He was flushed and feverish, shivering fit to rattle his teeth, and his purple eyes were glazed-looking. As soon as he saw us, he said, "Where's Burrus? My servant, where is he?" He tossed impatiently on his bed, throwing his arms out wide and tipping the blankets onto the floor.

I moved to the bedside and bent to pick them up. Be reassuring, Aurelia, that's the thing. "I'm afraid Burrus isn't here just now. Why don't you get some rest till he comes, and you really must try to keep these blankets on."

He reached out and grabbed my wrist with a grip so strong it hurt. "What have you done with him?" he almost yelled. "Why isn't he here? He was with me yesterday."

"I wish I could help, really. But you were found on your own." With my free hand I tried to prize his fingers loose from my wrist; he resisted for a couple of heartbeats, then suddenly went as limp as a lettuce leaf and lay still.

"I feel awful," he said mournfully. "I need him to patch me up. I've got to make it to the Oak Tree Mansio by dark."

"You've already made it," I answered. "You're at the Oak Tree now."

He stared at me. "This is the Oak Tree? *Here?*"

"Yes. This is the Oak Tree Mansio, and I'm Aurelia Marcella. I run the place."

Not a flicker of recognition this time, but his eyes flashed with excitement. "Then I could make Eburacum today. It's only fifteen miles or so. But I do need Burrus, he's used to mending my cuts and bruises. Are you quite sure he isn't here? Ow!" He tried to sit up, but couldn't, and lay back, scowling.

"There's no sign of him yet, I'm afraid. You were found on your own." Gods, am I going to spend all morning repeating myself? No, gently, Aurelia, he's still recovering from that knock on the head. "I expect he'll be here soon. For the time being you'll have to make do with me and Albia." I bent and tucked in the blankets, and this time he didn't try to stop me.

"Jupiter's balls, my head!" He felt gingerly round it with his hand, exploring the large bump. "My hands hurt too. And I ache all over. I think somebody's tried to kick my ribs in. Was I in a fight?"

"It looks like it, but we don't know for sure. You just turned up outside our door this morning. Can't you remember what happened?"

"It's all mixed up. There was some sort of ambush, I think… several natives, and a man with no head, just a skull….but it's all confused." He screwed up his eyes with the effort of recalling it, then started to shake his head, and winced with the pain. "It's no good. When I try to remember, it hurts my head."

"Just take it easy for a while. If you rest a bit you'll get your strength back."

"I can't wait long. It's beginning." He had a worried frown now, and his voice was almost a growl. "What we've been afraid of. The attacks, and the Shadow of Death….and now they know I'm here."

"Shadow of Death?" I repeated, remembering with a jolt the words beneath the crude skull drawing. "The Shadow of Death attacked you?"

"I don't know," he muttered. "It's just a blur, like a dream…. *Merda,* I can't think straight. It feels as if there's a chariot race going on in my skull."

"We've got a cure for that, at least," Albia said. "Some warm wine?"

"Wonderful! Yes, please." He smiled. It made him look younger, and much more attractive. "I suppose I'm not going to get anywhere for an hour or two. Maybe I will rest for a while. Look, I'm sorry, I didn't mean to be rude. It's just, I feel so helpless, not being able to….You see, it's started. There was this weird man with a mask. If he was the Shadow of Death…."

When Baca brought the wine, we propped him up on some pillows, and he drank half a mug, and smiled again. Some progress at least. "This is good. My head still hurts, but now I don't seem to care so much."

We smiled back at the feeble joke, and he drank some more, and then yawned loudly. The wine and poppy-seed were beginning to work. "Has my horse turned up?"

"Not so far," I said. "What's it like?"

"Chestnut, with two white socks. And all my stuff in the saddlebags…." Suddenly he tensed, and his hand jerked up and went to the spot where his money-belt must be, hidden under the blue tunic. "Look here….my pouch. You haven't touched it?"

"No, of course not."

"Good. There's something important in it. My notes. Important notes."

"Notes? What notes?" Well, a girl can't help being curious.

"For….for my book."

"Ah. Yes, right." A book? Of course! And I'm the Queen of Brigantia!

"Can you put the pouch in your strong box, please? And keep it secret, nobody to know."

"Yes, I'll take care of it."

"The only thing is," Albia pointed out, "short of undressing you, we're going to have a job to get that money-belt off you."

He grinned, and there was a flash of mischief in his eyes. "You think I'll object to being undressed by two pretty women?"

"He's recovering already," Albia said, and between us we got him out of the money-belt. Though we tried to move him gently, the pain of it froze the grin on his face.

He finished the wine. "You're very kind. I'll sleep a bit until Burrus turns up. My head feels sort of fuzzy. As if it's got wool in it. I remember on my uncle's farm, when I was a boy…they sheared the sheep, and there were piles of white fleeces. I used to lie on them and look up at the sky. It was so blue, and the clouds looked like the mounds of white wool….Sheep on the hills and all the wool in the sky…."

His eyes closed, and he was asleep.

"Sleep well, Cousin Quintus," I said softly.

Chapter III

As we came back into the bar-room, Junius appeared, elegantly dressed for riding. "I say, we're on our way now. Back before dark, all right?" He gave Albia an enthusiastic good-bye kiss, and me a broad wink.

"Good hunting," I said. "And take care in the woods. It seems our mystery visitor wasn't the only one to be attacked last night." I told him what the German trooper had said.

Junius frowned. "Sounds as if we all need to be on guard. So take care yourselves, won't you? You're vulnerable here, with everything open to your customers."

Thanks, Junius! Very comforting, and you're the second soldier today who's remarked on it.

He went out to join Marius and their two men, and we followed outside to wave them off.

"I'm afraid he's right about our being vulnerable," I said, as we paused near the oak tree. "It's hard to see what we can do about it though."

But Albia was gazing at Junius as he rode away. I must say he was worth gazing at, sitting tall on his good horse, with the sun sparking off the silver trim on his belt and boots.

"Mmm," she commented, "rather good-looking, isn't he?"

"Marius? All right I suppose, but I get the impression he prefers boys."

"*Marius!* You're joking! No, Junius Pulcher. Quite a suitable name, Pulcher, beautiful...."

Here we go, I thought, she's in love again. Well, it could be worse, he'll be back with his legion in Eburacum in a few days.

"And he rides like a dream," she went on. "Did you see how he just vaulted onto his horse, didn't bother with the mounting-block?"

"I saw. But when you've seen one show-off, you've seen them all."

"There's something about a soldier," she said dreamily.

"Oh definitely. They're either away on campaign all the time, or if they're on leave, they're roaming the countryside pretending to hunt, with a girl in every village."

She giggled. "And even more so if they're on special duties like Cousin Quintus."

The forecourt was filling up. There were already a dozen or so mules and ponies hitched to the railings, and a dilapidated ox-cart was parked in the shade of the big oak. It had a couple of sacks in it, which occasionally wriggled and made piglet noises. A young lad in a crumpled tan tunic was busy watering its oxen from a pail, and chatting to another youngster in rough brown homespun hemp, one of the native boys who occasionally helped out with odd jobs. I remember thinking how alike they were physically, both small, wiry and red-haired, and yet their clothes marked them out unquestionably, one as a Briton, the other as a Roman. Clothes are what identify people, I thought. Look at me, in my workaday yellow linen tunic and sensible sandals, anyone would know I'm Roman; yet if I put on a shapeless hooded cloak and clumsy shoes like the local women, I could pass for native myself. Or could I? Is it more than clothes, maybe something about the way people move, how they carry themselves?

Albia interrupted my musing. "It's perfect weather. Just right for giving everyone a real thirst."

"How are things in the kitchen? Did you manage to liven up that cow's meat stew?"

"Yes, Cook added some extra herbs and it's quite tasty now. I don't think cow's meat will ever be anyone's idea of a delicacy, but the natives seem to like it. And there's plenty of good fresh bread."

"Fine. That deer the tribunes brought in yesterday will go down nicely tonight." We went on discussing the catering as we turned to go back inside.

"Mistress Aurelia? Could I ask you something, please?" It was the lad in the tan tunic. He spoke good Latin with only a slight Brigantian accent.

"Make it quick then. Your boss will be inside there, wanting his beer and his food."

"He's not my boss. I just watered his oxen 'cos he forgot. Poor beasts get thirsty this weather. I bet them piggies in the sacks could do with a drink too, but if I let 'em out…."

"No, don't even think about it. What is it you want?"

"I hear you're short of a stable-lad."

So he was after a job. "Yes, I am a lad short."

He looked at me earnestly. "They said one of your horse-boys has run away."

"That's right."

"Why?"

"Cheeky young pup," Albia remarked, and went on into the bar. Hiring and firing are my department.

But it was a fair question. Presumably he was wondering whether the lad had run off because we beat him, or gave him mouldy bread for his rations.

"To be honest," I said, "I don't know why. He seemed happy enough, but a few days ago he just disappeared without a word. It happens sometimes. Now I haven't got all day to chat. You're a horse-boy, are you?"

"Aye."

"Well, horse-boys are common enough in these parts, lads that I know already. I've never seen you before. Why should I hire you?"

He smiled. "Because I'm good."

I couldn't help smiling back. "And modest, obviously. All right, convince me."

"I can handle horses. Mules, too, and oxen. I can drive, and mend tack, and I've done a bit of horse-doctoring. And I don't mind hard work. You'll wonder how you managed without me!"

I looked at the youngster properly. He was small and compact, with bright red hair and light green eyes. He had a rather angular face, with a stubborn chin, and ears that stuck out. His tunic had once been a good one, but was faded now, and one sleeve had a tear in it.

"What's your name?" I asked.

"Gaius Varius Victor. But everyone calls me Titch."

"A Roman name! Are you a real Roman then, Gaius Varius Victor?"

He smiled proudly. "I'm Roman, born in Britannia. In the camp at Eburacum."

"How old are you?"

"Fourteen."

"*Fourteen?* Don't make me laugh!"

"It's true, honest. I've always been small. Like me mother was. She used to say size isn't everything."

"Did she now? Who's your father? What does he do?"

The smile got even prouder. "My dad's a veteran, a cavalry trooper. He was attached to the Ninth Hispana at Eburacum. He's done his time and come out, and settled down just outside the town. My ma was there, and they got married when he came out, but she died in the spring. My dad was real cut up about it, and he's talking about re-enlisting, in an auxiliary squadron this time, where there's more chance of promotion. So he may be posted away, even abroad, and he says I have to go out and fend for meself till I'm old enough to join up. I'm going into the cavalry, too."

"Have you any proof of who you are?"

He fished in his belt-pouch and brought out a battered-looking roll of parchment. It was from his father's former commanding officer, certifying that Gaius Varius Victor was the son of Gaius Varius Secundus, cavalryman, who had served his time in the Ninth Hispana; the boy was born in the eighth year of the Emperor Vespasian's reign, he was a citizen, and of good character. So far so good.

"You worked with horses at Eburacum?"

"Yes, all the time."

"Well let's see then. Come with me." I led him round the side of the house, through the stable yard to where the horse-paddocks sloped down to the river. In the nearest one several of our own black horses were grazing, making the most of the lush summer meadow.

"See the black mare there?" I pointed her out and called "Merula!" and she raised her head briefly in answer to her name.

The boy nodded. "Blackbird, is it? A beauty, she is. Real good looker. And her foal's only a few days old."

"That's right. Now can you bring the foal over here?" It would test his boast about being good with animals. The mare wasn't keen on strangers near her new baby, and would know if the lad was afraid; if he had the true horse-boy's touch, she'd accept him.

He considered it seriously. "She looks a bit fiery. Will she play me up?"

"What, an experienced horse-boy like you? She's not the most placid of mares, and she's wary of strangers near her just now. But if you work here, you'll be handling different horses every day. You'll need to be good with animals you've never met before. In the cavalry lines you presumably got to know your mounts, working with them regularly."

"Aye. Still, best not to get too attached to them, if they're going into battle."

I recognised the echoes of a drill instructor's lecture to new recruits. "Right. Off you go then."

He climbed lightly over the rail fence and walked towards the mare. Several of the other horses looked up from their grazing as he passed, but didn't seem bothered enough to stop eating, which was a good sign. He paused near the foal, which pricked its ears and came towards him, curious and unafraid. The black mare laid her ears back and advanced on the boy, warning him to keep his distance. He moved in closer to her and I heard him talking quietly, and then he held out a piece of bread on the flat of his hand. She sniffed at it, not touching it, but her ears came forward and she let the lad come to her and rub her neck. She sniffed him all over, and didn't move when he went over to the foal and stroked him gently.

He came back to the mare, grasped a handful of black mane and, without fuss, led her over to where I stood by the fence. The foal walked quietly after her. Both animals came to me to be petted.

"Easy," Titch grinned, giving the mare a pat.

"I didn't tell you to bring the mare," I objected.

"You didn't say not to. And I'd be a fool to try and separate them, when she doesn't know me."

Yes, he had the touch all right.

Hippon, my stable-master, had come up quietly to watch beside me. "The lad's a natural," he murmured in my ear. "He's been hanging around here since first light. Been sleeping rough, by the look of him. I tipped him the wink that there might be a job for him."

Hippon is a cautious man, especially where the precious horses are concerned. If he thought the boy would do, that was good enough for me.

"Well then," I said, "we'll give you a try."

Titch leapt right over the fence in one exuberant bound. "Oh, thanks, Mistress! I won't let you down, I promise."

"Make sure you don't," I warned, "because as I say, you're on trial. Hippon here is your boss, and you do what he says and don't give him any lip. You bunk over the stables with the other boys; you get your keep and the same wages as the other boys. And remember, horse-boys are the bottom of the heap, so do as you're told, and don't go getting into mischief. Understand?"

"Yes, Mistress," he answered demurely. But I had the feeling even then that I might as well have told the wind to stop blowing, or the river to flow uphill.

Chapter IV

Albia was in the bar-room, checking that we'd enough clean jugs and beakers, but her mind wasn't on the crockery. "You know," she remarked, "I hope that man in the guest-room really is the new cousin. He's pretty fanciable."

"Oh? I can't say I noticed." I was looking at a nasty lamp-black stain, high up on the whitewashed wall.

"Oh, of course not, Miss Couldn't-Care-Less." She frowned at a chipped mug and put it to one side. "So you didn't notice his nice eyes?"

"No," I answered, but too quickly. She knows me well, my sister.

"Unusual shade of dark green, I thought," she persisted.

"Dark blue," I corrected, and she laughed when I blushed.

The bar-room was filling up fast, so I escaped more teasing by chatting to the customers and making sure they were all happy, while the maids fetched jugs of wine or beer and brought plates of stew in from the kitchen. I like to supervise the bar myself when I can. Not that I need to, with Albia there, but it's such a wonderful place to pick up the latest news. Couriers ride in from Eburacum or Derventio, locals bring the gossip from the surrounding woods and farms, the occasional long-distance traveller arrives from Lindum or Londinium, or even across the sea in Gaul. We get them all, and their news as well. Today, we were giving out as much news as we were getting, thanks to our mystery traveller.

But eventually there was a lull, and I signalled to Carina, one of the senior maids, to take charge, so Albia and I could go into my study to talk privately.

"Well then," I encouraged, as we sat down on the reading-couch. "Come on, you're dying to tell me about the new cousin. Quintus Antonius Delfinus, you said?"

"Are you sure you're interested?"

"Definitely. Passionately…just get on with it, can't you, before I die of curiosity!"

"Well, if you insist. He's from Italia. Campania somewhere, I think. I met him when I was down in Lindum, last summer, you remember? For Claudia's wedding."

"I remember all right." She'd gone for ten days and stayed a month. But I'd already done my share of moaning on that score.

"Claudia's sister introduced me to him at a dinner party. I remember because she fancied him, but he was flirting with a flashy Greek girl in red ear-rings and didn't give her a second look." She sniffed. "Didn't give *me* a second look either, come to that! Anyhow, he said he was a surveyor, inspecting bridges. But really…" she dropped her voice to a conspiratorial whisper, "…he's a spy, on secret work for the Emperor."

"Half of the Empire's doing secret work for the Emperor.…"

"…Spying on the other half." She joined in the punch-line. "I know. But this one's different. He's not just a palace hanger-on. He gets sent into the provinces to hunt out traitors. He works alone, not with the usual military investigators, or the Governor's agents. Claudia's sister was sure of it."

"And you really think he's the cousin Lucius mentions in his letter?"

"Of course. Which is why someone tried to kill him."

"Yes, it could be. But—look, you know what Claudia's sister is like. She's got a pretty lively imagination, and she'd much rather have been turned down by a mysterious secret agent than a boring bridge surveyor any day." The same went for Albia, of course.

Then I realised I hadn't got round to locking away his precious money-belt. "Maybe we can settle it," I suggested, and fished the money-belt out of my own belt-pouch.

She raised an eyebrow. "Aurelia Marcella! You're not thinking what I think you're thinking?"

"I'm thinking," I said, "that it must be our duty to find out as much as we can about this new cousin."

"Oh it must. And there's no escaping one's duty, is there?"

It was just a standard purse sewn into a narrow belt, worn and discoloured now, but made from good soft leather with a pattern of stars on it. "He certainly seemed very anxious about it," Albia observed, as we spread the contents carefully on my desk. "Notes for a book, I ask you!"

There was a wax note-tablet, blank, a stylus, a folded square of papyrus, and a small slim case, like a flattened cylinder. This was made of some very dark wood inlaid with ivory. I picked it up and examined it. It was light in weight, and didn't rattle when I shook it.

"Well open it," Albia encouraged, and I pulled off the case's top. Inside I found not one but *two* travel permits, beautifully written, and each bearing the imperial seal. They were identical except that one was in the name of Quintus Antonius Delfinus, and the other was for Quintus Valerius Longinus.

"Told you so!" Albia was triumphant. "Only a spy would be using two different names. And these are very high-powered passes he's carrying." So they were: the bearer could use any and every facility of the public service, requisition the best horses, eat the best food, sleep in the best accommodation, and generally be treated like a consul at every mansio and mutatio in the Empire. They even included a command that all Roman citizens should give him "any necessary help in the course of his work." It looked as if Claudia's sister had been right.

"I must admit I'm impressed, Albia. We don't see many passes like that—in fact I don't think I've ever seen one with this much clout, let alone two of them! Should we move him into a grander room, do you think?"

"He'll probably requisition the whole place when he wakes up, and us with it. Or you, anyway. Come on, let's see the paper. Maybe that'll tell us more."

I unfolded the square of papyrus, expecting at the very least a citation from Caesar. But there were only a few lines on it, and they made no sense at all.

L's list
PGATT
SSFCV
CVBFS

"What a let-down," Albia grumbled. "Just a jumble of letters. I presume it's a code of some sort?" She brightened up. "Pass me a note-tablet. Let's try and work it out."

"It's none of our business...."

"It's a bit late to worry about that now...."

"...And besides, we've got a mansio to run."

But she wasn't giving up. "L's list. Now who's L, when he's at home? It could be Lucius. Our Lucius, do you think? After all, if Cousin Quintus was on his way here...."

"There are thousands of men called Lucius. Or it might be Lollius? Lepidus? Or how about Lugotorix?"

"Ah, Lugotorix! Now why didn't I think of Lugotorix, that world-famous compiler of coded lists! All right, I know we're never going to puzzle it out. Pity though. Maybe he'll drop some hints when he wakes up again."

"And if he does," I warned, "we haven't seen any of this, remember."

I put everything back in the money-belt, and locked the lot in the strong-box, safely hidden under its loose floor-board. Then we went back to the bar-room.

I moved among the customers again, saying a few words here and there. They were nearly all people I knew, a mixture of Roman settlers and native farmers. Most of them had heard about our wounded traveller, and several also knew of the murder on the Eburacum road. But despite the grim topics of gossip, the atmosphere was cheerful. Everyone enjoys a good market, whether they're buying or selling. Beer and wine sales were going nicely, and the cow's meat stew was appreciated.

At a corner table I spotted an unusual group of five young natives, dressed as old-style Brigantian warriors. We get plenty of native customers, but they're either peasants in serviceable dull homespun, or if they're a shade richer, they dress like Romans in tunics and travelling cloaks. These were different, so impeccably turned out that they seemed to be making some kind of deliberate statement. They wore their fair hair whitened with lime, and had plenty of blue skin paint on their faces and arms; and they were dressed as fighting men, in leather kilts, greaves, big boots, studded sword-belts and leather jerkins reinforced with bronze across the chest. Their colourful checked cloaks were piled up in a corner with their helmets. They weren't foolish enough to be carrying weapons, but all the same they were unmistakably trained fighters, exuding an aura of excitement, a strung-up feeling of waiting for something to happen. They were drinking mead, too, which can get men into a warlike mood quicker than wine or beer.

Their leader sported several bits of gold jewellery, a couple of bracelets on his right arm and a heavy gold collar round his neck. The others had smaller ornaments, mostly silver or bronze. The only jarring note in their appearance was that the leader was clean-shaven, so he must be from a family that had some pretensions to Roman status, with parents who wouldn't tolerate any barbarian beards. He looked vaguely familiar. In fact, as I walked over to their table I realised they were all familiar, all young men from local families, including Segovax, the son of our native neighbour. And the leader was none other than Vitalis, the son of our chief town councillor, Publius Silvanius Clarus. I hadn't seen Vitalis around for a while; now I remembered, he had been away somewhere in the west of Brigantia, staying with relatives in the hills. His father was one of the modern type of native, born in Britannia but now proud to be a Roman citizen, and living a thoroughly civilised life. His new villa wouldn't have looked out of place in Italia, neither would the clothes he wore, and his Latin was more grammar-perfect than mine. I wondered if he knew what company his only son was keeping.

Vitalis didn't acknowledge me, so I just addressed the group as a whole. "'Morning, gentlemen. Can I get you something to eat? We've a delicious beef hotpot today, with fresh bread."

Without thinking, I'd spoken in British, which surprised them. Vitalis said "Yes, please, and another jug of mead," also in British.

I signalled one of the slaves to bring it. "Are you going far?" It was the standard question, but it never fails, and I must admit I was curious. We don't get many old-style warriors at the Oak Tree, even kids like these who were just playing at it. At least I hoped they were just playing.

"Not far today," Vitalis answered, "but soon we'll be going all the way."

The tall lad Segovax reached for the mead jug and poured. "All the way! From here to there and back again, till we've chased all our enemies over the sea. Right, lads?"

They all nodded and grinned, and Vitalis said, "Then we'll vanish like shadows in the night," and they laughed outright.

What in Hades was all this about? When in doubt, make a joke. "I'll have to be sure you don't run out of mead then. I don't want to be included among your enemies."

"The Chief says that all of you Romans…" the tall lad began, but Vitalis cut in swiftly.

"…All of you Romans seem to be getting a taste for mead now. It's a good drink."

"Yes, it is," I agreed, wondering what the youth had been intending to say. Surely not "All of you Romans will be killed"? No, you're getting paranoid, Aurelia. Snap out of it.

I soon forgot the lads, because across the room were a couple of farmers I wanted a word with about some extra grazing for our horses. They were both called Cavarinus, father and son, and they had land on the opposite side of our little river.

They greeted me cheerfully as I pulled up a stool, and we chatted for a while about the pasture I wanted. I'm trying to expand the horse-breeding side of our business. The native ponies are tough, but small, and there's always a market for good Roman horses. I have half a dozen excellent mares and two good stallions, and…sorry, you don't want to know all that.

After some friendly haggling we made a deal and shook hands on it. They were simple men who'd never be more than peasants, the father stoop-shouldered and worn out before his time with hard outdoor work, but their word was to be trusted.

"What's the news in town?" I asked them, refilling their beer-mugs.

"The price of pigs is down again," the father answered. "Hardly worth rearing the beasts, it ain't…." He went on at some length. Did you ever meet a farmer who didn't moan about prices?

Eventually his son cut in. "There was one bit of excitement. Not very nice either. In the forum. You know the big marble statue of old daft Claudius?"

"The late great conqueror of Britannia? What about it?"

"Well you know Balbus has his pottery shop right opposite that statue. Except he don't live behind the shop no more, it's not grand enough for him now he's on the town council. His foreman lives there, and seemingly last night, just before dawn, he hears a noise in the forum and comes out to see. And there's a man out there, just by old Claudius, with a funny sort of mask thing on."

"If you ask me that was just the drink talking, or the hangover," his father remarked. "He's normally legless by bedtime these days. Terrible thing is too much drink." He swigged his beer.

"That's as may be. The man ran off anyway, but lying there, by the base of old Claudius, was a body. A dead body. With no head on him."

I felt a shiver down my back. "Another one? Are you sure?"

"Certain sure. I went and had a look at the place, although they'd shifted the body by then. They said he was a big German, with a green snake tattoo on one arm. Been badly knocked about, and stabbed to death, and his head cut off. But you know the strangest thing—there weren't a drop of blood anywhere. I'd have expected the place to be swimming in it." He sounded quite disappointed.

"And you haven't told her the weirdest thing of all," Cavarinus senior continued. "Pinned onto his cloak was a sort of medal thing, made out of bone, with a message written on it."

"Message?" I could hardly get the word out.

"About all Romans being killed if they don't go home. So he must have been a citizen, I suppose. He certainly wasn't from round here."

"Something like this?" I took the bone disc from my purse and held it out. They both stared at it, and young Cavarinus said, "Where'd you get that?"

When I told him, they looked worried. "I wish I knew what it meant," I said. "I suppose you haven't any idea who could be behind it?"

"No," they both answered, though from their grim expressions, I guessed they knew more than they were saying. But I couldn't get anything else out of them, and pretty soon they went on their way, leaving me with a nasty taste. I'd always thought of our neighbourhood as a peaceful one, yet this was the third brutal attack I'd heard of today, and the third sinister message. I remembered Quintus Antonius' disjointed words: "It's beginning…what we've been afraid of…." What was beginning? Whatever it was, I was starting to be afraid, too.

‹›‹›‹›

Everything was going smoothly indoors, so I went to check round outside. The stables had been mucked out, and the post-horses and mules groomed; the cow and goats had been milked and moved to a fresh field. Looking down to the little river, I could see three of the maids doing the laundry in the big shallow pool, and the bushes near the bank were draped with newly washed tunics and towels. Taurus was whistling as he mended a gate, and Hippon was in the training paddock, with Titch and the other horse-boys and some little native ponies they were breaking to harness. I stopped to watch our newest lad; his movements were lithe and quick, and he managed the ponies and their harness easily.

I strolled to the orchard next to the large paddock, taking it all in. The apple trees were full of fruit and would crop well this year; even the new pear tree, which was much more temperamental, was promising a good harvest, and we'd already started on the plums. The bees were busy everywhere, making the air calm with their steady buzzing. We should have a good honey harvest as well.

It was all so orderly and peaceful. I relaxed as I stood looking across the narrow valley, breathing in the good air, and thinking how much I loved our small piece of this raw new province. Yet was the appearance of orderly peace deceptive?

Travellers attacked? Headless bodies? Young lads playing warriors? And somebody called the Shadow of Death telling us to get out or die? What was going on?

I didn't know, but I had no doubt of my reaction. Nobody is going to tell *me* to get out! Nobody is going to make *me* leave this place, my home, which I love and work for and want to spend my life in. They can threaten all they like, but I'm staying here where I belong. And if they want a fight, by Mars I'll give them one!

I heard a familiar scuffling noise close by in the trees, and my favourite hound came romping up—Lucky, the black one with the tattered left ear, who's always full of himself. He stood in front of me whining and wagging his tail, then he walked a little way downhill, looked over his shoulder, whined and came back to stand by me again. I knew that signal, he had something he wanted to show me. He and his mate had probably killed a young deer. They were quite good at this, but then needed human help to get the trophies home.

"What is it, Lucky?" I patted his jet-black coat. "Something in the woods here?"

His tail wagged harder.

"I should be getting back inside, you know. But it's such a beautiful morning....Oh all right, why not? Come on then, show me."

He barked joyfully, and ran ahead of me down through the orchard, almost to the little river, and turned right, in among the huge old oak trees that had been here since time began. This was one of my favourite walks, along a path that wound its way more or less parallel with the river, and I strolled along happily, revelling in the quiet shade.

The dog led me perhaps a couple of hundred paces, till we came round a bend and out into a small clearing, where sunshine flooded in to light up the grass. I stopped dead, horrified. There on the ground was another body.

A big chestnut horse lay on its side, legs stretched out, throat cut. Flies buzzed and crawled all over its head, and a knife stuck out of its neck. I remember I noticed it looked a good knife, with some jet inlay in its smooth wooden handle.

It had been a fine horse, glossy-coated and well cared for. It had two white socks, and a white star; it was a first-class riding-horse, but there was no sign of saddle-bags or bridle. The grass and plants all around its body were trampled and there was dried blood everywhere. I got the smell of the blood in my nostrils, and it was all I could do not to be sick.

This must be Quintus Antonius' horse right enough. He'd been attacked here, and the attackers had killed the horse, perhaps to quieten it, and thought they'd killed the man. No, that wasn't right; they hadn't used their knife on Quintus Antonius. They had hurt him badly and could have killed him, even cut off his head, but they hadn't. Which meant they must have been interrupted in their gruesome work before they could finish him.

I set off further along the path, more slowly now, looking carefully. I saw trampled grass here too, snagged twigs, several footprints in the bare patches, and once a definite bloodstain, hard to spot among the brownish remains of last year's leaves. The path ahead curved away from the river, slightly uphill for a few paces, and would come out on the main road. From there it was only a short distance back down the road to our turning, and the paved track that led to our parking area. Was that the way Quintus Antonius had crawled last night?

I stopped walking as the questions chased through my mind. Who had attacked him? Did they realise they hadn't killed him, and if so, would they come back? I knew there'd be more to learn if only I had someone who could read the tracks and signs on the ground. It was time to send for Hawk.

Chapter V

Hawk is a native hunter, and he reads tracks the way the rest of us read books. His sharp black eyes miss nothing. He can look at a few scuff marks in the dust, or some bent blades of grass, and tell you who's been passing by, which direction they were heading, and what they had for breakfast. And probably whether they enjoyed it.

Hence his nickname: everyone calls him Hawk, either in British or Latin. He understands both, but will only speak his own language. Not that he's anti-Roman exactly, but he's his own man, with his own way of doing things. He sees himself as equal to anyone, Roman citizen or not.

He lives with two wives and a brood of children in a round house in the woods, about a quarter mile from us. The red-haired boy I'd seen talking to Titch was one of his sons, so I sent him home with a message, and Hawk appeared in the middle of the afternoon, just when the flow of customers was slowing down.

He is a slight, dark man, with long hair and a neat black beard, and he moves as silently and lithely as a cat. Today he was wearing hunting clothes, tunic and breeches made of tough homespun and dyed greenish to give him camouflage in the woods, and he had his bow with him, and his big hunting-hound Bran trotting along at his side. He didn't enter the bar-room, but sent his son in to fetch me out to the stable yard.

"I hear you've had an unexpected guest," he said after we'd exchanged greetings. "Quite a mystery, it seems. My son's full of it."

"Yes, unexpected, uninvited, and decidedly odd." I told him how I'd found the wounded man, and about Lucky leading me to the horse. As usual he spoke in British, and I replied in Latin. It must have sounded strange, but it suited us.

"I want you to try and find out what happened to him, Hawk. He's had such a bang on the head he can't remember anything clearly. But there's quite a lot of disturbance around the horse's body. I'd appreciate any help you can give me to piece the story together."

"All right. Let's take a look." We walked down through the orchard and along the path towards where the horse lay. I was amused to notice my hound Lucky walking behind us at a respectful distance, while Hawk's dog trotted beside his master. Lucky, like all the local dogs, knew a pack leader when he saw one.

"If dogs had kingdoms," I remarked, "your Bran would be King of Brigantia."

"He would." Hawk smiled, and gently stroked the dog's head. "But it takes more than brute strength to be a good king. I don't think dogs have learned that yet."

"Plenty of men haven't learned it either. Look at the way the tribal chiefs used to fight among themselves in the old days here. It was always the strongest who won, whether they were good chiefs or bad."

"Whereas Romans, of course, never fight each other, but just sit round a table debating who's the best ruler, and then appoint him, and all the rest of the candidates acknowledge him with gracious smiles."

I laughed. "With the Senate and People of Rome, it's a case of 'do as we say, not do as we do.' We're allowed to tear our Empire apart in civil wars, but woe betide anybody else who tries to do the same."

"You're unusual for a Roman, Aurelia. You don't think that everything Roman is perfect."

"Hardly! They say love's blind, but patriotism doesn't have to be."

The banter stopped abruptly when we reached the clearing and he saw the horse's body. He gave a sort of moan, and went to stand at its head with his hand outstretched, palm down, and chanted a brief prayer to Epona, the horse goddess. Then he turned to me, and his black eyes were blazing.

"Evil men did this. It's cruel and it's wasteful." His voice was low and angry.

"But I think the attackers were interrupted," I said. "One of them left his knife behind."

"Knife? Where?"

"There, in the..." I broke off, staring, because there was no knife. Yet there had been one. I knew there had.

"It was in the horse's neck. A long, narrow blade, and a wooden handle with a jet inlay." I felt shaken as I considered the implications. "Someone's been back to fetch it since I was here before. Jupiter! They might still be around now."

"Not now." He looked down at his wolflike hound. "Bran will tell us if he hears anyone. Won't you, boy? On guard now, while I look round."

Both dogs lay down, and I stood watching, fascinated, as Hawk searched the ground, carefully and thoroughly, like a man looking for a gold piece in a hayfield. Occasionally he bent low to examine the trampled grass, the broken twigs, and the blood-stains. Sometimes he gazed at what looked to me like perfectly ordinary clumps of weed, or patches of earth with vague lines in them. He walked along the path beyond the clearing quite a way. He must have got to the road, but I lost sight of him, and the dogs and I stayed put. Then he came back almost to where we waited, and branched off the track, down the slope a few paces towards the little river. As he did so, his dog stood up and gave a low growl, and from behind us Lucky rumbled an echo.

"What's up?" I asked.

He looked at his dog. "Who is it, Bran?" Bran gave another soft growl in his throat, and twitched his big pointed ears. Man and dog stood still, listening. I listened too, but all I could hear was the faint breeze rustling the leaves, and a murmuring of the shallow river water.

Then Hawk shrugged. "It's all right. Only one of the wood-cutters." He turned and walked back towards me. "Well, this was a wild goose chase, I'm afraid. I can't tell you much."

I was surprised, and disappointed. "Aren't the tracks clear?"

He shook his head. "This ground looks as if an army's marched all over it. The tracks are all mixed up. There was more than one man, and they had a fight of some sort, and the horse was killed. That's about it." He sounded irritated, as if it was my fault his usual powers weren't working.

"No, really? I'd worked that out for myself!" I was about to say, but then my brain started, belatedly, to function. The dogs had growled, there were strangers about, and Hawk was being cautious in case of eavesdroppers. Which meant he probably *had* found something.

"Oh well, if you can't, you can't." I tried to inject the right note of resigned annoyance into my voice as we began to walk back towards the house, the dogs prowling behind, still uneasy. If we were being spied on, I must somehow invite Hawk into the mansio where we could be private, without arousing anyone's suspicions. I racked my brains for a convincing reason.

As we reached the stable yard, inspiration struck me. "By the way, do you need some more cough syrup for your little boy? Albia said he was wheezing like a hedgehog when she saw him yesterday."

"Yes, thanks," he said, "I will take a bottle. It eased his chest before. I'll bring you a nice fresh hare tomorrow in exchange."

"It's a deal. You may as well take the stuff now. It'll help the poor kid sleep."

"All right. I mustn't be long though."

Soon we were sitting comfortably in my study, he with a mug of beer, and me with some wine.

"Did I guess right?" I asked. "You wanted to talk, but there was someone listening?"

He nodded and sipped his beer. "The trees have ears. There was somebody there that my dog didn't know."

"So you found something worth telling me?"

He put down his mug. "Oh yes, I can tell you more or less what happened, as well as anyone can who wasn't there to see. That horse has been dead since last night, throat cut with a knife as you said. From the tracks I could see five attackers on foot, and there was someone else there too, a lookout of some sort I'd say, keeping well back from the path—small footprints, maybe a woman or a boy. I don't know who any of the attackers were, but they all had on Roman boots, with the uppers nailed and stitched onto the soles. They make quite different prints from native boots. They must have been bought in somewhere like Derventio or Eburacum, because our local cobbler in Oak Bridges makes boots in the traditional way, you know, each one just a single piece of leather. I've not seen any of those tracks before, but I'll know them again."

"How?" I asked, pouring him a refill.

"Boots with stitching or nails are all different from one another if you know what to watch out for. For instance, one of the attackers had very worn heels, and part of the stitching missing on his left sole. That sort of thing. The other two, the riders, had army type riding-boots, fairly new."

"*Two* riders? We've only found one."

"Two horses came down off the road, at a walk, both being ridden, with the attackers walking. Both men got off the horses, or were dragged off, in the clearing there, and the one horse was killed. There was a fight, and they both put up quite a struggle, but they hadn't much chance against five. Luckily for them both, something interrupted the attackers. I don't know what, maybe some odd noise scared them. One rider managed to mount up and gallop off towards the road, and the other was left here, bleeding. Quite a lot of blood, all in one place, so probably he was unconscious and they thought he was dead. Anyway the attackers ran away down towards the river. Eventually the wounded man crawled back along the track, up onto the road, and found his way to your forecourt. He was lucky they didn't come back for him later."

"That's brilliant, Hawk! Thank you." I truly was impressed, and relieved that my faith in him had been justified.

"Tell me one thing." He fixed me with his piercing gaze. "The man you found, was he carrying any kind of message?"

I handed him the bone disc with its grim threat, and he didn't seem surprised, but nodded and stared awhile in thoughtful silence.

"What does it mean, Hawk? You know something about this?"

He put the disc on the table. "Just a few rumours. Have you heard of the Shadow-men?"

"Shadow-men? No. Some sort of religious group?"

"Not exactly, though the Druids encourage them. A war-band, but a secret one. The main thing about them is that they're Britons of the old sort, who want to put the calendar back to before you Romans came. They're mostly young and headstrong, just boys, but there are some older ones involved as well, training them to kill. Not like their ancestors killed, riding chariots into battle. The Shadow-men kill by stealth, at night. Their members are supposed to keep themselves secret, but some of the younger ones are easy to spot. They can't resist showing off in their war gear."

"I've seen them." I described the group of native warriors in the bar.

Hawk's eyes glinted. "Vitalis leads them, but young Segovax is the better fighter. They've been riding around for a few days now, just daring someone to give them any trouble."

"Yes, that was the feeling I got. They had a kind of tension, like a taut bowstring. But they're only fooling about, surely?"

"Not fooling, though they're not dangerous on their own. But there are some more experienced men leading them, and *they're* keeping themselves carefully hidden. This Shadow of Death, for instance." He glanced down at the bone disc. "He's their leader, but who he actually is, nobody knows."

"So this threat, 'Get out or die'…they really want to drive us out?"

"Yes."

"They seriously think they can?"

"Yes."

"But that's absurd!"

"Is it?" He looked at me soberly.

"It's laughable, Hawk! We've got three legions stationed in Britannia, not to mention all the auxiliaries, and the navy. And then there are thousands of Roman civilians settled, helping to make something of the province. The Britons couldn't defeat us fifty years back when old Emperor Claudius invaded, or in Nero's time when Queen Boudicca rebelled. That was thirty years ago, and we're even more firmly established these days. They must see they'll never do it now."

He rubbed his chin thoughtfully. "They're trying different tactics. Think about it. Your army's unbeatable in battle, yes, but can it fight secret enemies in the dark? Can it protect all you civilians from small groups who murder at night and melt away in the morning?"

"*All* the civilians? Surely we're just talking about a local band of rebels?"

"Maybe so, at this stage," he agreed. "But their plan is to succeed in Brigantia, and then encourage other tribes to rise up against you. I pick up rumours, you know, just as you must do here, only my sources of rumour are different. What's happened here today is meant to be just a beginning, and the situation for Romans will get worse before it gets better. *If* it gets better."

We were interrupted by a tap at the door, and Albia looked in. She smiled when she saw Hawk.

"Relia, Councillor Silvanius is here, and he says you're expecting him."

"Gods, I forgot he was coming. Is it about his wine order?"

"He didn't say. He seems a bit agitated. I've put him in the garden with some wine and cakes. Felix is with him."

"That's a relief. Silvanius can be a shade pompous, but Felix always brings him back to the real world. I'll be with them in just a little while."

"And Albia," Hawk added, "best not to say you saw me here. Our esteemed Chief Councillor doesn't approve of me."

"Don't worry. I told His Pomposity that Aurelia was in a meeting with the oil wholesaler. Just sneak out through our private door, he'll be none the wiser."

"I suppose you and Silvanius are like chalk and cheese." I smiled as I tried to picture Hawk wearing a toga.

"You could say that! It's not a personal thing, we hardly know each other. But I'm a Briton, and I'm proud of it. I don't even *want* to be a Roman."

I sipped some wine. "Whereas Councillor Publius Silvanius Clarus is determined to be more Roman than the Romans."

Hawk snorted contemptuously. "He makes himself ridiculous! That vast new villa, and his Greek major-domo, and his Italian chef, and wanting Oak Bridges to be a proper Roman town, and building his very own temple. Yet underneath it all he's no more a Roman than I am."

"Well, he's a citizen, and so was his father. I suppose that does make him more Roman than you are. And if he wants a Roman life, I'm hardly going to criticise him for that, am I? Live and let live, surely?"

Hawk shook his head. "That's just what he doesn't do, though. He wants everyone to live exactly like he does. And I refuse to follow his shining example, so he thinks I'm against Roman rule. He can't see the difference between someone like me, and these Shadow-men. But I'm not against Romans, Aurelia. You're here, and we should all make the best of it. You came, you saw, you conquered. Isn't that how it goes?"

I laughed. "Quoting Julius Caesar! Silvanius would be impressed."

"Astonished, more like. He thinks I'm ignorant because I didn't have a Roman education. But all I am is just proud of being born and raised in the way my ancestors were. I don't want to be a Roman citizen, but I don't think every single thing that comes from Rome is wrong, and I certainly don't believe everything about Britannia is perfect. I hate Druids, for a start, and I think endless wars between tribes are a futile waste. At least you Romans have brought us peace. Until now," he added sombrely.

"You take these Shadow-men very seriously, don't you? You think they could upset the Roman peace?"

"It's not impossible. But they're wrong, as wrong in their way as Silvanius is. Killing isn't the answer." He paused and fingered his beard, searching for words. "There must be a middle way, between what you could call the extreme pro-Britons on one side, and the extreme pro-Romans on the other."

"I hope you're right. Because I'm proud to be Roman, but my family have been here for half a generation, and it's where I want to stay. It seems to me this province will only have a real future if we can take the best of both Britannia and Rome and blend them together."

He smiled his rare smile. "That's what I think too. That's why we can be friends. For all our differences, we're two of a kind."

It was true, and comforting, with all this talk of trouble brewing. I raised my wine-mug to him. "To our friendship," I said, and we both drank the toast.

Chapter VI

Silvanius and Felix were sitting comfortably at a table near the ornamental pool, with the best wine-service—the green with the black slip decoration—and some of the little honey and hazelnut pastries that Cook is famous for.

Publius Silvanius Clarus was fair, fortyish, and starting to run to fat, but still large and imposing. He had been born in Brigantia, a local chieftain, but his family had lost no time in throwing in their lot with the new conquerors, and now his whole appearance was Roman, his hairstyle, his lack of beard, and his toga. Yes, he was wearing his *toga* in the middle of an ordinary working afternoon! But of course, the citizenship was an honour he treasured, and it meant, among other things, that he was entitled to wear a toga, so he'd wear one at every conceivable opportunity. I caught myself wondering if he went to bed in it.

Titus Cornelius Felix was the complete opposite. He was fair and fortyish too, but slim and lithe. Rumour said he'd been an actor once, in Nero's time when such a thing would be respectable, more or less, for a gentleman. He was a Roman from Rome, one of the prestigious Cornelius clan, which meant his pedigree went back to when Romulus was a lad, and he could dress as he liked. His style was usually somewhere between a romantic poet and a racetrack dandy. Today he was wearing a bright yellow cloak fastened with a huge gold-coloured brooch, and matching yellow boots trimmed with golden studs, and his yellow hair was done up in a complicated arrangement of ringlets that must have taken his barber half the morning.

Not for the first time I thought what an odd friendship theirs was, but I knew it was based on a firm footing. Silvanius was rich and wanted desperately to be accepted as a Roman, and to adopt Roman tastes in everything. Felix had plenty of class and impeccable taste, but no money, and he wanted equally desperately to maintain a flamboyant lifestyle. So they'd become pretty well inseparable, each giving and taking. It appeared to work better than many marriages.

They both got up as I approached. Silvanius shook my hand, and said formally, "It's good to see you, Aurelia, as always. I trust you're well?"

Before I could answer, Felix flung his arms round me and kissed me on both cheeks, exclaiming, "Aurelia, my dear, you look as ravishing as ever! Marry me this afternoon!"

"I'll think about it, Felix." I disentangled myself from his embrace, but not too roughly. "Let's have some cake first, shall we?"

This sort of nonsense was pretty usual from Felix; sometimes it could be a shade embarrassing, but not to Silvanius, who smiled indulgently.

We all sat down again. I refilled their beakers, and passed round the pastries.

"You've come about the wine for your banquet, Councillor?" I prompted. Silvanius was giving an important dinner soon, and we were supplying several kinds of wine for it; this must be the third time he'd come to check on the order. "It arrived safely three days ago from our wholesaler, and it can be transported to your new villa whenever you like. Just say the word."

"Wine? Ah, yes, of course. As soon as possible, then, please. Arrange it with my major-domo, if you would." He paused. "That was why I came, I suppose. But now…there's something else."

He relapsed into silence, and I waited. I had learned to let Silvanius tell things in his own pompous way, so I just gazed at the pond, trying to spot the frogs among the water plants.

Eventually it was Felix who set the ball rolling. "It's these horrid murders, my dear," he said, reaching for another pastry. "It's too awful, isn't it? Three corpses! All stone dead!"

"As corpses tend to be," I couldn't help saying, and he laughed. "Except that our victim isn't a corpse. He was alive when we found him, and still is, although he's unconscious most of the time. When he is awake, he seems to have lost his memory."

"How very intriguing! So you don't know who he is?"

"Not yet, but we're working on it."

"You were the person who found the man, I'm told," Silvanius said. "It must have been an unpleasant shock for you."

I shrugged. "I was just relieved he wasn't dead."

"The whole situation is extremely disturbing," he continued, absently twisting his wine-beaker between his hands. "So I wanted to make sure you are coping with everything, and not feeling too alarmed. We Romans," he declaimed, "must stand together at a time of crisis."

Here we go, I thought. I've heard his "Romans standing together" speech so often I could recite it for him.

Felix, thank the gods, had heard it before, too, and decided to divert the flow. "Absolutely," he cut in. "And while we're standing together, we must put our heads together, if that isn't physically impossible. We've got to decide what to *do*."

"Exactly," Silvanius said.

I thought so! Silvanius wanted my advice, but didn't want the world to know he'd asked me for it. Well, it wasn't the first time, and discretion is part of an innkeeper's stock-in-trade. I waited with what I hoped was the right air of attentive anticipation.

"Three murders," Silvanius said. "Correction, three attacks. You've heard about all of them, presumably?"

"We get news pretty quickly here. I've heard of one headless body found on the Eburacum road, and another one in the forum outside Balbus' shop."

"Balbus must be mortified," Felix murmured. "So bad for business, something like that! Has he offered to sell you an urn for the man's ashes?"

"Now do be serious, Felix," Silvanius said. "This really isn't a joking matter. We've had two brutal murders committed in our town, and another attack which might easily have resulted in a murder. Most distressing."

I told him how I'd found our unconscious guest, and described how the dog had led me to his horse. I didn't mention Hawk.

"May I see the, ah, threatening message?"

I showed him the disc. He looked even graver as he read it, then passed it to Felix, who examined it intently.

Silvanius said, "I feared as much. The man in the forum had one exactly like this, pinned to the front of his tunic." He drew a disc from his belt-pouch and held it out to me. Sure enough, the discs were twins.

I asked, but knowing the answer already, "What about the third man, on the road to Eburacum?"

"Yes, he had a similar one. I haven't got it with me. I left it with Vedius Severus."

Vedius was the aedile in charge of the town watch, which in plain Latin meant the two men and a mule-cart that made up the Oak Bridges fire brigade. He was an old soldier, seventy-five if he was a day, and he could just about handle being fire chief—there are very few fires in our district. But I reckoned that faced with a series of savage nocturnal attacks, he'd be as much use as a wax fire-bucket.

I handed Silvanius back his disc. "When I found the wounded man this morning, I thought it was just a single horrible incident. But this has the feel of something organised, almost professional, doesn't it? Three attacks in the area, one this side of town, one the other side, and one in the forum. It looks too well planned to be just a casual band of outlaws. And cutting off the heads of two of them…like in the old days, when the warriors collected heads as trophies from enemies they killed in battle."

He nodded. "Someone is threatening us, and making it as frightening for us as they can. It's like a military campaign, yet not fought on a battlefield. Waged in secret, through fear. A campaign of terror."

"A campaign of terror," I repeated. "A good phrase. And a campaign implies several engagements, not just one night's work. You think we're in for more attacks then?"

"I fear so," he said gloomily. "One has heard rumours. Discontent among some of the more hot-blooded young men.... As we all know, there are still elements of the native population who haven't accepted the finality of the Roman conquest." He sipped more wine. "But from what you say, your man will survive. Have you found out anything about him?"

I'd have to watch my step here. If Quintus Antonius was who we suspected he was, he wouldn't want anyone drawing attention to him. "Not much, no. He's got well-made Roman clothes, and his horse was a good one. So a reasonably rich traveller. And he called out for someone named Burrus, so he may have had a servant with him. That's about all I can tell you. We'll just have to wait and see when he wakes up properly. Have either of the other two been identified?"

"Not yet. The one in the forum was a servant, from his clothing, and young and strong. From the injuries he received, he had put up quite a fight. The body on the Eburacum road looks more eastern, from his clothes, and older; perhaps a trader or a contractor."

I sipped my wine, wondering what was coming next.

"As head of the Oak Bridges Town Council," Silvanius mused, "I feel I ought to do something. People will look to me, I know. But I'm unsure of the best course to take. That's why I thought.... You always talk good sense, Aurelia. So refreshing in a woman."

I'd have to let that go with a smile; there were more important battles to fight just now.

He went on, "We're being threatened by, well, we don't know by whom...."

"We can make a shrewd guess," I interrupted. "The Druids and their followers, the believers in the old religion."

"Oh, I hope not! We've all had enough bloodshed. What we need now is peace. Peace and prosperity."

"And some of the Druids' rituals are so uncivilised," Felix remarked. "Human sacrifice, for example. Quite disgusting!"

"All the same, if there's trouble, I'd bet any money they're involved. Even though they're outlawed now, they still have their followers. You can't just abolish a religion by a stroke of the Emperor's pen. In fact just trying to abolish it makes the believers more determined."

"How can they be such fools!" Silvanius exclaimed. "Can't they see this province of ours must go forward with Rome, not backward into the ancient past? Somehow we've got to stop them!" He stared at nothing in particular for a while, thinking hard. Felix and I exchanged a glance, but we both kept quiet. Finally he said, "I think I shall call a meeting of the Town Council."

"That's a terrible idea." Oh, me and my big mouth! When will I remember how seriously these new citizens take their town councils?

Silvanius looked quite hurt, but Felix smiled slyly. "Your view couldn't be coloured by the fact that you aren't a member of the council, so you wouldn't be able to attend, Aurelia dear?"

I couldn't deny it. "I'll admit I'd like to be in on it, but that's not the main reason. I think we must act quickly, and we must act in secret. The council, *any* council, can't do either. Too public, too slow, too many people involved, and anything it did decide, however secret, would be all over Oak Bridges in a day."

"More like an afternoon," Felix agreed.

Silvanius said, "But is our council so very incompetent?"

The straight answer was "Yes," but I gave the tactful one. "Of course not, for most of the town's affairs it's excellent. But it's not a war council. You said yourself this is a kind of war. It needs a different sort of leadership."

"Then if not a council meeting, what do you suggest?"

"A small secret meeting. Half a dozen people you can trust, to work together quietly and quickly. The people who have most to lose if peace breaks down. You two...Vedius, as head of law and order…Balbus, as the leading businessman in the area…me, if I'm invited. Meeting behind closed doors, we can discuss and plan without anyone else knowing, friend or enemy."

He sat up straight and drained his wine-beaker. "Yes, of course. That is what I shall do. Call a private meeting of the most prominent Roman citizens. There! I knew I'd come up with the right plan in the end."

"You always do, Publius," Felix said, catching my eye.

"We'll meet at my new villa," Silvanius decided. "You'll come of course, Aurelia, won't you? I know that traditionally this sort of thing isn't women's business, but…."

Try and stop me, I thought. "Thank you, Councillor. I'll be representing my brother, naturally."

"Relia!" I turned as Albia came hurrying towards us from the house, looking agitated. "Sorry to interrupt, but…Councillor Silvanius, please don't think I'm ungrateful, but I'm a little concerned. This doctor you've kindly sent to look after our sick man. I'm sure he's very learned, but…."

"What doctor?" Silvanius asked, surprised. "I've sent no doctor."

"He says he's your personal physician, Lykos of Cos."

"That's the right name, but my physician is away at present, in Isurium, attending my sister."

"I thought there was something fishy about him," she said. "He was insistent that you'd ordered him to treat our wounded traveller, and even stay with him if necessary. But there was just something wrong…."

I jumped up, forgetting my social manners. "Where is he now?"

"Don't worry. I left him in the bar-room with a beaker of wine. And I put Taurus outside the sick-room door and told him not to let anyone in there."

Albia and I ran for the house, the others following at as fast a walk as Silvanius' dignity would allow. But when we got there, none of us was surprised to find that the mysterious doctor had vanished into thin air.

I thought again about Taurus' comment this morning. Somebody didn't like Quintus Antonius very much.

Silvanius was red-faced and fuming. "This is appalling," he almost shouted. "How dare they? How dare they use my name! Use my name to try to trick you…to commit Jupiter knows what crimes in *my name*….By the gods, Aurelia, this is too much!"

"Call your meeting, Councillor, and the sooner the better," I said.

"Tomorrow. No wait, tomorrow won't do. I shall want Felix there, and he's going to a play in Eburacum tomorrow, aren't you, Titus? Well then, the day after tomorrow. Dinner at my humble abode. I know! Perhaps you'd like to come and see the latest work on my new temple first? If we all meet there about noon, we can go to my new house, have an early dinner, and then get down to our meeting afterwards. That will make the whole thing look like an ordinary social gathering."

"Excellent. Thank you, I'll be there." Dinner with the Chief Councillor wouldn't be just an "ordinary social gathering." Silvanius had the best chef north of the Humber.

"I shall count the hours." Felix clasped my hand. "And meantime, my dear, you must all take care of yourselves here. These are dangerous times. Don't run any risks."

I could have done without another well-meaning friend reminding me how vulnerable we were.

After they rode away, I went the rounds inside and out. The evening meal was well in hand; the olive oil delivery had arrived finally, with the correct number of amphorae for a change. In the stables and the horse-paddocks, I found everything in order. It was the usual quiet spell before the evening's customers started piling in.

But the calm was abruptly shattered by an unexpected sound, a cavalry bugle call. Who in Hades could it be at this hour? Not our hunting tribunes returning from the woods, surely? Perhaps a guest just arriving, demanding attention, but then why was he blowing "Prepare to advance"?

I didn't have far to search for the answer. Young Titch was in the stable yard, blowing a brass bugle before the admiring eyes, and ears, of the other stable-lads.

He paused for breath, and held up the battered instrument proudly. "Me dad gave me this. I know all the cavalry calls. Listen, this one's the Rally...." He demonstrated it, and several more. Then the other lads tried to blow it; most of them got no noise at all from it, and Milo managed a sound like a dying duck.

"Useful thing, a bugle," Titch said importantly. "I once saw a feller being attacked, and I blew me bugle and the men ran off, thinking I was the cavalry coming."

The other boys scoffed, and I doubted it myself, but it made a good tale.

He grinned at me. "Would you like a go, Mistress?" He offered me the bugle. I couldn't work out whether he was paying me a compliment, or being exceedingly cheeky. Probably the latter, but I thought, why not? Let's show them! I wiped the mouthpiece on my sleeve, and blew a couple of calls, the way my father had taught me: a quite creditable "Form up," and then "Return to camp." By this time I was enjoying myself, and I blew "Charge" till the buildings echoed.

The lads looked at me open-mouthed, and Titch said, "Wow! Where did you learn that?"

"My father was an army man," I answered, "and so's my brother. I probably know more calls than you've had hot dinners."

"That's brilliant!" Milo said. "Do some more."

I shook my head and handed the treasure back to its proud owner. "One bugler in the place is more than enough. I'd better warn you though...."

"Yes?"

"I'm aware that blowing bugles isn't considered a very lady-like accomplishment. So if Councillor Silvanius ever gets to hear about this, I'll skin you all alive! Understand?"

As I turned away it was good to hear their laughter. There hadn't been much to laugh about all day.

Chapter VII

Darkness came, and Quintus Antonius grew fire-hot and talked almost continuously as he tossed about in his sleep, but none of it made any real sense. He kept calling for Burrus, for Lucius—our Lucius? Who could say?—and in between whiles he babbled about urgent messages. I wished we did indeed have a doctor, but Albia and I did what we could for him. I bathed his face with feverfew water and tried to get him to drink some watered wine, but he spilt most of it, and Albia bandaged a small bag of dried arnica and violet petals over the bruise on his head.

The tribunes came in at dusk, disappointed and grumpy after a poor day in the woods; two small wild pigs and a geriatric hare were all they'd managed to catch in their nets. There was only one other guest staying, a quiet elderly contractor buying hides for the army, so Albia and I joined the three of them for supper, leaving the maids to run the bar. I lighted all the bronze candelabra in the dining-room to brighten the place up, and everyone enjoyed the venison. Cook roasted a haunch and served it with a damson sauce, and leeks and carrots from our own garden. I looked out some good Campanian red to go with it, and certainly the atmosphere needed lightening, because the tribunes were in a foul mood.

"Our trackers were useless," Marius complained. "Couldn't find any decent game at all, and they were surly and uncooperative all day long. I don't understand it. Yesterday they were full of the joys, and we caught this brilliant deer." He cut himself another slice of it, and drank his beaker of wine in one go. "And you didn't help matters, Junius," he grumbled.

"Me? What did I do?"

"You upset them, losing your temper like that when we got separated." Marius poured himself more wine. "I know it was annoying when they got you lost like that, but...."

"*Annoying!* Totally pathetic, more like! How can men who call themselves huntsmen get lost in their own woods, I ask you?" He spooned more sauce onto his plate, and chewed thoughtfully in silence for a while. "Actually, I don't think they did get lost. I had the feeling it was deliberate, some sort of trick to keep us separated, but I can't think why."

"Perhaps," the army contractor suggested, "there's some particularly good hunting, an old wild boar or a wolf with cubs, and they want to save it for themselves instead of letting you go after it."

"Yes, that's probably it," Junius agreed. "Or maybe they think we're not paying them enough. If we upped their wages a bit..."

Marius shook his head. "Not likely! Give natives an inch, they'll take a mile. If they don't start doing better, we'll pay them less, not more."

They bickered on for a while, and I thought, if they've been squabbling all day, I expect their mood will have infected the natives. But gradually the wine relaxed them. Unfortunately before they had completely cheered up, we had to tell them of the two corpses found after last night's attacks.

Junius suggested we should post a guard outside overnight, and we agreed Taurus would share the sentry duty with the tribunes' men. Albia and I agreed to take watches by Quintus Antonius' bedside. I thought this was pretty good of Albia, as I could guess which bedside she'd rather be heading for.

Marius left the dining-room straight after the meal; according to Junius he had an assignation with one of the slave-boys. Albia went off to the sick-room, and I went to bed, but I hardly slept. Every little sound had me wide awake and jumpy, and I was dressed and ready when Albia came to call me about halfway through the night.

I found Quintus Antonius still restless, but a little less noisy. I sat quietly with him through the dark dead hours, and managed to doze fitfully, but even in my sleep I could hear his ragged breathing and incoherent muttering. Then just before dawn I woke up fully when he started moving around in the bed. As I looked at him he turned onto his back, stretched his arms above his head, and opened his eyes.

"What day is it?" I don't know what I'd expected him to say, but that wasn't it.

"The Nones of August," I answered.

He looked stricken. "Then it's started. It started two days ago! And I should have been picking up reactions, watching what they did…."

He tried to get into a sitting position, but couldn't make it, and sank back onto the pillows. The bedclothes and his tunic were damp with sweat, and he was still flushed-looking; his eyes had lost their glazed stare, but they didn't seem to focus properly.

"What happened two days ago?" I asked, automatically tidying up the blankets.

"The eclipse, of course. You did see the eclipse?"

"Eclipse? No. What eclipse?"

"An eclipse of the sun. You must have seen it! The third day of August, late afternoon. A partial eclipse, not total, but the astronomers said it'd be quite a spectacular one. You can't have missed it, surely."

"We must have done." I tried to remember; but I mean, who remembers the weather two days ago, unless it's been blowing a gale or raining frogs? "It was cloudy all day, I think. It did get a bit dark in the afternoon, but that's hardly a novelty in Britannia in August. Did you see it yourself?"

"No, I didn't." Suddenly he smiled. "It was cloudy with us too. Perhaps it was cloudy all over Brigantia, so the natives wouldn't have seen it."

"But what's the difference if they did see it?" It seemed no great matter to me, but he was getting excited enough for both of us.

"Because they'll think it was a sign from their gods, or the Druids will tell them it was. I was supposed to be watching their reaction....And now I don't know what to do for the best. I'm helpless here. I must get up. I *must*....Help me up, please."

"I don't think that's a good idea," I said.

"Just do it!" he barked. "I've got to try. If I could get to Eburacum today, perhaps I could make a difference."

He sat up slowly, then he gritted his teeth and swung his legs out of bed. He put his arm across my shoulders to steady himself, and I supported him as best I could, though he was clumsy and heavy. He managed to stand on his feet for about five heartbeats; then he gave a little moan, put both hands to his head, and fell backwards. I stopped him sliding to the floor, and got him back into bed. He was unconscious again.

I went in search of Albia, and found her in the kitchen organising breakfast. "Holy Diana, Relia, you look as sick as Cousin Quintus! Is he any better?"

"He woke up for a short while, but he's passed out again. He was fretting about some eclipse of the sun that happened two days ago. Only we missed it."

"Yes, Junius was telling me about it. Shame it was cloudy. Junius says it would have been quite dramatic. He knows all about the stars." She smiled fondly. Gods, I thought, she's really got it badly for that young man. Oh well, she's a big girl now.

She helped me change Quintus' blankets, and dress him in a fresh tunic. He didn't stir, and his breathing was still uneven and noisy. I found Baca and told her to take up sick-room watching again for the morning. The pile of mending in the sewing basket was going down nicely.

I went and unbarred the main door. No golden dawn today, and no inert body on the forecourt either; just a mist with a clammy drizzle in it, and under the oak-tree the comforting, bulky figure of Taurus on watch.

"'Morning, Taurus," I called. "All well?"

"All fine, Mistress." He shook his wet cloak as he came towards me. "Nothing and nobody stirring anywhere."

He was right, there wasn't a single person or vehicle on the main road. It wasn't a market day, so there'd be much less early traffic. The first two couriers came through just after breakfast, heading for the coast. Unusually they were riding together instead of racing each other for a bet, which is the normal messengers' game. We soon discovered why: there had been two more murders overnight.

A headless body had been found in the forum before first light; another, headless also, had been discovered outside town on the road near Silvanius' new villa. Both carried bone discs with their sinister message.

"Get out or die....You know yesterday," I said to Albia, "that was just a wild threat, unpleasant but not seriously believable. Now it starts to feel real."

"I know." Her usually cheerful face looked grim. "Are we going to wake up every morning to find more and more of our people killed?"

"I wish I could answer no, but...it's scary."

"Yes, it is. But whoever the bastards are, Relia, they're not getting *me* out. I belong here, and I'm staying."

"So am I. Father brought us here to give us a chance of a good life, a stake in a new province. We've worked hard for those things. We're not giving them up. We're Romans, and Romans can't be frightened off by a pack of barbarians."

Brave words, but that wasn't the worst of it. The next traveller to come by with news, a wagoner, told us both the victims had been identified. The one in the forum was Gaius Terentius, the innkeeper of the Kingfisher Mansio in Eburacum. He'd been in Oak Bridges visiting friends, and was caught on his way home. It hit us like a physical blow. I mean all the murders were horrible, but the death of another mansio keeper, a friend, someone we knew well, and a Roman from Italia, made me feel close to panic.

The tribunes' mood was sour too, because the other victim was an old soldier, retired and settled near town on a smallholding. But though it sounds dreadful, I was almost relieved to hear about it. Now, I thought, the army will take some notice, and start patrolling the district properly.

Hippon came to see me. I noticed he was limping slightly; hard knocks were an occasional part of his job as a horse-trainer. He was grumbling because some harness that was being made up for us in town hadn't been delivered. "It was promised last month, and we do need it. I ought to go in myself and give the fellow a piece of my mind. I think I'll take the small carriage, then I can bring back whatever he's got ready. If anything."

Normally he'd prefer to ride. I looked him up and down. "What is it? Feeling under the weather?"

"No fooling you, is there? I bruised my leg, coming off the black stallion with a thump yesterday. That animal can be a real bastard." His words were softened by his smile; I don't think there ever was a horse he couldn't love. He rubbed his left knee gingerly. "I'm getting too old for this job, Aurelia."

"Nonsense! But take the raeda, by all means. You could try out those new ponies you were training yesterday. They look about ready for some road-work."

He cheered up at once; he always enjoys training horses. "Yes, I will. And I think I'll take young Victor along, and give him a try as driver. See if he's as good as he says he is."

"If he's *that* good, then I'm the Queen of Brigantia!"

Hippon smiled. "The best ones tend to be cocky at his age. Don't worry, I'll keep a good eye. We'll be off in about an hour, when the morning chores are done."

As he left us, little Baca came scurrying in, all smiles. "Mistress, the man in the bed is awake again, and he's got his wits back. I asked him if he felt better, and he said yes, and I said I hoped so, because then he wouldn't be so grumpy today."

"That wasn't very polite to a guest, Baca."

"That's what he said," she nodded, "but in a sort of smiley way."

Quintus was still smiling when I got to his room, and his smile widened when he saw me.

"Aurelia!" he exclaimed. "Aurelia Marcella. It is you, isn't it? I've had some weird dreams, with practically everybody I know appearing in them. But you're real, aren't you?"

"I'm real, Quintus Antonius, and I'm delighted you're back to your proper self again. You've given us all quite a fright."

He looked at me sharply. "Why do you call me that? Quintus Antonius…that's not my name."

"But…oh, I'm sorry." I must tread carefully here. "My sister recognised you, or thought she did. She was sure she'd met you before, but she must be mistaken." Well, I could hardly tell him I'd seen his high-powered official papers, after he'd made such a song and dance about keeping them secret. "What is your name, then?"

"I'm Quintus Valerius Longinus." He sat up and held out his hand. "And I'm afraid I've been poor company so far. According to your little sewing-girl, anyway."

I took his hand. "Never mind, I'm delighted to meet you. And I'm sorry you've had a rather rough welcome to the Oak Tree. How do you feel now?"

"I've felt better, but I'm on the mend. Could I possibly have a drink of water? I've got a thirst like a camel, and this jug's empty."

I fetched him some and he drank thirstily. Then he asked for a cloth, and rubbed his face with it, going carefully as he touched the bruises.

"Ouch! I seem to have been in a bit of a scrap."

"I expect you gave as good as you got."

"I hope so." He stretched his arms above his head, and smiled again. "I still ache all over, but I'm feeling decidedly better. I wonder….If I remember rightly, Lucius said you have a bath-house here."

"Yes, we have. You've met my brother, then. Is that why you're here? Did Lucius send you?"

"Not directly. But he's talked about you often. And this place. I was on my way here when we were attacked."

"If you're a friend of Lucius, are you a friend of Aunt Julia as well, by any chance?" I asked.

"Aunt Julia? No. The only one of Lucius' relatives I've ever met is his Uncle Paullus from Cyprus."

"Oh well, never mind. Now, before your bath, would you like some breakfast? Bread and honey, and some wine?"

"Wonderful. I could eat a horse."

"Or an elephant?" I suggested.

"I think I'll just stick to bread and honey."

So he hadn't picked up the identification code. Did that mean he wasn't the man Lucius had mentioned in his letter, or was it just the effect of his bang on the head?

As I crossed the courtyard to the kitchen, Taurus appeared through the back archway. "Is he better, Mistress? The man who was under the tree?"

"Yes, he is. Awake and asking for breakfast."

"That's good." He gave his slow smile. "You were worried for him."

"Well, of course I'd worry about a wounded guest, Taurus."

"'Course you would." He winked. He may be simple, but he's not stupid.

Quintus ate hungrily while I repeated the story of how I'd found him, and showed him the bone disc that had been pinned to his tunic.

"I remember Burrus and I were riding along quite fast," he said between mouthfuls. "We'd got held up crossing the Humber, so it was pretty well dark. But we knew we must be nearly at the Oak Tree. Then we saw a soldier lying in the road, and another soldier with him, who waved and shouted for help. So naturally we stopped. Then they attacked us, and three more men came to help them. We tried to fight them off, but....After that it's a bit confused."

"*Soldiers* attacked you?"

"I doubt if they were real ones. It's easy to look like a soldier, given the right clothes and weapons."

I told him what Hawk had pieced together about the fight, and about his dead horse and his companion galloping off.

"Good! That must mean Burrus got clear. I expect he's out somewhere looking for me."

"You said he was a German, with a snake tattoo?"

"Yes, he is…but you just said 'he *was.*' What's happened?" He looked at me keenly. Oh, me and my big mouth!

I told him as gently as I could about the body found in the forum. It upset him more than I'd expected.

"Poor Burrus! He was almost at the end of his army time. This was his last assignment. A good man, brave and sensible. When he got out, he was going back to the Rhine, to his parents. He used to tell me about their farm, and the girl who was waiting for him." His jaw set. "D'you know, I mind about them killing Burrus more than I mind about them attacking me. After all, I chose this lousy job. Burrus just went where he was told. Well, I'll have those bastards, Aurelia. I'll have the lot of them!"

"Good." The only way I could think of to comfort him was to change the subject, so I asked if he'd heard of the Shadow-men, and their leader, the Shadow of Death.

He nodded. "We've heard of them, and we're taking them seriously. The Shadow of Death is a good rebel commander. Far *too* good, from our point of view. He's also something of a mystery man. They say he wears a mask."

"A mask? You mentioned something yesterday about one of the attackers wearing a mask."

"Did I? Why yes, I remember now….A gruesome-looking thing, like a skull with empty eyes. He just stood there, but I got the impression somehow he was the leader, and the others were carrying out his orders, even though he didn't say anything. So that was the Shadow of Death? Well, his shadow wasn't long enough to swallow *me!*"

By this time he'd drunk his mug of wine and eaten two large pieces of bread and honey and a handful of plums. He sighed contentedly, and lay back on the pillows.

"I really do need a bath," he said almost dreamily. "When will the water be hot?"

"In an hour or so. I've told Taurus to make sure the stoker gets a move on, but it'll take a while. We don't keep the furnace going all night in the summer."

Taurus himself appeared just then, leaning his huge dark head and massive shoulders in through the door.

"Sorry to intrude, Mistress, but Miss Albia sent me. There are two military investigators in the bar, asking to see this gentleman. From Eburacum. They say they're looking into all these attacks and murders and they want to talk to him urgently. Miss Albia says, should she send them in here?"

"Yes, Taurus, tell her…."

"No, wait!" Quintus interrupted. "What do they look like?"

"Look like?" Taurus said, surprised. "Well…just ordinary army investigators."

"But their appearance? Tall—short—describe them!"

He thought about it. "The one in charge is small with black hair and a scar on his hand. The other one is tall and his hair is sort of mousey."

"That settles it," Quintus snapped. "I can't see them." His whole body had tensed up, for all the world as if he was going to make a run for it. "That is, I can't let them see *me*."

I was taken aback. "Why ever not? I'd have thought you'd be glad enough if someone catches the gang who beat you up."

"Those two have been following me. Because—well, never mind why." He turned to Taurus. "Tell them I'm asleep. Still unconscious, and too ill to be disturbed."

Taurus shook his head. "I can't, sir."

I wondered if Quintus was losing his grip again. But no, the blue-purple eyes were bright, alert, and hard.

"Are you sure about this?" I asked him.

"Quite sure." He looked at Taurus. "Do as I say. Tell them I'm unconscious, and get rid of them."

Again the slave shook his head. "I'm sorry, sir. I've already told them you're awake."

"*Merda*," Quintus swore. "What did you do that for?"

"I didn't know it was a secret," Taurus protested, looking miserable. "The Mistress told me that you were better. She was pleased about it. We all were. So when the men came asking, I thought they'd be pleased too."

"It's all right, Taurus, you weren't to know," I put in. "And we can soon…."

"Did you tell them my name?" Quintus barked.

"I don't know your name, sir. But they knew it anyway. They said you're Quintus Antonius Delfinus. I said I didn't know."

Quintus swore again, but I waved him quiet. I couldn't work out what was going on here, but clearly we needed a bit of time, so I could get to the bottom of Quintus' extraordinary reaction. Taurus could take a message to delay the military agents; he isn't over-bright, but he's as solid as a rock if you know how to explain things to him.

"Taurus, look. This gentleman is a friend of Master Lucius, and he needs our help."

"A friend of the master's? Ah, that's different."

"So we need to keep the investigators away for the time being. You know what the army can be like. They could make all sorts of trouble for him. And for Lucius as well," I added. Taurus nodded in understanding; this was familiar ground. "So go back and say he's too ill to see anybody."

"But I've already told them…."

"I know, but it'll be all right. You can say that the gentleman's passed out again. Say that he woke up, and tried to get up and was dizzy and flopped back into bed, and now he's asleep. It's all true, except for the last bit. He did pass out, when he tried to get out of bed earlier on. Didn't you?"

"Yes, I did," Quintus said grumpily.

"All right, Taurus. You do that, and then get back to work. I'll come and talk to them very soon."

Taurus grinned suddenly. "It's like when Master Lucius comes home. We have to be careful who we tell."

"You've got it. Now off you go. Don't let's keep them waiting."

Quintus looked doubtfully after him. "Is he reliable?"

"Completely, yes. He's a simple man, not good at lying unless he sees the reason for it. Sometimes I think the world would be better if we were all as truthful as Taurus."

"Ouch! That puts me in my place. Deception's an important part of my job."

"No, really?" I went and shut the bedroom door, and leaned my back against it. "Now I'm not leaving till you tell me why you don't want these men to see you."

"I told you already. They've been following me."

"That could mean you're a criminal. In which case my duty is to hand you over. You've got to understand, this is an official mansio here. I'm not under military orders exactly, but if I refuse to help the military…well, it could be awkward."

He sighed. "All right. I'm on an unofficial job for the Governor. Unofficial, and very secret."

"As revelations go, that's hardly earth-shaking. Are you hunting these Shadow-men?"

"No. Yes. Well, yes and no."

"Thanks for such a clear answer!" I looked at him for a few heartbeats, but his purple-blue eyes gave nothing away. I felt distinctly uneasy. What possible reason could he have for avoiding military investigators? Didn't he want them to catch the men who had nearly killed him, and had presumably killed Burrus? I could only think of one good answer. He wasn't, as he claimed to be, an investigator hunting criminals. He was a criminal, being hunted himself.

My brain told me to be cautious, not to take him at face value. And yet my instinct said he was no criminal, and I should help him. Usually with me, instinct wins out over caution. But still….

"I'll give you one more chance to explain," I said. "I'm from an army family, which means I've no great love for military investigators, but before I refuse outright to help them, I need to know why. Perhaps I'm like Taurus. I don't like lying unless I see the need for it."

"Military bureaucracy," he said. "It gets in the way in a case like this. I'm in their territory but they haven't been notified, and that'll upset them. They'll want me to do things their way, and I'll be writing reports and giving them briefings for days. I simply haven't got time for all that."

"Which, as our grandmother would have said, is a load of round objects! If your mission is so secret, how come they know you're here—they even know your name?"

"They don't. My name's Quintus Valerius Longinus."

"More round objects. Balls, in plain Latin! I told you, my sister recognised you as Quintus Antonius Delfinus. So let's stop playing games, or I'll fetch those investigators in here now."

He gave me a hard stare, which I returned. I felt both confused and annoyed. Was any part of his explanation remotely true? He claimed to be working for the Governor, so why couldn't he use one of his all-powerful government passes? He said he knew Lucius, but he hadn't recognised the identification signal. And now he was being pursued by military agents....

He smiled, a touch sheepishly. "Well, your sister's too clever for me. I am Quintus Antonius Delfinus. But I'm travelling as Quintus Valerius Longinus at present, and it's important they don't find out who I really am. Promise me you won't tell them. Please?"

"You can be Quintus Valerius Caesar for all I care. But if these two officers know you already...."

"They don't know what I look like. So you could tell them I'm Valerius Longinus....I suppose you can't stop them coming in here to look at me, if they insist. If that happens, I'll pretend to be asleep. But they may try to kidnap me."

This was going too far. *"Kidnap you?* For the gods' sake, why?"

"Because I'm on their trail, of course. And if they do, I'm relying on you to prevent them. Understand?" He looked at me intently, and suddenly he wasn't a wounded man talking to the woman who was nursing him; he was a battle commander briefing a subordinate.

But we weren't in a battle, and my irritation boiled over. "Understand? I don't understand anything, and that's a fact. So I'm going to see the two agents, and make up my mind when I've heard their side of this." I turned round and grasped the door-handle.

"No, Aurelia, wait. Please!"

I paused and half-turned, but didn't release the handle.

"I suppose I'll have to tell you a little more. What I'm investigating isn't primarily the Shadow-men. The real danger just now isn't the natives themselves. It's Roman treachery."

"*Roman* treachery? You mean the military...."

"And others. Please, no more now. Just help me by keeping those two from doing me any damage. Promise me you won't let them touch me."

Roman treachery.... Now that made more sense. Except that this man was a Roman too. Which meant he could just as well be a traitor as an investigator—or he could be both. How could I know?

I couldn't.

There was a knock at the door. Quintus lay statue-still on his bed as I opened the door slowly, but it was only Baca.

"Please mistress, Miss Albia says could you come. The two gentlemen are getting impatient."

"I'll come." I turned back to Quintus. "I'll promise this much. I won't let them take you away from here today. You're not well enough to be moved anyway. After that—it depends on what they have to say for themselves."

"Thank you." He relaxed, and smiled at me. "I know it's a lot to ask. From now on, I'm asleep." He snuggled down into the blankets, pulled a fold of one over his head, and began to snore loudly.

"Don't overdo it," I warned. "Heavy breathing will be fine."

And I still couldn't decide, as I crossed the courtyard, whether I believed a single word of what he'd told me.

Chapter VIII

Two men in short red cloaks got to their feet as I entered the bar-room. They had military hair-cuts and army boots and swords, but they weren't ordinary infantry; they were unmistakeably the sort of charmless bullies that serve as military investigators. I disliked them on sight.

But I gave them my most welcoming smile. "Good morning, gentlemen. I'm sorry to have kept you waiting."

"Good morning, Mistress Aurelia," they said pleasantly enough. The smaller one asked, "You're the proprietor of the mansio here?"

"I'm joint proprietor with my brother Lucius Aurelius Marcellus. But he's away on military service at present."

He held out his hand. "I'm Nonius, and this is Rabirius. We're agents from the Special Services Unit at the legionary headquarters in Eburacum." They both smiled, looking like lions in the arena, about to take their first juicy bites of doomed criminals.

"Military Intelligence, in plain Latin." I smiled again, as I remembered that the army nickname for military investigators was Kickers and Punchers, reflecting their normal methods of interrogation. "What can I do for you? But first, have you had some breakfast?"

"Thank you, yes." He indicated plates and wine-mugs on their table. "Your girls have looked after us nicely. You keep a good drop of Gaulish red here."

Gods, Albia must have been panicking, serving the best Gaulish red at this time of day! I glanced at her, where she stood behind the bar counter, writing some list or other on a wax tablet. She looked up at me and said casually, "Relia, can you just check this list—I don't want to miss anything out."

"Do sit down," I said to the visitors, as I strolled over and examined the tablet. At the top she'd written: *Something smells fishy. Take care.* So she didn't like them either.

"Yes, that's fine, Albia, thanks." I went back to the table and sat down.

"We hear there's been some trouble locally, and we're looking into it," Rabirius began. "Tell us about the man who was attacked here."

I gave him as little detail as I could without sounding suspiciously unhelpful. "It's all very worrying," I added. "We'll be glad of help from the military. Have you any idea who's behind the killings?"

Rabirius shook his head. "It's early days, but we're following up every lead, of course." Which meant, "We haven't a clue, and if we had one, we probably wouldn't know what to do with it."

The short one, Nonius, took out a wax notepad. "Let's get down to business. I'm sure Mistress Aurelia's got enough to do without our taking all morning." Presumably it was meant to be pleasant, but it came out as a threat. With every sentence they uttered, I felt more and more in sympathy with Quintus Antonius.

"This man you found," Nonius said. "What did you say his name is?"

Oh no, you don't catch me that easily, sunshine. "I'm afraid I've no idea. I haven't had a chance to ask him."

"Oh? But your man tells me he's awake."

Nice try, but I knew Taurus would have given him the revised version.

"Not any more." I sighed deeply. "He did wake up briefly this morning, and asked where he was, but didn't seem to have any memory of what had happened to him. Then he tried to get up, but it gave him head pains and he said he felt dizzy, and the next thing I knew, he'd collapsed back into bed. He's unconscious now."

"How bad are his injuries?" Nonius asked.

"He's had a hard blow on the head, and his face is badly bruised, his ribs too. And he must have been lying out in a heavy dewfall all night till we found him. But he looks quite tough. He'll pull through."

"Has a doctor seen him?" Rabirius put in.

I was about to say no, but then thought it might be better to tell yet another lie. "Yes, one of our friends sent his personal physician over yesterday. He prescribed rest, in fact he said it was vital in cases of concussion. He was afraid there might be damage inside his skull, and said we should keep him warm and still till he comes round naturally." Not bad for the spur of the moment, Aurelia.

The two men looked at each other, and Rabirius smiled his slimy smile. "It sounds like our man."

Nonius nodded. "I think so too. Quintus Antonius Delfinus."

I didn't register any expression. "You know who he is?"

"Oh yes. One of our people, helping us with some investigations. And if we're right, the best thing is for us to take him with us to Eburacum so he can be properly looked after. These head injuries can be very tricky."

My mind was buzzing like a beehive. They wanted to take Quintus away with them. Was it genuine comradely concern, or an attempt at kidnapping?

"Perhaps we can see him." Rabirius made it a statement rather than a question.

"Yes, of course." As we stood up, young Titch came running in, panting and looking worried. "Please, Mistress Aurelia...."

"Not now, Titch. I'm busy."

"But it's the black stallion, Mistress. He's sick, having some sort of fit, and Hippon doesn't know what to do. He said to fetch you quick."

"Holy Diana!" The black was our best stud horse. If anything happened to him.....I'd have to see what was the matter.

I turned to the waiting men. "Gentlemen, would you please excuse me? Sit down and have a drop more wine. I'll be as quick as I can, but it seems one of our best horses is in trouble."

We hurried outside, and rounded the corner towards the stables. Then Titch stopped dead.

"I'm sorry, Mistress, there's nowt wrong with the stallion. I had to get you away from them two and it was all I could think of."

"What? What game is this?"

"Not a game," he said urgently. "Them two men, they're up to no good. I've seen them before."

"They say they're from Kickers and Punchers."

He shook his head. "They were here in the woods two nights ago, and they attacked a man. Beat him up, and killed his horse. I saw it. Now Taurus says that's the sick man you've got here. So I thought I better warn you."

"You saw them? If you're making this up...."

"No, honest. I *saw*."

The boy was deadly serious. The words "Roman treachery" resounded in my head, and I couldn't begin to deal with the implications of what he'd just said; the important thing was the sick man in the house, and I was convinced now that whatever his quarrel with the two investigators, it was Quintus' side I was on.

"You swear this is true?"

"I swear."

"Right. I'll talk to you later."

I raced back through the front door. And the bar-room was empty. The men had vanished.

I began to panic. Where had they gone? Where was Albia? And what were they doing to Quintus Antonius?

I ran into the courtyard, and that was empty too. I raced into the guest wing, along the corridor to Quintus Antonius' room, and found them just inside the door, making for the bed. Nonius had his sword half out of its scabbard, but he pushed it back as I charged in, apologising fulsomely for having left them alone.

I saw a look of annoyance pass between the two men, just for a heartbeat, then they were impassive again, but they still moved purposefully towards the bed. "Wake up, Quintus Antonius," Rabirius shouted, loud enough to rouse the shades from the underworld. "Wake up, man! We've come to look after you!"

"Please, Officer," I protested. "The man's unconscious, you can see that for yourself. He's also very ill. There's no call to make such a noise."

Quintus lay quite still, breathing heavily but regularly. The two men looked at the bed, and then Rabirius reached down and pulled back the blankets. Quintus didn't move a muscle.

Rabirius said, "That's him all right. And he's had quite a pasting." He didn't sound sympathetic.

Deliberately I went and covered the still figure up with the blankets, and stood close to the bed, facing the two men. They read it, correctly, as a challenge, and both took a pace backward.

"One of your men, you say?" I asked. "Was he on a case in this district?"

"The details needn't concern you, my dear." Rabirius' attempt at being soothing was unconvincing. "He's one of ours, that's all that matters, and we always look after our own. We must get him to Eburacum."

"As quickly as possible," Nonius agreed. "It's essential he has proper medical care. I know you've done your best, and we're grateful, but we'll deal with everything now. We'll take him back there straight away. You presumably have suitable transport we can requisition?"

You're taking him nowhere, I thought. *Roman treachery....* But how was I going to stop them?

"Well of course I appreciate your concern," I answered, "but this man's sick, and while he's under my roof I'm responsible for him. I can't let you move him till he's recovered."

"You really mustn't worry," Rabirius said, still trying to be reassuring, and failing dismally. "I can promise you he'll be very well looked after. The medical facilities at Eburacum are absolutely top class. Come now, let's not waste any more time."

"No, I can't agree...." I began.

Nonius waved my objection aside. "Leave it to us now. Get your people to prepare comfortable transport, and we'll be on our way. I'm sure you'd like to do the right thing for this poor man. I don't want to have to make it an official order."

Refusing to let them move him would be a serious step. Once I'd taken it, there'd be no going back. For the last time, that nagging doubt struck me: what if they were genuine, and it was Quintus Antonius who was a criminal on the run? But in that case, surely they'd simply say so and arrest him. No, I'd come this far, and I'd go through with it.

I took a deep breath and looked Nonius in the eye. "I'm sorry, but Eburacum's a good fifteen miles away. The journey could kill him, and I can't allow such a risk. He's staying here till he comes round. I promise he'll be well cared for, and when he's conscious and it's safe for him to be moved, he can decide for himself whether to go to Eburacum. Not before."

Rabirius said, "Now my dear, it does you credit that you're so concerned, but this is state business. Men's business. We know what's best, so you can just leave it to us, all right?"

Oh no! Now you've well and truly cooked your goose, my friend! Nobody tells Aurelia Marcella not to be concerned with "men's business."

"Taking care of my guests is very much my business," I retorted. "What would it do to my reputation here if the word got around that a poor wounded traveller had been taken out of his sick-bed against doctor's orders, and died as a result? So I repeat, I won't let him be moved till he's well enough."

Rabirius' face reddened and he took a step towards me, angry and threatening. I stayed where I was. "We don't need your permission for this," he almost shouted. "He's coming with us, and that's that."

Nonius advanced on me too, and snarled, "You'd better not dare to refuse military orders. You'll be in real trouble if you go down that road."

His threat simply made me angry, and I stood tall, and threw my winning dice. "I'm not under military authority. I'm a free Roman citizen, running my own business and doing what's best for my guests. So you can't march in here throwing your weight around as if I'm some native in a mud hut. I have a brother in the army, so I'm fully aware of military procedures, and I don't take kindly to threats. Either you leave my property now, or I'll report this incident to headquarters myself as a case of military harassment of a Roman citizen. If you go straight away, I'll put your heavy-handed style down to your zeal and sense of duty, and we'll say no more. Is that clear?"

"You are refusing my orders?" Nonius was now deadly calm.

"I am not under your orders." I was calm too. I was in the right. I knew it, and they knew it.

"By the gods, you'll regret this attitude," Rabirius was shouting again now, but Nonius glared at him and he subsided. Nonius, it seemed, had realised what would happen if I did indeed report them. I hadn't told them where my brother was stationed; they would assume it was Eburacum.

"We'll leave then," Nonius said, attempting a dignified retreat. "I'm sorry you've adopted this unhelpful attitude, but as you say, when it comes down to it, we can't force you to release this man against your will. Not yet. But consider this. If any harm comes to him because he hasn't had proper treatment, if he doesn't recover, or if he is so damaged when he recovers that he's no longer fit for his work as an investigator, then you, and only you, will be held to blame for it. Meanwhile, I shall certainly be reporting to my commanding officer, and I can promise that you haven't heard the last of us."

He turned to the door, Rabirius close behind him. I followed on their heels, and ushered them along the corridor, out through the door that faced onto the stable yard, and round to the front of the house, where their two horses were waiting for them. They mounted and left without another word.

Then I summoned Titch, who was helping Hippon harness the ponies.

"You were right about those two men," I told him. "They were up to no good. I want you and the others to keep a sharp lookout for them, and if they come anywhere near the house again, I want to know at once."

"Yes, Mistress."

"And Titch…well done. But what were you doing in the woods two nights ago?"

"Sleeping. I didn't have nowhere else."

"But why didn't you tell us what had happened, when you began working here? Why in Jupiter's name didn't you mention you'd seen someone attacked?"

"You might of thought I had something to do with it. Anyway, it wasn't till today I realised the man I saw was the sick man you were looking after here."

I told him briefly what Hawk had made of the tracks. He said, "I reckon that's right. I only saw the part in the clearing. They got him off his horse and then they killed it, and there was another man caught with him, but he escaped. This one fought like a madman. And there was a weird man in a mask, saying nowt and watching it all."

"Something interrupted them though. Did you see what it was?"

His cheeky grin appeared. "Not see. Hear."

"Hear? Oh, Titch…not your bugle?"

"It was all I could think to do."

I could have hugged him, but he'd hardly have appreciated it. "Good lad. But look, have you told anyone else about this?"

"The other stable-lads. But I reckon they thought I made it up. Nobody else."

"Well don't. Those men were going to kidnap our sick man, perhaps even kill him. They don't know you saw them. Best if they don't find out."

"They might want to shut me up, like?"

"They might."

"Wow!" Suddenly he laughed. "I've never been that important before—for someone to want to kill me!" He went off, smiling hugely, and I had to smile too. You don't meet many people who are pleased at the prospect of a death threat.

Albia emerged from the main door, glancing anxiously around. "Relia! Have they gone? I'm so sorry...."

"They have. But *merda,* Albia, why in Saturn's name did you leave them alone?"

She smiled ruefully. "The oldest trick in the book. One of them knocked the wine-jug onto the floor, and the wine and the bits of pot went everywhere. It looked like an accident, and he kept apologising over and over, and saying, 'Just fetch a pail and a cloth and I'll clear it all up.' None of the slaves were about, so like an idiot, I went into the kitchen myself....I wasn't gone long. They didn't *need* long, the bastards."

"No. Well, no harm done. But it was close." I found I was shaking now it was all over. We went inside and I poured us each a drink, and told her what had happened, and what Titch had said.

She nodded. "Titch isn't the only one to have seen them before. One of them, anyway. It was a good disguise, that's why I didn't realise at first."

"Disguise? What disguise? When?"

"Yesterday. The short one, dark-skinned and longish black hair, put him in a Greek tunic, give him a black beard and a medical bag....I suspect you'd end up with the famous disappearing doctor, Lykos of Cos."

Immediately I knew she was right. "It strikes me," I said, "this Quintus Antonius must be rather an important cousin, if people are so set on getting rid of him."

When I got back to his room, he was sitting up and grinning all over his battered face, and when he saw me he got out of bed. "Aurelia, thank you. That was magnificent! You were quite wonderful!"

"Thanks. I just hope I've done the right thing."

"You have, you truly have. Oh, when I heard you laying into them about military procedure, threatening them with a case of harassment....I could kiss you, I could really!"

And he put his arms round me and kissed me on the mouth. I didn't see any reason to stop him.

I heard Albia's familiar giggle at the door, and I broke away, trying to think of something suitably cool and casual to say, but when I looked, the corridor was empty. So there was nobody around to see how many more times he kissed me before he finally stood back, smiling, and said: "And now, there's only one more thing I need to make this morning perfect."

So he went off, whistling, to his hot bath.

Chapter IX

I organised a larger room for him, in our private wing, away from other guests. It had a sitting-room attached, with cheerful red walls and scenes of distant hillsides painted in the panels, and it had a glazed window and a door which led out onto our personal garden. "In case you feel like taking a stroll later," I said to him.

"Or need to come and go unobserved," he agreed. "Thanks. This will be excellent."

The morning wore on with a series of the usual guest-house dramas. Cook was moaning that someone was stealing plums, and then he threw a real temperament because he was making sausages, and didn't like the quality of the smoked pork that Albia and two of the maids had prepared. He maintained it had an odd smell. Albia said it was fine, and I thought so too, when I was called in to arbitrate. One of the barmaids dropped a tray of six beakers; I gave her a box on the ears, and she went crying to Albia for sympathy, which she didn't get. Taurus reported that a garden-boy had put an axe through his foot, so now they were short-handed for harvesting vegetables. I told him to see the farm foreman Ursulus and borrow a field-hand for the day, but Ursulus said he couldn't spare a man, and sulked when I insisted....And so on, and so on. I wonder how many of our customers realise the behind-the-scenes turmoil that's taking place while they're sipping their drinks and chatting up the barmaids.

Twice I went to look in on Quintus Antonius in his new quarters, but he was fast asleep on his bed. It wasn't the feverish unrestful sleep he'd had yesterday; he was relaxed and peaceful. Albia had found him a lightweight green tunic to wear, but he'd discarded it, and lay there mother-naked. Even with all his bruises, he had a good body, well muscled, no fat on him, with powerful shoulders and arms, and legs to die for. I found myself remembering his kisses, and imagining....Yes, I know; that's not relevant to this report.

By noon there were several mules and a couple of horses on the forecourt, and one official government raeda. I'd seen its occupants in the bar, a tax collector and his clerk stopping for food on their way to the coast. (I regretfully set aside various private schemes Albia and I had hatched, only half joking, about putting hemlock into certain guests' drinks.) Among the native ponies tied to the railings were five sturdy animals hitched in a row, which belonged to Vitalis and his warrior lads. Last and best, there was a grey scrawny donkey, standing with its head down in that lugubrious way all donkeys have. I smiled as I recognised the beast, and the worn leather pack and bulging saddlebags it carried. It meant my favourite pedlar was inside.

He was propping up the bar, chatting to Albia, and several customers were clustered around buying him drinks. With half an eye I noticed the group of young native warrior boys sitting at the same table as yesterday, but they were keeping themselves to themselves and I didn't pay them any real attention.

"Ulysses!" I called out. "The welcome wanderer returns! How are you?"

"Ah, Mistress Aurelia, good day!" His big smile was as genuine as ever. He wasn't much to look at, short and weather-beaten, with hair and beard as grey as his donkey, and he was wearing the same old blue cloak with yellowish trimmings that had once been white. But he didn't need to be a Greek sculpture. He was just—well, just Ulysses.

"Good day, and a lovely day too, even better now that you're here! And how is my very favourite mansio lady?" He bowed and kissed my hand, a quite outrageous gesture which would have earned anyone else a caustic comment, but not old Ulysses. He was a perfume and trinket seller, originally from Syria some-where, and though he travelled the Empire, he'd never lost his oriental charm, or his air of having had a good education, yet having deliberately chosen the simple life. He was a born rover, and he always came with a pack full of the best scents and potions this side of the Alps, and a head full of amazing stories, most of them about as factual as the Odyssey. We hadn't seen him for six months, so we'd a treat in store.

After a couple of beakers of wine, and an account of his recent adventures, including a ludicrous but very entertaining tale about a dragon, Ulysses fetched his packs, and started laying out his wares.

"Any fancy ribbons today, ladies? Gentlemen—they would make perfect gifts for your wives. Look at these wonderful new colours, the very height of fashion in Rome, fresh in from Italia...."

The patter was professional, and the colours were beautiful; there was a glowing bright turquoise that would set off my fair hair, and I saw Albia eyeing a vivid scarlet, which would suit her dark curls.

He pulled some small clay flasks from a box where they'd been carefully packed in straw. "Or if it's perfumes you're after, I've got a wonderful rose scent, straight from the flowering gardens of Damascus....Or how about this now?" Out came some little round clay pots, their lids held in place by thin string. "A real treat for you, Mistress Aurelia. Straight off a boat from Alex-andria, it is. Made from a secret recipe for the Queen of Egypt herself. A marvellous new face cream, guaranteed to banish all wrinkles and lines, and leave every lady looking like the beauti-ful Queen Cleopatra."

"Ulysses, you're treading on dangerous ground," I warned. "Do I *look* as if I need a face cream to banish wrinkles and lines?"

He chuckled. "Well of course not, Mistress. Not *now*. And if you use this cream, I promise you never will. But if you don't buy a little pot today, can you be certain that one fine morning years and years from now you won't wake up and look in that pretty bronze mirror of yours, and say, 'Oh no, I'm sure there's a tiny wrinkle there, and how I wish I'd taken the advice of good old Ulysses?'…Who's to say, lady? Who's to say what the future holds? Why not take a pot just to be on the safe side?"

Albia and I and the senior maids spent a happy half-hour going through his stock, taking turns to attend to the customers when their good-natured complaints about dying of thirst became too strident. Some of the men even bought small items too, presents for their womenfolk. Several of us girls were persuaded to buy a couple of pots of the cream; then Albia bought a piece of scarlet ribbon, and I took some of the turquoise. And finally I went quite mad and bought a pair of lovely silver dress brooches with pieces of jet in them, and even some rose perfume.

Then we sat Ulysses down with more wine and some bread and cold venison, and asked him for the news.

He sighed. "I wish I could say all is well with the world, but in truth I can't. There's something disturbing going on. For years I've been travelling this province, going all over, from the white cliffs at Dubris to the hills of Brigantia; and I've always felt safe, give or take the odd highway robber. Now…I don't know, but something's changed. I hear tales of horse raids and barns being burnt, and now these murders, and the strange messages….Well, you'll say to me, Ulysses, there have always been small crimes—feuds between families, squabbling over tribal boundaries, that sort of thing. But now it's different. Always it's Romans who are the victims."

"Yes, that's right," I agreed. "I wish I knew what's causing it. We've always got on well with the local people."

"The Druids are behind it," Ulysses declared.

"The Druids are outlawed now, though," Albia pointed out. "Not in a position to do much harm, surely?"

"That's as may be. The politicians in Rome, they think all they have to do is announce that a religion is forbidden, and it'll evaporate like the morning mist. But the Druid beliefs are still strong in this province. And their priests are saying their gods are angry, because the gods of Rome have become too powerful now."

"If you ask me," I said, "the Druid gods always seem to be angry about something. Isn't that why they have those disgusting human sacrifices at their ceremonies? To try to appease them?"

"Yes, but this isn't the same. The Druids have been stirring things up for some time, especially in Brigantia, prophesying that Britannia will soon be free again, and that the gods will send a sign. So when the eclipse happened two days ago, of course they made the most of it. It wasn't a total eclipse, but very nearly. Quite spectacular. Did you see it?"

"No. It was cloudy here, and we missed it."

He drank some more wine. "I was in Eburacum. Well, just outside it, where the soldiers' families live. It was quite a sight."

"Did the Druids know the eclipse was coming, then?" Albia asked.

"Oh yes, for sure. They're knowledgeable about the skies. There are ways of working out where the sun and moon will be as they travel round the earth....I used to know about such things myself once." He smiled, remembering. "I wasn't always a poor pedlar, you know. When I was a young man in Damascus, I had good Roman schooling, like a fine gentleman...but I've forgotten most of it now, and I certainly didn't realise there was an eclipse coming. I was actually in a tavern, just wetting my whistle, when one of the soldiers' women ran in all excited, and called us to come outside and look because the sun was being eaten alive. So we went out, and sure enough, the sun seemed to be disappearing into a giant black disc, getting smaller and smaller like a melting piece of ice, till eventually it was nearly all hidden, with just a small part of it at the top shining brightly still. The sky went dark blue, and it got quite cold." He shivered at the memory, and took a sip of wine.

"Weird," I agreed. "And a bit frightening?"

He laughed. "Not to us Romans, no. I mean we all knew it was only a temporary thing, and would put itself right. It's to do with the moon moving in front of the sun, and blocking out its light for a bit. But the natives were in a terrible state, thinking the sun was going to vanish altogether and never come back. Shouting and crying and praying, they were. What a din!"

"I can imagine." It doesn't take much to scare a bunch of barbarians.

Ulysses dropped his voice dramatically and we all craned forward to listen. "The natives all thought the gods had sent a huge monster to gobble up the sun. The more it gobbled, the more terrified they were, calling out to their gods for help." He paused theatrically; the whole bar had gone silent, listening.

"Then this old Druid came out among the people, all in his white robes, and held up his hands and started praying to Taranis and the Three Mothers, saying the people would avenge the old gods and destroy their enemies, if only they'd have mercy and not take away the sunlight. He didn't actually say drive out the Romans, but it was clear enough. And, what a surprise, slowly, slowly, the sun came out from behind the moon, and everyone let out a great cheer. Even the Romans. Even me! I couldn't help myself. Soon the sun was whole again, and the old Druid stood there, taking all the credit for having rescued it, and saying to the people, 'You all know what's required of you. Take heed of this sign from the gods.' Sign from the gods, indeed! Makes you laugh, doesn't it?" But he wasn't laughing, and neither was I.

"It could have been a sign from the gods," Vitalis spoke up from his corner. "The gods could make an eclipse happen, couldn't they?"

"Well, yes, they could." Ulysses turned to face the five young warriors at their table. "In fact I suppose they do, but not just when they feel like it. The patterns of the sun and moon are fixed, and come round again and again every few years. Can the gods know, years in advance, that they are going to be angry on such-and-such a day, and will need an eclipse to give a sign to mortal men? Well, yes, before you say it," he waved a hand to stop Vitalis interrupting, "perhaps the immortals do know the future, and they did predict that they were going to be angry about the Roman conquest. But if they knew about all these happenings long ago, why couldn't they have done something to stop the Romans conquering Britannia in the first place?" He smiled triumphantly and drained his beaker.

It got a big laugh from everyone, except the young warriors, who sat glowering in their corner, muttering among themselves.

We passed round more drinks, and the bar became noisy again. "You gave those warrior lads one in the eye," I said to Ulysses. "Take care you don't cross their path on a dark night. They didn't look too pleased."

"I should hope I can speak my mind without worrying about a few foolish boys," he answered. "Mostly I don't mind what religion a man follows, but I don't care for Druids. They'd trick the hair off your head if they thought it would do them any good."

"More like the head off your shoulders," I joked.

"That too, yes." Ulysses looked at me seriously. "I knew a Syrian boy once in the far west of Britannia, by the ocean. Well, a man I should say. He'd been a soldier and got his discharge, and bought a small farm, just a few cows and a field or two, and he worked hard, and married a lovely girl, and started dreaming about raising a family. But the Druids in those parts told him his bit of land used to be one of their holy shrines, there was a spring and some oaks, and you know how they are about oak trees. They threatened the boy that he'd be killed if he didn't leave, but he wouldn't budge, and he bought a couple of strong field-hands for extra protection. So then the Druids apologised to him and said they didn't want to take away his living, but their tribesmen were upset at the holy place being used for a farm, and they promised if he'd move out peacefully, they'd give him a bigger and better patch of land a few miles away."

Again his voice had dropped, and the whole bar-room was listening. "Well his wife was a local girl, related to half the families around, and he didn't want a feud on his hands, so eventually he agreed, and he and his slaves and his girl and the cows set off for the new farm. But they never got there. They were ambushed on the road, and all killed."

There was a collective sigh, almost a moan. Suddenly the air felt chilly.

"Surely Druids aren't all like that?" Albia asked. "I thought they were scholars, and even healers."

"Well." Ulysses considered it. "To be fair, I have met a few Druids who are truly wise, and have the gift of healing too. But most of them are evil men who care more for their own power than anything else."

He stayed for one more beaker of wine and then went on his way. As he left I was surprised to see Junius standing near the door; he'd been listening to Ulysses too. Albia got him some wine, and said, "Have you given up hunting for today?"

He nodded. "The trackers were worse than ever. If you believe what they say, there isn't an animal worth hunting for ten miles in any direction. I wish I knew what's got into them! Perhaps the pedlar is right, the Druids are making them jumpy. Anyhow there was no point wasting more time. Marius is going off somewhere with his latest boy." He smiled at Albia. "I'll have to think of some other way to pass the afternoon. Do you ever get any time off, or does Aurelia keep you working all day and all night?"

"She's a real slave-driver," Albia smiled back. "But I might manage an hour or two."

"Good!" He turned to me. "But first...I say, Aurelia, could I have a quick word in private?"

"Why, yes, of course." I took him to my study. "What's up, Junius? Something wrong? I mean apart from the hunting?"

"No, nothing at all. But I've been trying to get a chance to talk to you on your own. I've a message from your brother Lucius, but he said to keep it discreet. About your Aunt Julia. Her birthday's coming up soon, apparently."

I must have looked completely thunderstruck, because he asked uncertainly, "Doesn't that make sense to you?"

"Is this the same Aunt Julia who's set her heart on an elephant?"

"That's the one!" He smiled, relieved. "So Lucius did write to you. He said he would, but I didn't know if the letter had got here."

"Well if that doesn't beat everything! Welcome, Cousin Junius. Welcome indeed! As you've seen for yourself, we've got troubles here, and we need all the help we can get."

"That's why I thought I'd better make contact," he answered. "But you'll keep all this to yourself, won't you?"

"Of course. Except you don't mind if I tell Albia—or perhaps you've done that already?"

"I think she guesses."

"And Marius—is he involved in what you're doing here?"

"Yes, but he's not a full cousin yet. In training, you might say; Uncle Titus gives the new recruits a trial period before they are truly part of the family. So he's acting as my assistant. He's a sound man, old Marius. From Gaul originally, and speaks several languages, so he gets on well with the natives."

"Lucius said in his letter you have business in Brigantia. Are you allowed to tell me what you're doing here?"

"Looking into these rumours of native unrest. We think the rebels may be getting help from someone in the army. I've orders to see if there's any evidence of that on the ground here. Lucius will be working on the problem from the Eburacum end, though I don't know when he'll be able to start."

"His letter said he was in the west, but that was half a month ago."

"Isca Silurum, yes. His present investigation is dragging on rather. He'll come north when he can."

"It can't be too soon! But at least we've got you here now. You'll let me know if we can help in any way?"

"There's one thing you can do straight away, if you will. Tell me all you can about that wounded man who turned up yesterday."

"Was it only yesterday? Gods, it feels longer! I'm afraid I can't tell you much. He's still asleep."

Junius said, "Not all the time, surely. I gather from the houseboys that he enjoyed some breakfast this morning, and had a bath."

That's the trouble with letting one of Lucius' so-called cousins into your house—bang goes your privacy. But this situation was getting out of hand. I was under an obligation to Lucius, and another conflicting one to Quintus Antonius, and I was in the middle trying to do what was right. I'd have to assume that a promise given face to face outranked an obligation to an absent brother.

"He did come round," I admitted, "but he was pretty dozy, and seems to have no memory of how he got here. Now he's gone to sleep again, which will do him good. He'll need to rest until his bruises go down, especially that lump on his head."

"What work does he do?"

"He's a bridge surveyor and inspector. But I can't see him doing much inspecting for a while."

"Has he told you his name?" Junius wanted to know.

"He's Quintus Valerius Longinus."

"Pity. I was wondering if he might be Quintus Antonius Delfinus."

"Who's he?"

"Just someone I'm looking for." He shrugged. "Never mind, we must do the best we can." He stood up. "And now, you don't mind if I take Albia away from the bar for a few hours?"

I laughed. "I don't seem to be getting much choice in the matter!"

"Good. And I'm glad we've had this little chat. Cleared the air, haven't we?"

"We certainly have." The air's as clear as winter fog, I thought, as I watched him go back to the bar. If he's Lucius' cousin, who in Jupiter's holy name is Quintus Antonius Delfinus?

Chapter X

I couldn't even begin to get an answer to this till next day. Quintus Antonius slept like a baby through the afternoon, into the evening, and all night. I looked in on him every now and then; he was relaxed and didn't stir, and there was no need for anyone to watch beside his bed. As our grandmother used to say, "Sleep is the best medicine, and cheap too."

Albia and Junius disappeared till dark, came back briefly for supper, and then disappeared again. I was glad for Albia. She's so good at her job, I admit I sometimes leave her to do more than her share of the work here. She deserved some time off, and if being in love made her happy, then I was happy too. But being a bit more cynical than my sister, I just hoped it wouldn't end in tears.

The sentries we posted reported nothing stirring from dusk till dawn. I woke up refreshed and full of energy, looking forward to the day ahead, the day of Silvanius' meeting, and the dinner at his new villa. Before I got involved in the morning chores, I sorted out the clothes I wanted to wear so they'd be ready for a quick change later. I decided to put on a show. Well, why not? I was pretty sure I would be the only woman in the party; I could either try to be invisible, or aim to be conspicuous. I never was much good at being invisible.

I chose my cream embroidered tunic with the russet-red over-tunic, and white sandals; I added my green wool travelling-cloak, in case it was cold on the way home. I even found some silver ear-rings and a chain necklace, to match my new silver brooches.

At breakfast-time I took a tray of food to Quintus' room; if he was still asleep, I could leave it in case he woke up hungry later. But he was wide awake, and greeted me with a smile.

"Hello, Aurelia. You're a welcome sight."

"Cupboard love." I put down the tray. "I thought you might be ready for food, after a hard day and night sleeping. There's fresh bread, cold sausage, and fruit, and some Rhodian."

"I'm starving! Thanks." He took a beaker and drank gratefully, then started on the sausage as if he hadn't eaten for a month. "Delicious," he said, with his mouth full.

"You're looking better." I sat on a stool next to his couch.

"I'm feeling better too. I'm still sore, especially my head. But I'll mend. I've slept for hours. I just stretched out for a rest after my bath, and dozed off....Well, it's done me good. So what's been going on? No more visits from the military?"

"No, we've had a peaceful time. And an interesting visitor yesterday." I began telling him about Ulysses, and was surprised when he said he knew the old pedlar.

"I'm sorry I missed him, he's a marvellous old boy. I've met him down south."

I laughed. "And was it his coloured ribbons that interested you, or his perfumes?"

"His travellers' tales, of course! He may embroider his stories a bit, but he's actually one of the most observant men you could wish to meet. He has to be, to survive on his own. And he travels the whole province. A very useful source of information, a man like that. If I couldn't see the eclipse myself, I can't think of anybody better to report on it than old Ulysses. Tell me exactly what he said about it."

I did, and he looked grave, and actually stopped eating. "That's just what we thought would happen—the Druids encouraging the natives to turn on the settlers. We knew an eclipse would make a perfect omen to frighten them into doing what the rebels want."

"Which is to try and drive us out of Brigantia?"

"Out of Britannia, if they can. But Brigantia will do for a start. If they can recapture Brigantia, they hope that other tribes will follow their example. Brigantia is where their leader is based. And I'm afraid it'll get worse before it gets better." Just what Hawk had told me. It was depressing to hear it repeated.

"We've had trouble from the natives before," I pointed out. "In a newly conquered province, it goes with the territory. But this seems somehow more organised."

"It is. That's why I'm here." He finished the last of the meat and took a long drink of wine.

"Roman treachery, you said. Romans are helping the rebels, like those two yesterday, pretending to be from Kickers and Punchers?"

"Oh, they're genuine investigators all right. Not for much longer, I hope, but for the present, they're based in Eburacum, and they've got a nice little racket going, supplying the natives with military stores."

"Weapons, you mean?"

"No, much more subtle. Military clothing."

"*Clothing?* You're joking!"

"I wish I was. Tunics, cloaks, helmet crests, boots, belts, all the things that make a soldier *look* like a soldier. Think about it. When someone's dressed in military gear, you don't question who he is, you probably hardly look at his face. He's just one more soldier from our occupying army, and you do what he asks you to do. Whether it's giving him information, food, drink, shelter even….You don't think twice. I mean you, Aurelia, and me. I stopped on the road the other night when I saw what I took to be a wounded soldier. Roman soldiers can get other Romans to do almost anything without having to spill a drop of blood, in a way natives never could."

"So you've found them out. Is that why they attacked you? They were in the gang that tried to kill you on the road."

He looked up sharply. "Ah, now I did wonder….I didn't get much of a look at them in the dark. You're sure?"

"One of my horse-boys saw them, and he's quite sure. That's why I sent them packing. Even though they behaved as if you were their long-lost friend, and you wouldn't tell me properly what was going on."

"You were wonderful." He reached out and touched my hand lightly. "And this is really good news. I've been looking for evidence against them for a while, but they've been pretty clever, keeping in the background. At last they've slipped up and shown their faces. I wonder now...." He sat staring at nothing, lost in his thoughts.

I got up quietly and went over to the door that led into the garden. I opened it a few inches, and a cool morning breeze stole in. I looked out at the quiet flowers and the cloudless sky, a scene that usually gave me a calm pleasure, but now all I could do was wonder if any enemies were lurking in the woods.

A soft footfall made me jump. Quintus was there beside me, and he slid his arm lightly across my shoulders. "I'm going to need your help again, Aurelia. If you will."

"What sort of help?" It came out more abruptly than I'd intended, and he moved away slightly.

"I'd like to stay here at the Oak Tree for a while. It's just the base I need, bang in the middle of the area I'm investigating."

I was aware how much I wanted him to stay. So was he, probably. But there were questions I had to ask before I agreed. "Quintus Antonius, I don't know who you are and I don't know what in Hades you're up to. I didn't mind keeping those brutes from harming you yesterday, but if I'm going to get involved any deeper, I need more information."

"I've told you all I can."

Again, he was evading my questions, and it irritated me. "It's not enough. If I help you, and I only say *if,* I could be putting myself in danger, and Albia, and all our people. That's something I'm only prepared to do if I know it's absolutely necessary. So convince me."

"What would you say," he smiled, "if I told you that you look beautiful when you're angry?"

I said what I usually say to that kind of nonsense. I won't write it here; it might shock the Governor. "And I don't think it's a joking matter," I added, "being asked by a total stranger to take risks with my home, just because he's been incompetent enough to get ambushed in the woods."

He grew serious, and looked me squarely in the eyes. "No, it's not, and I apologise. If I tell you what I can, will you help me then?"

"How can I answer that until you *do* tell me?"

"All right." He walked back to the couch and sat down, and I went and sat beside him, saying nothing, waiting for him to explain.

"What I need is for you to tell everybody that your guest, Quintus Valerius Longinus, is recovering slowly from being attacked, but will have to rest for a while before travelling on. He's going to take a few days' leave to recuperate—walks in the woods, perhaps a ride, that sort of thing. If anyone asks his job, he's a bridge builder and surveyor." He took a plum from the fruit dish and ate it. "I've got to be as inconspicuous as possible. I know I've made a dramatic start, but now I just want to blend into the scenery."

"No problem about any of that. People will soon find some other topic of conversation, and we'll tell the world your bang on the head has made you lose all memory of being attacked, so they'll get tired of asking you about it."

He nodded. "Good. And may I borrow some clothes please, and perhaps a sword? And a horse now and then."

"Fine. But what will you actually be doing?"

"Oh, nothing much. Just finding and killing a dangerous rebel leader, before he and his band drive all the Romans out of Britannia."

But I wanted an answer to my question.

"Quintus," I persisted, "watch my lips. What will you actually be *doing?*"

"Talking to people, gathering information. From Romans, from native Britons, from Hyperboreans if they have anything useful to tell me. And doing it in such a way that the traitor, whoever he is, doesn't suspect."

"Presumably you'll arrest those two bent investigators first?"

"Soon, yes. I'll send word to Lucius at Eburacum about them...."

"My brother's at Eburacum?"

"Not yet, but he's due any day. He's supposed to be covering the military side of this investigation. There are probably more traitors in the garrison than just those two. I've been wondering about your two young tribunes...but I'm after the big fish, not the small fry."

"The Shadow of Death. And you've no idea at all who he is?"

"We know a few things about him. He's a Roman civilian, and he's high-powered enough to have access to secret information. He's in control of a well-trained Brigantian war-band, which he often leads himself, wearing a mask. Above all, he's the reason this bit of native violence could turn into a very dangerous rebellion."

"Why are you so sure he's a Roman? Isn't it more likely he's a Brigantian chieftain, someone from one of the old families who resents the Empire for taking away his political power?"

"That's what we thought at first, but he can't be." Quintus rubbed his bruised eye thoughtfully. "He's too well informed for a native. He gathers extraordinary amounts of secret information, which he could only get from Roman sources, and highly placed ones at that. I tell you, he frightens me."

"What sort of information?"

"Well...." He hesitated, then seemed to make up his mind. "Who do you know who could successfully ambush convoys carrying gold for paying the troops at Eburacum?"

"*Merda!* They've robbed pay convoys? Those wagons are guarded better than a Vestal's virginity. Usually *much* better!"

"Quite. And it was very professionally done. They had accurate details of routes and times, and they picked perfect spots for their attacks, where the road goes through deep woods, miles from anywhere. All the troops in the escorts were killed, and the bodies beheaded. And every horse, wagon and gold piece vanished like the morning mist, or as they would probably say, like shadows."

"How many convoys?"

"Two. The second was last month. That's when the Governor started taking the Shadow of Death seriously."

"But we've heard nothing about any of this. The mansio here gets the news from half the province, and there hasn't been a whisper."

"Of course there hasn't! It's hardly the sort of thing the military would want spread abroad, is it? Ambushes in broad daylight in a conquered province, top secret information being passed to well-organised rebels?"

"Holy Diana! If they can do that, they can do anything."

"Yes. And the point is, the leader, the Roman traitor, is based somewhere near here, within easy reach of Eburacum and Derventio, and not too far from the coast...."

"Near here? Near *Oak Bridges?*"

"Yes."

"Then he could be someone I know personally!"

"I hope so, yes."

"*What?*"

"That's where you can help me still more. I need to know about the leading Romans in this part of the province. Who has a reason for wanting to betray the Empire? Who's got good contacts among the natives? Who's short of money, or who's suddenly got more money than he should have....I don't know. I need someone with local knowledge to tell me."

"You want me to spy on my friends? I don't much like the sound of that."

"I'll do the spying, you just give me a base to work from, and whatever information you can. Don't you see, this is the reason, the *real* reason, why I've got to make myself inconspicuous. I want people round here not to notice me, but if they do, just to think I'm a harmless government surveyor, recovering from a knock on the head, on his way to inspect some bridges. Above all I don't want any of the settlers to realise that the slightest suspicion could fall on them. This is a dangerous man, and a clever one. My only hope of finding him is if he gets over-confident and does something careless. If I'm the one to do something careless, I may not live to tell anyone about it. And I haven't got long. The trouble has started, and I must find him and kill him. And quickly!" The last word came out sharply, like a trap closing. Then with an effort he relaxed, and held the dish of plums out to me. "These are delicious. Have some, before I wolf them all."

I shook my head, too busy thinking to eat. "So this Shadow of Death must be living a kind of double life. Behaving like a Roman during the daytime, and turning into a rebel leader at night. It certainly can't be anyone I know. I mean you'd be bound to notice something like that...."

"No, you wouldn't. I've told you, this is a clever man. Think how easy it would be in practice. A man who's high up in Roman society here, on friendly terms with every other important Roman in the area, who travels about freely, who has plenty of money, and plenty of slaves to carry messages. A town councillor maybe? A government official? Or a rich trader? How about your chief town councillor, Silvanius Clarus?"

"Silvanius! Not in a thousand years! He's a second-generation citizen, and he's more Roman than the Capitol. He wants the whole of Britannia to become indistinguishable from Gaul or Italia. He wants Roman government, towns, temples...."

"That's what he *says*," Quintus interrupted.

"And that's what he does! He's even building a new temple himself."

"Which could be the perfect bluff."

"An enormously expensive one!"

"Well he's one of the richest men in the district, isn't he? He also has contacts and clout, with the Romans and with the natives. He's a Brigantian, isn't he?"

"He is, from one of the old aristocratic families. But he married a girl from the Parisi tribe, a chieftain's daughter I think—there's a lot of intermarriage in a border area like this. She died when Vitalis was born. But you've only got to look at him, or talk to him for half an hour, to know how keen he is to be a Roman."

"So he has family ties with both the Brigantes and the Parisi. It seems to me he'd make an ideal Shadow of Death."

"Not all the Brigantes are anti-Roman though," I said. "And the Parisi definitely aren't. They've always been allies of Rome."

"But you have to consider every man as an individual, not just part of a tribal hierarchy. The more you tell me Silvanius is above suspicion, the more suspicious he seems to me."

Suddenly the door flew open and Albia burst straight in without knocking, something she'd never normally do. She was pale as ashes, and her eyes were red from crying. She mumbled "Sorry," and flopped down onto a stool, looking miserably from me to Quintus and back again.

"Relia, it's awful…."

"What is it?" I went and stood beside her, putting my arm round her. "What's happened?"

"Another murder."

"Who?" I felt cold inside. It must be someone we knew well. Not Junius?

"Ulysses." She started to cry.

"Oh, Albia, *no!*"

"A farmer found his body on the Derventio road. They'd cut off his head, and left one of those messages pinned onto him. They even killed his donkey. How could they? Such a gentle old man…he wouldn't hurt a beetle on the ground, never mind another person. How *could* they?"

I felt more like cursing than crying. I heard in my head his comment about Druids. "Most of them are evil men, who care more for their own power than anything else." And I remembered my own words about the warriors: "Take care you don't cross their path on a dark night."

"Quintus," I said, "whatever it takes to stop these Shadow-men, we must do it. I promise I'll help all I can."

"Yes," Albia said. "And so will I."

He got up and came over to us, and took my hand, and Albia's hand too. For a few heartbeats we were close together, linked by touch, and it was comforting. But we all knew it was no easy bargain we were making.

Chapter XI

It was only a mile or so to the centre of Oak Bridges where Silvanius' temple stood. I could easily have walked it, but I wanted to go in style, so I took the medium-sized raeda. Hippon reported that Titch had driven the ponies well yesterday, so I took him as driver, and told him to harness the two best mules and polish the carriage till he could see his face in it. I also ordered two of our brawniest farm slaves to accompany us on horseback as guards. They weren't exactly legionary trained, but they were tall and strong and handy with their cudgels, and clearly enjoyed the fearsome impression they made as they rode beside the carriage. And I felt safer knowing they were there.

Oak Bridges isn't much of a town yet. True, it has a forum—well, a very large open space in the middle—and a civic hall where the town council meets, and talks as much hot air as the Senate of Rome. There's a regular market every eight days, and there are all the basic shops and several taverns, not to mention a statue of the Divine Claudius, and a small triumphal arch commemorating some victory of Governor Agricola's. But it has no public baths yet, and no amphitheatre, essentials for a proper Roman town. Still, thanks to Silvanius, it would soon have its very own temple to Jupiter and Juno.

The Marble Monster, as we all called it, was on a slight rise of ground just a few paces from the forum. It had been under construction for months, and had become the butt of everyone's jokes, but in all fairness I must say Silvanius had done a good job, or rather his workmen had. Most of the labour force was shipped all the way from Gaul, as he never tired of reminding us. It was of conventional design: it stood raised on a podium about ten feet high, so we reached it by steps, leading up to a big open court with an altar in the middle. Towards the rear was a white building, the sanctum, with a covered walkway on three sides of it, and its door facing the altar. On either side of the door would stand bronze statues to the two divinities for whom the temple was built. Only Jupiter had arrived so far. Next to the altar, where a small spring ran out, there was a huge pink marble basin to hold the spring water, with a pipe to one side carrying the overflow over a miniature waterfall made of stones and away down a drain. The effect would be pretty, and the basin would in due course receive offerings from devoted worshippers. At present it was empty and covered by a rather dirty sack.

I hadn't been to the place for perhaps a month, and last time I'd visited, it had looked like a building-site with here and there a glimpse of a finished temple. Now it resembled an almost-complete temple, and I could get a good idea of how it would be in all its final glory. But the site was still strewn with piles of stone and marble, stacks of wood, scaffolding poles and ladders, tools of every shape and size, and the usual builders' clutter that always seems so completely chaotic you wonder how anything ever gets built at all.

What I could see of the work was excellent. The columns were clad in elegant Italian marble; the carvings were good; and the paintings on the white sanctum's external walls had been well done, their colours glowing in the summer sunshine. The bronze statue of Jupiter was a beauty. Juno would presumably be just as fine. The whole place was beginning to look impressive.

I couldn't spot Silvanius, who was probably inside the sanctum, so I just wandered around watching the craftsmen at work. I always enjoy seeing buildings going up. We've had several extensions done to the mansio in the last few years, and I never tired of watching the work. I suppose it's the feeling that here's something permanent being made, something that will last perhaps for generations. When we're dead and gone the buildings we created will still be there, for our grandchildren and their grandchildren to see.

The fifty or so workmen looked busy, masons carving, painters finishing off the walls, labourers taking down scaffolding, a carter unloading tubs of ornamental trees, and the foreman yelling and gesticulating and rushing about putting on a good industrious show for his patron. It wasn't the usual foreman, I noticed, but he appeared to have things well in hand. I knew Silvanius planned to have the formal dedication in a matter of days now, so it was just as well.

I gazed at it all in fascination until a familiar voice beside me broke my concentration.

"Aurelia! Light of my life, say you'll marry me, or I shall die of a broken heart!"

Felix was wearing peacock-blue today: a brilliant blue cloak, matching sandals with gold and blue studs, and a couple of rings with blue stones in them. As usual, his cheerful clowning made me smile.

"Ask me again after dinner, Felix. I never consider proposals of marriage on an empty stomach."

"Very wise. And how's life at the Oak Tree? How's your not-quite-dead traveller?"

"He's much better, I'm glad to say."

He began to steer me towards the pink marble basin. "I hope the plumbers are being careful. That marble cost a fortune…. Have you found out anything about him yet?"

"A little, yes. I'll tell you at the meeting."

He smiled. "Oh, you *are* coming to the meeting, then?"

"I certainly am. Why wouldn't I?"

"Our esteemed aedile Vedius Severus," he answered, with a smile of pure mischief, "would say it wasn't a woman's place. In fact he *has* been saying it. So I wondered…."

"Stupid old fart," I retorted, but quietly. "Still, you can't teach new steps to an old dancer, as our grandmother used to say."

"Did she? How sad!"

"I'm sorry?"

"For you, my dear. To have a grandmother who insisted on talking in clichés."

Just then Silvanius came over to greet us, in a gleaming toga as always, with Vitalis in tow. He was wearing a toga too, and looking the complete young Roman gentleman; I'd hardly have recognised him. But his surly expression told me he'd been made to join the party by his father, and he wasn't going to let anybody think he was enjoying it.

"You've met my son Gnaeus, of course, Aurelia," Silvanius said. "Though perhaps not for a while. He's been away, staying with some of our relatives in the hills."

"Hello, Vitalis," I said.

He actually smiled. "Good to see you, Aurelia. I hope I and my friends didn't drink you out of mead yesterday."

"No danger. Come any time. We keep a good supply of it."

Silvanius beamed. "You've been sampling the hospitality of the Oak Tree, have you, Gnaeus?"

"I have, father. Very pleasant too."

"That's excellent!" the fond father said. I made a mental note, when we had a quiet space, to mention to him what sort of company Vitalis had been keeping there.

"The work's coming on fast," I said to Silvanius. "It looks as busy as a hive of bees."

"It's going tolerably well, I think," he agreed, "though we have had one or two trifling setbacks. The native labour, you know… and today I'm without Casticus, my foreman. He simply has not appeared for work! I sent to find out if he was ill, and his wife said he never came home last night. She said he's probably been out drinking somewhere and will turn up in his own good time. I ask you! And he's a Gaul! I've imported the real craftsmen from Gaul. My family has estates there, you know."

I did know; he mentioned it often enough. Still, it was all credit to him that he was constructing such a grand public building. Some men would dedicate an altar, or maybe put up a small shrine; Silvanius was going the whole hog and providing a complete temple.

Balbus strolled up to join us. He wasn't wearing a toga; a serviceable dark blue wool cloak was more his style, and his fair hair, with a touch of white now at his temples, was combed back in a plain no-nonsense fashion. But the gold brooches that fastened the cloak and the wide seal-ring on his finger were expensive. He was the richest businessman in the area, what with the pottery he made and the fine glass and ceramics he imported to sell to the more prosperous settlers, but he liked to present himself as the plain honest craftsman and trader who'd hauled his way to riches by his own sandal-straps. Well, fair enough, so he had.

"Hello, Balbus," I said. "How are you? How's trade?"

"Oh, not bad, I suppose. I'm thinking of making a new range of pots."

"Oh?" I knew what was coming, but friendship includes laughing at each other's favourite jokes.

"Something more fragile. People don't break them often enough!"

"We'll have to arrange an orgy where we all throw the crockery about," Felix suggested. "Aurelia has some soldier-boys staying at the Oak Tree. We could try to get them drunk—I doubt if we'd have to try *too* hard—and they could smash the place up in no time."

Balbus looked shocked. "Felix, that's in pretty poor taste!" and turning deliberately away from him, he said to me, "How are you coping, Aurelia? Bad business, all these murders. One victim ended up right outside my shop. And someone was attacked on your doorstep, they tell me."

"Yes, but at least he survived. How's Ennia taking it? Not too upset by it all?"

"Well, she's a bit unsettled, of course. It's harder on womenfolk, this sort of thing…." He saw the glint in my eye and hastily changed direction. "The temple's coming on pretty well, all things considered. I hate to think what it's costing." He gazed round the site approvingly, then turned to Silvanius. "Nice quality marble, Clarus. Not local, surely?"

"It's from Italia, naturally."

"Thought so. It must have cost you an arm and a leg!" From Balbus this was a high compliment, and Silvanius basked in the warmth of it. They discussed quarries and transport costs and problems with shipping. Balbus imported many of the pots he sold, so the state of the shipping industry and the cost of transport generally were topics that never failed to interest him. I knew I should feel the same, because I rely on imported wine and oil for the mansio, but today I was in holiday mood, so I steered the conversation back to the Marble Monster.

"When will it be finished, Councillor? Have you planned a date for the dedication yet?"

"Please, Aurelia," he smiled at me. "My friends call me Clarus, and I hope I may number you among them?"

"Thank you. I'm honoured, Clarus. And the dedication of the temple?"

"Five days from now. The day before the Ides."

Gods alive, no wonder the foreman was rushing about like a stampeding chariot-horse. Only five days!

"Excellent!" I said. "A temple to Jupiter and Juno is just what we need in Oak Bridges. Roman gods, Roman ritual, for a Roman town. You're doing us proud."

The others nodded in agreement, and Clarus positively glowed. "We Romans have a duty to maintain standards. No, not just to maintain, but to improve them. This province of Britannia may not have centuries of history behind it, but it can be one of the most prosperous in the Empire. We need the gods of Rome to unite us all." He stood up tall, posing like an orator, and declaimed, "We are citizens of a great Empire, my friends. We must stand together."

"Definitely," I agreed. I even managed not to smile, when I thought how Silvanius' grandfather must have been a blue-painted chieftain with a taste for collecting enemy heads.

"And after the temple, I'm trying to talk him into giving us a theatre," Felix said. "To put Oak Bridges finally and forever on the artistic map. Imagine, our own centre of acting and musical excellence…culture, real Roman and Greek culture."

Silvanius smiled, but didn't, I noticed, commit himself.

"I only wish everyone in Oak Bridges saw the benefits of the Empire as clearly as we do," he said. "I'm afraid even this small project of mine has attracted some hostility."

I sensed a real concern under the pompous phrases. "People are always moaning about anything new. Have you had opposition to the temple?"

"Some, yes."

"Who from?"

"Oh, anonymously. Just muttering and whispering here and there, you know. There's been no real damage, but we've had some unpleasant graffiti here at the site."

"Recently, you mean?"

"For the last two nights. I'm leaving guards here from now on when the workmen have gone home, so it should stop." He sighed. "Just some of the local hotheads, I'm sure, but it's upsetting."

"Was it the same message that was left with the murdered victims, about all Romans being killed?"

"I'm afraid so."

We all made sympathetic noises, except Vitalis, who was leaning against a column looking bored. He was obviously following his own line of thought, because he suddenly remarked, "Father, if you had to build a temple, I wish you'd dedicated it to one of our old gods, not imported Roman ones."

"Gnaeus!" Silvanius said sharply, but Vitalis ignored him.

"I mean why did you have to choose Jupiter? Why not Taranis the Thunderer, he's a sky god too? You can't blame our people for wanting to keep faith with the old gods, and the old ways. Not everyone thinks Britannia should become a poor man's copy of Italia."

"That's enough, Gnaeus," Silvanius warned. "You know perfectly well that the old days are gone forever. The only future for this province is as part of the Roman Empire."

"Don't you be so sure," Vitalis said. "There are gods more powerful than Jupiter, and there are leaders who can command more power in Britannia than the Emperor of Rome."

"Really, Gnaeus...." But the lad was already striding off, and Silvanius gave an embarrassed little laugh. "Young men, you know! They always have to be rebelling about something."

Well, yes. But I found myself wondering how far his rebellious feelings would take him. Loud talk, or secret killing? I recalled Quintus' remarks about how well placed Silvanius was to be a rebel leader, if he chose to betray Rome. I still found it hard to accept this even as a possibility, but Vitalis...now that was a much more likely proposition.

We were all relieved when a distraction appeared, in the shape of Vedius. He came striding up, white-haired but erect, and hardly using the walking-cane he carried. I'd assumed Silvanius would invite him; he was one of the leaders of the town council, the aedile responsible for the fire-cart, and for public order. He'd been a career soldier, serving mostly in Britannia; it was said he'd been in the army at the time of Boudicca's rebellion over thirty years ago, but the uprising hadn't put him off settling here when his service ended. He still kept in touch with his old army cronies, and rumour said that his influence had been one of the factors that helped Oak Bridges become a town with its own council, whereas many other settlements near legionary bases stayed under military control. He still managed to assume a soldierly swagger as he greeted us in turn.

He shook my hand formally. "Aurelia, what a pleasant surprise. Silvanius didn't say there were to be any of the fair sex present."

Old fool, I thought, I know you think all women should be kept at home to weave cloth and mind babies! Still, I'd never change his mind, especially not by being rude.

"It's good to see you, Vedius," I answered. "Isn't the temple looking good?"

"It is," he agreed. "A credit to you, Clarus."

Silvanius spent the next quarter of an hour showing us around the site in detail. Felix was the most knowledgeable on the subjects of sculpture and painting, and had been mainly responsible for designing the temple, and finding the workmen to build it. He and Silvanius went into a lot of technical detail which was beyond me. Balbus and Vedius and I admired the craftsmanship and complimented Silvanius. Yet I felt, I think we all did, that there was a tension in the air; we were impatient to get to Silvanius' house, where the real business of the day would begin: an excellent dinner, followed by some serious talking.

Just as we were about to leave, the foreman came running up, looking more harassed than ever. Ignoring Silvanius' disapproving frown, he planted himself in front of his master.

"My lord, there's a bit of a crisis. Would you please come and sort it out, my lord? It's very urgent."

"What sort of crisis?" Silvanius growled.

"Well…just some trouble with the latest delivery."

"You're paid to control deliveries, Lentus. So control them. I'm busy."

Lentus looked fit to explode, but he kept his voice respectful. "Please, my lord, it is very important, otherwise I wouldn't presume….If you could just step this way…."

Silvanius sighed. "You see what I have to put up with, my friends. Please bear with me, I'm sure this won't take long."

He turned back to Lentus, who led him at a fast pace across to the far side of the site. There was a gate there, from which a broad ramp led down to street level, so that heavy materials could be brought up on wheels. A cart had just been hauled up the ramp and stood inside the gate, its oxen still panting in the shafts. There was a cover over it, and we watched as Lentus talked earnestly, and then lifted one corner of it to let Silvanius look underneath.

"Somebody's going to get bawled out for poor materials, or maybe…" but Balbus never finished his sentence, because Silvanius recoiled from the cart as if a snake had bitten him. Then he approached it again, very cautiously, and took a second look.

"My dears, don't tell me it's another corpse!" Felix exclaimed.

"Shut up, Felix," Balbus and I said in unison.

But that's just what it was.

The missing foreman Casticus lay face down in the cart, except there was no face, because there was no head. He'd been a tall, deep-chested man, with hands like shovels and legs like tree-trunks. He was wearing a homespun work tunic, and we could see clearly how he'd been stabbed, from the dried blood all down his back.

We stood around, not quite knowing what to do or say, but presumably all thinking one thought: "This is part of the same pattern. 'All Romans will be killed….'"

Balbus eventually spoke the unpleasant question out loud. "Was he a citizen, Clarus?"

"He was," Silvanius said bleakly. "I gave him his freedom last year."

"Is he carrying the same message?" I wondered. "Well, I suppose there's only one way to be sure." I bent over the body. "Help me turn him over, Balbus, will you?"

In fact Vedius helped Balbus with the gruesome task, and just for once I didn't insist on my right to do a man's job. Sure enough, there was a bone disc pinned to the front of the brown tunic. Vedius studied it closely. "Same as the others," he muttered. "That makes seven."

Chapter XII

We headed in a rather subdued convoy for Silvanius' "humble abode." This, as you'll have gathered from what I've said about its owner, was actually a very sumptuous villa standing in grounds the size of a small village, on the winding native road that runs north from Oak Bridges and then east, eventually connecting with the main Roman road to Derventio. The house was enormous, and had taken even longer to build than the Marble Monster, but now Silvanius was in residence, and he and Vitalis and their slaves must rattle around in it like peas in a drum. But he felt his position called for a large place, as like as possible to the kind of villa he'd have owned if he'd lived in Italia. There'd been no woman's touch in its construction or furnishing; he had never re-married after his wife died bearing Vitalis. But as we approached it, I knew, if I hadn't known it before, that it was the grandest house for miles around, and the absolute best that money could buy.

We turned off the road and trotted up a long paved drive through colourful gardens, opening out for what appeared to be miles on either side, but cleverly designed to focus attention on the house itself. There were some lovely ornamental trees, and a veritable maze of criss-crossing paved walkways bordered by small box hedges, with ever-such-tasteful statuary dotted about. I shouldn't mock, most of it was very good. Further away was an orchard of fruit trees, and we could see some beehives near them. Next to the house were beds of lovely roses, and stone tubs bright with lilies and poppies. He must have a cohort of well-trained garden slaves, and they'd done their work well.

We drew up on a wide paved circle outside the house, and before I dismissed Titch and the farm boys, I beckoned them close to me. "If any of you get drunk," I warned, "you're headed for a flogging that'll take the hides off you. We'll be driving home when it's nearly dark, and I want all three of you sober and ready for anything. Understood?"

They nodded, and Titch said, "I never drink on duty, Mistress. They say the great Julius Caesar never let his legates drink on the march."

"Very sensible of him." As I turned towards the house, I heard one of the farm lads suppress a groan; I gathered they'd been told more than they wanted to know about the Divine Julius and his military style. Still, as our grandmother used to say, a bit of education doesn't hurt, and sometimes is actually quite useful.

Vitalis met me and the others at the door, and escorted us into a beautifully painted large hallway, with rooms and corridors leading from it and a wonderful mosaic floor with swirling patterns of red, yellow, cream, and black. He was in a happy mood now, playing his part as the son of the house, and when he chose, he had real charm. "Welcome to our new home. May this be the first of many visits! Do come through and enjoy the sun on the terrace."

The villa had a paved terrace all along its south-west side; a shade optimistic for northern Britannia, but very fashionable of course, and today it was certainly warm enough to sit there and enjoy a beaker of excellent wine. We could see yet more gorgeous gardens, flower-beds and statues, a small summer-house surrounded by low-growing trees, and a stream flowing down through a couple of little pools, making a miniature cascade.

"This is lovely, Clarus," I said, as he came up to greet me. He looked as if he'd recovered from his shock at the temple site, but all the same I decided to start with a neutral subject. "I love pretty gardens. I just never seem to have the time to organise ours."

"You have fine fruit and vegetables at the Oak Tree," he answered.

"We do, but they're not very decorative. Something like those little ponds there....That's so attractive. Did you have an Italian architect to design it?"

"Felix did the design. He's so talented, so artistic."

"Yes, he is." I glanced round us; Felix and the others were safely out of earshot. "Look, Clarus. Before we go inside, I wondered...may I speak frankly?"

"Of course, Aurelia. You know how I value your opinion."

"It's about Vitalis. He mentioned that he's visited us at the Oak Tree."

"Yes. I'm glad. I'd sooner he came and had a drink with you, rather than frequenting some disreputable wine-shop in town." He looked worried suddenly. "He's not been making trouble, has he?"

"Not at all, no. He's welcome. But he's been with a group of young Brigantian lads, all dressed up like old-style warriors, though without weapons of course. I thought....I mean I wondered...."

"You wondered if I knew," he smiled. "Yes, I was aware of it, but it's nothing to worry about. I'm sure it's just a phase he's going through, you know what young men are like. Ever since he visited his cousins in the hills, he's been asking and talking about our family history, and this is his way of showing that he isn't ashamed of it. Neither am I, as you know. I should hate him to lose contact with our Brigantian relatives, even the ones in the hill country, although they are a little—ah—wild in their ways."

"Oh, quite," I said hastily. "It's just, seeing them all dressed up like that....But you don't think he's seriously anti-Roman?"

"No, of course not. There's a fashion among the young just now, a yearning for the old days, when lads proved their manhood by fighting, and gained advancement in war, not by a political career. I fear Vitalis and some of the other youths of his age regret that they're growing up in a time of peace. When they *are* grown up, they'll be glad of it. Vitalis will soon settle down and come to realise the importance of peace for all of us."

"I'm sure you're right," I agreed, though I wasn't.

At dinner, as I'd expected, I was the only woman present—a situation I'm quite happy with. But in the interests of truth, I must confess that I was up-staged. Not by another person, but by the decorations of the dining-room, which were truly stunning. The handsome wall-paintings were on the theme of Theseus and the Minotaur, and a marvellous floor mosaic showed Cretan bulls, and bull-dancers jumping and twisting and grasping the horns to swing onto the bulls' backs. I'd never seen a floor so intricate and with so many colours in it, and neither had any of the other guests. More of Felix's design ideas, we were told; they'd used the services of a pavement-maker from Africa, and the result was marvellous.

The meal was superb, naturally. We started with oysters, quails' eggs, and shrimps, with a salad of lettuce, sorrel, and olives; then there was a whole roast pig, with the most mouthwatering stuffing made with peaches and wine; and there were swans, and ducks with plum sauce. All sorts of vegetables went with the meat—the artichoke hearts were especially good, and the fish sauce was from Spain, the very best. There was Italian white wine, and Gaulish red. We finished with some wonderful soft cow's milk cheese, and fresh figs, and several sorts of sweet-meat; my favourite were the dates stuffed with almonds and preserved cherries. It was all quite delicious, and I noticed—as I'm sure I was meant to—how much of it was imported. It isn't just buildings that show off a man's status.

The conversation was general at first, and we all made a determined effort to be cheerful. Mostly we talked about Eburacum, because it turned out that Silvanius, Balbus, and Felix had each been there recently, and been impressed by the way the place was changing; it was developing from a raw military base into a civilised town. Silvanius had heard a rumour that it would soon have a smart new amphitheatre, replacing the primitive semi-permanent arrangement there now, and the prospect of regular good-quality gladiator shows only a few miles away pleased all of us. Everyone loves a day out at the arena, enjoying traditional Roman sport. Felix said he'd heard there was also to be a permanent theatre, but I suspected this was wishful thinking on his part. Balbus was impressed by how quickly the warehousing and dock facilities were coming on. Listening to it all, I realised I hadn't been to our nearest big town for months, and it was high time I took a trip there.

I shared a dining-couch with Vitalis, and when the main course came and general talk changed to conversation between dining-partners I wondered what in Hades we'd find to say. Then I remembered he'd been away visiting his relations in western Brigantia. He chatted enthusiastically about the wild Pennine country, remote valleys, rivers teeming with fish, and vast impenetrable oak forests full of game. Then he began telling me about his cousins' way of life.

"They're much freer than we are, up in the north-west of Brigantia," he said, signalling a slave to bring us more meat. "There's far less interference from the Roman authorities—well, it's pretty remote—and the Romans seem happy to let the chiefs govern the people, as long as there's no trouble and the taxes get paid. So men like my uncles, the old tribal chiefs, still have a lot of power, and can make a real difference, a proper contribution to the government." I stole a glance at his father, but Silvanius was discussing mosaic styles with Balbus.

"You sound almost envious," I said cautiously.

"Oh, I am. Very much so. My cousins still have their proper standing in the tribe. They're only in their twenties, my age, but they're respected as leaders because they come from a chieftain's family. They've had to prove themselves of course, hunting and fighting, but they're real men. Whereas *I'm* just…." He paused, and lowered his voice. "One of my cousins said to me, 'Vitalis, you should be a chief among warriors, but the Romans have stolen your birthright. Watch out they don't turn you into a eunuch.'"

This felt like dangerous ground. Time to change the subject. "And what did you get up to while you were there? Some good hunting, I expect."

"Oh yes. Wolves, and stags, and wild boar. The woods are overflowing with game, and they breed superb hunting-dogs there. I killed a big wild boar by myself—I had to show my cousins I'm as good a hunter as they are." He sipped some wine. "Once we went after a bear. She had her den in a cave—it was brilliant. And we spent a lot of our time exercising, training ourselves and our men and horses, to keep ourselves fit and ready."

"Ready? For what?"

He looked abashed, as if he'd said too much. "Why—ready for anything!" he finished with his winning smile, and rushed on to tell me about the bear hunt.

When the meal was over, Vitalis stretched and stood up and declared he needed some exercise, and was going out riding with his friends, so he hoped we'd excuse him. I for one was glad to; after the suspicions I'd been mulling over about his anti-Roman activities, I'd have been very uneasy discussing the native unrest in his presence.

Silvanius suggested we move next door to one of his sitting-rooms. Yes, he did actually say "one of my sitting-rooms." Nobody asked how many there were altogether. As we seated ourselves on ornate chairs round a citrus-wood table that must have cost a consul's ransom, I saw Vedius looking at me doubt-fully.

"Is Aurelia staying for the meeting too?" he asked.

Silvanius nodded. "Yes, of course. Why should she not?"

"Well, it's just...." He turned to me. "You know, this isn't really women's business, is it? Planning how to stop a band of barbarians murdering our citizens—too upsetting for the fair sex, surely. There's no need for you to be concerned."

"I am concerned, whether I want to be or not. One of the victims, the only one to survive, appeared on my doorstep."

"Yes, and it must have been very unpleasant for you. But you can leave matters to us men now."

I bit back my instinctive comment; this wasn't the bar-room at the Oak Tree. I saw Felix wiping his mouth with a handkerchief, hiding a smile. Dear gods, I should be used to this sort of nonsense by now. But however often it happens, it always infuriates me. Well, this time I'd show the old idiot. I'd got something to tell the meeting that would make them all sit up and take notice. I had a government investigator under my roof, looking into the devious depths of Roman treachery.

"I think you'll find, Vedius Severus," I said, in what Albia is pleased to call my "honey-sweet" tone, "that it's worth including me in your discussions. I've got some important information to impart. Still, if you want me to leave…." I half-rose.

"Of course we don't," Silvanius interrupted. "I'm sure your information is extremely valuable, and we all want to hear it. Don't we, Severus?"

"It's a bit irregular," Vedius muttered, but not very loudly.

"Being irregular won't hurt for once," Balbus commented. "Aurelia's got her head screwed on."

"She certainly has," Felix added. "Of course she must stay."

Oh, me and my big mouth! What had I been thinking of, boasting like that? I couldn't tell them about Quintus Antonius, could I? For one thing, I'd promised not to, and for another, he was investigating Roman treachery, and had made it abundantly clear he needed to remain incognito.

You idiot, Aurelia, you complete fool. What are you going to do now? You've told them you have important information. So think of something!

Silvanius said, "Before we discuss anything in detail, let me make one point. Our discussions here today must be kept absolutely private, just between us five. I assume we're all agreed on that?" He surveyed each of us in turn.

"We should take an oath of secrecy," Vedius suggested, "just to be on the safe side."

"Surely that's going a bit far," Felix objected. "We're all friends here."

"I think it's a good precaution," Balbus said. "We don't want any tittle-tattle."

"It can't do any harm," Silvanius put in, "as we'll be discussing weighty matters."

"Oh well, if you all insist on playing cloak-and-dagger!" Felix suddenly sprang up from the table, ran over to the door, and pulled it open with a flourish. "Pssst! Anyone listening out there?" he asked in a loud stage whisper, and stuck his head into the corridor.

"Empty as a beggar's purse," he cried, retracting his head and closing the door. "How disappointing! So we *really* don't need to take an oath now." He sat down at the table again.

Typical Felix! Silly, childish, but it broke the tension and it made me smile, and Silvanius and Balbus were amused too; not Vedius though. "I wish you'd all take this seriously," he complained. "Men are being murdered. Secrecy here may be a matter of life and death."

That sobered us, and Silvanius went out to fetch from the family shrine the statues of his household gods to witness our oath. The other three began a desultory discussion about the beauties of the citrus-wood table we were sitting at, but I wasn't listening. My mind was racing, trying to come up with something I could use to impress this high-powered meeting. I'd boasted that I had something important to contribute. If I couldn't produce anything, I'd never hear the end of it.

Perhaps I could tell them just a little about Quintus Antonius, drop a few hints about having an important guest staying who wasn't all that he seemed to be? But no, I'd given my word. Holy Diana, I prayed silently, help me. I know I've got myself into this pickle, but please help me out of it....I had a sudden vivid image of Quintus on the morning I found him, lying as still as death, with blood matting his fair hair. I remembered how we'd all speculated about why he was attacked, and decided it couldn't be a robbery, because of his emerald ring. And Albia had said... what was it now?....In a sudden lightning-flash of understanding I remembered her words, and realised I *had* something important enough to impress the meeting. As Silvanius returned with the precious statues, I sent a quick prayer of thanks to Diana.

We each took a strong oath of secrecy, and Silvanius then made a short and pompous speech about Romans standing together to resist a Campaign of Terror, which I won't bore you with.

"Now," he continued, "we should try to establish the facts of this very unpleasant situation. There have been seven attacks so far. Can we identify the victims?"

Between us we could. Of that day's casualties, we'd all seen Casticus the foreman, and they'd heard the sad news about old Ulysses. Of yesterday's victims, we all knew Marcus Terentius, the innkeeper at the Kingfisher, and Vedius had recognised Flavius Nepos, the retired soldier. When it came to the corpses found the day before, the man on the Eburacum road was apparently a naval contractor called Hirtius, carrying papers about harbour construction. That left Quintus, and his servant Burrus. They accepted my explanation that Quintus Valerius Longinus, bridge builder and surveyor, and his German servant had been attacked; the servant was killed and his master was recuperating at the Oak Tree.

"Good," Silvanius said. "Now can we work out what the victims had in common?"

"Being Roman, of course," Felix commented. "Yes, my dears, I know it's obvious, but in view of the horrid messages…."

"But all from such different walks of life," Silvanius pointed out. "A freedman, an old soldier, an innkeeper, a pedlar…a naval contractor, a bridge surveyor, and his servant. What could such a mixture of people possibly have in common?"

"Perhaps Aurelia can suggest something," Vedius challenged. "Does your important piece of information help us here, perhaps?"

I looked the old fool straight in the eye. "It does, yes. They all have one very obvious thing in common."

"Indeed?" Vedius sounded sceptical.

"They were all on the roads."

"Well, as it happens, yes, but...."

"No, Vedius, it's not a case of 'as it happens.' That's the point. I believe this Campaign of Terror is aimed at travellers. To scare us all off the roads, and make everyone feel it's not safe to go on a journey."

They were impressed. There were nods and murmurs of agreement. Silvanius said, "Of course!" and even Vedius conceded, "It's possible."

"More than possible," Balbus answered. "It makes good sense."

"The road system," Silvanius declared, "is one of the great civilising influences that we Romans bring to the provinces. It makes military conquest possible, and then it encourages the founding of new settlements, the spread of Roman culture...."

"And trade," Balbus added. "Don't forget trade. Trade unites a province like mortar holding together a wall."

"A good phrase, Balbus," Silvanius smiled. It was, and it would probably re-appear in a future Romans-standing-together speech.

"So if you want to disrupt Roman rule," Vedius said, "and you haven't the military force to take on the legions in battle, you destroy communications."

"Civilised life would be impossible without road transport," Felix put in. "Imagine, not being able to visit friends, or go to the theatre. Not being able to buy imported wine or food. What an appalling prospect!"

"Roads are our life-line," I agreed. "In my particular business, catering for travellers, they're our life-*blood.*"

There was more of the same, but you and the Governor don't need anyone to tell you how important the road network is.

While I had everyone's full attention, I reported the scraps of information I'd collected about the Shadow-men and their leader. All the others admitted they'd heard the war-band mentioned, but had not, until now, taken it very seriously.

"Their leader, this Shadow of Death, is presumably an outsider," Felix said. "Not from this district. I mean. If he were local, we'd surely have an inkling who he is."

"Not necessarily," Vedius countered. "The man must be a Briton, obviously, as he's attacking Romans. And some of the older families keep themselves very much to themselves."

"Even so—" Balbus drained his wine—"whoever the leader is, if he's powerful enough to run a war-band, he couldn't conceal the fact for long. He can't be anyone we know."

"But the war-band itself, the Shadow-men—they are presumably from hereabouts," Silvanius mused. "If there had been any large influx of natives into our area, we should have heard of *that*."

"Not necessarily," Vedius said again. "The countryside is full of small settlements, just hamlets with a handful of houses. If some of them acquired a few more tribesmen, would we notice?"

"Let's approach it from the other direction," Silvanius suggested. "If we don't know who the Shadow-men are, can we deduce how they choose their victims? Do we assume they're picking their targets quite carefully? Or do they attack any Roman traveller they find—anyone who just happens to be, so to speak, in the wrong place at the wrong time?"

Balbus frowned. "If they're picking out their victims personally, they must be very well-informed about them, to know how and when to ambush them alone."

"You're right," Vedius said. "Their intelligence network would have to be superb, and very widespread."

I wanted to add my agreement, when I thought of how Quintus had been deliberately ambushed by men who knew him, but I had to hold my peace.

Balbus' frown deepened. "And does this war-band have any serious following? Because if so, then most of the natives in the area could be passing them information. Not just the farmers and country people, but our own workmen, our slaves even. I've got a pottery workshop full of Brigantian slaves! As far as I know they're all completely loyal, but...how can we be sure?"

"We can't," Vedius said bleakly.

Silvanius fetched the wine-jug, and poured us all a refill. "It's a most alarming possibility," he said, "but still only a possibility.

It could just as well be that the Shadow-men are killing travellers more or less at random."

"Is that supposed to be comforting, dear boy?" Felix remarked. "Whether one is deliberately chosen, or murdered at random, one is still decidedly dead."

Vedius looked round the table. "So the Shadow-men are attacking Roman travellers. Roman roads may no longer be safe. Now what can we do about it?"

There were several suggestions for action, ranging from quite good to completely ludicrous. Silvanius proposed compiling a list of known anti-Roman sympathisers in the area, "so we can be watchful and try to observe if they are involved." He found a note-tablet and jotted down entries as everyone threw in names of natives who were thought to be anti-Roman, or just very strongly pro-Brigantian, which, as I pointed out, wasn't necessarily the same thing. We soon had a score of people listed. The only name I contributed was Segovax—in fact the Segovax clan, several of them, one of whom had land adjoining ours. Like the other suggestions, they were men from the old aristocracy. Most of the names meant very little to me, as I've never moved in those circles. The same should have been true of Felix, but he was such an inveterate gossip that he knew everyone, and joined in eagerly as Silvanius, Balbus and Vedius enthusiastically named names. I suspected, as the list grew longer, that a few old scores were being paid off.

"I'll have my secretary make copies of the list," Silvanius said. "I suggest you all notify me if you have any more names to add, and I'll circulate up-to-date lists as needed."

Balbus proposed we should infiltrate observers into some of the suspect households—spies who would report back if anything sinister was going on. There was some rather disjointed discussion about how this could be done, and also the ethics of bribing slaves to inform against their masters. Everyone agreed to think about it.

Next Vedius suggested that he and his town watch should patrol the roads all around Oak Bridges during the hours of darkness. I almost laughed out loud at the silliness of this, but he meant it quite seriously. He actually thought his handful of men and their one fire-cart were a match for the Campaign of Terror. "I'll recruit a company of volunteers," the old man said, sitting up straight on his chair. "They won't need much training; just to be observant, and to be seen to be everywhere. If the killers know the roads are being patrolled and unusual movements reported, they won't be so free to travel around themselves."

"There are miles and miles of roads," Felix pointed out. "You'd need half a legion!"

"And the Shadow-men seem very professional," I said. "If the patrols have no military training, the rebels will run rings round them."

Vedius glared at me, but Silvanius put in, "It might help a little, and any help is welcome. We should need to spread the news of their activities all over the area, and the patrols would need to take different routes every night, so the rebels wouldn't know their exact whereabouts."

"It'd be enormously expensive," Balbus objected.

There was a long and fiercely argued debate. Eventually, Silvanius used his chairman's clout and put it to the vote. The scheme was carried unanimously, though from the look on Balbus' face, he was less than overjoyed, and I had serious doubts myself.

But there was one good result: The old aedile finally admitted he was "not in the first flush of youth," and he offered his son Saturninus, a sensible Roman-educated man of thirty, as captain of the new recruits. So if the patrols surprised any Shadow-men, they'd be able to run after them, not just hobble behind on sticks.

"Now this decision," Silvanius said, "is the one part of our discussions that should not remain a secret—quite the reverse. What's the quickest way to make sure everyone, far and near, knows that we are taking defensive measures? Shall I post a notice in the forum? Or send out letters to our friends?"

"Call a meeting of the town council," I suggested. That made even Vedius smile.

Silvanius nodded. "I shall. And I'll suggest they vote some money to pay for the new night-patrols."

"Now you're talking!" Balbus said approvingly.

Silvanius glanced at the handsome water-clock in the corner. "But now I think we should close our meeting for today. Time is wearing on, and I imagine everyone would prefer to be home by dark."

"But we must meet again soon," Vedius said. "Report progress, and keep things moving."

"Five days from now?" Silvanius offered. "As you know, that's the day of the inauguration of my new temple. I'll be entertaining a few people to dinner afterwards, and of course I hope you'll all be there. If you'd care to stay on after the others leave, we'll have time for a meeting then."

We all agreed, and thanked him kindly. Then Vedius said, "Before we break up, there's one more thing we should settle. If we're going to be sending confidential messages among ourselves, we need a password. For identification."

Felix giggled. "Oh, Vedius, don't we know each other well enough already?"

"You can laugh, Felix, but just use your brains for once, and think! If we do need to send each other messages, they'll be brought by servants, perhaps men we don't know by sight. How can we be certain they are genuine? The Shadow-men might easily try to cause confusion by sending us wrong information, or maybe bogus instructions for some course of action. Suppose you got a note asking you to a meeting somewhere, and it was a forgery, and led you straight into a trap."

"Sensible idea," Balbus agreed. "I'll go along with that. What word shall we have?"

"Our enemies are the Shadow-men, so we ought to be the Men of Light," Silvanius suggested. "And 'light' could be our password."

"Too obvious," Vedius grumbled, "and too difficult to fit into a message. No, a personal name is best."

Felix stood up. "How about something from a book? There's a whole library to choose from over here." One wall of the room was entirely taken up with square book-pockets, each containing several scrolls neatly rolled and tagged with labels. Our host had all the books a Roman gentleman should possess. The gods alone knew whether he'd read any of them.

Felix stood facing them. "Now, as we haven't any dice to throw...Vedius, give me a number."

"A number? Now what are you up to?"

"Just a number, please, Vedius," Felix repeated.

"Oh very well. Five."

Felix pointed at the scrolls in the fifth square. "The Aeneid! How splendid! You next, Balbus. Pick another number."

"Eight."

"Book Eight, then." He found the right scroll and unrolled it carefully. "And now Aurelia, a number please."

This was getting too silly. "Ninety-nine."

"Don't be ridiculous, we'll be here all day. A *sensible* number, please."

"All right, sorry. Three."

"We'll use the third name that occurs in Book Eight." I expected him to read the poem aloud, but instead he began reciting the words from memory like an actor, hardly glancing at the scroll. He had a good voice and declaimed it well, even moving round the room and gesturing. As he passed near me, I reached out and gently took the scroll from his hand, and followed the text as he spoke. Sure enough, he was word perfect.

Book Eight, in case you don't have Felix's memory, begins with a description of Prince Turnus and all his warriors, so there's no shortage of names, and it didn't take him long to reach the third one, Messapus.

"There!" He smiled triumphantly. "That's our password. Messapus."

"Do you know the whole of the Aeneid by heart, Felix?" I couldn't help asking. "I'm impressed! I mean everyone can do

'Arms and the man I sing,' but I couldn't get through Book One, never mind all the way to Book Eight."

"Most of it, yes. The Emperor used to set parts of it to music, and we had to listen to him rehearsing so many times, we ended up learning it by heart."

"The Emperor?" Vedius looked scandalised. "Which Emperor? Not Domitian?"

"Hardly!" Felix laughed. "No, I mean dear Nero. The only truly civilised emperor we've ever had."

Personally I always understood Nero was a monster, and was wondering whether to say so when Silvanius cleared his throat. "We're getting off the point. Messapus is our password."

After that the gathering broke up.

"All in all, a very productive meeting," Silvanius declared, as we trooped out into the hallway, ordering our vehicles and collecting our cloaks. "We've made a good start, and we've got some plans to put into action. I knew I was right to suggest this sort of small high-powered gathering, Aurelia."

"You were absolutely right, Clarus," I agreed solemnly. What else could I say?

Chapter XIII

The sun was low as we set off for the mansio, and it made me uneasy. After all our talk of threats to travellers, I had no wish to be out on the road after sunset.

Silvanius suggested I stay the night at his villa, but of course I couldn't be away from home that long. Vedius offered to escort me to the mansio, but I didn't want him thinking I was some timid female too scared to go anywhere without his masculine protection, so I assured him we would be safe. But I wasn't sorry that his route and ours were the same for part of the journey. We travelled through Oak Bridges together, and to the outskirts of town on our side, where his house and smallholding stood. When we said good-night outside his gate, I remember saying, "It'll take more than a few barbarians to stop me travelling the roads."

We hurried the mules along at a canter, the men on horses keeping pace one on either side of the raeda. The sun was setting in a golden haze, but it would be light for some time yet. The summer twilight is long here in the north, and we'd be home before full darkness came. I pulled my wool cloak around me; it was cool now, and I thought longingly of the fire that would be waiting for me at the Oak Tree.

For the first part of the way the road ran through farmland, fields of ripening barley and oats, grass meadows with sheep or cattle in them, and a few horse-paddocks too. Pleasant land, prosperous and well looked after.

But then we came to the oak woods, and I grew tense as we entered the thick gloom of the trees. We were still on the native road, and though the surface was good—Silvanius' council had seen to that—the trees hadn't been cut back from the road's edge. I wanted to reach the good wide Roman highway, with its strips of cleared land to either side. You're a fool to be out here like this, Aurelia, I thought, and I told Titch to use his whip and make the mules go flat out.

The tall old oaks seemed to crowd us in, closer and more threatening as the light faded, looming to left and right in a more or less unbroken line. No other roads crossed ours; there was just the occasional faint track, made by animals or woodcutters. Among the trees the shadows were impenetrable, and anything—or anyone—could be waiting for us unseen. I'm not one of these city folk who panic if they find themselves among a few trees, but when it's getting dark and you're feeling apprehensive, there are too many shadows, and too many strange noises. Every creaking branch and call of a night-hunting animal made me jump. Once we heard the faraway howl of a wolf, but it wasn't wolves I was worried about.

Then the night was split by a loud and horrible scream from the trees on our left. A woman's scream, fit to curdle our blood.

Titch pulled up the mules, and we all listened, torn between horror, curiosity, and fear. The scream came again, a dreadful sound; no words, just an animal noise, piercing and terrified. Someone was being hurt. Another attack by the Shadow-men? And on a woman this time! Common sense cried out that we should ignore it, but we all knew we couldn't simply drive on and pretend we hadn't heard.

I looked at my two guards. "That woman needs help, lads. Better go and see what you can do. I'll stay here with the animals."

"Right," Bessus said, dismounting. "Come on, you two, if we're quick we can catch the bastards."

"Now don't be too hasty," Marsus began, getting down more slowly. "We don't know how many there is. It needs thinking about...."

"No time," Bessus answered, already heading into the trees. "Come on!"

"Wait." Titch jumped down and threw me the reins. "Bessus, it could be a trap. To split us up, like. One of us better stay with the mistress. I'll go with Bessus, Marsus can stay here. If you need us back again quick, Mistress, just whistle."

It made good sense, and we three adults unquestioningly did what he suggested. That boy will be a general, I thought, as he and Bessus set off at a run into the trees. Marsus, probably much relieved, grasped his cudgel firmly and stood by the mules' heads.

There was a narrow track into the wood heading in roughly the direction of the screams, but even so the two figures were lost to sight before they'd gone ten paces. Another scream shook the air. Bessus yelled "Hold on there, we're coming!" and then the trample of their footsteps faded out and suddenly it felt very lonely.

An owl hooted close by, and another answered it from a distance. A few leaves rustled in the faint night breeze. Apart from that all I could hear was my own heartbeat, fast and loud.

But soon we caught the sound of returning footfalls, and saw figures emerging from among the trees. One...two...three of them, moving fast. Only as they came to the road we realised that none of them were Bessus or Titch.

Marsus thumped the nearest mule hard, and I cracked the whip, but two of the men leapt forward to seize their heads, so all the animals could do was rear up and kick. Marsus swung round to face the attackers and got in one good blow with his cudgel, but they all had swords, and they disarmed him easily enough. I put two fingers into my mouth and whistled as if my life depended on it. Which I suppose it did.

The tallest man snapped "Quiet, you stupid bitch," and grabbing my wrists, pulled me roughly out of the carriage. One of his companions produced some rope and bound my hands behind my back. They tied Marsus' hands too.

That's something, I thought. They could have killed us already but they haven't. They must want us alive—for now, anyway.

And maybe Bessus and Titch have heard my whistle. I must play for time.

Then the leader said, "Right, boys. Kill them."

Marsus let out a cry. I didn't. To this day I'm proud that I didn't, because believe me I wanted to.

The other two men moved, but not towards us; it was the mules and the two horses they were after. They slit the poor beasts' throats so skilfully that they hardly had time to make a sound.

Would it be our turn next? My mouth was dry. But I couldn't just stand there and say nothing.

"That was a cruel thing to do, as well as a stupid waste," I said. "Those were valuable animals. I'd have paid you good money to leave them alone."

The leader spat in my face. "We don't want your money. You Romans think money buys everything, don't you? But we don't want anything from a stupid Roman slag. The animals are a sacrifice, an offering to the god of the woods."

"Well I hope he appreciates it! If you don't want money, what do you want? And who are you?"

"We're the Shadow-men, and as for what we want, you'll know soon enough. When the Chief gets here, you'll be told. Till then, keep your mouth shut."

"The Chief? The Shadow of Death, would that be?"

He leaned towards me for a heartbeat, staring into my eyes, his face twisted with hate. "If I had my way, Aurelia Marcella, you'd be dead already." I could feel his hatred, radiating out of him like heat from a brazier. It was a horrible sensation, being the target of such loathing from somebody who didn't even know me; all he knew was that I was a Roman, and that was enough to make him want to kill me.

But wait—he did know me, or at least my name. Gods, that meant these men had lain in wait for me—me personally, not just any Roman traveller who happened along. Why? Because I had Quintus Antonius as a guest at the mansio? Or because

I'd just attended a secret meeting to make plans for destroying their war-band?

I felt slightly sick, as I leaned against the carriage side, watching his two companions wiping their swords clean. When they'd done that, all three of them stood silently watching us and now and then glancing down the road. One muttered "I wish he'd hurry," but the others were as mute as the trees.

I looked at them carefully; I didn't know any of them, but I felt I must try to memorise their appearance in as much detail as I could, to recognise them later. If there was a later....No, concentrate, Aurelia. Quintus Antonius will expect a detailed description.

The thought of Quintus calmed me down, and I surveyed the men like an officer learning the faces of a new cohort. They were typical natives, tall and square in build, dressed in drab homespun cloaks, but with good leather boots and sword-belts. Even without blue paint or armour, they had the bearing of fighting men.

The biggest one, the leader, had fair straight hair and beard, and a slanting scar on his right cheek, starting just below the eye. The next biggest had fair hair but a reddish beard, and he'd had his nose broken at some time in the past. The smallest was a head shorter than the other two, and he had regular features and exceptionally fair hair, almost white, and red eyes—an albino. I stared at each one in turn, but they didn't meet my eyes.

Time dragged on. Where were the others? Had they heard my whistle, and could they do anything about it, two against three? I felt sure they would try. Unless they'd been caught too....It was almost dark by now; the stars were showing, and a thin sliver of moon, very low in the sky. And I was scared—no, not scared, completely terrified. But I wasn't going to give these barbarians the satisfaction of seeing it.

"You won't get away with this," I said. Hardly very original, but I was pleased to find my voice was steady. "I'm supposed to be back at the Oak Tree by dark. When my people realise I'm missing, they'll comb the woods till they find us. They'll bring the hunting-dogs…."

"I told you, be quiet," Scar-face snapped, and he slapped my face, hard enough to make my head ring and my eyes water.

"Don't mess up the merchandise, sunshine," I managed to say. "Your Chief won't be at all pleased if you deliver him damaged goods."

It was an arrow in the dark, but just for a heartbeat they looked shifty, almost scared. So the Shadow of Death wanted me alive and unharmed. Better not think about what he might want to do with me.

Then from the trees we heard trampling noises. My heart lifted, Bessus and Titch, at last! But out of the gloom came two more natives, dragging Bessus. His face was bleeding, and he was still struggling and trying to kick, but he couldn't make any real impression against his captors, who were taller, and built like wrestlers. These were more men I didn't recognise; one was dark-haired, with a black beard, and the other had long brown hair and small dark eyes.

And that left only Titch free. I sent a quick prayer to Diana that the boy wouldn't try any crazy heroics; his job now was to stay free, watch what happened to us, and get help. Perhaps in the near-dark our captors hadn't even noticed him. I would try and distract attention.

"Well isn't this cosy? Now you've rounded us all up, would somebody mind telling me what it's all about? You, perhaps?" I looked at the leader.

He slapped me again, and one of his men muttered "Go easy, Veric," and got a venomous curse in return. The two new arrivals tied Bessus' hands and pushed him up against the carriage, and he and Marsus and I stood there helpless, like beasts waiting for slaughter.

More time went by, and I could see our captors' growing restlessness; they peered into the dark along the road, and shifted about, and exchanged glances. The owl hooted again, but otherwise the whole shadowy world was still.

And then, clear and shrill, we all heard a bugle. A cavalry bugle, calling "Rally," the notes echoing through the woods.

By the gods! Titch! But surely he couldn't pull off the same trick twice?

Our captors started and looked alarmed, glancing along the road. Veric turned on the white-haired man, and swore at him savagely. "I thought you said the road was clear," he snarled.

"It *was* clear! Not a man or a beast…."

"Well it's not clear now, is it? That's a cavalry bugle blowing, if I'm not mistaken!"

"I tell you it was clear," the small man stubbornly repeated. "We've been stood about so long, there's been time for the whole ninth legion to march over from Eburacum. Where's the Chief? We ought to be getting out of here."

"How should I know, you stupid…."

"Calm down, Veric, they won't catch us," the broken-nosed man put in. "Just get the prisoners into these trees, then all the cavalry in the world can gallop about till they drop, and still never make contact."

"That's true." Veric laughed nastily. "Once the Shadow-men hide you, you stay hid. And you needn't look so pleased, you silly tart," he added, turning on me. "Something's coming that'll wipe that smile off your face for good." I'd been trying to look extremely pleased, as one would when expecting the army to come thundering to the rescue. I knew it was only one small boy, but they didn't.

"We've got some cavalry staying at the mansio," I improvised. "Ten of them. They've been hunting these woods today. Sounds as if they'll be here any time."

As if on cue, the bugle came again, and nearer. Not too close, Titch, I thought; just scare them, don't let them catch you. You're our only hope now.

"Let's go then," Veric barked. "Into the trees with them. Acco, stay here and watch, and mind you keep out of sight. Usual signal if we've got company."

"We're not going anywhere." I wanted to spin things out, get a little more time for help to come, if there was any chance of it. "You'd better go though, Veric or whoever you are. Once the military get here, you're dead. Run for it now, while you can. Otherwise...."

"Shut it!" Veric was really angry now. He drew his knife and for a heartbeat I thought he meant to stab me, but instead he grabbed my cloak, and wrenching it off me, he cut a long thin piece of the green cloth and gagged me with it. I tried to bite him, and I must have hurt his hand because I drew blood, but he didn't seem to notice. The cloth tasted foul, and I could have kicked myself for being too reckless.

They started dragging us up the narrow path into the trees. We all struggled, twisted and kicked, trying to move slowly and make as much din as we could. In the end they all drew knives and pushed us forward with knife-points pricking into our necks. The track grew narrower and veered left. It was almost pitch black in the trees, but the men clearly knew their way, and urged us on in silence.

We moved slowly, but with every step we took my heart sank lower. I knew that in only a dozen paces we were hidden from the road; a few more twists and turns and we'd be lost for good in the trees. Titch would make it home to the Oak Tree if he was careful, and bring a search party out, but by then we'd be long gone, and nobody would ever find us. They would see the dead animals and the raeda, and even perhaps make out our footmarks for a short way, but following our trail any distance would be impossible in the dark. Maybe it'd be feasible tomorrow, for a good tracker like Hawk...but it would be too late by then. I felt despair closing in on me, as thick as the black trees.

Then Titch's bugle called again. But no, wait! Even in my despair I realised the sound was coming from a completely different direction this time. Yet that was impossible, my ears must be playing tricks, deceived by the thick trees. There it came again—three short blasts, repeated several times. And that wasn't Titch, it couldn't be! Even at a fast run, he couldn't have covered such a distance on foot. Gods alive, could it be real cavalry after all?

The sudden hope was almost too much to bear. Supposing Junius and Marius, riding back towards the Oak Tree....Holy Diana, I prayed, let it be them! But how could I attract their attention? They'd never find us without some help; they'd gallop by in the darkness. All the natives had to do was keep us quiet and hidden here. I wanted to call out, but I couldn't. How stupid I'd been, to get myself gagged! Just when I needed to be able to yell for help....

But the slaves still weren't gagged, and Bessus suddenly gave a piercing whistle, and then a loud yell. "Help! This way! Help here....They're taking us off the road...." It ended in a horrible stifled gurgling noise as one of the natives cut his throat. But it was enough. *It was enough!*

"We're coming!" came an answering yell; the nearer bugle blew again, and now I could hear horses' hooves on the road, faint but getting louder as they cantered closer.

Veric swore. "They'll see the animals. Leave these here and scatter!" He shouted the last word, then he turned back to me and, as he released me, gave me one final hard blow across the face. "I'll be back for you soon," he growled, and then he began to run, following his men who had disappeared already.

I hardly heard him, because I was listening to shouts and hoofbeats, as down the dark track from the road came four men on horseback, and one boy, running.

It took forever to get home, because we had to go at walking pace. We only had four horses between eight of us, counting Bessus, because of course we would not leave his body behind for the barbarians to molest in the night. We tied him onto one horse, and Junius insisted that I ride another. To be honest I was glad to; now it was all over, my legs felt as weak as wax.

Junius helped me mount. "Are you all right, Aurelia? You've had a bad shock."

I wanted to answer, "Oh yes, we're tough as old boots, us innkeepers," but that hardly seemed gracious. "Fine, thanks to you and Marius. And young Titch too, of course."

As we plodded along, Junius explained how they'd returned to the mansio to find Albia very worried because I hadn't come home. "She insisted someone came out to find you. And the fellow that was hurt, Valerius Longinus, was on the point of setting off to search. Well that was silly, given the state he's in. So out we came without even stopping for a drink. And we could easily have missed you still, if it wasn't for this young fellow." Junius put a hand on Titch's shoulder. "You did well, soldier." Titch grinned hugely at the compliment.

At last we turned down the familiar Oak Tree track, and as we entered the bar-room everyone stood up and cheered. The customers and our servants came crowding round us, full of questions and congratulations. The soldiers went straight to the bar, Titch with them, and I heard Albia call out "Drinks on the house!" before she rushed up and flung her arms round me, laughing and crying at once. Next she embraced Junius, and they dissolved into a babble of explanations.

Marsus came over and said, "Am I allowed in here, Mistress?" The bar-room is normally off-limits to the farm slaves.

"You are tonight. Drink a toast or two to Bessus. He was a brave man, and he saved our lives. You were good friends, weren't you?"

"We were brothers."

"Brothers? I didn't know that!"

"No, well, we kept it quiet when we were being sold off at the Eburacum market. Folk often don't fancy buying two brothers. They say they can be troublemakers. But I'm glad I was with him...." He looked on the edge of tears. "He always was too reckless."

"Not reckless, brave," I said. "Go and drink to his courage. We'll give him a good funeral tomorrow."

And then Quintus Antonius came up and gently took my hand. "I'm so sorry, Aurelia," he spoke quietly, under all the noise of celebration. "This is all because of me, I'm afraid. Are you all right?"

"I'll survive. Tough as old boots, us innkeepers."

"You were right, you know."

"I'm always right. It's a well-known fact."

He didn't smile. "You said that if you helped me, it would put you in danger. And that's the very last thing I want. Tomorrow I'll move on, find another base to operate from."

"No." Shaken though I was, I knew for certain that the one thing I didn't want was for him to leave. "I promised to help, and I will. After all, as Silvanius is always saying, we Romans must stand together. Look, I've got a bar full of thirsty drinkers to see to. Let's talk later."

Predictably, the night developed into a party. Titch was hailed as the hero of the hour, and everyone fed him so much beer that I eventually took him to one side and reminded him gently of the great Julius Caesar's views on drunkenness, and he went happily off to his bed. The tribunes and their men were celebrating too, but Marsus slipped away after a couple of beakers.

I myself was more upset than I cared to admit, and it took all my willpower to join in the jollity with a cheerful face and a smile for everyone. Wine might have helped, but I wanted to keep a clear head, so I made do with a couple of beakers till eventually the last of the local customers were safely on their way home.

I had one more task before I could relax. I called all our people into the bar-room, house servants and field-hands, everyone. I arranged for a rota of men, the two troopers and Hippon, to take turns on night-watch outside the main door. Then I told them all how important it was that we stayed alert and on guard against the Shadow-men, and the particular danger to travellers. Finally I made a point of how brave everyone had been on the road tonight. I praised Titch's resourcefulness, and Bessus' heroic call for help, which had cost his life. "I'm proud of you all, and Lucius will be too, when he hears about it," I finished.

They actually cheered me, and then dispersed, and as they moved off, Quintus came out of a far dark corner where he'd been sitting unnoticed.

"A good speech. You should be a general."

"But I'm not, am I? I'm just a civilian, caught in the middle of someone else's war, when all I want to do is get on with running a peaceful guest-house."

He looked at me intently. "It's not surprising you're upset."

"Upset? Me? Of course not!"

"You saw them kill Bessus?" he asked gently.

"Of course I saw it. It was....I can't describe it...."

"Come and sit by the fire for a while," he said. "Just till you're ready to sleep."

"Sleep! Fat chance of that! I keep going through what happened out there, over and over in my head. Hearing the tribunes cantering up, and being sure they wouldn't find us, and then Bessus called out for help....He only got a few words out, before they cut his throat. He made a sort of gasping noise....I felt so helpless. I mean I've seen dead people before, but never a killing like that."

"It was brave of him," Quintus agreed. "And it certainly saved you. Junius told me."

"Yes, but if I hadn't been so stupid, provoking the gang leader with my silly remarks, I'd have been able to call out to Junius myself. I *should* have done!"

"Whoever called out," he said softly, "would be dead now."

I found I was shaking, and my legs refused to hold me up. I flopped down on a settle by the fire. Without a word he poured me a beaker of wine from one of the big jugs, and held it out for me. I drank the whole mug in one go. He poured more, and took a beaker for himself.

"It's always bad, seeing someone killed in cold blood." He sat down beside me, and took my hand. "In battle it's different, it's what you've trained for, and you're carried along by the excitement of it all. You can kill enemies as easily as swatting wasps. But *you* weren't on a battlefield. It's hard to take, especially the first time. And it's natural to feel guilty because you survived when someone else didn't." He drank some wine. "I felt the same after Pompeii."

I couldn't believe it. "After Pompeii? You were in *Pompeii?*"

"It was my home," he answered sadly.

"It was mine too!"

We sat there, amazed. Out here on the remote edge of the Empire's northernmost province, the river of fate had swept together two people from the same town in Italia. And not just any old unremarkable seaside resort; a town that no longer existed, having been destroyed in a day by an erupting volcano.

"Our home was in Pompeii," I said, "but we weren't there when Vesuvius erupted, we were staying with relations across the bay in Misenum. We saw the volcano erupt; fire and smoke, and ashes falling out of the sky, and then stones raining down. At first we didn't realise how serious it was, and by the time we did…well, it was much too late to go home. We just had to make a run for it, with all the other refugees. Everything was lost. Our town house, the farm, all our friends….We went back, a month or so after the volcano died down, thinking to salvage what we could from the house. But we couldn't even *find* our house. We couldn't even find our own street!" I paused to drink more wine, trying to prevent my hand trembling as I raised the beaker.

"I know," Quintus said. "I was actually in the town. I was just seventeen, still living at home. I got my grandmother out safely, and my sister and brother, and quite a few of the servants as well. Father told me to escort them to one of our villas inland. But he insisted on staying himself, to protect our house. He thought the eruption would stop soon, and then people would come back, and there would be looting if property was left empty. So he must have died there. By the time everyone realised the eruption wasn't going to stop, it was too late for me to go back and find him. But sometimes I still think, if I'd tried harder to persuade him, if I'd offered to stay there instead of him, I could have made him leave. After twelve years, it still makes me feel bad." He touched the emerald ring on his left hand.

"From your father?" I asked. "Your ring?"

"Yes. He gave it to me on my seventeenth birthday." He sighed, twisting the ring so that the green stone flashed in the lamplight. "He was a good man, very straight, and a scholar, but....I don't know, strict. Stern. Nothing I did ever seemed quite good enough. He always wanted me to have a political career and end up a senator. The gods know what he'd think of me now!"

We talked for a long while about our vanished life in Pompeii. We compared notes about the shops, the theatre, the temples, the gladiator shows, even the taverns.

"Not that I had any direct experience of those," I said, "but my brother occasionally sneaked off to somewhere called the Harpy's Cave when he was supposed to be at school."

Quintus laughed. "The Harpy's Cave! Gods, that takes me back. I used to go there—I think all the young lads did. It was an amazing place—the madam was an old crone, and the bar-room was done up to look like a real cave, complete with stuffed bats and spiders' webs. It even had a narrow secret passage at the back leading out into an alley, so we boys could make our escape when our tutors came looking for us....It was a good life, wasn't it?"

It was a very good life, and it was sad to think none of it was there any more, and yet I found it oddly comforting to remember it like this. It was years since I'd met anyone else who'd lost their home in that catastrophe, and it was impossible to explain it to somebody who hadn't been through it. So I hadn't talked about it, or let myself think about it, for a long time. And Quintus seemed to perceive things I didn't fully understand myself, things about needing to have a home, somewhere permanent to belong to, and the desperate panic I felt now, thinking our life at the Oak Tree might be snatched away from us.

"Are we going to lose our home here too?" I asked him. "Are the barbarians going to force us to leave? I can't let that happen, not again. I can't. I *won't.*"

"*We* won't," he corrected. "I'm with you in this, Aurelia. You know that. Whatever it takes, we'll win in the end." He bent close and kissed me. "I promise."

Eventually he took me to the door of my room, kissed me once more, and went away.

When I was alone I cried. I cried for Pompeii, and the travellers the Shadow-men murdered, and for our dead slave; I cried for the sense of impending disaster I felt. It left me bone-tired, and eventually I slept.

Chapter XIV

Next morning I woke late, with a splitting headache and a feeling of dread. By the time I went outside, the sun had cleared the horizon and was chasing away a thin white mist from the river. Albia was organising breakfast, and had already sent Ursulus with men and mules to retrieve the carriage, assuming there was anything left to retrieve by now.

"Relia, you look half-dead still," she greeted me cheerfully. "Go back to bed and catch up on some sleep. I can manage fine here."

"Thanks, Albia, I might just do that. I feel pretty rough. I'll see if a bit of breakfast wakes me up." We were in the kitchen, and I picked up a piece of crusty bread, dipped it in some olive oil, and had taken just one bite when there was a tap on the outside door.

It was Milo, the oldest of the stable-lads. His mousy hair was tousled and his expression was anxious. "Please, Mistress, Hippon says can you come round to the stable yard straight away. There's something he wants to show you."

"What's wrong, Milo? Are the horses all right?"

"Oh, they're fine, Mistress. It's—well, can you come, please?"

I abandoned breakfast and followed him to the stable yard, which was empty, except for a few half-groomed horses tied to the railings. I soon saw why when Milo led me around to the back of the stable building. There I found Hippon, the other horse-boys, and most of the older stable-hands. And I saw what they were all staring at.

Painted on the wooden back wall of the stables was a skull drawing, and beneath it two lines:

AURELIA MARCELLA WILL BE

KILLED

GET OUT OR DIE

So it wasn't a threat to "all Romans" now. It was a personal message for me! I stared at it, as if by sheer willpower I could make it disappear. But it was there, bright and clear for everyone to see. And then I looked down at the base of the wall. There was a dark green bundle of cloth, stained with something reddish-brown.

"Is that my cloak?" I could hardly get the words out. "They took it last night…." I bent to pick it up, but it was badly stained and still wet, so gingerly I lifted one end of the bundle, and it fell apart into dozens of small pieces; they had hacked it literally to ribbons, and doused it in some animal's blood.

Hippon said quietly, "We've only just found this. None of the guards heard anything last night—I certainly didn't. And yet….I don't like to think what they might have done if they'd found any of us outside."

"Especially me." I thought suddenly of Titch's remark yesterday: "I've never been that important before—for someone to want to kill me!" I glanced at the lad now, where he stood with the other horse-boys, looking unusually subdued. But he was fourteen, and at his age he knew that whatever the Fates threw at him, he'd be able to catch it and throw it back. I wished I had that resilience, but I didn't. All I knew was that somebody was taking trouble to let me know that they wanted me dead.

"Are you all right, Aurelia?" Hippon asked.

"Yes, but…*merda,* Hippon…."

"I know. Awful. Why not go inside for a while; we'll soon have this lot cleaned up, and the—the bundle thrown away."

"No. No, we must try and find out who did this." I made myself stand up straight and look steadily at the men and boys around me, and then survey the open area behind the wall. "I wonder how many of them there were? And if they've left any tracks? We could do with Hawk here, but I suppose it's worth a look—no, keep still, you boys, don't trample all over everything. Use your eyes, not your boots!"

I studied the ground, not seriously expecting to make anything of the footprints. There were plenty of them, mostly far too muddled to make sense of. But in one muddy patch a few feet from the wall I spotted a single clear left boot-print, with a worn heel, and some stitching missing from the sole.

"What's that?" Titch's sharp eyes had been busily scanning the area. He pointed to something shiny, and I nodded for him to pick it up and hand it to me. "A belt-stud, that is. Me dad has a belt with studs just like that."

"So do half the men in the Empire, though. Especially men with army connections. Except, this one's gilded, look. Usually they're bronze." It rang a bell, but I couldn't think why. I just knew that somewhere, recently, I'd seen something decorated with ornamental gold studs. "It might have been there some time, of course."

"But see where I found it, Mistress." The boy pointed to the soft ground, which had blurred boot-prints in it. "If someone had lost it yesterday, them fellers last night would have trodden it into the mud. But it was on top of the mud, see?"

We found nothing else, and Hippon told his lads to get back to work and see to the horses. "We'll need to think about guards for tonight," he said. "If anything happened to the horses.... Well, one thing at a time. The lads'll soon have this wall cleaned up. Why don't you get Taurus to look round the whole property, just in case...." He didn't need to finish it.

"Yes, everything must be checked over. I'll do it now."

"Take one of the men with you then. We can't be too careful."

"Gods, Hippon, has it come to this—that I can't even wander around my own house and land without a bodyguard?"

He shrugged. "Let's just play safe, shall we?"

I sent Titch to find Taurus, who came ambling round in his usual unhurried way, and stared at the wall. Hippon read him the message. "That's lousy," he said. "And they've spoiled your good cloak. Trying to scare you, I suppose."

Trying and succeeding, I wanted to say; but not in front of the servants. "I never liked that cloak much. Now I've got a good excuse to buy a new one." It didn't sound convincing even to me, but Taurus gave me a smile.

"Odd to use paint," he remarked. "I wouldn't have done. If I could write, that is."

"What would you use?"

"A bit of white stone. There's plenty of it about here." He walked over to the paddock fence and picked up a piece of chalky stone with a sharp edge. He went to the wall and drew a line on it. It stood out clear and white on the brown planking; better than the paint, which was pale green.

"Paint would be harder to clean off," I suggested.

"If I was writing on walls," Titch said gravely, "and I used a bit of chalk, like Taurus said, then nobody would know it was me, but they wouldn't know it was somebody else neither."

"I'm sorry?"

"If I used paint, I can't use me own, else people would know it was me. I'd use somebody else's, and then when it's recognised, he'll get the blame instead of me."

I saw where he was driving. "Somebody deliberately used this paint to throw suspicion on whoever owns it? Yes, you could be right. It's a fairly unusual shade—green with a slight trace of yellow. It ought to be possible to find out where it comes from. Titch, get a knife and scrape off some of it onto…let's see, onto my wax writing-tablet. If I think I see the same colour anywhere else, I'll be able to do an exact check. " I fished out a tablet from my pouch, and the boy scraped some green flakes onto it.

Just as he was finishing, we heard hoofbeats, and to my astonishment, Felix came riding up, accompanied by an armed servant, a giant of a man. Felix, on a horse? A pretty unusual sight these days, but he rode well, like any Roman gentleman. When he saw me he dismounted with a flourish, but without his usual smile.

"Aurelia, dear heart, I came as soon as I heard."

"Heard?" I asked stupidly, my mind still on the wall.

"About how you were attacked last night. Are you all right? Were you hurt? Oh my dear!" he exclaimed, catching sight of the wall. "How horrible! When was this done?"

"In the night."

"Jupiter's balls! It's—" he stopped suddenly. "It's quite dreadful," he finished lamely.

"Yes, it is. But some water and elbow-grease will clean it all off. And I can always get a new cloak."

"You're so brave, my dear! We heard you'd been attacked. The town's positively humming with rumours. Some farmer found your carriage, more or less wrecked, and your mules and horses dead, and we all thought....Well, never mind. Here you are, safe and sound. Now let me look at you." He took my face between two fingers and studied it seriously. "You seem none the worse, except is that a teeny bruise on your cheek?"

"One of the barbarians hit me, but really I'm fine. It could have been a lot worse."

"Oh, you poor thing. But you're all right otherwise? They didn't do anything else....I mean, they had no chance to...." He paused dramatically.

"No." I smiled in spite of myself. "They had no chance to, you dreadful old gossip! Thank the gods. And thank the cavalry, who turned up just in time."

"So what happened? Don't keep me in suspense!"

"Come inside, and I'll tell you."

I told Taurus to inspect the rest of the buildings, and also the orchard and paddocks, and to report to me if he discovered anything amiss.

It's hard to stop being an innkeeper even in a crisis; the first thing I did when we came into the house was get us both some breakfast, which we ate in my study. I knew that Albia had organised food for the other guests in the dining-room, but I felt happier talking to Felix in private.

"It's good of you to come so early," I said. "Especially as you normally don't open an eyelid till noon!"

"I must confess—" he helped himself to more bread— "that usually the only sure way for me to admire the rosy fingers of dawn is to stay up all night. But when the news came, I simply couldn't relax until I'd seen you with my own eyes. Do tell me what happened!"

I told him briefly, and he listened excitedly, and in the end said, "We were right, weren't we? At the meeting yesterday. These appalling men are going for travellers after dark. Well, I'm taking four strapping guards with me today, I can tell you. And we're stopping for nothing!"

I passed him more cheese. "Today? Where are you off to?"

"To Eburacum. To the theatre."

"Again? Clarus told me you were there two days ago."

He clapped his hands. "Checking up on me, my dear? I knew it—you do care after all! O joy! Marry me at once!"

"Idiot! But I care enough not to want you taking risks on the roads just now. You'll be careful, won't you? Is it a special performance you're going to see?"

"Yes, a new play for one of the officers' wives—her birthday party I believe. A comedy called 'Julia Joins the Cavalry.'"

"Don't tell me, lots of jokes about new recruits who can't get a leg over!"

"I'm afraid so. And the handsome hero getting his spear bent on night patrol. But my main reason for going is to see my friend Dardanio—he's playing the randy general. You've heard of Dardanio, the actor? He's brilliant! An old friend of mine. He's been in the theatre since we were boys together."

"I don't get time for the theatre, I wish I did. I like a good comedy."

"So do I. Why else do I spend so much of my life applauding Publius Silvanius and his antics?" His tone was bitter, not his usual teasing.

"Oh dear. Have you two fallen out?"

He looked contrite. "I'm sorry, that was beastly of me. No, of course we haven't. It's just that sometimes…." He hesitated, but this time it wasn't a contrived dramatic pause.

"Sometimes?" I prompted.

"Publius has been very good to me. Generous, understanding. I couldn't live the life I do if it wasn't for his friendship. And his money. But—I know this sounds dreadfully ungrateful…."

I looked at him in his finery. He had a fashionable brick-red cloak and matching sandals, and his hair was as immaculate as always. But his yellow-green eyes were troubled. I thought, this is a Roman from an old aristocratic family, brought up to wealth and privilege at the centre of the world, and now he's living on the bounty of a friend in a raw new province with barely a denarius to his name.

"Sometimes it's hard to have to be grateful all the time," I suggested.

He sighed. "That's it exactly. I'm a Cornelius—our family is an old one, and a rich one. I should be…." He shrugged. "I had to leave Rome in some haste, you see. I couldn't bring anything with me. Everything that belonged to my branch of the Cornelii was confiscated." He took a huge sip of wine. He looked close to tears, real tears, not the turned-on waterworks of an actor.

"Tell me," I said, "if you want to. I know very little about your life before you came here. Now, of course, you're one of the leading men in Oak Bridges."

"So they say. Three cheers and a fanfare of trumpets. Let's drink to big fish in small ponds!" He raised his beaker.

"Better to be a big fish than a little one. So tell me."

"Our family were at the court of the Emperor Nero. Oh, don't say it, I know he's regarded as a monster now, and he did go to pieces at the end. But he loved the arts. Especially the theatre and music. He tried to make Rome more civilised, more Greek. And all of us who loved the arts, loved him, too."

"Some of his courtiers used to perform with him on stage. Did you?"

"I did a bit of acting, yes. And wrote some plays. It was wonderful." Then the old mischievous Felix reasserted himself. "Mind you, most of us were pretty dreadful. We'd have got pelted with rotten fruit if we hadn't had the Emperor in the company."

"Was Nero himself good? I've always understood he was nothing special."

"He could have been brilliant. He had talent, and to start with he made a terrific effort. He wrote songs, he rehearsed them day and night. He did all sorts of exercises to improve his breathing, and strengthen his voice. Then he realised that everyone would applaud him like mad whether he was good or not. So he stopped trying. And then, at the very end, I think he was just plain mad. Power can do that to a man." He had regained his teasing smile. "It wouldn't to me, though. Give me imperial power, I'd say thank you very much, and live happy ever after."

I laughed. "With every other building a theatre, and you and your friends in specially created leading roles! But presumably life changed for you after Nero fell. He'd made too many enemies, and you were in line for revenge from everybody who hated him."

He shuddered. "Yes. It was a horrible time."

I didn't like to see Felix so upset, even though I doubted if many people would share his regret at the passing of Nero. "But all that is in the past, Felix. Twenty-odd years ago. Surely you could go back to Rome now, if you wanted to?"

"Well yes, I'd be safe physically, I suppose, but I'd still feel like an outsider, only half a man. Even if I could persuade some distant branch of my family, which managed to hang onto its lands, to help me out, everyone would start telling the old stories again. That I ran away, that I....Anyway, Nero's friends are no better loved now, a generation later, even though we've got another tyrant on our glorious imperial throne these days. And this one's got no redeeming features whatever!"

Gods alive, first I get Felix's life story, then he starts spouting high treason! Just pretend you didn't hear it.

"You're too sensitive. These things blow over. Everyone will have forgotten."

"Perhaps. But *I* can't forget. When they destroyed Nero, they made the arts seem somehow contaminated, defiled, just because he had championed them. A city which does that is no place for me."

"So here you are in Britannia, bringing Roman arts to people who'll appreciate them better. That's why you're trying to get a theatre built in Oak Bridges?"

"It would be wonderful. I think Publius is quite keen, but of course it would need a great deal of money."

"How about the other big fish in the Oak Bridges pond? Wouldn't some of them chip in a few aurei in the name of culture? Balbus, maybe?"

"Balbus spend his hard-earned gold on a theatre?" He laughed. "Balbus wouldn't recognise a good play if it jumped up and bit him! But listen, Aurelia, that's reminded me of something I noticed outside just now. I didn't want to say anything in front of the servants, but...." The dramatic pause was irresistible.

"Go on, what?"

"That graffito on your stable wall. It gave me quite a shock, and I don't just mean because of the horrid message. Do you know who did it?"

"The Shadow-men, presumably."

"Yes, but *who?* You haven't seen that particular shade of green paint before?"

Something in his excited semi-whisper made me look at him keenly. His eyes glittered and he sat forward, tense as a cithara-string.

"You mean you have?"

"Yes. In Balbus' shop."

"*Balbus'?*" No wonder he was so excited. "Are you sure?"

"Dead certain. Oh dear, an unhappy phrase. Quite certain, yes. I complimented him on it."

"But look, who'd use the kind of paint you decorate pots with for daubing words on a wall?"

"Ah no, it's not his special pigment for making glazes. It's the colour of his big display alcove, the walls and shelving. Don't you remember? He had a whole new tier of shelves built and everything painted pale green, to show off that lovely dinner-ware he imported from Gaul, the white with the vine-leaf design."

I did remember, and I thought he was right. "It's very similar....It would be easy enough to check. But I can't believe Balbus would help barbarian rebels. Can you? He lives for his business, and his business needs peace and prosperity. I know you're not one of his bosom pals, but...."

"Perhaps it's not him personally, but one of his workers." Felix scratched his head. "He employs a lot of natives, of course, including his foreman, who lives behind the shop now. And then you see, there's something else. It may be too trivial to bother with. I wouldn't even have thought of mentioning it, if it wasn't for the paint."

"Well now you have thought of mentioning it, spit it out!"

"I've heard our dear potter is on rather good terms with some of the Brigantian aristocracy. The anti-Roman ones, I mean. Especially the older generation, who, as Publius puts it, haven't accepted the finality of the Roman conquest. He visits them at home, that sort of thing."

"Does he? How in Hades do you know that?"

He smiled slyly. "I pick up snippets of gossip here and there. From my friends, and my theatre chums at Eburacum."

True, he had plenty of friends everywhere, and he made no secret of his love of gossip.

"But still....No, Felix, you can't assume that just because he sells pots to natives, he sympathises with the Shadow-men. I agree he'll trade with anyone, because he's a businessman first and last, and he might not be too choosy about who he deals with. But he's a Roman citizen. Which means he's at risk like the rest of us."

"Except that if he's in league with the rebels, he's at no risk at all, is he?"

"I can't fault the logic, I suppose, but...surely not Balbus! I'd as soon believe it was Silvanius. Or you."

Felix laughed and finished his beaker. "Yes. Of course you're right as ever, my dear. I mustn't let my prejudices get the better of me, must I?"

He departed soon after, leaving me with some unpleasant thinking to do. Prejudiced or not, he could have stumbled on something important.

I found Quintus Antonius in the garden, bathed and dressed, and looking almost back to normal, except that his bruises would still need a few days to disappear completely.

"Albia brought me breakfast in my room," he explained. "Now I've had a breath of fresh air, and I'm ready for anything. Shall we walk around the garden?"

"Why not? I need something to calm me down. The morning hasn't started well."

I gave him the latest bad news, and when I told him about the torn-up bloodied remains of my cloak, he repeated Hippon's question, "Are you all right?"

"I'll survive. It's getting a bit too personal, though."

"I'm sorry," he said seriously. "I've got you into this mess. I wish there was more I could do to get you out of it."

"The words on the wall were painted." I described them, and added Felix's theory about Balbus.

"The pottery shop?" Quintus said. "I'll maybe ride into town and buy a nice tasteful jug for my aged grandmother in Lindum. But as your young lad said, someone else could be using the paint to throw suspicion onto Balbus."

"I'll find an excuse to visit his shop soon, if I can. It needs checking. But I still find it a pretty unlikely thought."

"As I've said before, there's no such concept as 'unlikely' when you're looking for traitors. Who else was at your meeting yesterday?" With everything that had happened since, I hadn't had time to tell him.

"I'm under oath of secrecy," I said. "Will you swear not to pass any of this on?"

"I swear."

I tried to give him quick sketches of the five people: Silvanius the ambitious chief councillor, desperately worried about any threat to Roman people or property. Vedius the old soldier, organising night patrols even if he had to do it on crutches. Balbus the rich businessman, anxious about what would happen to trade. Felix the dandy, declaiming Virgil and lamenting the death of Nero. And of course Vitalis, envying his wild Brigantian relatives and yearning for the good old days. I told him as much as I could remember of the conversation, including my chat with Vitalis over dinner.

"An interesting group," he remarked. "Leaving aside Vitalis, who wasn't at the meeting, Silvanius presumably chose you all because you're the most prominent Romans in Oak Bridges. You have most to lose if the Romans are expelled from this area, so you can be trusted to take strong measures."

"That's about it. He probably wouldn't have included me in the group, but as the meeting was my idea, he couldn't very well keep me out."

"I imagine he didn't dare try." He smiled at me.

"Vitalis was the one person in the house who was openly anti-Roman. At the temple site he came fairly close to blasphemy, and then fairly close to treason over dinner."

"And he spent the afternoon out riding. Had he come back by the time you left Silvanius' villa?"

"He could have done. I don't remember actually seeing him, but it's a huge place."

"You told me last night that the leader of the ambush party called you by name."

I nodded. "But I didn't recognise him."

"It means the men were waiting for you, though, doesn't it? Not just any unfortunate traveller. You personally. So who knew you were going to Silvanius' house? Everyone at the Oak Tree?"

"Hardly anyone. Albia knew, and of course Titch and the two slaves who came with me. Nobody else. I come and go as I like here, and quite often drive into town, so it wouldn't cause comment."

"Did all the people at the meeting know beforehand you were going to be there?"

"Vedius certainly didn't, and probably not Balbus either. Felix did, because he was there when Silvanius asked me."

"But once you were there, they all knew, and all their servants did too. Did everyone leave for home at the same time?"

"No, Felix stayed on a while. Balbus and Vedius and I all left in a group. Balbus lives quite close to Silvanius. Vedius and I travelled through Oak Bridges together. The old fool offered to escort me all the way to the mansio. Gods, I wish I'd let him...."

"So do I. It was reckless of you to be out in the dark like that...."

"I know, I know. I don't need a lecture. You're saying that someone at the villa arranged to have me ambushed as I went home?"

"I don't see how else it could have been done. Do you?"

"Then Vitalis must have been there, I suppose."

Our pacing about had brought us round to the door into Quintus' room, and we went in and sat down on the couch. "This Shadow of Death," Quintus mused, "must be a master of disguise. It could be Vitalis, but any of the people at the house, especially the ones at the meeting, could be just as anti-Roman, only concealing it better. Look, there's something I want to show you. If I do, can you promise to keep it just between the two of us?"

"Of course. Only, if I need to, can I tell Albia? You're going to need her help as well as mine, if you're here for long."

"Well...I suppose as she's your housekeeper...."

"She's my sister, more to the point. We're very close, which is why we make a good job of running this place."

"Your sister? I thought she was just your assistant."

"She's both! Father used to say that I was a centurion, and Albia was my optio, my second-in-command. It's not a bad description. She's a brilliant organiser, and I'm afraid I take her for granted sometimes. And if we're in for trouble, she must know everything there is to know."

"Does she mind you being her centurion?" he asked, amused.

"No, she's happy having someone else to make the big decisions. And she doesn't see herself spending the rest of her life running a mansio. If you want to bet on whether she or I will be first to marry and start having babies, don't bother wasting your money on me. She'll win hands down."

"Don't you want to get married?"

"Perhaps, one day. But it's Albia we're talking about, not me. Take my word, she's one of those people who's a born second-in-command."

"Whereas you're a born dictator!" He smiled. "All right. You can tell Albia if necessary, but nobody else."

"I promise."

"Then could you fetch my money-belt from your strong box, please?"

I went to get it from my study, and I felt a thrill of excitement as I thought of its contents, especially the papyrus and its puzzling coded list. Now I was going to find out what it meant. But more important, at last, at *long* last, Quintus was taking me into his confidence.

Chapter XV

He held out the papyrus for me to see, and I gazed at its confusion of jumbled letters.

```
L's list
PGATT
SSFCV
CVBFS
```

"L's list," I read. "Does L stand for my brother Lucius, by any chance? "

"It does."

"But I can't make anything of the rest. Is it in code?"

"Just sleight-of-hand really. Try reading the letters from top to bottom, not left to right."

I spelled them out, mentally re-arranging them on the page. They still didn't make words, just five groups of three letters.

```
PSC
GSV
AFB
TCF
TVS
```

Groups of three letters. What can you list using just three letters? Of course! "Initials!" I exclaimed. "Each group stands for someone's full name. So it's a list of five people."

"Five suspects, yes. Your brother sent me the list when he heard I was coming up here. He said, if he was asked to put money on who would make a good rebel leader, these would be his choice."

"So they're people I know." I looked at the first name. "PSC. Publius Silvanius Clarus?"

He nodded.

"That's why you were so insistent that Silvanius could be the Shadow of Death—because Lucius put him top of the list."

"And I haven't changed my mind. I still think he's ideally placed. He has money, power, easy access to Roman government circles, and yet good contacts with the natives."

"But his foreman was killed yesterday," I objected. "Would he kill the man he was relying on to get the temple finished for the inauguration ceremony? It's only four days away now. Without Casticus, there must be a risk it won't be ready in time."

"Suppose Casticus found out somehow what Silvanius is up to? But let's go through the whole list first. You'll agree with the second name, I think."

"GSV, Gnaeus Silvanius Vitalis. Oh yes, I do. The only problem is that Vitalis is so open about his anti-Roman feelings. From what you've said already, I expected someone more devious."

He laughed. "Spoken like a true investigator!"

"Number three," I said, "is AFB—Aulus Fannius Balbus. This business of the green paint—but he's no fool. He wouldn't use a colour that everyone knows he possesses."

"Not even as a sort of double bluff?" Quintus smiled. "Or would you consider that theory too devious even for me?"

"I don't think there's anything that's too devious for you. But more likely one of his household might have used it from sheer thoughtlessness. Or as Titch suggested, somebody could be trying to incriminate him."

"And he certainly has the wealth, and the good contacts everywhere."

"Who's the fourth name? TCF. Well, that must be Titus Cornelius Felix. Can you see Felix master-minding a gang of murderers?"

"Stranger things have happened. He's not rich, and maybe that's why the first rebel ambushes weren't aimed at individuals, but at the pay convoys. He travels a lot, going to theatres all over the place."

"He has access to influential Romans too, through Silvanius," I agreed. "And there was that sad story he told me earlier today about being misunderstood by all true Romans because of treading the boards with Nero. All the same, Felix is one of the most truly Roman people in this town!"

"He *appears* to be. But he's admitted to being an actor."

"Well, yes…." I tried my best to picture Felix as the Shadow of Death. I couldn't, so I considered the final suspect.

"TVS. Tiberius Vedius Severus? I wonder why Lucius included him? An old soldier, with a string of military decorations as long as your arm, and living a life of old-fashioned Roman virtue that would have impressed the elder Cato!"

"He's got first-class military training," Quintus said, "and good contacts at Eburacum. Of the five of them, he'd be the most likely to be able to organise the ambush of the pay convoys. But he's there because of his murky past, of course."

"Gods, I can't imagine Vedius ever doing anything even slightly murky. Wait though…I do remember some bar-room talk about his first wife being murdered, and someone wondering if he'd had a hand in it. People love to make malicious rumours up in a situation like that. And it was a long time ago, before he moved here….He served in the Twentieth Legion, I think. And won some sort of bravery award when they put down Queen Boudicca's rebellion thirty years ago."

"That's right. By then he was a centurion, and a good one apparently, with just a year to go till he got his discharge. The general respected him, and his men would do anything for him. He had a woman and children, and was all set to marry when he left the army. He must have been looking forward to retiring and living a prosperous life as a respectable hero."

"He sounds like my own father. What happened?"

"His woman fell in love with someone else—one of the young military tribunes. It wasn't just a discreet flirtation either, it was a full-blown public romance. She abandoned Vedius, which was bad enough, and humiliated him in front of his men, flaunting herself with her new protector. Vedius was devastated, but he couldn't persuade her to come back to him, and after a month everyone thought he'd accepted it. Then one morning the tribune was found in the woman's house, which was outside the fort of course. He'd been murdered in the night."

"By Vedius?"

"Everyone assumed so, but it was impossible to prove. His woman had run away, and his two best friends swore he'd been with them all night long, getting roaring drunk in a bar."

"Perhaps he had, and then killed the tribune in a drunken rage."

"That's what most people thought at the time. And the tribune wasn't popular, he was an arrogant little show-off, and everyone felt he'd been asking for trouble, and took Vedius' side."

"So they hushed it all up."

Quintus nodded. "He asked for a transfer to another legion, which would have been the sensible solution, as he only had a year to go. But unluckily for him, the tribune had powerful relatives, some of them at Nero's court, and they wanted Vedius out of the army. So he was discharged a year early, 'on medical grounds,' which was a complete invention, and everybody knew it. There was no official stain on his character, but he hated having to slink away under a cloud of suspicion, when he should have been marching out in a blaze of honour."

"Yes, he'd have felt the disgrace." As a centurion's daughter, I could imagine it only too well.

"He moved to Oak Bridges, where nobody knew him, so he could start afresh as a retired hero who'd lost his wife in a tragic accident. He built a house, married a local girl, became popular with the settlers…and now he's an aedile."

"How did you find all this out? Did Lucius tell you?"

"He warned me about the rumour that Vedius might be hiding some kind of ancient scandal. I made contact with some of his former comrades from the Twentieth, and got the full story. After all this time, they're still saying Vedius was badly treated."

"And he could be bearing a grudge against the army, and helping the rebels as a kind of revenge?"

"Lucius thinks it's possible, though not very likely. That's why he's at the bottom of the list. But you see what I mean, it could be him. It could be any of them."

"That's an awful thought…." I trailed off unhappily. I was realising fully what life would be like now, if I had to go around suspecting everyone—every native and every Roman settler, including my friends. But the alternative, doing nothing and letting the Shadow-men continue their savage campaign, was even worse. Because in that case I might be their next victim.

As I was digesting this, Albia knocked and came in with bread and cheese, and some wine.

"I think we need a council of war," she said. "And Relia hasn't had breakfast yet."

Good old Albia. She always gets her priorities right. I hadn't the heart to tell her I'd eaten already.

While she passed me a plate and poured wine for all of us, I told her what Felix had said about the paint, and about Balbus being on visiting terms with the old tribal aristocracy. "You're right, Albia, we do need a council of war. We'd better include Cousin Junius too."

"The young tribune?" Quintus said. "He's a bit inexperienced for this sort of work, I'd have thought."

"Don't you believe it. Junius is a contact of my brother's. Lucius specifically asked us to help him." I explained about the letter, and the recognition code.

"Aunt Julia and the elephant! I wondered what all that was about yesterday. I should have realised it was an identification signal."

"To begin with we thought you were the mystery cousin," Albia said.

"No. I'm not a cousin."

"But you're part of the family though?" Yes, I realise I'm not supposed to ask that question direct, ever. Too bad—I wanted to know where we all stood.

"In a way," Quintus said. "I'm a colleague of Uncle Titus, if that helps."

"Then why didn't Lucius tell us you were coming?" Albia asked.

"He didn't know the exact details. Nobody did. I prefer to keep my movements unpredictable. But to get back to the matter in hand. I'd rather we didn't involve Junius in our discussions. Planning our tactics is an excellent idea, but the fewer people who are in on it, the better."

"But surely," Albia objected, "anybody Lucius recommends is one of us. We *must* include Junius."

"I agree," I said. "He's a soldier, his advice will be useful."

Quintus ran a hand through his fair hair. "It seems so. But…I told you we're investigating the help the Shadow-men are getting from the military."

We both nodded, and I said, "Yes. Those two bent investigators."

"I also told you those two are small fry who could lead us to a bigger fish. Now supposing…."

"You can't mean Junius?" Albia looked like a new bride being informed that the bridegroom is ravishing her sister behind the temple. Her astonishment would have been funny, if it wasn't so serious.

"I don't know, Albia," Quintus answered. "Probably not, if he's a contact of your brother's. But there's a traitor reasonably high up in the Eburacum garrison, all the evidence points to it. It could be either Junius or Marius. After all, they're staying here, very conveniently, in the centre of all the unrest. I can't overlook the possibility."

"Junius is no traitor," Albia declared.

Quintus said gently, "I can't rule him out, just because of your personal feelings. I wish I could."

"Who's talking about feelings? I'm talking about facts!" She drained her beaker and thumped it down on the table. "I'll tell you what *I* think. We've only got your word for who you are, and what you are up to. But Junius—we can be certain of him, because Lucius vouches for him."

"You can't use a word like 'certain' when you're talking about treachery," he answered. "We can't be certain, and we shouldn't take risks. So we won't tell Junius what we're planning. I must insist on that for now."

"Insist?" Suddenly his quiet assumption of authority made me angry. Insist, indeed! "Quintus Antonius, Junius comes recommended by our brother, and he saved my life last night, which to my simple mind indicates that he's on my side. I accept that we need to be wary of Marius, but Junius will be present at our planning meeting. If that means you don't want to be present yourself, it's entirely your decision."

His dark blue eyes flashed dangerously, and his mouth was a slit. I returned his stare, because I wasn't going to be ordered about in my own house on something as important as this. We paused, confronting each other like dogs sparring over a bone.

Albia broke the tension, by saying mildly: "She's right, you know. As our esteemed Councillor Silvanius is fond of saying, 'She talks very good sense. So refreshing in a woman.'"

Her impersonation of His Pomposity was so accurate that I had to smile, and suddenly Quintus laughed, and said, "Jupiter! May the gods preserve me from bossy women!"

"It's a bit late for that," Albia commented. "You've met Aurelia!"

So she fetched Junius, and Quintus greeted him politely. Marius, it turned out, had already gone off for the day, leaving a vague message about meeting a friend.

When we were all seated, Quintus said, "I suggest there's one important matter we need to settle first." He looked at me, and then at Albia. "Aurelia…Albia…you've had a bad time in the last few days. The indications are that it'll get even worse. The Shadow-men are trying to terrorise Romans in general, and, because I'm here, your household in particular. You've both said you intend to stay and stick it out. If you do, it'll be unpleasant and frightening, and perhaps very dangerous indeed. But you don't have to stay here and face the risks if you don't want to. Nobody will think any the less of you if you decide to leave the Oak Tree for a while, go to Eburacum or even down south, somewhere safe, and wait…."

"Leave the Oak Tree?" I almost shouted. "Never. *Never.* This is my home, it's where I belong. I'm not leaving."

He nodded. "And you, Albia?"

"Of course we're staying. I agree with Relia. Whatever happens, this is our place and it's worth fighting for."

I stood up. "We'll make this absolutely clear. Come with me, all of you." I led them into the hallway, to the little shrine that held our household and family gods. The small, familiar statues, with the daily offering of wine and food I always gave them, were suddenly very important, and very precious. I put my hand on the figure of Diana. "I swear," I said, "by the gods who guard this house, that I will not be forced to leave my home against my will. I will either live here, or I will die here."

Albia was beside me, and she repeated the same words. We smiled at each other. It was a sacred and binding oath. We both felt better for it.

Back in Quintus' room, we got down to discussing how best to protect the mansio and the outbuildings and livestock from enemies, especially at night. The main building and stables weren't too difficult to guard, but the problem got worse as you moved further away from the road. The horses in the paddocks were vulnerable, and the slaves in their living-quarters.

I was pleased to see that Quintus and Junius worked well together. Quintus had obviously put aside his reservations, and

they were very much of one mind. They'd both had army training of course, so they knew how to fortify a site quickly. They
started talking about building a fence and ditch right around
all the main buildings. Their military experience and practical
efficiency were comforting and I let them get on with working
out how much timber we'd need, and how many men would be
required. When the details got too technical I must admit I found
it hard to concentrate, because my mind kept filling with sad
images: a headless corpse in the forum, a builder spread-eagled
in a cart, and a little grey-bearded pedlar with a grey donkey.

"It boils down to three things," Quintus said eventually.
"Number one, nobody goes out after dark unarmed, and the
women should have an armed escort. Have you got weapons
for your people, Aurelia?"

I roused myself to pay attention. "Enough, I think. But most
of them are farm boys, they've no military training."

"We'll help there," Junius offered. "Marius and I and our
men can give them some basic weapons drill."

"Number two, you'll have to bring all the horses and mules
into the stables, or the stable yard, at night. We can't protect
the paddocks properly, and they're too much at risk out there."

"I agree." Some of the horses were valuable in themselves,
and even the scrawniest old mules represented our living, not
to mention our lines of communication.

"The third thing, and the most important, will be to build
a stockade and ditch to surround the main house, the slaves'
quarters, and the stables. You've got plenty of timber hereabouts,
haven't you?"

"Oh yes. Oak, beech, ash, alder, and hazel. The woods
between the little river and the road are ours for quite some
distance."

"Excellent. It needn't be a particularly elegant fence, as long
as it's strong and tall enough to make intruders think twice."

"A proper fence? Like in a marching camp?" Albia asked. "Do
we have enough men for that?"

Junius nodded. "Given a dozen of your field-slaves, we could have the job done in two days."

"More like three," Quintus amended. "There's the timber to cut and carry here."

"We can hire in some woodcutters," I suggested. "There are plenty of lads on the native farms who can handle an axe."

"Fine," Quintus agreed, "as long as they're properly supervised. But the fence-building must be done by our own people. Men we trust absolutely."

We left the two of them tossing dice to see who should be Prefect of Loggers and who should be Prefect of Builders. They were friends now, I could tell, and enjoying themselves like boys building their first den. "Men," I muttered to Albia. She just giggled, and headed for the kitchen.

I made for the bar-room, which was empty, and I sat quiet for a little while, giving some thought to Bessus' funeral. He was part of our household, though only a slave, and he'd died a brave death. He deserved a dignified ceremony, and we'd need a pyre. I must set Taurus and a couple of men on to carry wood to the far field, where the other slaves' ashes were buried.

I heard the main door open, and looked up, expecting to welcome a customer. And there, large as life, was a Druid.

Chapter XVI

Yes, a Druid! I couldn't have been more astonished if it had been Caesar and his whole court, dropping in for a quick drink on their way to an orgy, or whatever it is they do all day. (Better erase that bit before you show this to the Governor.)

Though I'd never seen a Druid in person, there was no doubting what he was. He wasn't wearing a ceremonial embroidered vestment, but his white hooded robe was adorned with a sprig of oak leaves, and he carried himself with the unfaltering air of authority that you see in senior priests of all gods, who are used to being listened to by deities, and obeyed by men. That, and the way his grey hair and beard were cut—it all said "Druid" as loudly as if a herald had blown a trumpet and announced it. His face was old and lined, with a high forehead and very dark eyes. I was so consumed with curiosity I had a job not to stare outright. But I couldn't talk to him in full view in the bar.

"Welcome to the Oak Tree," I said. "I'm Aurelia Marcella, the innkeeper. Will you come through and take some wine in my study? We won't be disturbed there."

Which in plain Latin meant, "For the gods' sake let's get you out of sight of the public." Everybody knows that Druids are outlaws, put to death if they're caught. Whether merely having a Druid under my roof could earn me the same fate I didn't know, and I didn't want to find out the hard way.

He smiled, and without a word followed me out of the bar.

He was unsteady on his legs, limping slightly, and as he walked the few paces to my study, he leaned on a stick to support himself. He sank down into a chair and smiled again.

"You are most kind." His voice was beautiful, strong yet controlled, and his Latin was pure, without the usual guttural British accent. "You don't mind my being here? I'm afraid my calling isn't highly regarded in Roman circles."

No, really? But I said, "We keep open house for any traveller, as long as there's no trouble."

"There will be no trouble, I promise you. One of our ponies has gone lame, and we needed to stop and rest him for a bit. Your new stable-boy is taking a look at him for us."

I glanced out of the open window and recognised on the forecourt a familiar group of young men in warrior gear, but only four of them. They were lounging at ease on a wall, chatting together, and looking about curiously.

"Ah, you've noticed my escort. Just a few lads keeping an old man company on the road. These are dangerous times, I fear."

And whose fault's that? But I merely asked whether the escort would like a drink.

"Thank you, I'm sure they would."

I rang for one of the maids, and told her to ask Albia to take some mead out to them. She catches on quickly, my chief of staff, and she'd know I was signalling her to keep an eye on them. I didn't fancy the idea of those young warriors snooping around unsupervised.

"May I know your name?" I asked the old man.

"Caradoc," he answered.

"Then welcome, Caradoc. Let me pour you some wine." I poured some for both of us, and saw that he was looking amused.

"You're suspicious of my lads?" he asked.

"Not at all. I know them. But usually when they come here, they are five. I was just wondering what had happened to Vitalis."

"Vitalis? He couldn't join us today. He has family business, I understand."

I watched the old priest as we sipped our drinks. His expression was calm and kindly, not at all the tense fanatical look of a rebel. And yet, from what I knew of their beliefs, there must be an iron heart under that gentle exterior. Maybe if I could get him talking, I'd learn something useful about the way their minds worked.

So I asked him the standard question. "Are you travelling far today?"

"Not far. Down the road a short distance, and then into the woods."

"Better down the road than up the Long Hill. It's a steep climb." Yes, all right, very banal, but I couldn't think how to get onto anything more interesting. You can't just toss out a conversational opening like "I believe you people carry out human sacrifices. When's the next one due?"

Caradoc smiled his sweet smile. "To be honest, I'm glad of an excuse to stop here for a little while. It's many years since I've been to this spot."

"You've visited us before?"

"Yes, long before your mansio was built. Before the road even. In my father's time, when there were just oak woods here. I expect you know what the original name for this place is? In the ancient language of our people?"

"I didn't know it had a name before Father came."

"It is called Dru Nemeton. The place of the holy oaks."

"You mean this was one of your holy groves? Here, where the mansio is now?"

He nodded, and then looked me squarely in the face. "Aurelia Marcella, I know you have had trouble here. I don't want to see it becoming worse for you. You and your family have always lived in peace with our people. You've treated us well, and kept open house for all comers. As with me, now. Most Romans would have thrown me out, and sent for the town watch to arrest me."

"You've seen our town watch, I take it?"

He laughed briefly, but then became grave again. "I'm old now, and close to death. We don't fear death, because we know that our souls will move on to another life after this one, and so we will live forever."

It sounded weird. Everyone knows that death means descending into the underworld, except for a few poor lemures. But I was much too interested to interrupt.

"Old age has its advantages," he went on, "and one of them is coming to realise that not everything can or should be resolved by violence. Oh, I know what you Romans think of our religion. You think our gods are savage, primitive beings, and you believe we native Britons are the same."

"We've fought some bloody wars against your people," I pointed out. "We've mostly seen you and your gods in anger. Now there are rumours of more trouble coming. It makes me sad. I don't want war, I want peace. I want to make my life here, and die here in my own bed. Live and let live, that's my motto. But if anyone attacks us, we'll defend ourselves. This is our home."

I hadn't meant to speak so bluntly, but it didn't seem to disconcert him. "I know. I even understand. Your father brought you here when you were young; he took this land—"

"He was *given* a land-grant by the Governor! He didn't just steal it."

"Yet the land was stolen, before your time, perhaps before your father's time. Stolen from our gods, and our tribesmen who used to worship them here. Do you see what that means?"

"You're saying you want the land back, and I should just walk away and let you take it? Never!"

"I'm not presuming to advise you. I am simply telling you that others are saying it. Younger men, with hotter heads, who long for the old days. They will bring those old days back at the sword's point, if they can."

"And kill us all in the process?"

"Not if you go peacefully." He shifted in his chair, and leaned forward to look at me intently. His black eyes were very piercing, reminding me of Hawk's. "If you were to agree to leave now, I could guarantee you'd have no more trouble here."

"Guarantee? So you can control these young warriors?"

"Up to a point."

"Then can't you stop them attacking us? Everybody knows that all I want to do is live here peaceably. I've no quarrel with the natives, if they'll leave us alone. Can't you make them see that?"

"When a tribe decides to go to war," he answered, "it's like a river flooding. It carries everything away, with a tremendous force, and nobody can stop it. I can redirect its course a little, that's all."

"And if I refuse to leave?"

"Don't refuse. Try to understand what is at issue here. The river of war among my people is approaching its full spate now, and it will fling you aside if you try to block its course. They will sweep all Romans out of Brigantia, perhaps even out of Britannia altogether."

"Get out or die....Yes, we've received their message. But we're not leaving. We've sworn an oath before our gods. We're staying."

He sighed. "I feared you'd say that. I wish I could persuade you otherwise. Because our young men will soon take an oath too, to return this place of the sacred oaks to the old gods. A formal oath, sworn before the whole people. There will be no going back from it, once they have sworn. Which means...."

"Destroying us and everything we've built. Well, let them try. Just let them try, that's all!"

"They will try, and they will succeed. Aurelia Marcella, I sense that you don't take these young warriors seriously. You dismiss them as a band of hotheads, energetic and brave, but no match for your legions. Am I right?"

"That about sums it up, yes."

"But you miss a much more important point. The young fighting men are the most obvious sign of Brigantia's opposition to Rome, but they are not alone. All Brigantia is behind them, supporting and encouraging. And, as perhaps you know, some of your own people, too."

I looked at him intently. "Vitalis, you mean? He's hardly more than a boy."

"A young man of courage and talent," he smiled. "And also a young man who's had a Roman education. So when it comes to serious matters, Vitalis will always do what his father tells him."

"I hope you're right, but I wouldn't bet on it."

"You safely could, I believe. But there are more Romans than young Vitalis who sympathise with our people's ambitions."

"Oh? Who?" Well, it was worth a try.

He shook his head. "That I can't tell you. But I'll say this much. When love feels itself betrayed, it turns to hate, and it is the bitterest hatred of all."

He got carefully to his feet, and began to walk slowly across the room.

I'd have liked to pursue that; but there was something more urgent I needed to ask.

"You said the young warriors will take an oath. When?"

"Soon. This is the time of year when the youths dedicate themselves and are accepted by the tribe as full warriors."

"But when exactly?"

He began to walk along the passage back into the bar-room. "Our ceremonies are not for the eyes of strangers. But it will not be long."

At the outer door, he turned to me. "I thank you for your hospitality, Aurelia Marcella. And I bid you a last farewell."

After he'd gone, I just stood rooted to the spot. His last farewell sounded a good deal too final for my liking. I don't know how long I stayed there, seeing and hearing nothing, trying to digest what the old man had told me. Eventually a hand touched my shoulder, and I jumped. Albia was there, looking worried.

"Relia, are you all right? I shouldn't have left you alone with that old Druid. Has he put a curse on you?"

"No, nothing like that." I told her the gist of it.

"When love feels itself betrayed," she pondered. "Did he mean love of a person? Has the Shadow of Death been betrayed by his sweetheart, and taken to a life of killing?"

"Gods, yes!" I repeated the story about Vedius murdering the tribune after his woman had betrayed him. But even as I recounted it, I felt doubtful. I didn't think Vedius' experience, however sad, would turn him into a rebel leader. And the Druid's words had been ambiguous.

"He didn't say love of a person. He could have meant love of a country—of Rome." That would fit in with Felix's earlier revelations. Felix and Vedius...both bitter from betrayal. Both equally unlikely, in my view, to be the Shadow of Death. Which meant, as Quintus would say, they were both equally *likely*....

"What was the Druid like?" Albia asked. "Friendly? Angry?"

"Neither, really. A bit scary, perhaps. So calm and courteous....Now tell me about those young warrior boys out there. Did they behave themselves?"

"Yes. They stayed together and were as good as gold. But of course they noticed the tree-felling near the house, and they saw Junius measuring out where the new stockade will be. I told them the army are helping us protect our property because of the troubles in this area." She giggled. "I made it sound as if we've got a whole century of men here."

"Good. Oh, no, not another visitor! Am I *never* going to get any work done today?"

She followed my gaze. Out on the forecourt a large carriage was pulling up, and Silvanius was getting out of it.

Like Felix, he had come to see how I was faring after my ordeal of the previous night. All this attention was very flattering, but I still had a mansio to run, and these interruptions weren't helping at all. However, I answered all his questions, reassured him that I hadn't suffered any ill effects, and took the chance to introduce him to Junius, who, it appeared, had become Prefect of Builders; at any rate he was very much in evidence around the outside of the house, whereas Quintus was nowhere to be seen.

The three of us walked round the buildings and showed Silvanius the line of the new stockade. And I realised that Junius, young as he was, had fully mastered the art of dealing with pompous but important civilians. He asked Silvanius' advice on one or two minor points, which I'm certain he didn't need, and in no time Silvanius was congratulating us on our efforts and offering any help he could give.

I tried not to show it, but I was in a dilemma. I needed his help, I wanted to accept it, but Quintus and Lucius were suggesting that Silvanius could be the Shadow of Death. I still found this hard to believe, but I had to consider it as a possibility. Could Silvanius' help be in the nature of a Trojan horse?

"You're very kind, Clarus, but I think we are managing well enough for now. I'll be sure to come to you if I need anything."

The sun was high and warm now, and customers were starting to arrive, but he seemed disposed to linger and chat. I offered him some refreshment in the garden. We sat by the pool, and it was hard to believe it was less than three days since we'd last sat there together sipping wine. We chatted in a desultory fashion, me trying to think of a tactful way to get him to leave without offence, and he, obviously, having something on his mind that he was finding difficult to talk about.

I wanted to say "Spit it out, I haven't got all day," but I said instead, "Clarus, I hope you won't think me presumptuous, but you and I are old friends, and I can tell there's something bothering you. Something you want to discuss with me?"

He looked relieved. "You're very perceptive, Aurelia. There is something, in fact there are two things, neither of them very easy."

"You know I can be discreet."

"Well then, it's Balbus. I heard something quite disturbing this morning. He's been seen consorting with a known anti-Roman sympathiser, one of the old aristocrats. One of the names on our list."

"Who?"

"Segovax Vericus."

The name made me start, and Silvanius saw my reaction.

"Do you know him?" he asked.

"Not personally. We've got some of the Segovax family as neighbours here, but not Vericus. It's just that the leader of the gang that ambushed me was called Veric."

"It's a common enough name, of course. Most of the Sego-vax clan live further west, in the heart of old Brigantia. They have never, how shall I put it, fully recognised the benefits of Roman rule."

"They could be rebels, in plain Latin."

"Yes, they could be. They were war-lords in the old days, and that's how they think of themselves still. They supported Prince Venutius when he quarrelled with Queen Cartimandua, and a couple of the sons of the house were killed in the fighting when our troops came to the Queen's rescue."

"And Balbus has been seen with them? Couldn't he just be selling them pots? We all know Balbus would sell his wares to the gods of the Underworld if the price was right."

Silvanius smiled in spite of himself. "Well, perhaps. But it makes it difficult to trust someone when you know he's keeping company with the enemy, even for quite innocent reasons."

"Absolutely." I hoped nobody would tell him I'd recently been entertaining a Druid. "But after all, we only had our meeting and drew up our plans yesterday. So what Balbus did last market day or last month needn't reflect how he feels now."

"No, that's true."

"Of course," I added, "there is this business of the paint." I told him about Felix's visit, and how he'd been so certain he'd seen the paint before. "I'm going to go down to Balbus' shop and look for myself when I've got a spare couple of hours. While I'm there, I can try and sound him out about his contact with the old Brigantian families. See if he admits it, or denies it, or doesn't think it's important. His reaction might tell us quite a lot."

"Excellent! You do that, Aurelia, and tell me the result. All the same…I can't believe Balbus is involved with rebels and traitors. Can you?"

"No, Clarus, I can't. Anybody less like a traitor it would be hard to imagine. But as my brother is fond of saying, the only sure thing about traitors is that they don't look like traitors."

"Ah yes. Your brother," Silvanius said unhappily. "That brings me to…oh dear. The last thing I want to do is cause offence, but…."

"I shan't take offence," I reassured him.

"Well, you know I'm calling a meeting of the Town Council tomorrow. So I've been spending the morning talking to various of my council colleagues. Some of them feel that your position here, running the Oak Tree, is a little—ah, irregular…and…well…."

"Really? What does that mean?" As if I couldn't guess.

"A business, especially an official enterprise like a mansio—it's more usual to have a man in charge."

"Have your colleagues got some fault to find with the way I run things here?" Attack was the best form of defence.

"Oh not at all, not at all."

"Well then?"

"Oh Aurelia, I fear I have offended you. But when your father died it was understood that your brother would take charge at the mansio, with you and Albia assisting him. He is here so rarely though. One or two of the council are beginning to feel that, in these dangerous times, the mansio should be in the strong hands of a man."

"Let me guess. Vedius Severus for one?"

He nodded.

"Is that what you think too, Clarus? That I can't protect my home properly?"

He considered seriously. "No, it is not. I believe that you do an excellent job, and I think you are capable of protecting it as well as anyone else. However I'm bound to be worried. You are vulnerable here, and even with your new fence….Will your brother be visiting you soon? Then perhaps…."

"On the first of next month, if not sooner. I heard from him a few days ago."

"Ah, that's good. Because I should hate anything to happen to you, or the Oak Tree, which would give others the excuse to…."

He was having trouble finishing his sentences today, but he didn't need to finish that one. Some of the charmers on the council would be happy to take over running the mansio if they could prove I couldn't look after the place properly. I was angry, and then suddenly I saw what it meant, and I laughed.

"What is the joke?" He looked at me warily, as if I might be going mad.

"Tell your council friends, Clarus, that I shall keep the Oak Tree safe, both from the rebels, and also from any business rivals who might be wishing me to fail. I'm glad to find that my family have made this mansio so successful that now some of the council want to try and take it over. They'll be disappointed, though. I'm here to stay. They can like it or lump it. Is that clear?"

He smiled and took my hand. "Absolutely clear, and absolutely right. And whatever happens, you have my full support."

For what that's worth, I thought, and then hated myself for such a mean-spirited reaction. It was horrible finding oneself suspecting everyone, even good friends.

At last he left, and I could get some work done. The logging and fence-building were going at a good pace, and there weren't many bar customers, so I went into my study to face the pile of jobs waiting on my desk. The most urgent were filing a report about the destruction of an official vehicle and animals, and making out the order for replacements from Eburacum. There was no escaping this tedious paperwork. I'm sure that if *I'd* been killed but the transport had survived unharmed, there'd have been a lot less of it.

Then I proceeded to checking orders, and paying bills. Among the bills I was pleased to find a small one from Balbus, which would give me the perfect excuse to go down to his shop. I consulted Albia about what crockery we needed to buy; there was quite a bit. Even when the maids don't drop trays of beakers, it's amazing the rate of breakages, and we're quite a respectable house, not one of those rowdy wine-shops in a garrison town where the patrons throw the mugs over their shoulders every night at going-home time.

During the afternoon I snatched a few breaths of fresh air, taking a stroll round the horse paddocks. I said hello to Merula and her foal, and several of the other mares and their young. I was soon joined by Titch, bringing some pieces of carrot to feed the mares.

"Mistress, I wanted to ask you about that old Druid," he began excitedly.

"He wasn't a Druid, Titch." I looked at him sternly. "Druids are illegal, as I'm sure you know. If I had a Druid in the house, I'd be in all sorts of trouble. That old man was a bard. A singer of ancient songs."

"Oh aye? But I got a good look at him, and I could see he was...."

"...a bard. Of course you could. So could I. What about him?"

He grinned. "Well that bard, then. I've never seen him before, but he says to me, 'You're new here, aren't you, lad?' How did he know that?"

"Good question. We're being watched for sure, but who by, I don't know. Now here's a question for you. Was there really a lame pony?"

"Nah. It wasn't even limping. One of them warrior lads made a performance of getting a stone from out of its offside rear hoof, but he could just as easily have had the stone hid in his palm. You know, like the cavalry boys do sometimes, when they want an excuse to stop."

"I thought so. The old man came to warn me that the spot where the Oak Tree stands now used to be a Druid holy place years ago. Some of them want it back."

"I don't like the sound of Druids. They have human sacrifices, don't they?"

"Yes."

"Let's hope we never meet one then, eh?" He winked, and went back to his work.

As I was heading inside again, a tall figure marched down the track towards me. He was an ex-soldier, I could tell at once by his bearing and his confident stride, not to mention the good sword he carried. He looked vaguely familiar, but then we see a lot of ex-soldiers in the bar-room. When he caught sight of me he came straight up and held out his hand. "Mistress Aurelia? I'm Flavius Brutus, at your service. The Chief Councillor was saying you might be glad of an extra pair of hands for a day or two, till these barbarians settle down. So I said I'd come and see if I can help. I can even stay if you like. Oh—I was to tell you it's all right with Messapus."

Gods, I thought, is Silvanius doing me a real kindness, or has the Trojan horse come uninvited? I can't have a total stranger staying here. How am I going to get out of this?

"That's very kind, Flavius Brutus, and I appreciate Silvanius sending you, but…."

"Oh, he didn't send me. I offered. You don't remember me, do you?" Before I could answer he smiled. "Well, it was a while ago. I served with your father. I came to stay with you once at Pompeii. You were only a child then. He was a fine man, and I haven't forgotten him. So when I heard what's been happening here, I thought I'd like to help if I can."

My spirits lifted; I was overjoyed. "Of course! I remember you now! You took me and Lucius and Albia out in a boat on the bay…." We reminisced a little, and I accepted his help gratefully. An extra man, especially someone with solid military experience, was as welcome as a gift from the gods. I introduced him to Albia, who of course remembered him immediately, and to Junius and Quintus. Then he went to help the tribunes' men give weapons drill to some of our slaves.

We held a short funeral for Bessus just before dark. All the slaves turned out, indoor servants and farm-hands. I left one of the maids to mind the bar, and the tribunes' two men on guard outside at the front. As I made these defensive arrangements, I reflected how quickly I was learning the attitude of mind of someone under siege. It was a depressing thought, but then funerals are depressing anyway.

Supper was cheerful; no overnight guests, thank the gods—just Albia and me, the tribunes and Quintus, and Brutus. Marius had come back in good spirits, dropping hints about amorous adventures, and he promised to help with the stockade tomorrow. The work was progressing well, and I longed for it to be finished.

The tribunes and Brutus went into the bar after the meal, which gave me and Albia the chance to tell Quintus about my various visitors—Felix, Silvanius, and of course the Druid and his escort, which made him laugh.

"Aurelia, there's no doubt that a talent for spying runs in your family! What did you manage to get out of him?"

When I told him, he said thoughtfully, "You did well to get even that much. Love turning to hate…very cryptic. So the Shadow of Death is a Roman who bears some kind of grudge against Rome?…That needs thinking about. Meantime, the most important thing is to find out when and where their ceremony will be. Then we'll know how long we've got before they attack."

Before they attack…what a horrible thought. I was frankly relieved when there was a tap at the door, and Carina appeared. "Mistress, the huntsman with the big dog wants to see you—his son works here sometimes. He says you promised him some cough-medicine for his little boy. He says it's important, but I can send him packing if you like."

Whatever Hawk wanted, it must be urgent, to make him come calling after dark.

"I'll see him, Carina. Where is he?"

"Outside, under the oak tree. Taurus is with him."

"Right, I'm on my way. Albia, have we got some of that syrup with the scilla powder in it?"

She fetched an earthenware bottle from the store-room, and I was about to go out of the kitchen door when Quintus appeared.

"I'll come with you," he said. "Remember what we agreed this morning, no ladies to go out after dark without an armed escort."

"I'm only going a few yards from the front door. Taurus is there, so I'll be safe enough, and whatever Hawk wants, he'll be wary of strangers."

"Then you'll just have to introduce me to him so I'm not a stranger any more."

"But—"

"Aurelia," he smiled suddenly. "I hesitate to use the word 'insist' after this morning, but I'll think of another word if I have to. You're not going out alone."

"Oh, all right. It's probably time you met him anyway." I pulled on a woollen cloak as we went outside; the wind had got up, and it was blowing quite hard as we walked across to the big oak. It stood out clearly in the faint starlight, but clouds kept racing across the sky now and then, making everything dark and uncertain. Under its shelter, Taurus and Hawk were chatting comfortably, oblivious to the moaning of the night wind.

Hawk got up as we approached, and he and Quintus looked each other over warily. I didn't know whether to be annoyed or flattered, but whatever the problem was, I hadn't time for it. They'd have to learn to co-operate, and like it or lump it.

I started to introduce the tracker and the bridge builder, but Hawk cut me short.

"I know. You're the man who was nearly killed the other night. I've seen you around, and I recognised your tracks."

"That's right," Quintus smiled. "You helped Aurelia piece together what happened to me. And I've seen you around too." I remember it was the first time I'd heard him speak in British, and his accent was pretty terrible, but Hawk understood him well enough.

"You've seen me? I doubt it," Hawk said. "I haven't been around to see."

"I noticed you in the woods this morning, when we were logging. You and your dog were watching us, or perhaps you were watching that Druid and his lads?"

Hawk laughed. "I must be slipping up. I prefer to be invisible unless I choose."

Quintus laughed too, and I was relieved that the ice was broken between them.

"Actually I was looking at your fence-building," Hawk said. "Get it finished as soon as ever you can, because I've got bad news for you. Some of the Shadow-men are planning a full-scale attack here any day now, or I should say any night. They say they won't leave a building standing or a person or beast alive."

My heart stopped. "When?"

"That's the worst of it, I don't know. It'll depend on the weather. They'll wait for a dark night, but they'll move soon, before the next Druid ceremony, and that's to be sometime before the next full moon."

"*Before* the ceremony? I thought they weren't going to attack till after, when the new young warriors had been sworn in or whatever it is. That's what the Druid said."

"Ah yes. The Druid." Hawk's face was in shadow, but his voice sounded grim, and I heard him spit on the ground. "Well, whatever he told you, my advice is, treat it with caution. They deal in half-truths, those people."

"He was deliberately trying to mislead me about the date of the attack, then?"

"Quite likely. Although my information is that it's the younger Shadow-men, the hot-headed ones, who want this attack. I suppose it's possible they haven't told the Druid."

"He said the land here used to be their holy wood."

Hawk grunted. "Another half-truth! There was some sort of small shrine here once, but nothing very remarkable. Not a full temple in a sacred grove."

"So he's making it sound more important than it was, to stir up the people?" Quintus suggested.

"It's their style, certainly."

I said, "He tried to persuade me we should leave voluntarily, and the Shadow-men would let us go without any more trouble."

Hawk stared at me through the dark. "What did you answer?"

"Need you ask, Hawk?"

"Good. You're right to stay and fight. It's your only hope. Even if you decided to leave of your own accord, it wouldn't save you. Most of those young hotheads think the presence of Romans here angers their gods. The place will only be purified when you've not just been driven out, but...." He hesitated.

"Go on."

"But also sacrificed to the god of the wood. The talk is that either they'll kill most of you here, or if you pack up and go, you'll be ambushed on the road before you've gone five miles. You, Aurelia, and Albia, and you, Valerius Longinus, won't be killed immediately, you'll be sacrificed at their ceremony."

"Holy Diana protect us!" I shivered, and it wasn't with cold. "What can we do?"

"Exactly what you are doing. Prepare to defend yourselves with everything you've got, and stay alert day and night, especially night. I'll help where I can, but I have to be careful. If they suspect, they'll kill me. Now I must go."

He reached out his hand for the medicine-bottle. "Thanks. I'd better be carrying something when I leave. In case the trees have eyes."

"Hawk," Quintus said urgently, "how long do you think we've got? And where will they hold the ceremony?"

"All I know is it's sometime soon, before the next full moon. They prefer a waxing moon, and they'll find an omen of some sort to fix the exact night."

"Like they did with the eclipse," Quintus muttered.

Hawk glanced up at the sky with its chasing clouds. "It'll be full moon in about ten days. As to where, I told you, they want to hold it here."

"But assuming they can't get us out? They must have other holy groves?"

"If they can't shift you, then they'll go to their usual place this time. But I'm afraid they'll keep trying."

"What usual place?" I asked. "You mean there's a Druid holy wood still used near here?"

"Oh yes, quite close. About quarter of a mile downstream, where the trees come right down to the water's edge. There's an old ruin of a roundhouse in a clearing, but nobody lives there now. It belongs to one of the Segovax family."

"I know it. Lovers go there courting sometimes. Quite a nice spot in the summer, although it's a bit uncomfortable when the insects are biting."

He nodded. "Your two young tribunes have been down there a couple of times lately. I suppose they were meeting girls, though I never actually saw any. That's the spot the Druids will use, if they haven't driven you out of here." He pulled his cloak closer round him. "So take care, all of you." And he turned and melted into the shadows.

We three stood gazing at each other in the fitful starlight, too stunned to speak for a while. An attack in the next few days! And if they were strong enough to capture us? Like everyone, I'd heard rumours about how the Druids sacrificed their victims, stabbing them or sometimes burning them alive. Was that the fate they had in mind for us?

"I'm scared," I admitted finally.

"With good reason," Quintus answered. "But we can beat them."

"Oh, I'm not giving in. If they want this place, they'll have to fight me for every stone, every blade of grass, every tree….I'm right, aren't I?"

"Quite right, Mistress," Taurus put in. "I'll fight too. We all will. If they just want the land back, that's bad enough. But if they mean to kill us even if we do give it back, they've got to be stopped." As usual, Taurus had summed it up in one simple sentence.

I looked at the two of them: the ruthless, devious investigator, and the honest, uncomplicated slave. With these two, and Albia, and the rest of our people, I thought, we'll make a real fight of it. We'll show the Druids what happens when they try to drive Romans from their home.

Quintus and I went back inside, leaving Taurus, who was on first watch. We went to sit by the brazier in the dining-room.

"Hawk's an unusual native," Quintus remarked, picking up his wine-mug. "You're quite sure you can trust him?"

"I am. I know him well. He hates the Shadow-men as much as we do. He doesn't want warfare here, it's the main thing we agree on, and it's why we've become friends."

Quintus nodded. "Good enough. But I tell you something, I'm going to find out when and where the Druid ceremony is. Then I'll put on a decent disguise and go and watch."

"You'll *what?*" I nearly choked. "You can't, Quintus. It's incredibly dangerous! If you're caught, you'll be killed."

"I won't be caught."

I tried to dissuade him, but he wouldn't budge. "We need to see what they're getting up to, Aurelia. And maybe we can identify some of their supporters. I assume the anti-Roman natives would all attend a ceremony like that. So say you'll help me find out when and where it is. Just make a few discreet enquiries. I will too. And don't fret, I've no intention of becoming their next ritual sacrifice."

Before I went to bed, I stood before our household shrine and prayed to Diana. As the moon goddess, she might be able to keep us safe. Cloudless light nights would help us and hinder our attackers. So I prayed for moonlight. I prayed as hard as I knew how.

The trouble with praying is, you never know till much later whether the gods have answered you.

Chapter XVII

The night was uneventful, and the dawn brought no graffiti anywhere. What's more, the wind had dropped and it was a magnificent clear morning, full of birdsong, with a blue sky and a few wisps of cloud. Just the sort of day for a jaunt into town to visit Balbus.

We were taking the medium-sized raeda—Albia insisted on coming too—and three guards, and to my surprise the slave Marsus offered to be one of them.

"I've got to, haven't I, Mistress?" He smiled at me. "When I was a little lad on the farm, before, well before I was captured, like, I used to ride a pony, and when I'd fall off, my father always said, 'Get back on, boy, before you've got time to be scared.' It'll be like that, going into town today."

"Yes, it will. For me too."

The first courier through from Eburacum brought a report of two overnight killings. And as usual—what a horrible thing to say, "as usual," but we were getting accustomed to the "usual" gruesome facts—as usual the victims were Roman travellers on the road. Both had been stabbed to death and then beheaded, and each was left with the customary threatening message. Nobody dwelt on this bad news as we prepared to go into town.

I decided I'd do the driving, and we took Marsus, Taurus, and the ex-soldier Brutus, all mounted on good horses and armed to the teeth. But the journey to Oak Bridges was uneventful. The woods in daylight were peaceful and pretty, in their full summer greenery, with birds singing, and sunlight slanting through the oak-leaves onto the quiet ground below.

As we came into town we met a band of Vedius' night-watchmen, returning to their base after dealing with a house fire. The leader was Saturninus, the old aedile's son, who was in charge of the new patrols, and we stopped to ask how they were going.

"Pretty well," Saturninus said, wiping soot off his face with his sleeve. "Though I must say, I'm knackered by this time of the morning, with a day's work to do as well. We have four patrols out each night now, circling round town. Nobody'll dare dump any corpses in the forum while *we're* on the job!"

Very reassuring, I thought. Where else will they dump them then?

Albia asked, "Have you caught anyone yet?"

"No, but my patrol scared off a group of lads who were hanging about near the new temple. Presumably up to no good, because they ran for it when we arrived. I couldn't get a close look, but one of them was wearing a skull mask. And we've had several reports from other patrols that they've seen a masked man lurking about. If all of them are this Shadow of Death, he certainly gets around! He must spend all night prowling the roads."

"Have you had any more slogans painted on walls?" I asked, "because we have."

"Yes, quite a few. All over the place, too. One on Felix's front wall, and on one of father's barns, which made him hopping mad as you can imagine. In the forum, and on several other bits of wall. And of course you know they've appeared at the new temple. Some are the full message about all of us being killed, and others are just a skull. All done in a putrid shade of green paint."

"They must have a good stock of it," Albia joked.

"Tell you who's joined our merry band of watchmen," Saturninus said. "Young Vitalis! Father and I couldn't believe it when he showed up for training. After all his nonsense about wishing he'd been born in the good old days! I suppose Silvanius pushed him into it. He must be delighted the boy's finally realised which side he should be on."

Merda, that's all we need. I said, "Whose patrol is Vitalis in?"

"His own. He brought four of his friends to enrol with him, and although I'd have preferred to give them an experienced officer, he insisted they'd be all right on their own. And with him being Silvanius' son, we thought, well where's the harm?"

I wanted to scream: Where's the harm? How long have you got? but I realised it would be better if we kept quiet, so I just said, "Well, good hunting, all of you. We must be getting along."

"Safe journey to you," he answered, and we drove on.

"Vitalis and his Shadow-men on patrol," I said. "And Saturninus is actually *pleased!*"

Albia shrugged. "I know. Just because he's Silvanius' son.... Did you notice he said green paint?"

‹›‹›‹›

In the pottery shop we found Balbus, his fair hair neat and his face freshly shaved, and wearing his working garb, a brown sleeveless tunic covered by a leather apron. Both were spotless, because it was rarely these days that he personally threw a pot or loaded a kiln. He was apparently in the middle of bawling out his foreman, and I caught something about "...straighten yourself out, or you'll be looking for another job." But he broke off and greeted us warmly.

"Aurelia and Albia! What a pleasant surprise! How are you both?"

"We're well, thanks, Balbus," I said. "We fancied a trip into Oak Bridges, and we've got a bill to pay, and an order."

"Fine. And you'll stay for a drop of wine, I hope? Ennia will never forgive me if I let you go without a drink and a gossip."

"Thank you, yes. How's trade?"

"Pretty good, actually." He rubbed his hands together. "Can't complain at all."

Gods, it must be spectacularly brilliant. Normally Balbus' answer when one asked about trade was "Not bad."

I paid our bill and Albia showed him our list of requirements: a dozen beakers, a couple of mortars for the kitchen, one large serving dish, three jugs, and four plates of various sizes. Having given our order to his foreman, Balbus proceeded to show us around, pointing out new or unusual items for us to admire.

Balbus' shop was no cramped booth with the stock piled in disorganised heaps; it was large and airy, with the pots and glass well displayed. I always enjoyed looking round it. Balbus himself had been a good potter when he started out in Gaul, with an eye for style and beauty. Now he was a good businessman, expert in every aspect of the ceramics and glass trade, and he made handsome profits. Most of his pottery these days was imported, everything from cheerful red Samian ware to some exquisite Greek and Egyptian vases that I thought of as too fragile, not to mention expensive, to use. Of course he had his own potters working behind the shop, producing the more basic everyday tableware and kitchen bowls and mortars; but it was the imported items that gave the shop real distinction. As for the glass, some of the flagons and goblets were so beautiful you just wanted to stand there gazing into the depths of their luminous colours.

Another customer came in, a very old grand Brigantian lady, and Balbus went to greet her. She was dressed—well, overdressed—in a mauve-embroidered gown, and as much gold jewellery as she could conveniently cram onto her chubby arms and hands, and round her plump neck. Well, if Balbus was in some sort of illicit contact with the natives, his shop gave him the perfect cover for it, but from the snatches of conversation I managed to overhear, this was just another customer. A dissatisfied one too, with some complaint about flawed crystal goblets.

But while Balbus fussed around the old dame, and his foreman put together our order, Albia and I had the perfect chance to wander undisturbed, looking at the shelves. Sure enough, we found the pale green paint, not only on shelves, but on the wall behind them too. A small alcove had been coloured green, and was displaying a set of large platters, superb work, each one with a different woodland scene in the centre, and trails of acanthus leaves round the borders. Their shape was stylish, their glazing detailed and delicate, and their price would be too huge to contemplate.

I surreptitiously fished out the wax tablet with the green flakes of paint on it. Yes, a perfect match. Good for Felix. But had Balbus really been involved in defacing our wall? Or had somebody else got hold of the paint, and used it in a deliberate attempt to throw suspicion on the potter? There was only one way to find out.

The old lady departed, leaving Balbus looking unhappy.

"Dissatisfied customer?" I said lightly.

He grunted.

"We've all had them. In our line of business they complain about the wine and ask for their money back, but usually not till they've drunk three-quarters of the jug."

"I shouldn't have let her have so much credit," he grumbled, more to himself than to us. "Now she thinks she can run up debts like a grand patrician lady. Oh well, her son's a friend of mine, I know he'll pay in the end. He lives up on the wolds. I'll drop round and see him, give him a nudge, if I can drag myself up the Long Hill."

"Your friend can't be short of a gold piece, if he's buying crystal."

Balbus smiled. "The locals are getting a taste for imported pottery and glass, I'm glad to say. And they know they get good value from me."

"You've got some beautiful stock," I said. "I hope you don't mind me asking, but I've just seen something I've been searching for all over the place. You must tell me where it comes from."

He looked interested, as well he might. He'd noticed me admiring the expensive platters.

"That lovely green paint," I babbled on, pointing at the alcove. "It's very attractive. I've been wanting just that colour for my study. Haven't I, Albia?"

"Oh yes," she improvised. "Ever since I told her about the decorations in Claudia's house in Lindum. There's a lot of green paint there. It's quite the most fashionable colour. They say even the Governor uses it."

I thought she was overdoing it, but Balbus laughed. "I'm beginning to realise that! You're the third person lately who's asked about it."

"Really? Who else is in the fashion?"

"Felix bought some last month, and Silvanius—well, Vitalis actually, but he said it was for his father, which is the same thing."

Ah, not the same at all! I felt a tingle of excitement, and was careful not to catch Albia's eye.

"Do tell us where you buy it," Albia persisted.

"I don't *buy* paint!" he exclaimed. "One of my slaves, Zandros, does all my colour mixing here. He mostly works on glazes for pots, of course, but he does wood-paints as well. I can let you have some of this green, if we've any left."

"Thank you, that would be marvellous." Well, what else could I say, having praised it so enthusiastically?

He turned to his foreman and barked, "See to it, will you?"

"Excuse me, Master," the foreman said, pausing in his work of packing our new beakers in a box of straw. "That green paint isn't one of ours, as it happens. Don't you remember? Zandros was ill about the time that vine-leaf dinner service was shipped in, and we wanted to get the display sorted, so you sent me to pick up some paint in Eburacum. I got it from Divico's place."

I cursed silently as I contemplated a promising theory falling apart. If the paint was available in Eburacum, half the houses in the district probably had some.

Balbus gave the man a look that would have soured wine. "Oh yes, I remember now. You didn't bring enough, did you? We couldn't do all the alcove with the piddling amount you fetched back."

"It would have covered the area you originally wanted," the foreman objected. "But they sent us more stock than we ordered, so you enlarged the display, and there wasn't...."

"Don't argue with me all the time!" Balbus snapped. "Anyway—" he turned back to us— "we made a mixture of Divico's paint with some very pale primrose yellow we had in, and came up with that colour on the shelves now. In the end I was quite pleased with it."

I smiled at the foreman, and said, "Presumably I could send to Divico and get more of the original green, and Zandros could mix me up some?"

He scratched his beard doubtfully. "I don't think Divico has his shop open these days. He's one of the Segovax boys, Divico is, and they've all taken themselves off into the hills just now. They say it's a hunting trip, but if you ask me…."

"Daft young idiots," Balbus interrupted. "We haven't got time to gossip all day about the Segovax boys. Get on with the packing."

"Segovax," I repeated. "My neighbour is a Segovax, so that name rings a bell with me. Aren't they one of the old aristocratic families? Some of them fought for Prince Venutius when he rebelled against us in the old days?"

"That's right. I know them quite well actually. Especially the old chief and his wife, they buy a lot of pots from me. There's still quite a deal of money left in those old Brigantian families. Enough for decent pottery, anyway." Far from sounding apologetic, he seemed quite proud of it.

"The old chief?" My mouth went dry. For a heartbeat I was back on the dark wooded road. "When the Chief gets here, you'll be told…."

"That's what everyone calls him. He was a leader in his day, quite a warrior, or that's how he tells it, with a big war-band. Now of course he's too crippled to do more than sit in his big roundhouse and dream. Rather sad, really. Who wants to grow old?"

"I do," Albia said. "At least I'd prefer it to being murdered."

Balbus laughed. "I can't argue with that! Now why don't you go through and have a beaker of wine with Ennia? She's in our sitting-room."

Even though they didn't live behind the shop now, Balbus and Ennia still kept a room and a servant there. Ennia gave us her usual warm welcome, but she was looking, I thought, rather strained today. Everybody liked Ennia; she was round and motherly, and several years older than Balbus. She kept the shop's accounts, and she always said cheerfully that "Aulus married me for my money," which was presumably true, but there was affection there too.

Over wine and pastries we discussed the horrors of the murders. "It's dreadful," Ennia exclaimed. "So much violence, so much killing! It frightens me. Aulus and I moved to Britannia to be safe."

"Safe?" Albia said. "But I thought you came from Gaul. Surely Gaul's as safe as houses these days? The Gaulish barbarians could teach ours a thing or two about settling down."

"It isn't always the barbarians who make trouble," Ennia murmured. "And when we lived in Gaul, it was only a small shop then, but it meant the world to us."

She stopped, as if that explained everything.

I asked, "What happened?"

"Some soldiers from the local camp came in drunk one day, very drunk, and broke the whole place up. Our pots, the shelves, the kilns, the tools....Smashed everything to smithereens. Aulus tried to stop them, but they were just like animals. That's how he got the scar on his neck."

"How dreadful! They were punished, presumably?"

"No. Nothing was ever done."

"Why ever not?" But there could only be one reason, some kind of fairly serious corruption. "Somebody senior got them off?"

She nodded. "The camp prefect, their commander, owed us a lot of money. We'd let him have too much on credit—you have to with these important people. His two daughters got married, and they'd ordered enough pottery and glass to hold an imperial banquet. He couldn't pay our bill, and every time Aulus went to see him about it, he got more and more abusive. Bastard!"

she muttered bitterly. "After the shop was smashed, we went to complain to him, and he told us that he'd organised the gang of drunks to do it, and they'd do it again unless we co-operated."

"Co-operated? Let him off his debt?"

"That's right. We had to agree, he even made us sign a paper cancelling his debt. And yet in public he was so generous, so sympathetic! He got us a grant from military funds, to pay for the damage and rebuild, provided we'd move on somewhere else and wipe his slate clean. And that's why we came here. So much for Roman justice!"

"Oh Ennia, how terrible!" With all our own troubles, hers seemed even worse. If you've been bullied by powerful men who can put themselves above the law, you must feel as if you're sinking in a quicksand. What's the point of law and justice, if it doesn't stop the stronger people bullying the weaker ones?

But could an experience like that turn a man into a traitor? "When love feels itself betrayed...." Was that what the old Druid had meant?

"Well you know, don't you," Albia said, "that everyone in Oak Bridges is glad you're settled here. You're among friends now. It couldn't happen again."

With an obvious effort Ennia smiled. "Don't mind me, I'm being silly. And don't mention to Aulus I've told you about this. He prefers to try and forget it. Anyway, he says Clarus' meeting has come up with some good plans to fight this Campaign of Terror, so things will get back to normal soon."

We made reassuring noises, and drank more wine. "You and Aulus," I said, "you've got quite a lot of friends among the old native families, haven't you?"

"I suppose we have, yes. I've never thought much about it. If you like someone, you become friends, whether they're citizens or not."

"Have they any idea what's behind all this killing?"

"It's hard to say." She fiddled with a grey curl that had fallen across her face. "Of course they don't admit it to us, but I think some of them do know who's stirring up the young warriors,

and even sympathise with the idea of getting rid of Roman settlers—though I'm sure they wouldn't openly take part in any
violence themselves. We've noticed the natives in general are
edgy just now, even our own workshop slaves. Something, or
someone, is making them resent us. Our foreman is drinking too
much….Let's hope it's just a phase. He's a good worker usually.
Have your own natives been behaving oddly at all?"

"Not really. One of our horse-boys ran off, but that's not
such a rare occurrence, and we've got a bright lad to replace
him. What do you think, Albia?"

"Two of the maids are enjoying being miserable because
their men have gone away into the hills hunting," she said
thoughtfully. "Otherwise nothing, unless you count Cook's
temperaments."

Ennia smiled. "Ah now, if we're talking about cooks…." The
conversation turned to domestic gossip, and we left soon after.

Chapter XVIII

As we were getting into the carriage, I said to Albia, "Why don't we pay a quick visit to Felix while we're here?"

"Good idea. So you noticed that too—Balbus saying he'd bought some of the green paint?"

"Yes. Odd he didn't mention it to me, but it's no wonder he was so quick to recognise the colour. Let's see what he has to say about it."

"And he always keeps a good drop of Campanian white," Albia added.

Felix's house was on one of the main streets, set back a little, with a large garden to the rear It was on a smaller scale than Silvanius' humble abode, but it had the same feel of well-designed luxury. Not surprising, as the same combination had gone into building it—Felix's artistic flair, and Clarus' money.

The door was answered by the huge manservant, who told us that the master was in, but had company, and he went off to enquire if he would receive us.

In no time at all Felix himself came bounding across the hall, and gave us each a huge hug and a kiss.

"The two most beautiful women in Britannia! You've quite made my morning. Come in, my dears, and tell me all the gossip. Vitalis is here."

"Vitalis?" Now that was a surprise. I hesitated. "If we're interrupting something, we can call back another time...."

Fortunately he brushed aside my half-hearted attempt at politeness. "Nonsense, Vitalis won't mind. He and I are just hatching an interesting little conspiracy."

Felix led us to his study, which was at the rear of the house, overlooking a large and lovely garden. The room was a typical bachelor's retreat; it had two whole walls lined with book-scrolls, a shelf full of exquisite ivory carvings, two comfortable couches, and several beautiful little tables.

Vitalis got up as we came in. He was in his warrior clothes, which looked even odder than usual alongside Felix's flamboyant apple-green tunic with matching accessories. Looking at them together, it struck me how handsome they both were, and in a similar sort of way, both thin and lithe, with regular features and fair hair. See them naked in the bath, they might be brothers. See them with clothes on, and they were as different as figs from fish sauce.

"Hello, Vitalis," I said. "I'm sorry if we're disturbing you. Felix says you're concocting a conspiracy."

Vitalis gave us his radiant smile, and Felix said, "Oh yes, a deep dark secret! You must promise never to admit you've seen him here."

"Of course we shall promise," Albia smiled. "Do tell us what it's all about."

There was a pause while two young girls brought in refreshments. They were pretty and properly trained. They served us the good Campanian and some fruit, and I thought, whatever Felix may say about how he dislikes living on Silvanius' bounty, he does pretty well for himself.

When they'd gone, Felix said in a conspiratorial stage whisper, "Vitalis is going to help his father with the rituals at the temple dedication ceremony. There's quite a lot to learn, and I've been taking him through his lines."

"Only it's a surprise," Vitalis added, with an embarrassed little laugh. "I shan't tell Father till the day before. He's been wanting me to take part, and to start with I said I wouldn't. But…Well, I don't like to disappoint him."

"I'm sure he'll be delighted." I was genuinely touched to find Vitalis had some family feeling after all.

Albia giggled. "He will—as long as you don't go dressed like that."

Vitalis laughed, and said, "We've finished our rehearsal for today, so if you'll all excuse me, I'll be on my way. I'm meeting my friends at the Oak Tree, so I'll see you ladies later." And with a wave and a smile, he was gone.

"He's not a bad lad," Felix said. "For all his nonsense, he wants to be a credit to his father."

"I'm pleased to hear it. And he couldn't have a better tutor for the ceremony. Talking of rehearsals, did you enjoy your theatre trip to Eburacum?"

"Oh yes, very much. The play was pretty dreadful, but Dardanio was there, in fact all my friends were, so I caught up with the latest actors' gossip. Some of the soldier-boys at the garrison are getting very keen on the theatre—rather sweet really. They're always so grateful when I introduce them to the professional actors. And my dears, I did hear one very juicy piece of scandal...." He reported a wonderfully entertaining bit of gossip, which we enjoyed even though we didn't know the people involved. It may even have been true. But it's not relevant to this report.

Eventually he said, "Now, before I die of curiosity. Have you been to Balbus' shop yet—and did you see *it?*"

He listened excitedly as we told him about the paint, and how Balbus had boasted of doing business and socialising with some of the old Brigantian aristocrats.

"I told you," he crowed. "Didn't I?"

"You did," I agreed. "But Balbus says he isn't the only person who's used that green paint lately."

"Does he? Who else?"

"Vitalis bought some for Silvanius," Albia said slowly.

Felix shrugged. "It's possible. They're still putting the finishing touches to the humble abode."

"And Balbus told us you've bought some too, Felix." I paused, watching for his reaction.

He was unperturbed. "Oh dear. Caught red-handed, or should that be green-handed?"

I felt a leap of excitement. "Felix, you admit it! So you could be the one who painted the horrible message on our wall?"

He laughed. "I suppose I could. All right, I deserve a slap on the wrist for not mentioning it. Sheer vanity, I confess—I wanted to impress you with my powers of observation when I recognised the colour. I own up, I bought the paint. Come and see what I've done with it!"

We followed him out into his garden, and headed for a small summer-house at the far end, half hidden by climbing roses. It was a lovely little outdoor room, just large enough for a couch and a writing-table, and a carved ebony scroll-rack. And the inside walls were pale green. The table was a clutter of reed pens, papyrus, and ink-pots, but what took the eye was a wooden plinth nearby, holding a marble statue.

"My pride and joy," he said, indicating the room. "Especially my Apollo, with the features of dear Nero. He gave it to me himself, and I've always treasured it. I like to look at it here when I'm writing my plays."

It was a beautiful piece of work, about two feet tall, carved by a master. Nero was handsome physically, whatever the faults in his nature, and he made a good-looking Apollo.

"So that's why I needed the paint," Felix said. "As soon as I saw it, I knew it was the right colour for this little writing-room. Fortunately," he joked, "I had just enough left over to daub on your wall, Aurelia dear!"

We went indoors for another beaker of Campanian, and then Felix sighed and said, "Well, I'm afraid I must leave you, and get ready for this afternoon's entertainment."

"Entertainment?" I asked. "Not another play?"

He gave an elaborate shudder. "Alas no. I'm afraid there will be a dearth of any sort of drama, tragic or comic. I've got to attend Publius' dreary town council meeting. You can imagine how much I'm looking forward to *that!*"

As we set off for home, I told our three guards to ride a short distance behind the carriage, so we could talk privately. There was certainly a good deal to discuss.

"I was hoping," I began, "that once we'd confirmed whether the paint was in Balbus' shop, things would become clearer. Instead of which, they're more muddled than ever. We've answered one question, and now we've got to answer a whole lot more."

"Three main ones, I suppose," Albia said. "Who painted the threatening message on our wall—Vitalis, Balbus, or Felix? Why? And how?"

"You'll be comforted to know, or maybe you won't—but Quintus thinks that the Shadow of Death must have been at Silvanius' villa the day of his meeting. So we're not just look-ing at Vitalis, Balbus, and Felix. We have to add Vedius and Silvanius as well."

I told her about "L's list," and predictably she wanted to know all about the code. She's always fascinated by puzzles.

"We ought to have a code between ourselves, Relia. There's one that Julius Caesar used to use…."

"Gods, you're starting to sound like Titch! No, let's not get side-tracked into codes. If you and I need a way to tell each other discreetly that something's fishy, we can fall back on our old favourite, the customer from Arpinum." Arpinum was our private code for trouble. Most innkeepers use variants of this—a word that sounds innocent to customers, but warns the staff to be on the alert.

"Fair enough, but…."

"No, no buts! Let's get back to your three questions."

"I think I listed them in the wrong order," she said. "Because to answer the first one, who painted the wall, we need to solve the next two—why and how did they do it?"

"As to why, that's easy—to give me a good fright, which it did. Especially as they added the remains of my cloak, to make sure I realised it was personal." I shivered in spite of the warm sunshine. "As to how, that's easy too. Given a dark night and a half-decent horse or mule, anyone could ride over from Oak Bridges to the mansio, collecting the cloak on the way, and ride back again, with plenty of time to spare. Gods, you could even walk it, if you thought riding made you too conspicuous."

"Not Vedius, surely?" Albia objected. "He's too old."

"He's still tough. He could do it on horseback, if he had to."

"But he's the only one who didn't buy any green paint."

"Perhaps that's significant. He begged or stole or borrowed it secretly, to avoid attracting attention, knowing other people were using it openly. And don't forget he's in charge of the watch patrols, even if he's too old to lead one himself. He's in the perfect position to know when it's safe for him to travel at night, and when others will be travelling as well....Look, we've got to start somewhere. Let's put Vedius at the bottom of the list of suspects, which is where Lucius put him anyway."

She nodded. "It looks as if Balbus is the most likely to have painted the message, in person or using one of his people—perhaps his foreman. I don't like the thought of a friend doing something like that, but he's rich, he travels a lot, he socialises with the natives...."

"...But he seems happy to brag about that," I put in. "You'd expect him to be more discreet about meetings with Brigantians, if he spent them plotting treason."

"No, if he's being really clever, he'll make everything look open and above board, won't he? And from what Ennia told us, the way they were treated in Gaul obviously still rankles. An injustice like that could turn a man into a traitor."

"But whatever else Balbus is, he isn't a fool. And it does seem foolish to use a shade of paint which is there for the world to see on his shelves. He could so easily have chosen another colour."

"Well..." She pondered for a little. "Say he wanted to distract suspicion from himself by throwing it on other people who he knew had bought it. Like Vitalis, for instance."

"He said Vitalis bought the paint for Silvanius," I pointed out.

"Well, perhaps he did. Or perhaps Vitalis was lying. Yes, that could be it! If he'd bought it, intending to paint graffiti with it, he'd hardly admit it was for himself."

"No. And to my mind, Vitalis is most likely to have painted the message," I said, "and left me my torn-up cloak as well. Of all of them, I think he'd make the most effective Shadow of Death, with his warrior training and his father's Roman connections. And he's got the best possible reason to be anti-Roman, if he feels he's lost his future as a warrior chief. He's also young and impulsive enough not to care who knows it. But then, what about this morning's revelation that he's going to help his dear papa dedicate the Marble Monster?"

"That could be a bluff, to make everyone think he's a true Roman at heart," Albia answered. "Or it could be genuine, I suppose. What if he did actually buy the paint for his father, and handed it over, and then forgot all about it. So he's completely innocent!"

"Dear gods, Albia, that opens up a whole new box of beetles! It means Silvanius himself used the paint, with or without Vitalis' knowledge."

"He *is* at the top of L's famous list," Albia answered thoughtfully. "He's powerful enough, and rich and well-connected; and his family are natives, even if he appears completely Roman now. But he's done so much to promote Roman ways and ideals in this area. Look at the Marble Monster."

"Quintus would say that's just a bluff."

"It's a far bigger and more expensive bluff than he'd need, though, isn't it? If he seriously means to drive all Romans out, would he be spending huge amounts of time and money building a temple to Roman gods, just as a bluff? He could get the same result with a lot less trouble. A good statue, or a small shrine, would be enough to impress Oak Bridges."

"I agree. Despite what Quintus thinks, I still feel Silvanius is a friend, and if every man in the Empire stood in line to paint a message telling all Romans to leave or they'd be killed, Silvanius Clarus would be the very last in the queue."

"Well then—" Albia pushed some loose strands of hair out of her eyes— "what about Felix? He's clever—probably the cleverest of all of them. With his aristocratic background, he could have all the contacts he needs. He has the paint, but he only admitted it when he had to. He didn't tell you straight away."

"He explained that, and I believed him—he's as vain as a pen of peacocks. But still, there's the story he told me about being tired of having to live on Silvanius' bounty, and I believed that too."

"What was it the old Druid said to you? When love feels itself betrayed, it turns to hate, and it is the bitterest hatred of all. I thought that meant Vedius, but...."

"It could apply to Felix and his grudge against Rome. And he used to be an actor, which would be useful for someone playing the part of a Roman in the daytime, and a rebel after dark."

"He made sure you knew that the paint came from Balbus originally," Albia said, "and told you all about Balbus' native contacts. Both those things could be Felix trying to cover his own tracks, or just being malicious, because he doesn't like Balbus much. Or they could be true."

Our discussion went round and round like chariots in a circus, with one suspect and then another taking the lead for a while and then getting overtaken. The race was still going on as we got back to the Oak Tree, but when we stepped into the bar, it stopped abruptly. I smelt trouble, stronger than any smell of drink, and Albia did too.

"Arpinum," she muttered. "I'll get some help." She slipped away, and I walked across the room slowly, looking around.

The place was full, silent, and tense. All eyes were fixed on one corner of the room, the corner containing Vitalis and his warriors.

They were at their usual table, with their customary big jug of mead, and one of them was drunk as a senator, and obviously out of control. He was standing up, more or less, swaying erratically, and shouting raucously. As I came towards him, he hurled a beaker of mead against the wall. It smashed loudly in the silence.

"That's what we'll do to the Romans!" he yelled, his speech slurring. "Smash their heads into little pieces and spill their brains all over the floor. Like this!" He flung another mug at the wall.

I glanced round. None of the other customers was showing any sign of stepping forward to help. Why should they, after all? I saw Carina, white-faced, near the bar. I hoped she'd had the sense to send for some of the men who were fence-building. If not, Albia would bring help soon. But meanwhile I'd have to manage this on my own.

I walked slowly up to the table, and you could have heard a pin drop. The drunk turned to face me. He was only a boy really, and his unsteady stance and glazed look made an almost comic contrast to his warrior clothes and blue war-paint. But he was spoiling for a fight, and his comrades were watching and waiting for their chance to join in.

"Now, my friend, I think you need a bit of fresh air to cool you down." I took a breath, and smiled into his bleary eyes. "I think you've had enough mead for now. Why not go outside for a while and come back later? Vitalis—" I turned to their leader— "could you take him outside please?"

"Don't you touch me!" the boy shouted. "Don't anybody touch me! I'm a soldier, I am, a Shadow-man, and nobody pushes me around! If I want to stay here and drink, then I will, and no Roman bitch is going to stop me. Get it?" He grabbed the neck of my tunic with one hand, and picked up the big mead jug with the other. He raised it above his head, and I got ready to dodge.

A cool voice behind me said, "Put that down, lad, and leave the lady alone."

I couldn't turn, but I knew the voice. "Hello, Quintus. I'm having trouble persuading this—gentleman—to leave."

Quintus stepped towards the boy. "Out, scum. *Now!*"

"Who are you calling scum, you Roman…." Yelling obscenities, the boy let go of my tunic and hurled the jug at Quintus. He missed, and it smashed harmlessly, though messily, on the floor.

There was a quick scuffle, almost a blur, and then Quintus was holding the native fast, with his right arm twisted halfway up his back. The abuse turned into a whimper of pain, and then silence.

Young Segovax jumped up and launched himself at Quintus. Calmly, without releasing the drunk, Quintus took a pace sideways, then twisted round and gave the lad a vicious kick in the knee. Segovax grunted and backed off but didn't sit down. Quintus said, "Don't even think about it, boy," and after a tense couple of heartbeats, I saw Vitalis wave him down again, and the group of them relaxed a little, and sat there unmoving. I realised I'd been holding my breath, and let it out with a rush. The crisis point was over.

"Come on, you," Quintus growled, and marched the drunk to the door. He threw him outside, more or less literally, and came back grinning.

"Anyone else got anything to say?" He looked at the remaining four warriors. "No? Right. Go and play soldiers somewhere else. Call yourselves warriors? I've seen girls of ten better trained than you lot! Jupiter's balls, a couple of hours with a Roman drill instructor, and you'd all be crawling on your knees and crying for your mothers."

Vitalis got up. He ignored Quintus, and spoke to me. "I apologise, Aurelia. They've behaved very badly." He fished in his belt-pouch and held out a gold quinarius. "And I'm sorry for the damage to your property. Will this cover it?"

"It will." Several times over, but he wasn't getting any change. "Thank you, Vitalis. And look, hard drinking and horse-play aren't the end of the world, but I won't have people in here talking treason. Understood?"

"Yes, of course, completely. And Aurelia, if it's not too much to ask, I'd be grateful if you didn't mention this unfortunate incident to Father."

"I imagine you would," I said. The warriors collected their cloaks and helmets and left. The maids started to clear up the mess, and the customers went back to their own conversations.

I thanked Quintus, but he shrugged it off. "They're just stupid boys. They couldn't fight their way out of a burst wine-skin!"

Through the afternoon the men laboured like Hercules, and by dark the stockade was almost complete. In the morning there would just be the two gates to fit: one for the point where our track joined the forecourt, and a smaller version for the rear fence, leading into the big paddock.

After a cheerful supper, everyone went to bed early. The night was clear and cloudless, with plenty of stars. We set sentries outside, but we all felt sure it wasn't the sort of night the Shadow-men would choose for their attack. Just for once, our optimism was justified.

The next morning was grey and damp, with a thin, steady rain. After breakfast I did my rounds outside muffled in an old hooded cloak, and as I came back into the bar-room, I almost collided with a courier, hurrying out as if the Parthian cavalry were after him. I didn't recognise him, and when I wished him good morning, he merely grunted. He was either one of the strong silent ones, or just plain rude.

"He's in a rush," I remarked to Carina behind the bar.

"He came to deliver a letter for Quintus Valerius Longinus." Carina held up a scroll. "Wouldn't even stop for breakfast!"

Quintus was outside, supervising the fitting of the big new front gate. When I could do it discreetly, I detached him for a quiet word. We went into my study and I handed over his letter.

He scanned it quickly, like a centurion reading battle orders from his general. Then he smiled. "Good. It's from Lucius. He wants me in Eburacum as fast as I can."

"He's in Eburacum now?" I felt as if a burden was being lifted off my back.

"Due there today. Can I borrow a few denarii, please, Aurelia, and a good horse?"

"Yes, of course. You're going straight away?"

"Lucius says he'll be at headquarters by noon. I want to be there when he arrives. I'll be back here tonight."

"What about the fence?"

"It's almost done; they can finish it without me. This message has to take priority. Look, I must hurry. I don't like leaving you just now, but I've got to. And I'll be back by dark." He tore up Lucius' scroll into several pieces, and said, "I'll burn this," as he dashed out.

I wished he'd let me read the message. I'd have found it comforting to get a glimpse of my brother's untidy writing, even in a letter addressed to someone else. I suddenly wanted very much to talk to Lucius, and the next best thing was to write to him. I took a wax tablet and stylus, quicker than ink and papyrus, and wrote:

"Things are bad here, brother. The Druids and the natives want to destroy the mansio and I don't know if we can hold. Come home, PLEASE."

I underlined the last sentence, tied up the tablet and sealed it.

Just as I finished, Quintus came flying in again, asking about the loan of a sword. There was a good old-fashioned one that had been father's; he tested the weight and said it would do. I tried to insist he take a man with him as guard, but he said it would slow him down. I did persuade him not to wear his own cloak, which would be recognised if we were being watched, so he took an old worn one of my brother's instead, the sort of thing a farmer might wear.

I gave him my note for Lucius as he hurriedly dressed for the journey. He blew me a kiss, and was gone into the rain.

Our defences were complete before noon, and they were impressive. The stout stockade was about nine feet tall, and it formed a secure compound, with all the main buildings inside—house, stables, slaves' quarters, barns and stores. Sharpened spikes stuck up from its top, and a ditch, with thorn-bushes in it, ran along the outside where it faced the open paddocks. On the inside, every few yards, were crude platforms made of stones or logs, that a defender could stand on and look down over the fence on the attackers. A heavy oak gate with iron spikes sticking up from its top barred the width of the track to the main road, and a smaller one, also spiked, led out from the rear of the enclosure to the big paddock.

It was good. Given the shortage of time and the lack of skill of most of our labour, it was brilliant. We'd just have to pray it would be enough, when the time came.

Taurus had made a big pen formed from hurdles in the open space in front of the stables, and Hippon's lads brought the horses and the more valuable mules in from the paddocks well before dark. A few animals were squeezed inside the stable block, but there wasn't much spare room there, because the official post-horses were already kept inside at night. So most of them stood out in the rain, dripping wet and unsettled by the wind and the change of routine. Hippon fed them oats laced with some herbal concoction which was supposed to make them sleepy and docile. It didn't seem to be working.

The rain lashed relentlessly down, the wind blew stronger by the hour, and I noticed occasional flashes of lightning. We only had a handful of customers, and they'd all gone home by mid-afternoon. Hardly surprising. We were so obviously preparing for an attack of some sort, a man would need to be very drunk, or desperate to become so, not to take the hint and depart.

I kept everyone busy checking and double-checking our preparations. The slaves stacked logs in the forecourt, and behind the stables; fires would be good for morale, as well as helping us to see in the dark. Brutus, the veteran, suggested some kind of fireballs, something we could set ablaze and throw down on the enemy if they tried to climb the fence. We decided on bundles of hay sprinkled with oil. When we tried one out, it burned well, though whoever was throwing it would have to be careful not to get singed himself. I set some of the younger girls to prepare piles of these and we put them outside around the compound, carefully shielded from the wet with leather covers. We stationed braziers at various strategic points around the inside of the fence, where there was shelter to stop the rain putting them out.

The braziers gave Albia a brilliant idea. "We need something we can drop on their heads if they come too close to the fence," she suggested. "How about boiling water?" So we got out every last brazier and hung metal cooking-pots over them, and positioned them around the fence too. More pots were ready in the kitchen, to be boiled as needed.

Darkness came early, bringing on a continuous pitch-black storm, without a star or a ray of moonlight, or even any lightning. We all knew that if the natives were bent on attacking us, they'd never get a better night for it. We barred the gates early and settled down to wait.

But as the daylight faded I had something else to worry about. Quintus Antonius hadn't come home.

Albia knew how anxious I was. "I expect Lucius was late getting to garrison headquarters," she suggested, "and Quintus had to kick his heels all afternoon waiting for him."

"But he said he'd be back by dark, and he knows how much I—we need him. Suppose something's happened to him on the road? Suppose the Shadow-men have attacked him again?"

"He'll be back, you know he will. He's clever, and he's tough, and he wants to be with you—anyone can see that. He'll be back."

I sent a silent prayer to Diana that I'd still be here to welcome him.

Chapter XIX

The attack came about an hour before dawn. I suppose they thought that after a tense, dark, sleepless night we would be tired and frightened. Quite right. It was the longest, most wretched night I've ever lived through.

At dark everyone gathered in the bar-room, waiting for instructions. I was pleased to see they were all there, farm-hands and house-servants, men and girls. We armed them as best we could: those that had any sort of military training had swords, and the others had pitchforks or heavy sticks, and most of them also carried daggers. And, best of all, two of the field-hands had hunting bows. Yes, I know, giving weapons to slaves is strictly illegal; but very comforting when they are your main defence against barbarians.

We divided all our people into two watches, who would stand guard turn and turn about; Junius and Marius would be watch commanders. Albia and I were supposed to take turns too, but we knew that neither of us would sleep, and we would both be active all night long.

While I had everyone together, I spoke to them briefly, telling them what was at stake. I can't remember much of what I said, except that I tried to finish with something rousing. "There are enemies out there who want to kill us all and destroy our home. But we can beat them off. We've got good defences, we've got the gods of Rome on our side, and best of all, we've got all of you. So let's show the world that we stand as strong and solid as our own oak tree!"

They cheered, and I was moved and also comforted. They were all as determined as I was, including the natives, even the ones like Marsus who could remember a time when they weren't slaves. They felt they were our people, which meant they would fight. Not long ago I'd have taken it for granted that our household would defend us, but the old certainties weren't so certain any more.

Titch wanted to go outside the fence to scout, but was firmly forbidden to do so, by me and also by the tribunes.

"Far too dangerous," Junius told him. "Anyhow, I've got an important job for you young horse-boys. You're to act as runners, when we need messages carried. It's vital that each part of our area is kept in touch with all the other parts, and with the house."

Titch, of course, immediately took charge of the runners, and we heard him lecturing them about what sort of communications in siege conditions were favoured by Julius Caesar.

We lighted two big fires, one on the forecourt and one near the smaller gate at the back. We put up torches in wall-brackets as well, though the strong gusts of wind tended to blow them out every now and then. We got storm-lanterns ready. We organised hot food and mulled wine, well watered, for everyone who wanted it. Then there was nothing for me to do but wait, trying with a cheerful, confident face to hide the dread I felt inside.

I remember I went to the household gods about midnight and asked them not to let any harm come to us, or to Quintus. Albia found me there; she'd come to say a prayer too. We prayed together, but my heart wasn't in it, to be honest. I'd already asked Diana to give us moonlit nights, and to send Quintus safely home, and either she wasn't listening, or some other god had over-ruled her. One of the Druid gods, perhaps, was looking after the interests of our enemies. I know it's fashionable nowadays to mock the old stories of the gods above fighting the battles of their followers down on earth, but that night, with the storm raging and in fear for our lives, we weren't mocking, I can tell you.

Junius was on watch when the first sign of trouble came; it was almost a relief when things started to happen. The bar-room door flew open, letting in a flurry of wind and rain, and Titch ran in, shouting something jumbled about enemies moving in the distance. Marius held up a hand and silenced him.

"Calmly, lad. If you gabble like that we can't understand you. Now make your report sensibly."

"Sorry, sir. Tribune Junius' compliments, and there's movement outside the fence in the big paddock. Four or five men, he reckons. He's reinforced the area and is getting ready to use some of the fireballs."

"Good." Marius got to his feet. "Tell him I'll keep an eye on the front of the building, in case it's just a diversion. And I'll send more fireballs out as needed."

Titch scurried out, and Marius reached for his cloak. I got up too. I couldn't stay inside if the action was beginning. I headed for the door.

"Better not, Aurelia," Marius said. "You'll be a liability out there. If they see you, they'll try to kill you or maybe capture you."

"They won't recognise me. I've got Lucius' old army sagum. With that on and the hood up, I'll look like just another man." The heavy military cloak would stand any amount of rain, and it brought Lucius nearer somehow. When I'd put it on, Albia exclaimed, "Gods, you look a sight!" which I took to mean the disguise was effective.

Albia had a cloak handy herself, but as she reached for it I shook my head. "You're in command here, Albia. You're the reserve, and don't worry, you'll get your share of the battle later. We'll be lucky to beat the bastards off at the first assault."

Outside, the wind and rain whipped fiercely around us, fit to knock us over, and we had to raise our voices to be heard above the noise. The blackness was so complete it seemed solid, and our fires and torches and lanterns gave pathetically little light. We checked the guards around the gate and the front half of the fencing; they were alert and itching for a fight. Marius went off to find Junius, leaving me alone in the forecourt, with the fitful firelight making huge shadows everywhere. I could find my way about without lights, but the inky blackness was unnerving. I decided to head for the stables to see if the horses were all right.

As I went towards the rear, where the fence backed onto the paddocks, I heard a raised voice and a string of choice curses. It turned out to be Junius, laying into one of the field-hands.

"Stupid bastard left the cover off this pile of fireballs and the rain's got to them," he snarled, pointing to a soaking pile of hay-bundles. "Ruined them! Sheer incompetence!"

"I never!" the man was protesting. "I never touched them, I swear I didn't!"

"Well, somebody did. You were supposed to be guarding them, so if you've let someone else get at them, it's just as bad."

"We've plenty more bundles," I said. "Don't let's waste time over it. What's happening outside?"

"Not much so far. There were men moving about in the paddock, coming up to the fence, but when we started throwing fireballs out they pulled back. They haven't gone far."

There was a loud yell from the front of the house. "Here! This way! Tribune, this way, quick!"

Junius and I ran to the open ground between the bar-room door and the new gate. Taurus was there, pointing over the fence. "I heard something," he said. I doubted it myself, in this wind, but there was only one way to find out. Without thinking, I started to climb up the big old oak tree. I'd climbed it ever since my childhood; I knew every toehold and handhold, though the clumsy, thick sagum kept catching as I went up. Soon I was high enough to look over the fence, but it was hard to make much out in the blackness. I could dimly see a group of figures manoeuvring something bulky from among the trees that bordered the road. It could have been anything from a small cart to a giant barrel. Someone was uttering rhythmic shouts, presumably giving the time for them to heave or push. "Fireballs at the front!" I yelled. Two of our farm boys clambered up onto the nearest platform, and a third began passing them lighted hay-bundles, which they tossed out over the stockade. By their blazing light I could see the attackers scatter, and I could make out that what they were moving was a large tree-trunk, roughly pointed at the nearer end. A battering-ram then, a very crude one, to be moved by the brute force of a team of men. Our stockade was stout, but the sections to either side of the front gate were vulnerable, because on the road side there wasn't a ditch, just a few thorn-bushes on good firm paving.

Still, the ram would be slow to move, and we had bowmen. I'd station one of them by the gate on permanent guard, I decided, with orders to shoot at anything that moved, and to let loose occasional arrows even if all was quiet, to keep the besiegers at a respectful distance. Meantime I watched with pleasure how the fireballs' light and flames were keeping the attackers back. I tried to count the men, nine, ten, eleven…and then my heart almost stopped. In the fitful light it was hard to be sure, but I could swear one of the attackers wore a skull mask. The Shadow of Death was leading his band in person.

Suddenly close behind me I heard a branch creak. There was someone else up here! I froze with horror for a couple of heartbeats, then I collected what was left of my courage, pulled out my knife and twisted round, calling out, "Keep still or I'll slit your throat."

A familiar voice said, "It's only Titch, Mistress. This is a brilliant place to keep lookout. I'll send someone up here to watch, shall I? You'll be needed on the ground."

The boy was right, and I should have thought of it myself. I said "Good idea," and started on my way down.

Taurus helped me down the last few feet. The paving was slippery with rain and I was glad to steady myself against his shoulder. "I haven't seen you do that for a year or two, Mistress." He gave me his slow smile. "You haven't lost the knack though."

"Titch," I said, as the boy landed beside me, "tell Junius I want one of the bowmen permanently covering the front gate. They mustn't get that ram any closer."

"Aye, Mistress," he said, and vanished into the dark.

"Aurelia! Aurelia, here! The horses!" That was Hippon's voice, sounding desperate.

"Mistress Aurelia, come quick!" Milo's shrill shriek carried from the stable yard above the storm.

I raced for the stable block; even in the dark I knew the way well enough to run. As I came near I could hear the horses were panicking, calling each other and trampling around.

"They've broken in somehow," young Milo panted. "Look!"

Two horses lay dead on the ground, their throats cut. The rest of the animals were milling about, too close to a stampede for my liking, with Hippon and the stable-hands trying to calm them.

"Go and help quieten them," I said to the boy.

Junius came hurrying over. He took in the scene and swore. "Nobody could have broken through, we'd have seen them."

"Shadow-men!" I exclaimed. "Well-named. Who's supposed to be on guard in the yard here? Marsus? *Marsus! MARSUS!*" But there was no reply.

Then Milo screeched again, from the other side of the horse pen. "Dead! He's dead!" I hurried to him through the circling horses, my heart pounding.

Marsus lay spread-eagled on the ground, bleeding profusely from a hole in his belly, with half his guts spilling out of it. The milling horses were managing to avoid trampling on him, but it was close.

Who'd done this? My mind started to race, but there wasn't time to think about it. I wanted to be sick, but there wasn't time for that either.

I knelt down by his head. He was still conscious, but not for much longer, by the look of him. I took his hand.

"Marsus, you'll be all right. We'll carry you inside where it's warm, and Albia will patch you up. Just hold on till we get a stretcher."

"No." His voice was more or less a whisper; I had to lean so close I could feel his breath on my face.

"Don't waste…men. I'm done. But listen, Mistress…."

"Yes?"

"The tribune did this. I tried to stop him…." His voice tailed off.

"Which tribune, Marsus? Which was it?"

But there was no answer, nor ever would be. He was dead.

The tribune….

O holy Diana, I whispered, help us! Help us now!

Before I could even find someone to move Marsus' body, I heard shrill triumphant yells from outside the fence, and then an animal screamed. The bastards were butchering the mules in the paddock. We hadn't been able to bring all the stock in, so the less valuable mules were still out there. I clambered up onto one of the log platforms and looked over, unable to see anything; but the yelling and the animal noises told me where the enemy were, and they were too far away for the fireballs to reach them. I pictured my tough reliable old mules, being chased and killed by the barbarian savages. I hoped one or two of them landed some hard kicks as they were caught. I cursed like a fish-wife, hurling insults over the fence, but the wind whirled my voice into oblivion, which made me feel even more helpless, and angry tears came to my eyes.

"Fire! Fire! Bring water here!" That was Albia, and it sounded as if she was near the slaves' quarters, out behind the bath-house. Gods, what now?

I raced towards her voice, and she wasn't hard to find because indeed there was a fire, inside the slave block, and the smoky flames lighted my way. Several of the farm-hands were busy with buckets of water and it didn't take long to douse the flames, but it was clear someone must have started the blaze deliberately. And surely nobody had broken in here, so near the buildings? It must have been done from inside. By whoever had killed Marsus? One of the tribunes—but which?

We got the fire out, and before we'd finished that, there was another assault on the fence, near the front gate, about as far from the slave block as it could be. And I began to see a pattern in the attacks. The Shadow-men couldn't get over our stockade quickly, but they had only to threaten to break in, sending small groups of attackers one after another at different points outside the compound. By constantly changing their focus of attack, they could force us to race from end to end of our enclosure to oppose them. That, combined with the damage being done by the traitor inside, would be enough to wear us down and break us. Good, sound tactics, and they almost worked.

I felt chaos closing in on us. It was dawning on me that, for all our hard work and brave words, we might not be able to hold the barbarians off. We lurched from one crisis to another, managing, just barely, to survive. The roaring of the wind in the trees, the challenges of our enemies outside the fence and the answering yells of our own men, the scared neighing of the horses, and the fact that we were more or less blind in the blackness combined to make one violent, terrifying nightmare. I was frightened beyond anything I'd ever experienced before.

By now all our men and quite a few of the women were outside. There were about fifty of us, against perhaps twenty attackers. The fire-balls kept them at a distance, and a dozen times our people poured down boiling water; one well-aimed deluge produced a satisfying scream, which we answered with a loud cheer. Yet even with superior numbers we couldn't guard everywhere at once. They knew it, and I knew it. They were managing to stretch our resources very thin, too thin to last long. All I could do was rush from one part of the compound to another, encouraging the men, making sure there were plenty of hay-bundles, and trying, in between whiles, to watch what the tribunes were doing.

Eventually we got our first real taste of blood. One of the natives, braver than the rest, flung a heavy sheepskin on top of the big front gate and clambered onto it, protected from the spikes. He sat astride it, taunting us and boasting what he'd do to us when he jumped down. But he never jumped. Taurus ran forward, brandishing an axe, and we heard his yell of triumph as he swung it at the man's dangling leg and severed it clean through at the ankle. Simultaneously one of our bowmen put an arrow into the native's chest, and he let out a howl and pitched backwards onto his side of the gate. His foot fell on our side. In the exhilaration of the fight, it was wonderful, and even better when Titch ran forward, picked up the foot, still in its crude leather boot, and hurled it over the gate.

We all joined in with shouts of triumph; you could have heard us in Eburacum. But when eventually we paused for breath, there was a new sound outside in the big paddock, a high rhythmic shouting. Not a slow chant for moving a battering-ram; this was fast and angry. Close at my side, Albia's voice came out of the dark. "Druids! Relia, it's Druids cursing us!"

"I know." I couldn't catch the words of it, but it was Druid chanting, and they must be repeating their vile ritual curses over and over. So, I thought, the Druids have come with the young fighters, hoping to reclaim their holy place. It was a horrible sound and it made me shiver. I pulled myself together with an effort.

"Let them rant and rave!" I shouted. "We're Romans, and Romans don't fear the old gods!" Fine words, but my next thought wasn't so brave. We're not all Romans. Most of our people are natives, and maybe they do fear the old gods....

What saved us were two things, which happened quite close together. A loud, confident Roman voice—Brutus—began a familiar chant in return. "Eagles win! Romans rule! Eagles win! Romans rule!" It was a war-cry so old it was probably shouted at Hannibal and his elephants, and its solid rhythm was enough to drown out the Druid curses. Soon we were all yelling it at the tops of our voices, as if by the sheer noise we made we could force them to retreat. Our spirits lifted, but even as I felt this, some separate corner of my mind wondered if we should be making such a din; it would prevent us hearing what the enemy were up to. Reluctantly, I put two fingers in my mouth and whistled, and the comforting chant stopped.

And then the second thing happened. Over the Druids' cursing we all heard the shrill, triumphant crow of a rooster.

Dawn! The one thing that could save us! Suddenly I realised that the clouds were splitting apart, and the faint glow of starlight showed above us. And to the north-east, the horizon was no longer jet-black but grey, and getting brighter with every breath we took.

"Cock-crow! The night's over!" I yelled. "Look, it's dawn! The gods of Rome are victorious, and the Druids' gods are beaten! *We can't lose!*"

Everyone cheered, and then above the cheering we heard, from the front of the compound, a shout and a huge splintering crash: they were finally using their battering-ram. Somehow they'd got it close enough to make one last, deadly attack.

Junius called to Marius to stay at the rear, and he and I and nearly everyone else raced to deal with the new danger. They were battering the fence near the gate; as I headed for it I tripped and almost fell over a body on the ground. The bowman we had left on guard was lying there with his throat cut. The traitor in the camp had struck again.

The men with the big tree-trunk ran at the fence a second time. After each blow they had to manhandle the ram back and make another run. It was a slow business, and I wondered how long it would take them to break through, under a hail of fireballs and a rain of boiling water. The answer came in the worst way possible. The fence broke at the third assault, bending inwards with a rending sound and sending wood splinters flying everywhere. A gap opened up, and there were many hands ready to widen it, and then the natives started piling through. Our men went forward in a disorganised mass, blocking the gap with their bodies and their weapons.

I stood a few paces behind the fight, but I couldn't see what was going on, so I ran to one side and mounted one of the platforms. I held my long knife ready in case anyone broke through, and remembered what Lucius had told me. "If you're ever stupid enough to get in a fight, Relia, either kick them in the balls or go for their eyes. That's the only hope for an amateur, and it's a last resort...." Well if this was the last resort, I'd be there at the bitter end.

But there were enough of us to hold them, and men to spare to hurl fireballs at them from either side of the gap. As the light grew, I could clearly see the struggling mass of fighters. I saw Taurus knock a man down with his huge axe, and as another warrior lunged at him, Brutus was there with a good sword-thrust at the man's belly, and he fell dead. Another of our boys stumbled and fell from a heavy blow to the head; but a second man dragged him safely out of harm's way, and Ursulus stabbed the attacker in the face with a pitchfork. Everywhere I looked, our people were holding the enemy back.

I realised with a surge of excitement that the besiegers had left it too late to use their ram. If they'd broken through in the pitch blackness, they would almost certainly have overwhelmed us, but by now we were exultant, invincible, and we had Apollo's light to show us what was happening. Our men fought them off with swords and farm tools and sticks, and though fresh natives were coming forward into the gap to replace the wounded ones, the attack lost momentum and faltered. From where I stood, I could see that one last push from our side would finish the fight.

"They're retreating!" I screamed out. "They're beaten! Drive them back! Drive them back now! *Now!*"

Our men made a last supreme effort. The natives stood fast for only a few heartbeats, then they turned and ran. One or two of our people started to go after them, but Brutus roared at them and they had the sense to come back. Soon there wasn't a barbarian to be seen anywhere.

Hippon came dashing across from the rear. "They've all gone! All of them! We've won! We've done it!"

And so, incredibly, we had.

Chapter XX

It was full daylight before I could really believe that we'd won, that the natives wouldn't be back, at least not for now. Hippon and the stable-hands calmed the horses, and a party went outside into the paddock, and came back to report sadly that all fourteen of the mules there had been killed. Those, plus the two horses, were a bad enough tally of animal losses.

We had only lost two men—Marsus, and the bowman by the front gate. But most of our people had bruises and cuts, and a couple were quite seriously hurt; one had a badly slashed arm, and another had taken a sword-thrust in the shoulder.

Albia got busy patching up the wounded, while I organised food and warm wine for everyone. The victorious defenders ate and drank and congratulated each other. I didn't blame them for playing the hero; they were all heroes to me, and I made sure I told them so.

It wasn't till quite a late stage in the proceedings that I realised Titch was missing. I checked with everyone, but nobody had seen anything of him since the final stages of the fight. We hunted high and low, and I sent a couple of men outside to look round in the paddocks and by the river, but there was no sign.

"Stupid young idiot," Hippon grumbled, halfway between exasperation and concern. "I suppose he disobeyed his orders and went outside to scout. When they retreated, he'd have to make a run for it. He could be anywhere."

He could be dead, but I hastily pushed that idea out of my mind. I couldn't bear that anything serious had happened to that cocky, cheerful little brat. After all, he was destined to be a general, wasn't he?

Then Taurus called me over to look at the broken stockade. His expression was grim, as he pointed to the gap the battering-ram had made. "I thought that fence came down a bit quick. Look at these five stakes. They've been sawn half through, close to the ground. There was hardly any strength left there at all. They'd give way easily, you'd hardly have to touch them."

"But the attackers couldn't have done that." I felt cold inside.

"No. It was someone inside. Who?"

Who indeed? "And someone told the enemy where the weak place was, too."

"I'll find out who put up this section," Taurus grunted. "I was round the back, mostly. But I'll find out. I don't like the idea of one of our own people...."

"No, wait, Taurus. We've got to box clever. We'll keep this to ourselves for now, all right?"

He looked doubtful. "But if we've got a traitor here...."

"We *have* got a traitor here, that's obvious, but we'll let him think he's got away with it just for the present. That way he'll get over-confident and careless and it'll be easier to catch him. We must be on the alert the whole time."

"Well, if you say so. But we should tell someone else," he insisted. "One more person, to cover the other watch from me. Then one man on each watch will know to keep his eyes open."

That was good sense. I called Hippon over and we showed him the sawn timbers. He was speechless with anger at first, then he growled, "By Epona, when I find who's done this, I'll cut them in pieces."

Taurus said, "I hope Master Quintus comes back soon. He'll know what to do."

"He will." Oh gods, with everything else going on, I'd had no time to worry about Quintus, where he was, and why he wasn't home. Perhaps he'd been out in the storm all night. Perhaps he was lying dead on the road somewhere....

Albia came out to me. "Relia, you'll catch your death, standing about talking all morning. Come and get some food."

"How are the wounded?"

"Pretty fair, all things considered. Except for Otho; his shoulder is quite bad. His woman is seeing to him now, but I'll need to change his dressings later, and keep an eye on him for a day or two. By the way, has anyone looked at the man that Brutus killed? I mean, I suppose he's really dead?"

"If he isn't, you're not wasting time nursing him," I called out as she walked across to where the inert body lay.

"Jupiter's balls, Relia!" Albia exclaimed as she bent over the man. "You didn't tell me it was *him*."

I turned to look at her. Albia never swears as a rule. "Who? I don't know who it is. Just some horrible barbarian who got what he deserved."

"But don't you recognise him?"

I went over and gave the corpse a kick. "No. Should I?"

"It's Balbus' foreman. We saw him in the shop."

"*Merda,* you're right!" We both stood staring down at him, trying to work out the implications.

"Let's go inside," she said at last. "We need to get warm and dry, and then we need to take stock."

We changed into warm, dry clothes and went to my study. Taurus brought in a brazier to drive away the cold, and we sat down with a beaker of wine each, and went over the events of the night.

We'd been extremely lucky. We'd survived in spite of several things that had gone wrong, and some of them could have finished us. The attack on the horses, the fire in the slave quarters, the big heap of hay-bundles soaked in the rain. Worst of all, the weakened stakes in the stockade, and the fact that the attackers knew where they were.

We had a traitor in the camp all right. Marsus had narrowed it down to one of two. But which of the tribunes was it?

"Most of the things that went wrong," Albia said, warming her hands over the brazier, "were around the back—the horses killed, the fire, and the fireballs ruined, though I still think that could have been sheer accident. And Marius was in charge at the back."

"That's true, but the place where they broke through was at the front. Junius was in charge of the fence-building. He could have...."

"I don't believe it! You saw the way he fought, Relia, you can't seriously be thinking...."

"No, no, all right." I *was* seriously thinking it, but I was too tired for an argument.

Suddenly Albia gave a great yawn, which made me yawn in sympathy. "Gods alive," I said, "we've got to get some rest. Tonight could be just as bad, or worse even. But one of us needs to stay on watch. I'll toss you for first to bed."

I won the toss, and I wasn't about to argue. I went quickly to the household shrine and said a short but heartfelt thank-you to the gods there; then I stripped off my outer clothes, crawled into my bed and fell instantly fast asleep. I was woken, what seemed like quarter of an hour later, by a hand shaking my shoulder, and Albia's voice in my ear.

"Relia! Wake up! Come on, wake up!"

"I'm asleep. Go away." But I knew she wouldn't.

"Wake up! I've got some good news. Quintus has come home!"

I was fully awake, out of bed and running through into the bar-room before I'd time to remember I had only a light linen shift on, and no shoes. I didn't notice the morning chill. I didn't feel anything but pure happiness. I ran to Quintus as he ran to me, and we ended up embracing in the middle of the room. I suppose other people were there; I didn't know or care. He was back, and he was safe!

Eventually I pulled away and said, "I must get some more clothes on."

"You look fine to me," he grinned.

It didn't take me long to find a warm over-tunic and shoes, and to give my hair a quick brush. When I came back the bar-room was empty except for him. As he heard me enter, he turned and held out a beaker of Rhodian.

"We were so worried..." I started to say.

"I've been so worried..." he began. We laughed.

"Sit down and let's do some catching up," he said.

"I must check outside first. I presume nothing's happened while I've been asleep, but...."

"No, I've had a look round, and all's quiet. You've had quite a night of it though, I can see. I've sent Albia off to get some sleep. I told her not to wake you, but I'm glad she did."

"I'd have killed her if she hadn't. We were worried sick about you. What happened?"

"Oh, nothing much." His purple eyes were laughing.

"What sort of nothing much?"

"Somebody tried to kill me. That sort of thing upsets one's travel plans."

I sipped more wine. "Some people will use any old excuse to avoid riding a few miles in the rain. I assumed you'd got held up by the bureaucrats at Eburacum."

His smile faded. "That wasn't the half of it. Lucius wasn't there."

"*What?* But his letter said...."

"I'm pretty sure the letter was a forgery, to get me away from here. Nobody at Eburacum was expecting him, or knew anything about a letter from him."

"*Merda!* What did you do?"

"Once I'd got inside headquarters, I wasn't leaving again till I'd seen somebody senior, and that's what took the time. There's trouble all over Brigantia. Everyone was rushing round in circles like dogs with fleas. I had to pull rank and jump up and down a bit and use Uncle Titus' name, which got results in the end."

"Results? Are they going to send us some help?"

He shook his head. "I saw the garrison commander. He was extremely sympathetic, but it seems the whole of Brigantia is seething like a pan about to boil over. There are other war-bands further west, picking on isolated settlers and threatening the roads. So he had no spare men to send back with me. With luck we'll get some help in a couple of days."

"A couple of days? Holy Diana! Can we hold out? Last night was terrible—I've never been so frightened. If they try again...."

"We'll hold out. I wish I could have done more, but it took all my time to get even that much. And I wish I'd been here. I should have been here! I started for home in plenty of time. But I noticed a couple of horsemen riding along behind me. They were following me, not very cleverly. I'd spotted them earlier too, when I came in through the town gates, because they were wearing cavalry clothes but didn't look genuine."

"Not genuine? Most troopers are handsome hunks with their brains in their backsides. So these two were intelligent-looking weaklings?"

"They just didn't have the right amount of swagger." He laughed. "They didn't wear their uniforms properly. You know what I mean—like new recruits, not very comfortable in their gear. Anyhow, while I was in town I'd asked a friend to watch my back till I was well on the road home, just in case, and I knew he'd be following fairly close, so I got off my horse clutching my belly as if I was going to be sick, and led the two idiots down a track into the woods. They must have thought it was their lucky day, until my pal showed up behind them. They won't be following anybody else. And when I looked at them closely, guess who they were?"

"I'm in the wrong mood for games."

"Spoilsport! It was our old friends Nonius and Rabirius, the failed kidnappers."

"Good riddance."

"I agree. I didn't want a lot of paperwork, so we left the bodies in a bramble patch in the woods. By then the storm was getting even worse and it was almost night, and I thought it was a foolish risk, to come riding that road alone in the dark. So I stayed in Eburacum, and set off just before dawn. I'm sorry, Aurelia. I feel I've let you down."

"It couldn't be helped. Albia's told you what happened, presumably."

"Some of it. You tell me now, all of it."

So I told him about all of it, in as much detail as I could. He stopped me now and then with questions, and when I was done he was silent for a while.

"You did well," he said eventually. "I just wish I'd been here to help."

"So do I. The worst bit was knowing we had a traitor inside the stockade, as well as all the enemies outside it."

"One of the tribunes," he mused. "It fits with what we've learned already in general about the situation at Eburacum. And as you know, I've been wondering about those two. They could both be in it. They seem to be close friends."

"Except they keep falling out all the time. I wonder if maybe one of them is trying to persuade the other to join the conspiracy."

"Or not to, perhaps. Yes, that could very well be it. *Merda*, I wish we could contact Lucius. I spent some time yesterday trying to find anyone who'd had a briefing from him, but he works alone, and never confides anything to anybody."

I said, "How very inconsiderate of him," and Quintus had the grace to look sheepish.

He ran his hand through his fair hair. "Were you able to recognise any of the attackers?"

"No, it was too dark. Except…I can't be certain, but I think I saw someone in a skull mask. Unless it was a trick of the shadows. And the one we killed is familiar, Balbus' foreman."

"So Balbus himself is involved too, you think?"

"It rather looks like it, but there's no solid proof."

The outside door opened just then, and my farm foreman came in.

"'Morning, Ursulus," I said. "How are things going?"

He stood on the doormat shifting nervously from foot to foot, a big, powerful man who looked at ease in a field and awkward in a room.

"Sorry to interrupt, Mistress. I thought I'd better tell you. Something bad's happened."

"Gods, what now? Spit it out."

"Two of the field-hands have run off. Two of the free ones, I mean, the slaves are all present and correct." Ursulus himself was a freedman.

"Which two?"

"Cimber and Ardan," he said unhappily. "Cimber had his own house, with a woman and kids. Ardan lived with his parents. They've both gone, and nobody knows where."

"Run off to join the Shadow-men, do you reckon?" Quintus put in.

"Maybe. Or got scared and didn't want to stay here. You've heard the rumours about how the Druids have put a curse on us all? I don't believe in that stuff, but some of the men are frightened."

I managed to smile. "Try to reassure them, Ursulus. This won't go on for long now. Master Quintus went to Eburacum yesterday, to get us help."

Well that *was* what he went for. I didn't say he'd actually got any.

"Good, sooner the better." But the big man still didn't make a move.

"Has something else happened?" I prompted.

He nodded glumly. "I went out to the paddock, to sort out them dead mules. Shocking mess, they are, but I'll see to them. The thing is…while I was there I checked the old round byre. They've wrote on the wall again. I mean painted."

"What does it say?" Quintus asked.

"There's a skull, and three lines of writing. The first two are like on the stable wall the other day. And then at the bottom it says 'Greetings from Messapus.'"

"*Messapus!* Gods alive! Well, thanks for telling me. Send a couple of men to clean the paint off, and make sure they do a thorough job."

"Very good, Mistress. One more thing...." He shuffled his feet.

"Yes?"

"Me and the lads think, well, we all think you did real well last night. And we want you to know we're all with you. We won't let them Druids drive us out."

"Thank you, Ursulus. That's good to hear. You and the men fought like gladiators. Is anyone too seriously hurt to work today?"

"Only Otho, and he'll mend. Even the ones who'd normally have tried it on aren't complaining overmuch. It's just those two that have gone missing."

"Right. Thanks, I'll come and do the rounds in a while." He went out.

"Two runaways," I muttered. "After last night, I suppose I should be glad it's not more. If there are rumours about being cursed by the Druids—Holy Diana!" I didn't want to think about what we'd do if the men deserted in droves.

Quintus was looking at me curiously. "Who's Messapus?"

"A character in the Aeneid. I thought everybody knew that!"

"And what's he doing sending you his greetings?"

"It's a password. I told you we agreed on one at Silvanius' secret meeting the other day."

"So you did. Gods, how very literary! It's a more elegant class of password than we humble investigators go in for."

"That wouldn't be difficult. Lucius always picks something really silly. Like Aunt Julia and an elephant."

He nodded. "My usual one is beans."

"*Beans!* As in, 'Here are the secret orders, and I thought you'd like my cook's recipe for bean stew'?"

"Something like that. But I take it," he said more seriously, "that only the people at the secret meeting knew about Messapus?"

"That's right."

"And Vitalis wasn't at the meeting?"

"Right again."

"Then our traitor was one of the men at the meeting, or some- one working for him. This latest bit of wall-painting confirms it. And I'd say the evidence points to Balbus as the most likely."

"Because his foreman attacked us?"

"Yes. The foreman would have been his second-in-command, doing the actual fighting and leaving Balbus to do the planning and organising. He must be a good organiser—all successful businessmen are. We know he has money enough, and he's proud of his friendship with the natives, including the anti-Roman ones. He travels about a good deal, ostensibly on business."

I couldn't deny that it fitted. "And he's the original source of the green paint. He must have used it because he thought we'd all assume he was the one man who *wouldn't* use it! Gods alive, how devious can you get?"

"When it comes to being devious, he's a mere babe in arms. Look how he's played right into our hands," Quintus said.

"By betraying all our plans?"

"By boasting about it, of course. He couldn't resist showing off. 'Look, aren't I clever, I know all your secrets?' He presum- ably meant to frighten you, but the whole thing will recoil on him like a badly made catapult. If you're doing secret work, the first rule is, stay secret, and the Shadow of Death has broken it. He's shown himself to be a complete amateur. Whereas *I'm* a professional!"

"Now who's boasting?" But what he said was true. We had a traitor among the trusted inner circle, and it was better to be aware of it.

"What's the next step? Arrest Balbus?"

"Not yet, no." He finished his wine. "I want more tangible proof, if I can get it. Balbus could afford the best lawyers in the Empire, and they'd make short work of my case as it stands. And I'd also like to be completely sure he's the only Roman traitor in this area. We'll give him a day or two more."

"That's far too risky," I objected. "Another attack...."

"...is likely to go ahead in any case, I'm afraid. The young rebels won't stop now. If their leader is captured, they'll want revenge."

"But I must get a message to Silvanius. He needs to know that the password isn't secure. So do the others."

"I suppose that can't hurt," he agreed. "In fact their reaction might be useful. We can ride into town this morning."

"We? You want to come too?"

"Yes, I do. It's time I met the famous Councillor Silvanius Clarus."

"Then let's go on horseback—it's quicker than the carriage. Well, don't look so surprised, Quintus! In case you hadn't noticed, I'm not some mincing lady of fashion who has to go everywhere on wheels."

He surveyed me with an air of amazement. "That's where I've been going wrong with you, Aurelia. I had you down as definitely the mincing type!"

It was nearly noon by the time we set off. First we had to wait till Albia was up and about. She came in, looking more or less awake, about two hours later. I gave her some breakfast, and we told her about the password on the byre wall.

"Balbus," she said gloomily. "I suppose this proves it. Relia, I feel as if there are traitors everywhere we turn. And...poor Ennia!"

Her remark reminded me of the tribunes. They were still sleeping, but if they went out later, I wanted to find out where, so I sent one of the horse-boys to ask if Hawk could come over. While we waited, we saddled a couple of the good black horses, and told Taurus to saddle up too and come with us as guard.

The tribunes finally appeared, looking remarkably fresh; they sat down to a large breakfast and announced they were going hunting later. I said they deserved some relaxation, and wished them luck, but I didn't feel inclined to chat. Knowing that one or both of them had tried to get us all killed last night put a definite damper on conversation.

Hawk appeared, with his red-haired boy, the one who reminded me of Titch. After the usual brief play-acting concerning bottles of medicine, they followed me to my study.

"You had a bad night," Hawk said. "I couldn't get close, but I saw the attack from a distance, and the man in the mask too. Are you all right?"

"Just about, but we've got a problem. We've discovered one of our tribunes is helping the rebels, or it might even be both of them." I briefly reported last night's events.

He didn't seem surprised. "I've noticed they seem to do more courting than hunting. And they sometimes split up and go separate ways."

"They're going hunting today, or so they say. Could you follow them for me, find out where they go, who they meet, and come and tell me tonight? We've got to know for sure if either of them can be trusted."

"If only one of them is a traitor, they'll probably separate. But Teilo's not a bad tracker, if I need a second pair of eyes." He indicated the boy.

I must have looked dubious, because he added, "He's quite good, and you're only wanting them kept under observation, after all. It's not as if he'll have to follow tracks that are days old. I should hope any of my older children can track an unsuspecting hunter without being seen."

"Fine. Take care, though, won't you? And while you're out and about," I added, "could you keep an ear open for news of young Titch? The new stable-boy. He disappeared last night during the fight, but he's a smart lad. I think he's much more likely to have been driven off and got lost somewhere than got himself killed. All the same, I'm worried about him."

"Oh, we'll be looking for him, never you fear. Teilo's been on at me about it already. The two of them have made friends, I gather."

I looked at the lad more closely. "Are you teaching him to be a tracker too?"

He grinned. "Yes, and he's teaching me to play the bugle." He touched his belt, and there was Titch's old bugle hanging from it. "Good, isn't it?"

"Wonderful." Hawk winked at me over the boy's head, and I tried not to think about somebody learning to play a bugle in a one-room roundhouse.

I went into the kitchen to tell Albia we were on our way, and found her shouting at Cook, something she never does as a rule. "Just get on with it, and stop arguing!" she finished, and turned to me, flushed and angry.

I looked at her enquiringly, and she managed a smile. "Don't mind me, I'm just edgy today. I'll feel better when the customers start arriving. The trouble is, it's too quiet. The Campaign of Terror is starting to work. There should be more people on the road by now."

She looked strained, and had dark circles under her eyes. I realised she was as exhausted as I was, with the added burden of anxiety over whether Junius was a traitor or not. And now the latest news about Balbus....I gave her a quick hug and said, "Try not to worry. We all did brilliantly last night. We've shown the natives we aren't an easy target. And Lucius will be home soon."

"Yes. I only hope there's still a mansio for him to come home to. Now you and Quintus be careful on the road, won't you?"

It was a pleasant day for a ride, breezy and sunny, drying out the soaking woods and fields after yesterday's deluge. We urged the horses into a gallop, enjoying the wonderful feeling of motion and freedom.

As we slowed down on the outskirts of Oak Bridges, Quintus glanced at me and said, "You ride like a man."

"I'll take that as a compliment."

"It is one. Most women perch uncomfortably on a saddle, but you ride as if you're part of your horse....What's the matter? You keep looking up and down the road."

"I'm just wishing there was a bit more traffic on it. This is the middle of summer, a good fine morning, yet there's hardly a man or a beast stirring. The Campaign of Terror is beginning to bite."

With this depressing thought we rode through Oak Bridges, which seemed almost deserted, and trotted along the country road towards Silvanius' villa.

"It's still too quiet for my liking," I commented.

"Here comes someone now," Taurus said suddenly. "Hoof-beats behind us, coming up fast. Listen!"

We turned as we caught the sound, and all instinctively looked about us. We'd just rounded a bend, and were hemmed in by trees on either side. We could hear two sets of hooves, but the riders would be on us before we could see them. If these two meant trouble, this was the kind of place they would choose for it. Quintus drew his sword, and Taurus and I drew our daggers.

Chapter XXI

But as the riders rounded the bend, we recognised Felix with his giant bodyguard. They slid to a halt, their horses panting.

"Felix!" I exclaimed. "Jupiter, you gave us a fright. What in Hades are you doing, galloping about like the Parthian cavalry?"

"Aurelia, my dear! The gods be thanked! You're safe? We heard there was trouble at the Oak Tree last night."

"You could say that, but yes, we're safe. We're just on our way to see Clarus. Let me present one of our guests, Quintus Valerius Longinus, bridge engineer. Quintus Valerius, this is Cornelius Felix, one of our town councillors, and a patron of the theatre."

They acknowledged one another courteously. I noticed that Felix looked tired and drawn. Had anyone in Oak Bridges had a decent night's sleep? But he gave us his most charming smile. "Are you here to survey our splendid oak bridges? Are they going to collapse one dark night and deposit some unwary traveller into a watery grave?"

"I hope not," Quintus smiled back. "But I haven't started my inspection yet. If I find anything amiss, I'll make sure the town council is informed straight away."

I began to walk my horse along the road. "Let's not waste time. We need to see Clarus urgently."

"So do I, so do I! Something quite dreadful has happened."

"What?"

"I feel I've been assaulted…violated…."

"Whatever is it? Have you been attacked?"

"Not personally, no. But my beautiful statue of Nero. My Apollo. Someone broke into my garden last night in the storm, and smashed it to pieces. Into a million tiny pieces!"

If this had happened to anyone else, I think I'd have wanted to laugh. I'd spent the night trying to avoid being killed, and he was lamenting the loss of a statue! But I knew how he valued this particular work of art, and whoever had broken it must have done it to hurt him.

"Oh, Felix, I'm sorry. It was a beautiful piece. And something you really valued. Was it the only thing that was damaged?"

"Oh yes. They knew where to find my most precious possession. It's irreplaceable, quite irreplaceable…."

"It was the Shadow-men, presumably?" Quintus asked.

"Who else? The barbarians at our gates."

"Quite literally, in our case." I told him about the attack, and the betraying of the password. He was still exclaiming over this as we turned our horses into Silvanius' drive. We were dismounting at the main door when the Chief Councillor himself emerged from the house. He looked haggard and harassed, and he wasn't wearing his toga.

"Thank the gods!" he exclaimed when he saw us all. "I was about to send for you, Felix, and you too, Aurelia. And this—" he glanced at Quintus—"if I'm not mistaken, must be your bridge surveyor, who survived the Shadow-men?"

"Quintus Valerius Longinus, at your service, Chief Councillor," Quintus answered, and they shook hands.

"What's happened, Publius?" Felix asked. "You were going to send for us? Don't say you've got more bad news. Aurelia and I are both the bearers of terrible tidings…."

"Dreadful news, yes. Old Vedius was killed last night."

"Gods, no!" I was never one of Vedius senior's keenest admirers, but that didn't mean I wished him dead. "Was he out on patrol?"

"No, on his way here. He was at home, and he received a letter, asking him to come to my house urgently. Although it was late, and such a filthy night, he set off—his wife says he left home just as it was getting dark. But he never got here. He was attacked on the road, and his body was found at first light."

"You sent him a letter?" I asked. "Who knew you'd sent it? Who knew he'd be coming here?"

"No, I said he *received* a letter," Silvanius corrected. "I did not write it. It was a forgery. Quite a competent one, and it included the password, so he thought it was genuine…." He stopped abruptly. "But forgive me, I'm forgetting my manners. This horrible business….Let us go into my study. You'll take some wine?"

While his major-domo brought it, I told him about the attack, and also about the greetings from Messapus on my wall. Then Felix piled Pelion on Ossa by recounting the destruction of his Apollo.

"This is frightful." Silvanius looked round distractedly as if he expected yelling barbarian hordes to come pouring into his garden there and then. "Your mansio attacked…Vedius killed… your beautiful statue broken…and someone in our trusted circle betraying our secrets!"

"There's only one person it can be," Felix said. "The potter with the feet of clay. And I hesitate to say 'I told you so,' but…."

"That's what we think too," I said. "If there's really a traitor among the five of us who met here three days ago, it can only be Balbus."

"I agree, though it gives me no pleasure." Silvanius sighed. "So what's the best course of action now? Arrest him, I think, and have him sent to Eburacum. What do you say, Aurelia?"

There was a knock on the door and the major-domo came in.

"Excuse me, my lord, I'm sorry to interrupt, but Councillor Fannius Balbus has sent a messenger, begging you to visit him at his shop urgently. He says something disastrous has happened there. The Councillor is uninjured, but very shaken."

"Disastrous? Did he give any more details?" Silvanius demanded.

"No, my lord."

"Nothing at all?"

The slave shook his head. "No, my lord. He simply delivered his message, and said his master had told him to return straight away."

"Then I must go and see him. We all will. Order the large carriage immediately," Silvanius told the slave. "And I'll need three mounted men as escort. We'll all go together."

The servant left, and we sat there in gloomy silence.

"He didn't use the password," Felix said at last. "Is that significant? Does he know it's been betrayed?"

"He could just have forgotten," I suggested. "If something awful has happened."

"Or it could be a trap," Quintus muttered.

"It could," Silvanius agreed. "If we're right about Balbus betraying us. But he is a friend, and he is asking for our help. We'll give him the benefit of the doubt for now, and we'll be on our guard."

He got to his feet; we three made to follow his example, but he waved us down again. "No no, stay there till the carriage comes. I am only going to change into my toga."

While he was gone Vitalis strolled in, looking every inch the well-groomed young Roman gentleman, in a white tunic with dark green trimmings, except that he had a livid cut on his left arm. Somebody had plastered it with healing ointment, which made it stand out even more. You've been in a fight, my lad, I thought, and we all know where. But he showed no emotion at the sight of me and Quintus.

"Felix, are you….Oh, good morning, Aurelia. And this is Quintus Valerius Longinus, I presume?"

"We meet again," Quintus said, as they eyed each other warily. Both were doubtless remembering the way Quintus had dealt with the drunken warrior in my bar.

"I didn't mean to interrupt," Vitalis said. "Is something wrong? You all look very serious."

"Aurelia has been telling us about an attack on the Oak Tree," Felix answered. "And now we've heard that Vedius has been killed, and Balbus has had some sort of catastrophe and wants us all to go to his shop."

"Oh, I see." Vitalis didn't look concerned, just mildly disappointed. "Are you going too, Felix? Only you did say you'd hear my lines again today."

"My dear boy, so I did. And so I will. I'm sure Balbus won't miss me, and I doubt if I can be of much help in a ceramics crisis."

"Good. I still need some final rehearsing," he said to Quintus and me. He had nerve, I couldn't deny it.

I decided to try to shake him a little. "You've been in the wars, Vitalis. What happened to your arm?"

His composure was unruffled. "I was on patrol last night. One of the new watch patrols, you know. Somebody threw a stone at me. I hope it doesn't put the girls off," he added, with his dazzling smile.

"Where did it happen?"

There was a tiny hesitation before he answered, "Near Father's temple."

"You're certainly doing a good job, you night-watchmen," Quintus commented genially. "It must take guts, going out there in the dark, never knowing what you'll have to face."

"Someone's got to do it," Vitalis said, with a becoming air of modesty.

"Well, all credit to you, I say. How's the poor man who lost his foot?"

"Pretty ill. We don't know if he'll survive, but...." He stopped. "So they say. I haven't seen him yet, myself."

"Vitalis, we'd better go and make our excuses to Publius," Felix said, getting up from his couch. "Then we'll find somewhere quiet for a rehearsal. Aurelia dear, and Valerius Longinus, you will forgive us, won't you?"

"Our bout, I think," Quintus murmured when they'd gone. "If Vitalis isn't up to his ears in this rebellion, I'll eat my boots! And I still wonder about his father. Surely he has to be in it too?"

It didn't take long to drive to the pottery shop in His Pomposity's grand carriage. The forum was quiet, and the shop looked much as usual from the street.

But when we stepped inside, it was like plunging into a nightmare. The whole interior was in ruins. Somebody had efficiently and mercilessly smashed up the entire place and everything in it. The floor was a finger deep in pieces of broken pot and glass; there wasn't a fragment longer than my thumb, and most of them were shorter. The shelves were chopped to splinters which lay everywhere in heaps. The walls, including the green alcove, were smeared with patches of black paint. On the biggest bare patch of wall was the usual threatening message—with Balbus' name instead of "All Romans"—and ending with a greeting from Messapus.

What made this appalling mess almost unbearable was the sight of Balbus and Ennia, standing in the midst of it all, white-faced and forlorn, surveying the wreck of their livelihood.

Chapter XXII

Ennia was crying, and Balbus was shaking; he was either going to explode, or start crying too. We went to them, surrounding them as if by our physical presence we could somehow help, though there was no comfort any of us could offer for this sort of horror. As I embraced Ennia she moaned, "Not again! Dear gods, not again! I can't bear it!" I remembered what she'd told me about their troubles in Gaul. I hugged her tight, trying to show her the enormous sympathy I felt for both of them. I knew how I'd feel if somebody did this to the Oak Tree. After last night, I knew all too clearly.

I could sense that Balbus was angry for two quite different reasons. He'd lost his beautiful pots and glass, many of them exceptionally lovely pieces which he'd gone to endless trouble to seek out and import. But he'd also lost his whole stock-in-trade, and rich though he was, he'd find it hard to start again from scratch, even if he had the heart to.

A slave came in from the living quarters at the back, with a tray of wine. Balbus roused himself to invite us through to their sitting-room, where we sat around awkwardly. I perched on a couch next to Ennia, who was still crying. I put my arm round her and just held her, and gradually her tears dried.

Quintus was telling Balbus about last night's attack, with Silvanius chipping in comments and asking questions. I found it hard to concentrate on what they were saying, until I heard Quintus remark, "Balbus, you know who's done this, don't you?"

He looked, if possible, even angrier. "I think it must be my foreman. He's gone missing, since yesterday afternoon. His woman and child have gone too, which makes it look as if he's run off for good. When I find the bastard, I'll kill him!"

"I'm afraid you're right." I told him how Brutus had killed the man.

"I knew there was something wrong," Balbus said. "He's been behaving oddly for days. Drinking too much, and so moody! Surly and resentful half the time, and then suddenly over-eager to please, trying to make up for it. I thought he might be wanting to tell me he was leaving me. He'd been talking about setting up on his own. I never guessed he'd betray me like this. I was his patron, I gave him his freedom because he was a good worker....How *could* he?"

"Maybe he had no choice," Quintus said. "If they had some sort of hold over him, if his woman was a local girl perhaps...."

"There's always a choice!" Balbus snapped. "There's always a point when you can choose what to do next!"

But Ennia interrupted quietly, "Not always, Aulus. Sometimes there's only one road open." And he subsided, thinking presumably of Gaul.

"You've got a good few native slaves here, haven't you?" Silvanius asked. "We could get evidence from them."

"Torture them, you mean? That's the only way to get admissible evidence from slaves—by torture. Believe me, I'm tempted! And if I do, Clarus, you'll support me as a magistrate?"

"Of course I will."

"But when all's said and done, what's the point?" Ennia asked. "We know who to blame, and nothing can undo this mess!"

We didn't stay much longer. As we were mounting to ride home, Balbus came after me and said, "Aurelia, I don't want that bastard's body back. He doesn't deserve a funeral. Throw him in your lime pit with the dead animals, will you?"

"Whatever you say, Balbus."

Silvanius offered us more refreshments at his humble abode, but we regretfully declined; we wanted to get back to the mansio as quickly as we could.

"But you'll be able to come tomorrow, won't you, Aurelia?" he asked anxiously.

"Tomorrow?"

"My temple. The dedication."

His temple! "Gods alive, Clarus, you're going ahead with the dedication? I mean I thought, with all these disasters...."

"I know. I wondered if I should delay the ceremony because of Vedius Severus' death. But if I do put it off, that will be a victory for the Shadow-men. They are trying to disrupt our lives. I must go on as I've planned. I asked Saturninus, and he said his father would wish us to continue. To show them we Romans are strong and unafraid. Don't you agree?"

"Yes," I said soberly, "I think you're right. Of course I'll come."

"And I'm still holding my celebration dinner afterwards." Silvanius turned to Quintus. "You'll come to the dedication, and to dinner, won't you, Valerius? Any friend of Aurelia's will be most welcome."

"Thank you. I'd be honoured, Chief Councillor," Quintus answered, and gave a slight bow. I suppressed a smile. It never ceases to amaze me how we manage to hang on to these formal courtesies even in the middle of catastrophe. Like the scene in the comic play, where two fat men try to escape from a burning house through a narrow doorway, each repeatedly saying "After you, Senator" until the flames burn their backsides.

"And the meeting afterwards, Clarus?" I asked him. "We were going to...." I paused, remembering that Quintus wasn't supposed to know about our secret circle.

"I'll need to think about that." He scratched his chin reflectively. "Having seen what has just happened to Balbus, I can't believe he is the one who betrayed our password. And yet *somebody* did. We'll see."

We rode home with Taurus twenty paces or so behind us, so we could talk privately.

"Well, nothing's ever simple, is it?" I said. "We're back at the starting-gate once again. And our field of runners is getting smaller by the day! Even with your suspicious mind, you can't seriously believe the traitor is Vedius now. Or Balbus."

"Not Vedius, no. But I wouldn't rule out Balbus just yet."

"What, with everything he and Ennia have worked for in ruins? If that's the work of the Shadow-men, then Balbus can't be their leader."

"But suppose he and his foreman were working together, Balbus organising, the foreman leading the warriors. All their bickering could just have been a pretence. The foreman leads the attack on the mansio, and gets himself killed. Balbus realises that'll implicate him, and there's still the matter of the green paint. He needs to show the world he's a victim of the rebels. So he arranges to have the shop trashed. He wouldn't tell his wife, of course."

"But you saw him this morning, Quintus. Do you honestly think he could have destroyed the shop? It'd be like hacking off his hand."

"It'd be worth it, to allay our suspicions. Remember, if he *is* the Shadow of Death, he must be capable of being utterly ruthless."

"Look, when you first asked me to help, you said my local knowledge would be useful. And I'm telling you—Balbus could be ruthless, he could even have such a grievance against Rome that he could organise a campaign of terror. What he could *never* do is destroy his own shop."

"Fair enough. Would you say the same applies to Felix not being capable of destroying his statue of Nero?"

"That isn't so easy, I admit. Felix is such an odd mixture.... Hello, who's that?" I'd spotted a green-brown figure at the edge of the wood, beside a big holly-bush which was unusual enough to be a local landmark. He waved to us briefly and then vanished into the trees.

We pulled up sharply. "That was Hawk, I'm sure it was."

Quintus looked uncertain. "I only got a glimpse. It might be a trap."

"Not if Hawk's involved. And I'm sure it was him."

"Yes, it was, Mistress," Taurus said. "I saw his big dog too. Shall I go and see what he wants?"

"We'll all go," I decided. "Just to the edge of the trees, within sight of the road."

"It's too risky," Quintus began, but I drew my dagger and walked my horse slowly over the cleared strip of land that bordered the road. I heard Quintus swear under his breath, but he and Taurus drew their weapons and followed.

I halted a few paces from the trees and called, "Is anybody there?"

A voice came from further on, though there was nobody to be seen. "It's Hawk. Come for more cough-mixture. Follow this little track into the wood."

We rode along a faint game-track, until Hawk and his dog emerged as silently as a swirl of mist.

"Your tribunes are hunting, and so far they've stayed together," he announced, without preamble. "Teilo is still with them. We found something interesting down by the river. I'll show you."

We followed, still riding, as he picked his way through the trees. The oaks were tall and widely spaced, so it wasn't hard going. In a hundred paces or so we came into a large clearing, and on the far side I caught the gleam of the river. We were on Segovax's land, close to where it adjoined our own, the place that Hawk had said was used by young lovers, and also by Druids.

I hadn't been here for years, but the clearing looked much the same, big oaks all around in a rough circle, except for a gap in the trees where the grass led straight down to the river. There was a ruin of an old house on the side furthest from the river, and this was the spot the courting couples used; Hawk had said Junius and Marius had come here. As I glanced round I was surprised to see a huge stone, like an altar, in the middle of the space, and some strange wooden statues—surely they were recent additions. But before I could take in any more Hawk said "Look!" and pointed at the tallest of the big old oaks.

However hard I looked, I couldn't see anybody in it, or under it, not even an animal. "There's nothing there," I said. "Just an old grandfather of a tree."

"Mistletoe!" Taurus exclaimed. "In the forked branch there, see? Odd, that. It never used to grow here."

It was just an ordinary bunch of mistletoe, in a fork about three men's height from the ground. It was quite a small clump, with some of its light-coloured, shiny leaves dangling down beneath it, but no berries yet of course. Not exactly a common sight, admittedly, but nothing to get excited about.

I said, "Is that all? I thought it was something important."

"The Druids would call it important," Quintus remarked.

"It wasn't there yesterday," Hawk said.

"It must have been," I objected. "It couldn't grow so fast, could it?"

"No," Quintus answered seriously. "Hawk, somebody has planted that mistletoe there overnight."

"I wouldn't call it planting, in the strict horticultural sense." He gave his lazy smile. "But yes, it's been fixed there in the tree to look natural."

"But why?" Taurus asked.

Quintus said, "My guess is the Druids are preparing for a ceremony here. Am I right?"

Hawk nodded. "I think so. That's why they've brought in all the statues, too. They...." He stopped suddenly as his dog gave a soft growl. He muttered, "You haven't seen me," and was gone.

"Time for some play-acting," Quintus murmured, and turning his horse back towards the road, frowned horribly, and swore loudly, exclaiming, "Aurelia, your eyes are playing you tricks, or is it your brain? There's no sign of any deer here, red, green, or sky-blue-pink!"

"I saw one, I know I did," I retorted. "A big one, too. You've frightened it off, that's all. We should have come up on foot. Riding up like this, we're about as silent as a cavalry charge."

"Well I say it was never there to frighten!"

"Say what you like, I know a deer when I see one!"

We kept this going till we were on the road again, trotting towards the Oak Tree.

"Did you notice the Druid altar?" Quintus asked, in his natural voice. "And the hideous wooden statues, too. I've seen the same thing in Gaul. Whatever it takes to be a Druid deity, beauty isn't essential."

"They are the old gods," Taurus put in. "But they haven't been there long. I was there myself, last full moon, with...." He stopped, and when I looked back I saw he was blushing. "Well anyhow, the clearing was empty then. If they're in it now, it means bad trouble."

"I saw the altar," I said. "And that old tumbledown house, with a path leading off into the trees from just beside it. Quite a wide track, well-used, considering the spot's supposed to be remote and only visited by courting couples."

Quintus smiled. "It proves their ceremony is imminent. I just wish we knew when! There's one good thing though. If the Druids are having to fake omens like mistletoe in trees, they must be getting desperate."

I didn't find the thought of Druids getting desperate the least bit comforting.

When we got home there was nothing much calculated to cheer us up. The bar should have been nicely busy, but there were no animals or carts on the forecourt, and only two native peasants drinking beer inside. Albia was there as usual, busy, smiling and outwardly cheerful. But I know my sister, and for once it was all an act.

"Albia," I called, "come and see what we've got you from town!"

"Lovely!" she beamed, and we went to my study. When she was out of sight of the bar, her smile faded.

"It's dreadful, Relia. Hardly anyone on the roads all day. We've had three couriers through, and those two natives. We should be a lot busier than this."

We told her the bad news from town. "Jupiter," she said eventually. "When will all this ever end? Destruction, death.... Every morning I wake up and think, it can't get any worse today, and then it does. Poor Balbus and Ennia. And poor Felix. He thought the world of that statue." She rubbed her face slowly. "I only wish I'd something better to report from here. Old Cavarinus looked in earlier to see you, Relia. A farmer we were going to rent some pasture from," she explained to Quintus.

"*Were* going to?" I didn't like the sound of that. "Not any more?"

"He says he's very sorry, but it's not convenient to rent us the grazing now."

"But we had an agreement. We'd shaken hands on it!"

"So I pointed out to him," she said sadly. "I told him you'd be very upset, and that *you'd* never go back on your word to him. Eventually, after a lot of humming and hawing, he admitted he'd heard that the Druids have put a curse on us, and anyone who helps us will come under the curse too. So he's playing safe. He did say he was very sorry," she added wryly.

"Holy Diana! Now we're really on a slippery slope."

We sat in a depressed silence for a while.

Eventually Quintus said, "But we have made some progress today."

"Two steps forward and one step back," I complained. "But I suppose we're nearer finding the Shadow of Death than we were this morning. We've eliminated Balbus, and Vedius, obviously. And Felix, I think."

Albia said, "I'm glad it isn't Balbus. Somehow after the attack, even with his foreman lying dead in the yard, I kept hoping against hope that a friend like Balbus couldn't be the traitor."

"Felix is still a possibility." Quintus looked at me. "Isn't he?"

"I don't think so. He was beside himself, telling us about how the barbarians had broken his precious statue. He's as much a victim as Balbus and Ennia."

"In that case, the rebel leader has to be Vitalis," Quintus declared. "But is he, or is he not, getting active help from his father?"

"He must be," Albia said. "He wasn't at the secret meeting, and we agreed the Shadow of Death must have been there, or how would he know the password?"

"No!" Quintus exclaimed. "Not necessarily. We've got it all wrong. *I've* got it all wrong."

"Gods alive! Did you hear that, Albia? I could have sworn he said he'd got something wrong!"

"Be serious and listen! I assumed that the Shadow of Death has betrayed the password as a kind of boast of how clever he is, knowing all the secret plans made at that meeting. But it did strike me as odd behaviour for such an intelligent rebel leader—and he *is* intelligent, that's what makes him so dangerous. Now if someone else got hold of the password, someone not at the meeting, then by making it public, he'd be throwing suspicion onto everyone who actually *was* there. Sowing seeds of confusion and doubt among you all—as he has done."

"By someone else, you mean Vitalis," Albia said. "But how could he discover the secret password? Relia, could he have overheard the meeting?"

"Definitely not. We checked to see there were no eavesdroppers outside."

"Later on then?" she persisted. "Silvanius might have been talking about it in the house afterwards, with Felix, or with his secretary, not realising that Vitalis was listening."

"Or one of Vitalis' slaves was listening, more likely," Quintus put in. "He's bound to have his own personal servants at the villa, and if he's the Shadow of Death, they'll be well used to spying on Silvanius, collecting information for the rebels. Silvanius might just be cautious in front of another Roman, even his own son. But slaves come and go around the house all the time, and you hardly notice them."

I pictured that vast villa, with its numerous rooms and its large retinue of slaves. "That's the answer, I'm sure of it. Vitalis' men could easily spy on Silvanius. It wouldn't occur to him to lock up his confidential letters, or to check for eavesdroppers every time he dictated something to his secretary."

"It's a good case," Quintus conceded. "Only one thing worries me. He's so openly in sympathy with the rebels. I'd have expected a traitor to be less obvious about it."

"Oh really, Quintus," I objected, "now you're looking for complications just for the sake of it. You've got to face it—sometimes the simple solution is the right one, and the simple solution here is that Vitalis is the Shadow of Death."

"All right," he agreed, "but the gods alone know how we're going to prove it."

Chapter XXIII

The afternoon was deadly quiet; the money from bar sales wouldn't have kept a slave in cabbage stalks. We got various odd jobs done, and Albia and I managed a couple of hours' sleep each, while Quintus went off to "see one or two contacts." I checked round outside in the late afternoon, not that there was anything to check, but I felt like a change of scene. In the stable yard I found young Milo, sitting on a pile of straw, taking his ease. Nothing remarkable about that, except that he had something in his hand, and when he saw me he slipped it under his tunic to hide it.

"What have you got there, Milo?" I asked, thinking I'd probably found the arch-villain who had been pinching the plums.

The boy muttered something, I couldn't hear what, and looked mulish.

"I said, what have you got there?" I walked up closer.

"Nothing, Mistress."

That sort of reply is calculated to arouse suspicion. "Show me," I ordered.

"It's a secret."

"You don't keep secrets from me, boy. Now let's see it."

Slowly, reluctantly, he brought out a knife. I felt a shock of recognition as I saw how the sun glanced off its long, narrow blade and gleamed on the jet inlay in its handle. Just as it had done when I'd seen it last, sticking out of the body of Quintus' dead horse.

"*Merda,* Milo! Where did you get that knife?"

"It's mine."

I felt a sudden jolt of excitement. I stared at him, willing him to tell me the truth, yet trying not to show how desperately I wanted to know who had given it to him. "Oh really? I think you stole it!"

"No!" He looked frightened. "I didn't! Tribune Marius gave it to me. But I haven't to tell anyone. It's supposed to be a secret."

Marius? That was Marius' knife? I heard in my head Marsus' dying words, "The tribune did this…." Well now there could be no doubt *which* tribune.

But did young Milo know Marius was a traitor? Surely not. He wasn't the brightest of lads, but I'd always thought he was loyal.

"Why a secret, Milo?"

"He said the other lads would be jealous and take it off me."

"When did he give you it?"

"After the barbarians attacked us. He said it was a reward for fighting well."

If there's one thing that angers me more than another, it's taking advantage of youngsters. If Marius had wanted to be rid of that very recognisable knife, why couldn't he simply have thrown it away? To give it to Milo….He'd put the boy at risk. And he'd taken a risk for himself too. Well, he'd soon be facing the consequences.

"He was good to me," Milo added. "He wanted to give me a present. I'd seen it in his room. I asked if I could have it. At first he didn't want to, but then….I persuaded him." He looked down, twisting the jet-inlaid handle between his hands.

"He was good to me…." I could guess what that meant, knowing Marius. Milo was a plain boy, big and square with mouse-coloured hair and solemn blue eyes, not Marius' type at all, you'd think. Unless he'd wanted to find out about the detailed workings of our stables….

"Does he take you to bed, Milo?"

He blushed and nodded, still not looking at me.

"And I suppose you tell him all your secrets?" I tried to make it sound light and casual, but the lad looked genuinely shocked.

"Secrets? Of course not! I don't *know* any secrets! He's just interested in me, and in my work—how we look after the animals, what sort of shifts we do, things everybody knows. He says I'm good with the horses, and he can help me get into the cavalry if I want."

"Well, you are good with the horses," I conceded. "But nobody knows the future." I suddenly felt sorry for Milo. He'd been made a fuss of by a handsome young officer, and presumably thought he was in love. And all the while he was being used. But this wasn't the time to tell him. Marius must get no inkling of the fact that I now knew him for what he was.

"May I keep the knife?" the boy asked. "If I make sure it stays a secret?"

"Yes, all right. But Marius gave you good advice—don't go showing it off to anyone. If I see you with it again, you'll have to hand it over to me. Now, haven't you got work to do?"

Actually he hadn't much; none of us had. I finished my walk and went back inside.

When I told Albia what Milo had said, she was overjoyed. "I told you it wasn't Junius," she said triumphantly, and added that she'd find us some special wine to celebrate with when Marius was firmly under arrest. It seemed to me at least possible that Junius could still be involved with his friend, but I didn't say so to Albia.

Quintus came home shortly after, and he was delighted too. "Well done! This is just the breakthrough we need! I wonder if Junius knows what's going on. I shouldn't be surprised....I'll arrest Marius as soon as he shows up. Oh, this is excellent news, Aurelia! At last I've got something positive for Lucius. There's been so little to report. I'm afraid he must be thinking I've been malingering up here."

"Whereas you've been incredibly busy, loitering in taverns and chatting up peasant girls in woodland glades."

"Not all the time. For one thing, I saw Hawk—well, to be truthful, he saw me. He said to tell you the tribunes spent most of today hunting, but have left off now, and gone down to that old roundhouse by the river."

"I wish they'd come home. Then you can arrest Marius."

"Yes, and if I can get him to confirm that Vitalis is a part of the rebellion, I can round him up too....You know, at last I feel this investigation is getting somewhere. I'm going to write to Lucius straight away, and send it off first thing tomorrow."

I wished I could share his happiness, but truth to tell, the more I thought about what Marius had done, and was presumably still doing, the more depressing I found it. He'd betrayed his army comrades—his friend Junius, and also the ambushed pay convoys—and he had betrayed us; he'd tried to get us all killed when the mansio was attacked. To me, a centurion's daughter, treachery like that is hateful, and the idea of such a man being under my roof was horrible.

To cheer myself up, I went to see my horses. I walked round the various paddocks, looking over them all, making a fuss of the new foals and letting them get to know me. It always makes me happy and relaxed, being with the animals, which are so much less complicated than people. This year's crop of foals were beauties. Our horse-breeding programme was beginning to show results.

The two dogs, Lucky and Dancer, came with me, but disappeared into the trees chasing small game. I went into the round stone byre, now thankfully clean of green paint, determined to make sure all was in order. Occasionally in the summer, vagrants slept in it, though it must be pretty draughty, because we'd taken out part of the front wall to make it easy for the animals to shelter there. But today there were no signs of intruders. The byre was partly boarded out to make a hay-loft above, and I debated scrambling up to check in the hay, but I'd need a ladder, and there wasn't one handy. It could wait another day.

And then a horse screamed in the paddock, a horrible sound that turned my blood to ice. I ran outside and saw one of the foals lying on the ground thrashing about, with an arrow sticking out of its side.

I was consumed with anger, far too furious to be afraid. My horses are precious, and the thought of the Shadow-men trying to kill them in broad daylight wiped all caution from my mind. I looked round; there was nobody to be seen. Well then, I'd go and find the bastards myself. Then another arrow flew towards me. It missed, but not by much.

"No!" I yelled. "No, you don't hurt my horses. *NO!*" And I began to race across the field towards the trees, the direction the second arrow had come from. As I ran full pelt, a separate detached bit of my mind said, "Run crooked! Twist and turn!", the words Lucius used to call to me when we played at soldiers as children. I swerved to the left, and as I did so an arrow whizzed past my right ear, so near I felt the breeze of it flying by. But I was still much too angry to be scared. I just thought, I've got the direction right, and I tore on faster than ever, in a series of irregular curves but still making for the trees. By the time I got across the big field, two more arrows had passed me, quite close but not close enough.

I was yelling like a Fury, telling the bowman what I'd do when I caught him, and my screeching scattered the horses in all directions, and brought the two dogs out. They raced ahead of me, barking fiercely. They looked alarming, and might scare the bowman off. Except if they frightened him away, I wouldn't be able to get my hands on him....

Then with the very tail of my eye I caught a flicker of movement in the trees over to my left, but I couldn't stop to pay any attention to it. "If there's more than one of them," that detached cool voice in my mind said, "you're done for." But I was seized by a kind of battle-lust, the sort of thing I've heard soldiers describe, but a quite new sensation for me. I was carried along on a wave of exultation, and I wasn't going to stop till I'd destroyed my enemies, or they'd destroyed me. And I felt invincible; I was the one who'd do the destroying. Soldiers must feel like this, otherwise nobody would ever go into battle more than once.

As I ran into the trees the man with the bow was standing there, an arrow ready on his string. I recognised him, the white-haired man from the gang that ambushed us in the woods. Then I saw a black blur as Lucky leapt at his throat and knocked him down, and Dancer's grey shape as she started to worry at his face. I heard him scream, and I yelled, "Kill, dogs! Kill! Kill!" Neither dog had ever killed a man, but the bastard didn't know that.

Then there was a noise in the trees to my left, and a second man was hurtling towards me, with a drawn sword. It was Veric, the scar-faced leader of the ambush party. Knowing his name gave me inspiration.

"Veric! Drop your sword! Drop it, Veric, and I'll call my dogs off! Otherwise they'll kill your pal there!"

The man on the ground screamed, "Veric! Help me!" He was rolling about trying to throw the dogs off him, and I hoped they were both taking large chunks out of him, but dared not turn to look. Veric hesitated, and I could have yelled for joy. He should have charged me first, put me out of action, and then gone to help his comrade, that's what a professional would have done. He'd had me at his mercy, but his indecision had lost him the chance. And now another scream split the air, as Lucky buried his teeth in the man's neck.

Frightened by the screaming and probably by the anger he could see in my face, Veric dropped his sword and raised his arms in the air. I grabbed the weapon and held it in both hands. It was too heavy for me, but I was angry enough to have wielded a barbarian double-axe.

I whistled at the dogs, and amazingly they stopped attacking. It looked impressive, but probably it was just that the fallen man was lying still now, blood all over his face and chest, so the hounds stood still too, looming over him and daring him to move a muscle.

Veric wasn't done yet. I saw him go tense and instinctively flung myself to the right as he sprang at me, hands outstretched like claws. I held the sword straight out pointing at his belly, so he couldn't come in too close, but he circled round me, forcing

me to keep moving, hoping I'd stumble on a tree-root and give
him an opening. There was every chance of it too; the ground
was uneven and I wasn't exactly used to this sort of thing. Now
that the battle-fever was leaving me I began to be afraid, and I
hadn't the faintest clue what to do next.

Then I caught another quick flash of movement in the trees,
directly behind Veric. I couldn't see anyone there, but it must
be another enemy. Gods, I thought, I'm finished. I can't deal
with more of them while Veric's still on his feet, and I haven't
the skill to kill him. I hoped I'd be able to give one of them a
serious wound before they got me.

Then that cool detached voice, which was like Lucius talking
in my head, spoke again. "If he's hiding, he must be a friend.
Hold on, and keep Veric busy. Help's coming!"

And as the thought came to me, a voice, a real voice this
time, roared out: "Stand still, you scum. Freeze!" It was like a
centurion's bellow on a parade ground, and instinctively Veric
half-turned. I raised the sword, preparing to stab him, but there
was a hissing noise, a silver streak flew through the air, and a
long, thin knife caught him in the cheek. He cried out, clutching at his face, but I wasn't watching him really; my eyes were
on Quintus, who was emerging from the trees with his sword
in his hand.

He ran to us, stabbed Veric expertly up through the chest,
watched the body fall, and pulled his sword out, all without a
word. Then he turned to me.

"Hello, Aurelia." He smiled as if we'd met in the course of
an evening stroll. "Having trouble?"

"I'm fine, now, Quintus. Thanks for your help."

"My pleasure."

I bent to pick up his thin-bladed knife, which had fallen to
the ground. As I reached for it, my eye was caught by a boot-
print near Veric's body. The ground was thick with them, of
course, but this one happened to be easy to spot. It was from a
left boot, with a worn heel and part of the stitching missing from
the sole. So Veric was one of the men who attacked Quintus.

I pointed it out to him, and he said, "I'll look soon. First let's deal with the other man."

I called the dogs away, and Quintus bent over him briefly, and nodded. "Your hounds have finished him off."

"Good."

"Lucky they were with you. I'm sorry I couldn't get to you sooner. I had to keep in cover and work my way round to you. I was near the stables when I heard you yelling, and I saw you run across the field, but there was no point both of us behaving like idiots."

I stared at him. "Is that what I did? Behaved like an idiot?"

He cleaned his sword-blade on Veric's tunic, then surveyed me like a drill-master looking at the lowliest recruit. "Racing across open ground, charging blind straight into the enemy when you couldn't see them....It was the stupidest thing I've ever seen in my whole life."

"You must have led a very sheltered life then," I snapped. "In my book, it's not stupid to take risks, if you're defending something you value."

I turned my back and started to walk away, too angry to say any more. I mean, when you've scared yourself nearly to death trying to save something precious, what you don't need is some arrogant man telling you you've been stupid. Even if he's just saved your life. *Especially* if he's just saved your life.

"Aurelia, look, I didn't mean it like that..." he said, but I ignored him. I headed back across the open paddock, and saw Hippon there, squatting down by the body of the shot foal. The other horses were calming down, now the excitement was over.

As I strode on, Quintus came up beside me and touched my arm. "Please wait."

I walked faster.

"Stop, Aurelia, let me explain. I didn't mean it to come out like that. I was so terrified, thinking of what they might do to you. If anything happened to you I'd...I'd...."

"You'd what? Laugh yourself sick, presumably, at my stupidity in getting myself killed!"

"I don't know what I'd do. I love you. I don't want to think about life without you."

At that I did stop. The rest of the conversation isn't relevant to this report.

Diana gave us a moon that night. She also provided a sky full of beautiful stars, or perhaps that was Venus' doing, because there was even a little time for Quintus and me to gaze at them, and make love in my favourite private spot in the garden. It was wonderful; we forgot our troubles for a while, and I wouldn't have believed I could be so happy, with my whole world threatening to collapse around me.

But we couldn't relax for long. We had to check our defences, post guards, and distribute supplies of fireballs and boiling cauldrons. Albia, Quintus and I took watches in turn. We'd have included the tribunes in the roster, but they hadn't come home by dark. Their two servants appeared eventually, and reported that their masters had gone off to spend the evening with a couple of natives down by the river. Marius' man smirked and said, "They're only young, they've got to sow their wild oats."

The officers still hadn't come home by morning. Albia was desperately anxious about Junius, and I was uneasy too, but I tried to reassure her. Junius must be involved in his investigations, but he and Marius were due to be at the temple dedication, and they'd have to return to the mansio first, to put on their parade armour. And as she wasn't coming to the dedication, she'd be there to welcome them. She'd been invited, of course, and would have liked to attend. But she realised that with things as they were, I needed to leave someone I could trust in charge at the Oak Tree.

It was a beautiful day, and I was in high spirits as I got through my morning chores. There was plenty of time, because the dedication was to take place about an hour before noon. In Rome or Londinium I daresay they do these things differently and it would have begun at dawn, but here in our small town, people would be gathering from many miles around, and needed time to travel there.

I chose my clothes carefully. This was a grand occasion, Silvanius' Big Day, and I didn't want to let the Oak Tree down. I wore my pale blue embroidered tunic, with the sky-blue over-tunic that exactly matched the colour of the embroidery. I also wore my pale blue scarf made of silk, a wonderful thing, so light and delicate; Lucius had brought it back from the east, and I kept it for very special occasions. I completed the outfit with two gold brooches with blue and white enamelling. Though I say it myself, I was pleased with the effect, as I studied the reflection that gazed back out of my bronze mirror. From the look in his eye, Quintus was happy with it too, and I was pleased with his appearance. Freshly bathed and shaved and in a gleaming new toga, he would do the Oak Tree credit, and me. ·

We took the largest carriage, with four of the best mules. Milo drove us; he was a good driver, but I felt a pang as I thought of Titch and wondered if we'd ever see his cocky smile again. Taurus, Brutus and two field-hands rode alongside as guards. As we set off for Oak Bridges, I felt a thrill of pride—and of excitement. After all our troubles, today would be a holiday, and I was all set to enjoy it.

Chapter XXIV

The temple looked superb. The workmen must have toiled day and night to get every last thing ready, but they'd done it, and the result was magnificent. In the bright sunlight the white marble-clad columns were dazzling, and the white walls of the sanctum displayed their beautifully painted pictures to perfection. They showed a whole variety of gods and goddesses who were intended to bring us peace and fertility. I saw Apollo with his lyre, Minerva with an owl, Neptune with a dolphin, and I was especially pleased to see Diana there with a crescent moon, and offered her a quick prayer.

As Quintus and I went up the steps to the big, open forecourt in front of the sanctum, the statues of Jupiter and of Juno gleamed brilliantly, that wonderful pale gold of newly cast bronze. They hadn't been painted at all; this was unusual, but the effect was stunning, because the figures had been so expertly sculpted. The big stone altar stood waiting to receive its first sacrifice, flanked by tubs of ornamental trees; the water in the pink marble basin glittered in the sun and cascaded gracefully away over the stones. A tripod held a holy flame in a bronze urn, and the smell of frankincense wafted from it. Well, all right, you don't want a lyric poem in praise of every stick and stone; suffice it to say that no expense had been spared, and the temple was rich, stylish, and impressive.

The wide open space was large, but it was quite full, and more people were arriving all the time. I looked round the assembled worthies to see who was present; everyone who was anyone, that's who. I pointed some of them out to Quintus. The town council of course were out in force in their best togas. Even Felix wore formal dress today, and very handsome he looked with his yellow hair combed straight for once. I waved to him and he waved back, but the crush was such that we couldn't easily get over to him. As the crowd grew, quite a few curious glances were directed at Quintus and me. I introduced Quintus Valerius Longinus the bridge builder to one or two couples within reach, including Balbus and Ennia. I was glad to see them there; I don't suppose they were feeling much like celebrating, but they'd come to do their Romans-standing-together bit for Silvanius.

The councillors' wives hadn't missed the chance to wear their best finery, and I was glad I'd gone to some trouble over my appearance. I saw that Ennia and several other ladies had a new hairstyle, a particular way of piling up curls with gold netting and ivory combs. I hadn't seen it before, and I made a point of complimenting Ennia and asking where the style came from. She said one of the other wives had recently returned from a trip to Rome with news of the latest hair fashions there. It did look good, new and interesting. I know it's ridiculous how we all still follow Roman fashion, even though by the time the style gets to us in the wilds of the north, Roman ladies will have long ago moved on to something else—they were probably all wearing red wigs with green feathers by now.

Silvanius was a member of one of the Colleges of Priests at Eburacum, a useful honour for an aspiring Roman politician, as long as he's rich. This meant he would take an important part in the dedication himself, and when everyone was assembled he took centre stage to start the production off. Sorry, no irreverence intended, but we all know that religion and theatre aren't all that far apart, and I could tell that Silvanius was relishing his leading role. He would be assisted by two full-time professional priests, one from Jupiter's temple at Eburacum, the other from Juno's. There was an augur to read the omens, and several underlings hovered about in the background. Vitalis was in the main crowd, near Felix;

his part must come later. The priests, including Silvanius, were in white robes with ritual head-dresses like crowns, with plaques of silver and gold hanging from them, flashing as they moved in the sunlight. Yes, I thought, this is just right. The gods should be worshipped in style, and today they will be.

The ceremony was along conventional lines, so I'll just summarise it. First Silvanius took up his place in the open space in front of the sanctum, between the bronze statues, and made a short speech of welcome; and yes, you've guessed, it did include a sentence about Romans standing together. Then he began the formal prayers invoking the blessing of the gods. He had all the prayers off by heart; he must have been rehearsing for ages, and he delivered them clearly, with just the right amount of expression. Felix had a hand there, I assumed, and had coached him well.

Then a pure white bull-calf was sacrificed on the altar, and some of the blood was caught in a bronze bowl. The augur examined the entrails and pronounced that the omens were good, which in view of later events just goes to prove what an unreliable business augury is.

There were more prayers to Jupiter and Juno, and a sort of eulogy in parenthesis in praise of the Divine Augustus—it never hurts to have the approval of the deified Emperors. For the climax of the proceedings, Silvanius moved to the entrance of the sanctuary to offer a white ram and to make the final dedication.

We, the worshippers, wouldn't follow him there; the sanctum was for priests and gods only. So we all stood outside in respectful silence, waiting for him to make the offering and come out to tell us that the gods had accepted the dedication and the place was now up and running, I mean, truly sacred.

Silvanius had his back to the congregation as he walked to the entrance, arms raised up for another prayer. He started the ritual words, and then he froze rigid, like a statue himself. For a few heartbeats I thought he'd just forgotten his next few lines; there's a lot to learn in these religious ceremonies, and even the best of priests get lost sometimes. If you know the rituals well, you can often spot how the experienced priests just make it up if they lose the thread. They have to keep going, because if they hesitate too long, it's taken as a sign that the ceremony hasn't been carried out correctly, and everybody has to start all over again. In practice this means you always allow plenty of time for these performances, and make sure there's a spare sacrificial animal handy just in case.

But when Silvanius turned to confront us all, he was as white as the marble wall behind him, and looked close to fainting. My heart stopped in my chest. Something was dreadfully wrong.

All the same he kept calm, managing to retain his remote, priestlike manner. "My friends," he said, "a great impiety has been perpetrated here today. A most monstrous, an unheard-of blasphemy against the gods. I call on you all to witness, and I call on the gods to witness, that I am a loyal Roman and a faithful Priest of Jupiter, and I must and will cleanse this horror from the temple."

There was complete silence. I could hear birdsong, and the gentle breeze, and I could almost hear everyone's brains whirring as we all tried to work out what in the gods' holy name this "horror" could be. What had he found in the sanctum? After the last few days it could be anything. And from Silvanius' stricken look, it was truly terrible, not just a minor slip-up, like a box of tools accidentally left by the workmen. I felt my stomach knot itself into a ball as I started to speculate. Beside me, Quintus was rigid, his face taut and pale.

"I must consult with my priestly colleagues about what is to be done," Silvanius went on. "I do not know yet whether this, whether what has happened means the gods are angry with us, and what we must do to appease them if they are. But we will perform the rituals that are needed for cleansing the sanctum, and proceed with the dedication in due course."

We all just stood dumbly there, still too stunned to move or speak.

"Meanwhile, my friends, the dedication is only postponed, not cancelled. So I ask you all to bear a short interruption with patience, and we will resume the ceremony as soon as we can."

Now the congregation moved, breaking up into small groups, and everyone began talking at once. The two priests who were helping went into a huddle with the augur and Silvanius, and Balbus and Felix joined them. They all went inside the sanctuary and came out again, looking appalled. After a few heartbeats Silvanius glanced round, caught my eye, and beckoned me over; Quintus came too.

"Clarus, this is dreadful for you," I said. "But what is it? What's gone wrong?"

"I don't understand!" he moaned. Now that we were close I could see that he was shivering. "We purified the sanctum at dawn and nobody's been into it since. How could it have happened?"

"But what *has* happened?"

He motioned for us to go in and look.

The entrance was narrow, but the high windows let in plenty of light. The inner walls were whitewashed and painted with figures of gods; the room was sparsely furnished, and what there was, including the floor, was made of gleaming white marble, so the effect was almost dazzling. In the middle of the floor there was a small marble altar, and against the back wall, almost touching it, a polished table holding a bronze bowl of water and two ornate incense burners, unlit. But our gaze went straight to the back of the room, under the table, where two bodies were lying. They were side by side, with their heads pointing into the middle of the room and their feet hidden by the table top. They were in military clothing, and they were dead.

They were Junius and Marius.

On each man's chest was pinned a bone disc; I bent to look, and sure enough, it was the usual threat, with a slight twist to the wording:

ALLROMANSWILLBEKILLED

WHENTHEYDEFYTHESHADO

WOFDEATH

I don't know how long I stood there just gaping. Eventually I heard Quintus mutter, "That's odd."

"Odd? It's hardly the word I'd choose."

"Look at the bodies. There's no blood."

He was right; there wasn't a drop, and their faces looked tranquil. My brain started slowly to work, like a wheel being dragged through mud.

"So they weren't killed here. That's something to comfort Silvanius. They weren't murdered in the temple itself."

"No," Quintus agreed. "And they weren't stabbed or beaten up. There are no marks of strangulation either. That only leaves poison."

Vitalis appeared in the sanctum entrance. His eyes darted everywhere as he took in the scene, though he said nothing. But seeing him there made me angry. Had it all been a pretence, his talk of helping his father with the dedication ceremony? Had he known what the Shadow-men intended to do here today? Because there was no doubt the Shadow-men were responsible for this horrifying act. Had Vitalis himself had a hand in it?

"Vitalis," I said. "Do you know anything about what's happened here?"

He shook his handsome head. "Me? Why should I?"

"Don't play games. We know you're involved with the Shadow-men, you've made no secret of it. This outrage is their work, and how you could bring yourself to take part in desecrating your father's temple, the gods alone know. And they'll punish you for it in their own good time."

"I don't fear the gods of Rome. I worship the old gods, and they will stand fast in the face of their enemies," he replied calmly, and turning away, walked out across the forecourt.

"For two bronze pins," I muttered, "I'd chase after that little scum-bag and denounce him in front of everyone!"

Quintus growled, "I know, but it wouldn't help."

"But how could he? It's just…so awful."

He touched my hand briefly. "Aurelia, we need the public cleared off the site here, with the minimum of fuss. Silvanius is in no state to do it, so somebody else must. Then you and I can investigate what's happened, without everyone looking on. Who can we ask to speak to the crowd?"

"I'll find Vedius Saturninus." I looked outside and saw him coming towards the sanctum. When I beckoned him in, he was aghast.

"Saturninus," Quintus said. "This is clearly the Shadow-men's doing, wouldn't you say?"

"Yes, I would. By the gods, the blasphemy of it…defiling a holy temple with death, with deliberate murder. It's beyond belief!"

"We need your help," I said. "Can you get everyone to leave quietly, without causing a panic?"

"But shouldn't Silvanius?…" He glanced outside, and said, "I see what you mean. All right, I'll do it. How much should I tell them?"

"As little as possible," Quintus said. "Just say there's been an unfortunate accident, an irregularity in the ceremony, and the sanctum needs purifying. So the dedication is postponed for today, until the rituals for cleansing have been taken care of."

He did it well. He'd had a Roman education, and all that emphasis on public speaking comes in handy in a crisis. In no time at all people were leaving calmly, till soon the forecourt was empty but for Silvanius, the priests and the augur, Felix, Saturninus and Balbus, who all crowded around the altar. Vitalis had vanished. The only other people left on the site were about twenty slaves and building workers, gathered in an anxious group near the steps leading down to the street. It was a sorry and depressing scene, so utterly different from an hour ago.

"This is the Shadow-men's work all right," I said to Quintus. "The deaths of the tribunes are bad enough in themselves, but they've been deliberately associated with the new temple, to make it seem contaminated and unclean. Poor Clarus! Everyone will think the gods have turned against him. How can we prove that this is a mortal crime, not a divine omen?"

"Evidence," Quintus said. "Facts. When were the murders committed? Where? How were the bodies carried into a closed sanctum in the middle of a temple full of people? The answers have to be here somewhere. All we have to do is find them."

The obvious thing would have been to start by talking to as many people as possible, collecting eyewitness accounts. But as we approached the altar, we could see that everyone was too upset to respond well to being questioned. The two priests stood close together, talking in hushed tones and looking frightened; Felix was mopping his eyes; Silvanius was weeping noisily, sitting on one of his ornamental stone tubs, a picture of misery. Balbus and Saturninus stood nearby, helpless, yet not wanting to leave a friend in such trouble.

"It's a complete disaster!" Silvanius was moaning. "Such a blasphemy! A dreadful omen! The gods must hate me very much, to punish me like this. But what have I done to offend them? All I wanted was to give them honour….How can I have brought down such anger?"

And more in the same vein. The poor man was devastated.

"Listen, Clarus," I said. "This *isn't* an omen from the gods. Truly it isn't. That's what it's meant to look like, but the gods didn't do this. Mortal men did it, the Shadow-men did it, to try to convince everyone that the gods are angry. But they aren't."

"You think not? You believe these are more of the Shadow-men's killings?"

"I do, and I believe we can prove it. We've got to investigate what's happened here, and the priests must carry out the rituals needed to cleanse a holy place after death has touched it. You should go home, Clarus, and rest for now. Quintus and I will take care of things here, and stay until the priests have got started on their rituals. Felix, why don't you take Silvanius home? Balbus, Saturninus, you go too. We'll follow on later."

They all went off meekly, relieved to let somebody else take charge.

We stood at the doorway of the sanctuary. "Now it's up to you and me," I said. "Where do we start?"

"With the bodies," he answered. "Let's go and say a last farewell to Junius and Marius."

Chapter XXV

"First of all, we need some privacy." Quintus beckoned the building foreman, Lentus, and also Taurus and Brutus.

"I want the whole temple site kept private," he told them. "Nobody is to come in. If anyone asks for me or Mistress Aurelia, escort them to us personally. Understand?"

They all nodded and were turning to go when I said, "Lentus, have you been here on the site since dawn?"

"I have, Mistress. We all have."

"Did you go into the sanctum?"

"I looked in there first thing. It was spick and span, as it should be. Then the priests did the purification ritual, and after that we weren't allowed. They left one of their little acolytes standing outside the entrance to guard it. Well, sitting, mostly—he was only a kid and he kept dozing off. But none of us could have got in past him. Or would have," he added righteously.

Quintus had picked up my drift. "So how do you reckon the two bodies could have been carried into the sanctum, with a boy standing guard, and only one entrance in full view of the forecourt?"

He looked uncomfortable. "Can't rightly say, sir."

Quintus sighed. "Silvanius is talking about having all the slaves here tortured, to give evidence in court. We were hoping, if anybody could tell us anything useful, he would change his mind."

"I'm a freedman," Lentus said quickly. "They can't torture me. Not that I know anything, anyway."

"They could torture you under the new Lex Domitiana," I suggested.

"The which?"

"The Lex Domitiana. It says that if a freedman doesn't give evidence voluntarily when asked by his patron, and then he's found later to have important knowledge which he's held back, he can be deprived of his freedom, and then tortured because he's a slave again."

"Never heard of that before," Lentus grumbled. "Is it true? Really?"

I turned to Quintus. "I've got it right, haven't I?"

"Absolutely."

"Well...I suppose there is one way it could have been done," Lentus said reluctantly. "I'm not sure, mind." We waited. "I'd better show you. And if I do, this new law, it can't apply to me?"

We shook our heads, and Quintus said, "Definitely not. Aurelia and I will both be witnesses that you've volunteered all the information you have."

"All right then. This way, round the back." We followed as he led us round the outside of the sanctum, to its rear wall. We were hidden from most of the site here; we couldn't see the forecourt or the altar, and nobody there could see us. Lentus walked along about half the wall's length to a massive stone tub with a bay tree in it. It looked well against the smooth white surface, but I noticed some spilt earth on the paving round about. Somebody had skimped on the cleaning-up. Not all that surprising in the general rush.

"Can you help me move this tree, sir, please?" Lentus said to Quintus.

They shifted the heavy thing away from the wall. Behind it, the surface wasn't so smooth, though it was still white; but a whole section of it, about two feet tall by three feet across, was marked out by a noticeable hair-line crack. When Lentus thumped it with his fist, it rang hollow.

"A false wall!" Quintus exclaimed. "Just a sheet of wood?"

Lentus nodded. He took a small knife from a sheath on his belt and stuck the point into the crack; he gave a practised twist, and the whole section of white wood came away. We could see through the gap into the sanctum, and found ourselves looking straight at Junius and Marius as they lay under the marble table.

"Who knew about this?" Quintus demanded.

"We all did. Except the master. Well, we didn't want to trouble him. With him being so busy, and all."

"I bet."

"It was only a small thing," the foreman said defensively. "We were going to make good the hole with stone as soon as all the ceremonials were out of the way."

"But why is it there?" I asked. "It can't have been designed like that?"

"Drains," Lentus sighed. "That floor ain't laid right, it slopes inwards, so any liquid would collect at the back here—blood from the sacrifices, water from the purifying, that sort of thing. It was meant to slope to one side, see, where there's a drain-hole to carry everything away. Stupid tilers the master brought in, couldn't lay an egg, never mind a decent marble floor. Mind you, to be fair, it was all being done in a hurry. By the time we realised, the walls was nearly up, so we had two choices—either take the whole building down and start again, or else put in a false wall, so we could sort out the drainage from the back."

I'll skip all the technical stuff about levels and pipe diameters. The point was, we now knew how the bodies had got into the sanctum.

Quintus said, "Thank you, Lentus, that's very helpful. Now, have you any idea who brought those bodies into the sanctum this morning?"

"No, sir, I haven't. And you can torture me or do what you like, but that's all I know."

Quintus dismissed him, and we went back inside.

"Lex Domitiana," he murmured. "An interesting little piece of legislation. Remind me when it was passed, exactly?"

"Given our present Caesar and his paranoia about Palace freedmen, any time now, I should think."

He grinned "So we know how they were moved, but not who by, or where from. Or who killed them. Still, it's a start." He bent down for a close look at the two figures lying side by side. "They have no wounds on them. It must have been poison of some kind. With two fit young soldiers, the killers probably didn't want to risk force. Poison would be easier."

"Their servants said they were with some young Brigantians last night. They must have been lured into a trap."

Quintus nodded grimly, and gently touched Marius' face, peering closely at the mouth; then he touched Junius' and recoiled as if he'd been burned. "Gods, Aurelia, he's still warm. I think he may be still alive!"

So he was, but his pulse was very weak. We carried his limp body outside into the sunshine, and Quintus said, "We must get the poison out of his system. Make him sick."

I'll draw a veil over exactly how we did this. Just take it from me that we made him very sick, and it worked. Lying in front of the sanctum, on some sacking we borrowed from the builders, he slowly dragged himself back to consciousness. A groggy and uncertain consciousness, but nevertheless, he opened his eyes and saw us, and knew us.

He looked very boyish and vulnerable; his sandy hair was damp with sweat, and his light-grey eyes had trouble focusing. I crouched down on the ground beside his head, and took hold of his hand, which was icy cold. I said softly, "Junius, you're all right. You're safe, and you're among friends. This is Quintus Antonius Delfinus. Can you tell us what happened to you?"

"Oh gods!" He gave a moan, and licked his lips.

"Shall I get you some water?" I asked.

"No," Junius said hoarsely. "It will…spread…the poison."

Gods, he thinks he's dying. Perhaps he is. But he was speaking again, and I had to concentrate to hear him.

"Tell Lucius I'm sorry. I've made a complete mess of things."

"What happened?" Quintus asked.

"We met two natives by the river. A girl and a boy. They said they'd take us to see the Chief, but we'd have to wait a while…. They gave us some of their mead. I realised it was poisoned, but too late. Don't remember any more. Where's Marius?"

"Dead, I'm afraid," Quintus answered gently.

"It's best. He was helping the Shadow-men."

"We realised," Quintus interrupted. "How long have you known?"

"After the eclipse. He kept getting separated. I tried and tried but…couldn't change his mind. They wanted me to join too. I thought, if I pretended to go along, I could learn…and report back…so I let them think I sympathised…said I'd help. Tried to stay with Marius…stop him doing too much harm."

"Oh, gods, Junius, if only we'd known. You were playing a very dangerous game!"

"I should have told Lucius. But I kept thinking, just one more day, just a few more hours, and I'll know everything. And then when Albia was in danger…I didn't want even to pretend any more. I told Marius I'd die rather than hurt Albia….I'm sorry." He began to cough, and was sick again.

I wiped his mouth and smoothed the hair back from his face. "Junius, tell us all you can. Have you seen the Shadow of Death?"

"Only with the mask on." His breathing was ragged. "He's tall and fair…carries himself well. And from what they say… it's not…not…." He had another spasm of coughing. "Not for money. For revenge. Find…a Roman who hates Rome."

"We'll find him," Quintus promised. "And you'll help us, when you're better. Now, did you get any idea where their hideout is?"

"I heard them mention the 'house in the rock.' They said…. it's so secret, nobody will find it."

"House on the rock?" Quintus said thoughtfully. "Surely there are dozens of houses built on rocks on the hillsides?"

Junius gave a tiny shake of his head. "No. Not on…*in* the rock. Maybe a cave…."

Quintus turned to me. "Are there any caves near here?"

"Not that I know of."

"What else did you get, Junius?" Quintus asked.

But Junius began coughing again. His skin was greyish; sweat stood out on his face, and his eyes were starting to glaze. He wasn't going to recover, and there wasn't much time.

"Have you any message for Albia?" I asked. Quintus glared at me for changing the subject, but Junius smiled.

"Yes. Tell her I love her. Too late now. Tell her…and tell my father…I died for Rome." His eyelids closed, and he slipped back into unconsciousness. We both tried to rouse him, but a short while later he died.

I felt a numbing sadness. Here was the ruin of a lively, intelligent young officer, not much more than a boy; whether he'd only pretended to be tempted along with his friend we would never know, but in the end he was killed by the Shadow-men because he wouldn't be a part of their campaign of terror against the girl he loved. Poor Junius, and poor Albia. I sent a silent prayer to the gods of the Underworld to receive him kindly.

"We can tell his father he died for Rome," I said to Quintus. "And Albia too. Can't we?"

He looked at me doubtfully. "You don't think he was seriously helping the enemy?"

"Who knows? I doubt it, but…anyway, he came back to us in the end. Does it matter now?"

He shrugged. "No. No, it doesn't." Suddenly he swore. "So close," he muttered. "So very close. Gods, what an idiot! If he had to try something so dangerous, why couldn't he have at least let Lucius know, then perhaps we could have given him some support. He must have realised they would kill him if they thought he was slipping away from them, and knew too much about them."

I felt tired and depressed by it all. "Gods, Quintus, why is everything such a mess?"

"If you don't like mess, you shouldn't be working with an investigator. It goes with the job."

"Your job. Not mine. And I just feel…."

"You just feel sad, and so do I, but there isn't time. We have to concentrate on catching the Shadow of Death. Later there'll be time to be sad." He took my hand and held it as he went on: "The Shadow-men are very sure of themselves, to kill two Roman officers and leave them in such a public place in broad daylight. If you ask me, the whole rebellion is about to erupt. Like a volcano that's been rumbling, and suddenly starts spitting rocks and fire."

He shivered in spite of the heat. Like me, just for a few heartbeats, he was remembering Pompeii.

"Junius said the Shadow of Death is a Roman who hates Rome," I mused. "Which ties in with that cryptic remark the old Druid made. 'When love feels itself betrayed....' He meant love of country, not of a person."

"There are still three people who have grudges against Rome. Balbus, and Felix, and of course Vitalis. All of them in a position to be using the natives here to get revenge."

"We've already agreed that the traitor isn't either Felix or Balbus. They've both had something they valued destroyed by the rebels. The one person who hasn't lost or suffered anything so far is Vitalis. And he's a Roman who hates Rome, if ever I met one."

"I agree. We can go on forever, supposing and speculating about bluffs and double bluffs, but I think we should accept the answer that's staring us in the face. The Shadow of Death has to be Vitalis."

I got to my feet, brushing the dust off my tunic. "Then let's not waste any more time."

Quintus stood up too. "He's presumably at Silvanius' villa now. We'll go straight there and arrest him. Then I'll borrow a couple of your men and escort him to Eburacum to be locked up."

But Vitalis wasn't at the villa. The door-slave said he hadn't returned there since the disaster at the temple.

We were shown into the beautiful dining-room. It was decorated with flowers and greenery, and the tables were crammed with delicious food. Silvanius was sitting in solitary state, looking utterly miserable.

"Valerius, Aurelia, you must forgive me," he said, getting up to greet us. "I'm afraid I'm poor company. I sent my friends home. I—I'm not feeling very sociable."

Quintus said, "I'm sorry, Councillor, this isn't a social call. I'm here to ask for your help officially. I'm afraid I've been less than truthful about my presence in Oak Bridges. I'm here to investigate the native trouble in this area." He produced one of his high-powered government passes and handed it to Silvanius, who examined it carefully and exclaimed, "My dear Valerius, if you're on the Governor's service, I'm yours to command. Whatever you need, just name it."

"Thank you. Aurelia has been helping me," Quintus went on. "And we're getting close to finding out who's leading the Campaign of Terror."

"Good," Silvanius said. "Very good. May I know who you think it is?"

"I'm not quite ready to make it public," Quintus replied. "But as Chief Councillor, you'll be among the first to know when I do. But now we need to have a word with your son. I gather he's not here. Do you know where he's gone?"

"I'm afraid I don't," Silvanius said sadly. "I haven't seen him since I left the temple."

"You're quite sure? You've no idea at all?"

"No. No, I haven't. And I must admit I'm quite worried about him. He's been keeping bad company, I'm afraid, seeing too much of some of the anti-Roman youngsters in this district. I didn't take it seriously to start with. I thought it was just young men showing off. But now...." He looked close to tears.

"You think he may be involved with the Shadow-men?" I prompted.

"The way he behaved at the temple just now!" Silvanius burst out. "He didn't seem concerned at the dreadful thing that happened. He didn't even seem surprised. He just stood there and smiled. I asked him to stay and help me, and he turned away and walked off. And now he's gone. It isn't...it isn't the way I expected my son to behave."

"No," Quintus said. "I'm afraid you've good reason to be worried. We think he's gone further than mere youthful foolishness. He's got himself deeply involved with the rebels."

"Oh, dear gods!" Silvanius put his head in his hands, then he seemed to get control again and looked up. "What are you going to do? Can you—I mean is there anything you can do to help him? He's only a boy, and if he's done wrong, then...." He trailed off, conscious of Quintus' unwavering stare.

"We must find him and talk to him," Quintus said. "If he decides to co-operate with us, and helps with my investigation... well, let's just say that's his best course of action. You understand me, I think."

Silvanius nodded silently. He knew as well as anyone in the province the price that's paid by rebels.

"Meanwhile," Quintus went on, "may we talk to your major-domo? He might have some idea where Vitalis has gone."

But the major-domo had nothing to add. He confirmed that Vitalis had not been home since leaving for the temple ceremony earlier in the morning.

"We all assumed he would be attending the master's celebration dinner," the man said. "With the—ah—the change of plan now, I'm afraid I don't know what he will do. His body-slaves could help, perhaps?"

But a search failed to find Vitalis' three personal slaves. They had vanished like their master.

Quintus said, "Councillor, I must ask you to get word to me immediately if you hear any news of his whereabouts."

Silvanius nodded. "Yes, of course. There may be a perfectly innocent explanation for his disappearance."

And if there is, I thought, I'm the Queen of Brigantia.

We had various practical arrangements to make, so Silvanius lent us the use of a room and a secretary. He even provided lunch—his major-domo brought us a tray of food and wine, and we ate as we worked.

We sent a message asking Saturninus to join us, and in the privacy of our borrowed room, we outlined enough of the case to explain to him why we wanted Vitalis arrested. He wasn't particularly surprised, and undertook that he and his lads would keep a sharp lookout for Vitalis, but we all knew it was unlikely they'd catch sight of him. He had presumably gone to ground in his hideout, but Saturninus was as baffled as I was by the name "house in the rock."

The tribunes' bodies were sent off to Eburacum in a good stout cart, with an escort of four of Saturninus' toughest patrol men, plus Junius' servant. Marius' man had disappeared. Quintus dictated letters of explanation for the garrison commander, and for the commander of the Ninth Hispana, the tribunes' legion. I wrote a few lines to Lucius, hoping my wandering brother would soon be there to read them.

By mid-afternoon we'd done all we could, and Milo drove us home. I felt sorry to leave Silvanius all alone, sunk in such complete despair, but I needed to get back to the mansio, where another gloomy task awaited me—to tell Albia about Junius. But by the time we reached the Oak Tree, she'd heard the gist of it already; I should have known such hot news would spread at lightning speed. I found her alone in the garden, crying her eyes out.

She was heartbroken at the news of Junius' death, and frantic to be reassured that her lover hadn't been a traitor. I repeated what he'd said before he died, word for word, and more than once, till she understood that Marius had been the only one to betray us. As Quintus and I had already decided, if Junius had blotted his papyrus and been tempted by the rebels, he'd made amends at the finish; it comforted Albia to regard him as a fallen hero, and this no doubt would be some consolation to his father as well.

As the shadows grew longer I was doing my rounds outside, with Taurus close by in case I needed a guard, when I caught sight of a thin brown-green figure flitting round a corner into the apple orchard. I followed among the trees, and greeted him.

"Hawk! You're a welcome sight. You've heard what happened at the new temple?"

He nodded sadly. "I have. A dreadful impiety. There doesn't seem to be any end to the evil these Shadow-men will do. How's poor Albia?"

"Pretty devastated. But at least she knows for sure that Marius, not Junius, was the traitor."

"I've some news for you," Hawk said. "Well, for Quintus Valerius, about the Druid ceremony. It'll be tonight, as soon as it's full dark. Down near the river, in that clearing where the mistletoe has magically sprung up."

"Tonight? Excellent! Thanks, Hawk."

He looked doubtful. "Not quite the reaction I'd expected. It means trouble for you, you know. They plan to attack the mansio again."

"I'd prefer to face the trouble head-on than have to wait for it, not knowing when it'll catch up with me."

"Is Valerius still intending to go to the ceremony?"

"We both are. We're hoping we may discover who are their secret supporters."

"You're going too? For Epona's sake! I hope you know what you're doing."

"I hope so too! But my mind's made up. We'll be well disguised. Are you planning to go along there yourself?"

"Yes, I'll take a look. But I'm used to being invisible. You two….Try just this once to make less noise than a herd of charging aurochs!" He turned to go, then swung back to face me. "You haven't seen my son Teilo anywhere, have you? He's been in the woods, still looking for your boy Titch, and he isn't home yet. I don't want him out after dark."

"Not a sign, I'm afraid. I'm beginning to be quite worried about young Titch. If he'd simply been driven away from the mansio and got lost somehow, he should have come back to us by now."

Hawk grunted. "Boys wouldn't be boys if they didn't get into mischief! Still, if you do see Teilo, send him home straight away, will you? And Aurelia...."

"What?"

"Don't take any chances tonight. May your gods protect you both." He melted away into the trees.

I went to find Quintus. He was delighted with Hawk's news, and like me, relieved to know when the next attack would come. We held a brief council of war with Albia, Brutus, Hippon and Taurus, and then set about getting together a couple of good disguises. It would be dark in the woods, and we intended to stay well hidden among the trees, but we didn't need Hawk to remind us not to take any chances.

By the time we'd finished, helped by Albia and Carina, I don't think our own mothers would have recognised us. Quintus looked like an old farmer in a worn brown tunic made of hemp, sloppy sandals, and a dingy brown cloak with a hood which hid most of his head. Albia dyed his hair with some black liquid which had the effect of darkening it to a sort of muddy brown, and after a bit of experimenting, used the same stuff on his face and hands to give them a genuine weather-beaten colour. I borrowed some red hair-dye from Carina, and actually it looked better on me than on her; a grey tunic, a tattered blue hooded cloak, and shabby black boots finished off my outfit nicely.

It seemed almost a game, this dressing-up; we found we were light-hearted, cracking jokes, and full of confidence. And Albia, who had the hardest part, staying behind and guarding the mansio, put on a brave face for us. I've never appreciated her or loved her more than I did that evening, because only I, who know her well, realised what an effort she was making.

We brought the animals in well before dark, and set sentries; Albia kept everyone busy preparing hay-bundles and boiling pots of water. There was no knowing when the enemy would come, and it was possible Quintus and I would not get back in time to help.

At dusk we said goodbye to Albia, and cheerfully parried the sentries' ribald teasing as they barred the gate behind us. Only in the fading evening glow when we began to ride away from lights and people did I find myself wondering if I'd ever see the Oak Tree again.

Chapter XXVI

It wasn't quite dark, and the moon was about half full, although low in the sky. We had plenty of light, and we went by road on horseback as far as we safely could. When we reached the big holly-bush, we tethered our horses out of sight among the trees and walked quietly into the dark wood, along the small game-track that Hawk had used to bring us to see the mistletoe. It wasn't easy to follow the faint, twisting path in the patchy moonlight, but we had time to go cautiously, and we reached the clearing without incident.

The oaks all around it were dark, but the open space in the middle was brightly lit, and the river gleamed like pewter through the gap in the trees. We worked our way round to a point on the clearing's edge, about midway between the round-house and the river, but on the opposite side. From here, safely concealed in shadow, we could see the house as a blacker bulk looming in the dark of the wood, and the path that emerged from beside it, most of which was in shadow too. We had a good view of the whole clearing, which at present was empty, except for some statues and the large stone altar slab in the middle.

But small groups of people were walking along the shadowed path, some talking quietly, others glancing around, and all with a sense of excitement in their movements. They mostly wore dark cloaks and hoods, even though it was a warm night. The only exceptions were some youths dressed in full warrior gear, kilts and bronze-reinforced jerkins, bronze helmets with crests, shields and short swords. These young men came out briefly into the moonlight, and then disappeared into the shadows near the roundhouse, presumably to await their dedication.

The cloaked figures fanned out as they reached the end of the path, walking round the edges of the clearing and taking up positions all around, until eventually there was a ring of people two or three deep everywhere. They kept clear of the big open space, as this was the centre of their temple, if you can use that word—it was as different from Silvanius' Marble Monster as it was possible to imagine. They don't use buildings in their holy places; worshippers of the Druids' gods prefer to be in the open, with the trees for colonnades and the sky for a roof.

The big, flat altar stone, about ten feet square, was supported on short stone pillars so it was at about waist height off the ground. Near it in an arc with its open side towards the river were some wooden statues, crudely cut out of blocks or stumps of wood. They were grotesque figures of godlings, and to any civilised eye pretty horrible. There was one with a huge deformed head; one with three heads; several with no arms and one with no limbs at all, just a torso and a head with horns. The only half-decent carvings were of animals: a horse, a boar, and a bird with outstretched wings.

I couldn't see the point of such ugly things, and when I remembered the beautiful bronzes in Silvanius' temple, I felt an oppressive foreboding. If the statuary was so hideous, what could we expect the ritual itself to be like?

There was another big, square slab of stone, lower than the first because it wasn't on pillars, which must be either a table or a smaller altar, near where the path came out of the wood. I noticed that most of the people strolling past it paused briefly to glance at the carvings on it, which were a series of human heads. Then I was nearly sick, because I realised they weren't carved heads; they were real ones.

I nudged Quintus and pointed, but he'd already seen them. I tried to count them—more than a dozen, but it was too horrible. So I sent up a quick prayer to Diana, hoping she was near even in this alien setting. "Don't abandon us just when we've come to confront the barbarians' gods," I prayed. "Protect us now, and help us."

And in my head, a thought, almost a voice came to me: "Don't be afraid. I will protect you." I've never managed to explain this properly, to myself or anyone else; all I know is, hearing the goddess herself speak to me was like wonderful music, or a draught of strong wine. I felt a sudden rush of courage, and was ready for anything.

It was full dark now, and no more people were arriving in the clearing. There was a tense, expectant feel in the air. We strained our eyes looking at the dark figures, but it was impossible to recognise anybody. "I can't identify anyone," Quintus whispered crossly. "Can you?"

"No. They're all wearing hoods. I'd be lucky to spot my own grandmother."

"I'd be rather surprised to spot mine," he whispered back, and he smiled at me and touched my hand. "Disappointing though. I bet we'd know some of the faces if we could only see."

We were talking in British. Although we were careful to keep our voices very low, we couldn't risk anyone overhearing Latin. I moved closer till we were just touching, which made me feel safer. "I wish they'd get on with it, whatever it is," I murmured, and as if on my cue, the ceremony started.

First came the low, powerful boom of drums: two of them, beating slowly and quietly but insistently, like a pulse. Then the rhythms became quicker and more complicated, and after a while a couple of flutes joined in, each weaving its own melody, making weird harmonies and patterns of sound. It was quite unlike any music I'd ever heard—wild, savage, undisciplined, and compelling. The rhythm was becoming gradually faster, leading on to a climax, and I felt the power of it, even though I didn't want to; the pulse got into my very bones, vibrating in my blood.

We couldn't spot the musicians at first, but eventually picked them out just in front of the ruined house, in the shadows where they could watch the clearing but not be seen. I don't know how long the music went on before we saw movement on the path, and a Druid stepped out from the dark trees into the full light of the moon and began chanting. He was an imposing figure, tall and stately, in white robes with a silver belt, and a silver head-dress with white birds' feathers that fluttered as he moved his head.

He stood alone for a few heartbeats, and then out into the light strode another imposing figure, tall and slim, in full war-gear, with bright silver buckles and studs which flashed in the moonlight; he had a silver crest on his helmet, and carried a long sword. And I recognised him by his movements. Vitalis!

He stood beside the priest, who raised his hands and prayed, using an archaic dialect, some form of religious language presumably, but it was near enough to the modern Britons' speech for us to follow. He prayed to Taranis the Thunderer to bring victory to their tribe, and to give courage and strength to the new soldiers who were to be dedicated tonight.

Vitalis turned and beckoned, and a dozen young warriors came out of the trees. The moonlight reflected off the metal of their armour and helmets, making them look like dream soldiers of silver. Vitalis presented each of the youths to the Druid, and each of them laid an offering of bread and mead in front of the altar, and took his place in a line facing the Druid and Vitalis.

Then the Druid moved to the foot of the tree with the mistletoe sticking out of it. He intoned another prayer, thanking his gods for showing their favour by allowing the holy plant to grow on the oak, and then three more Druids came out of the shadows, holding a large white cloth between them, for all the world as if they were off to shake down apples.

The next part was pure theatre. The first Druid took up a small sickle which glowed darkly in the moonlight; it was bronze presumably, although I'd heard stories about them using gold tools in their rituals, but a real gold sickle wouldn't have cut a piece of cheese. He held it aloft for everyone to admire, and then, with impressive agility, he climbed up the oak tree and cut off a tuft of the mistletoe, letting it fall into the middle of the white cloth which his three assistants were holding ready underneath. It was neatly done, especially as he had to be careful not to pull too hard on the mistletoe, or he'd dislodge the entire clump in one go, which would give the game away, even to gullible natives.

So far the whole event struck me as rather trivial—entertaining and dramatic, like a well-made play, but not alarming. Then abruptly the tone became more sinister. The three Druids with the mistletoe went and placed it reverently, still on its white cloth, in front of one of the crude statues, and then disappeared, returning straight away with a young white bull which they led on a rope. It was a nice-looking beast, strong and sturdy with long horns, and it had presumably been drugged, as it was placid, with drooping head and gently swishing tail. They led it to the altar without trouble, and the senior Druid cried, "O gods of our fathers, accept this sacrifice and grant us your favour!" Then he swung his sickle and cut its throat. It fell with a subdued bellow. One of the other priests held a small cauldron out to catch its blood, but then they put the cauldron aside and let the blood simply drip down over the edge of the big, flat stone, and each of the Druids in turn bowed low beside the altar, letting the blood spatter onto them. The congregation gave a kind of sigh of content, and I tried to distract my mind from the horrible spectacle by sparing a thought for the laundry slaves who'd be expected to wash all the blood off those snow-white ceremonial robes. But silly flippant thoughts couldn't help me now; this was deadly serious, and I felt the tension mounting with every heartbeat.

Then the young warriors came forward one by one, and the chief Druid dipped a finger into the cauldron of blood, and made a mark on each man's forehead. The drumming increased its tempo, and a cymbal added its clashing rhythm. Then the flutes took up another eerie tune, joined by some double-pipes, weaving yet more strands of melody in and out.

My throat was dry. Now we were getting to the heart of the dedication. The warriors in front of the altar began to dance in line, leaping and gyrating, making thrusts with their swords in a vivid imitation of battle. They formed a column and made a circuit of the clearing, displaying themselves to the tribe. Their movements were violent and strong, representing real fighting, not a theatrical parody, yet these were fit and well-trained young men, so they contrived to be graceful too. In any other circumstances I might have enjoyed the show, and the congregation certainly did; they started stamping in rhythm with the drums, their bodies swaying in time, and some of the men, presumably the older warriors, repeated the less energetic movements of the dancers.

The procession came back to the altar, and the warriors re-formed their line. There was a thunderous clash from the cymbals, and the youths leapt high in the air, uttering their war-cry; then they knelt down, laying their weapons and helmets in front of them. As they waited there, I was surprised to notice that Vitalis had disappeared, and somebody had cleared the bull's body from the altar. We had all been too engrossed in the dancing to notice. For all its primitive trappings, this ceremony was efficiently organised.

The senior Druid swung round to face away from the river, and raised his hand. The music faded and died. He called out, "Let the Shadow of Death accept the newest warriors into our tribe," and from the darkness near the roundhouse stepped a tall figure. He strode out, clothed in kilt and scale armour, with a big helmet and a drawn sword. His face was hidden by a mask in the form of a skull.

He was a horrible and yet awe-inspiring sight, with his death-mask and staring eye-holes, like something out of one's worst nightmare, grotesque and unfamiliar. I'd assumed that when I actually saw the Shadow of Death, I would recognise the man behind the mask, but this apparition didn't look like anyone I'd ever seen. Well of course it didn't, that was the whole point! The handsome, familiar figure of Vitalis had been transformed into something alien and frightening.

There was complete silence in the clearing, and a vibrating tension in the air that you could have cut with a knife, even a real gold one. I didn't know what was coming next, but it was easy to tell it was to be the high point of the ceremony.

The tall, masked figure announced in ringing tones: "The time has come to seek for guidance from our gods. We pray to the Dagda and to Taranis and to the Three Mothers, and to all the holy ones of this river and this wood. Send us a sign that these young men, the flower of our tribe, will be acceptable to you, to fight and die in your service. Receive this our sacrifice, and give us your blessing." He raised a hand in signal, and out from the shadows came two more Druids, holding between them a skinny boy with an angular face and hair that, despite the deceptive light, I recognised as red.

Titch!

The world seemed to lurch, the ground to heave under my feet, and I opened my mouth to scream. I knew that when I did we'd be dead; but I also knew I couldn't stand there silent and watch them murder Titch.

I felt a sharp pain in my arm. Quintus was pinching me so hard he drew blood, and I gasped, but it brought me to my senses and I made no real sound. I stood there feeling sick and numb, and not knowing what to do. But I must do *something*. Quintus probably wouldn't do anything, I thought with a sudden surge of bitterness. When I'd rushed out to protect the foal he'd told me I was stupid to take risks. Well, stupid or not, I'd have to think of some way to get the boy out. I measured the distance between the altar and us. If I raced out into the clearing creating as much din as possible, causing a diversion, perhaps he could make a run for it. He looked half-asleep, as if he was drugged like the bull, but knowing Titch he could be pretending, waiting for his chance. Working out what the great Julius Caesar would have done....

The great Julius Caesar would have had half a legion of soldiers to back him up in a situation like this. I knew I was quite mad, even thinking of rescuing him. And yet…I had to do something.

"It's Titch," I whispered in Quintus' ear. "We've got to get him out."

He leaned close, shaking his head. "No," he breathed. "Not Titch."

"It is—"

"No, Aurelia. I swear. It's not."

I looked again. They had brought the boy to the altar stone, for everyone to see in the silvery light; he wore a skimpy tunic and no shoes, and stood upright but swaying slightly between his captors. Yes, surely it was Titch!

"His hair's too long," came the whisper in my ear. "Look. Titch had short hair. It's like him, but it isn't. I promise."

As I stared and stared, I realised that Quintus was right. This was a similar-looking youngster, short and wiry, but his hair grew down past his ears. Titch's ears stuck out. Whatever else had happened in the few days he'd been missing, Titch couldn't have grown so much hair on his head.

An enormous flood of relief engulfed me; then immediately I felt guilty. This lad, whoever he was, was about to be murdered in a disgusting ritual. But we couldn't help. I knew we couldn't do anything.

The senior Druid stepped up to the boy, this time holding a long, shiny dagger. "Do you go willingly as a sacrifice to the immortal gods?" he asked.

The lad muttered something, so quietly we couldn't hear it. The priest chose to interpret it as "Yes," because he announced loudly, "Bear witness, all folk here assembled, that this prisoner goes willingly to meet his fate." Then he said to the boy, in a quieter, almost kindly tone, "Though in your life you were an enemy of us and our gods, yet now you have the chance to make amends, by giving yourself to death. Your soul will live on. Death is not the end of life, just a stage upon the way."

He nodded to the two priests holding the boy. They turned him so that his back was to the Druid, who grasped his knife and plunged it into the lad's body at the base of his spine. He made a sound halfway between a groan and a sob as he fell forward onto the altar, and his blood mixed with the bull's blood. All three of the Druids paid careful attention, looking closely as he fell and lay face down. The omens were being interpreted from the way he twitched as he died. I closed my eyes, I couldn't watch.

There was a pause, and then the senior priest addressed the others. "What are the omens?"

"The omens are good," each man answered in turn. I opened my eyes again.

"The omens are good!" the senior Druid proclaimed. "The sacrifice is pleasing to the gods." He turned to face the kneeling warriors. "The gods accept you, and I proclaim you warriors in the service of the Shadow of Death, full and trusted members of the Shadow-men!"

There was a huge cheer from the crowd, and from the youths too as they leapt up, put on their helmets and grasped their swords, and started to dance around the big stone. Their gyrations were wilder than ever, and their leaping bodies hid the altar and its sad sacrifice, until they started in procession round the clearing again. The tension was gone now, the air full of joyous, exultant music.

Eventually the triumphant dancers returned and formed their line once more before the altar, standing proud and tall in their armour, the sweat shining on their faces. The Shadow of Death, who stood beside the Druid, beckoned to a tall lad, apparently the leader of the group. He approached, and bowed first to the Druid, then to the masked chief.

"Are you ready to take your oath before the gods of this place, and before the people of your tribe?" the Shadow of Death asked.

"We are," declared the young warrior.

"And are you all of the same mind?"

"We are," they said in chorus.

"Speak the oath," the chief commanded.

The tall lad took a breath. "I swear that I will not rest content until we have restored to the gods the holy place known as Dru

Nemeton, which is now defiled by the Romans. I dedicate my life and my sword to killing every Roman who lives there, and tearing down their buildings, so that the gods may once again come into their own. I swear this by Taranis and by the gods of the wood and of the river." He stepped up to the Shadow of Death and knelt, holding out his sword. The Chief touched it, and gestured the lad to rise.

There was a low growl of assent from the crowd. Then each of the other new warriors took the same oath and presented his sword. That's how I come to know it by heart. Not that I needed to hear it more than a couple of times, for those foul promises to be burned into my brain.

With each dedication the crowd's approving roar was louder. As the last lad said his piece and offered his sword, the whole clearing erupted into a battle-yell. The Druid raised his arms, and called out, "Go then, to battle and to glory!"

The crowd cheered itself hoarse, and the ceremony was at an end. The priests walked back into the shadows of the wood. The masked chief raised his sword and signalled the young warriors to follow him, and they formed a column and began to move off at a jog-trot, towards the river.

The suddenness of it caught both Quintus and me by surprise; we were used to more measured and formal rituals, I suppose. But the lads' excitement was at fever pitch, so it made sense to send them into battle straight away. And somebody, perhaps, had observed that Quintus and I were not among the defenders at the mansio.

We moved quickly back from the edge of the clearing and started as fast as we could, making for the track that led to our horses. We tried to run but it wasn't possible; the moon had almost set, its beams hardly reaching among the thick leaves, and we blundered clumsily through the shadowy trees and undergrowth, until we knew we were well and truly lost.

At last we stopped, breathless. "We can take our direction from the moon," Quintus said, "and head for the road, or for the river. Which is quicker?"

"The river path. But it's riskier—that's the way the warriors are going."

"They won't be hard to avoid. We can hear them whooping and yelling from here."

So we forced a way through till we could see the river glinting between the trees, and started moving along roughly parallel with it. We could hear men to our left, following the river bank, and occasional battle yells split the air. Now the darkness was to our advantage, and we'd almost reached the first of our paddocks when there was a sudden shout very close to us, and three men ran past, so near I was convinced they must see us. One of them yelled, "They went this way, towards the mansio! Call the others and circle them in! Don't let them get across the fields!"

"I think it's the innkeeper and the spy," another voice called out, slightly farther away, but still much too close for comfort. "Someone tell the Shadow of Death. He wants to be in at the kill."

"All Romans will be killed!" the first man bellowed, and there were whoops of delight from at least three directions, and several more voices took up the chant. "All Romans will be killed! All Romans will be killed!"

"They must have heard us thrashing about in the dark," Quintus breathed. "If we move now they'll hear us again."

"But if we stay put they'll surround us and trap us here."

"Can we get across the big paddock?"

"Not without being seen. We'll head for the round stone byre on this side of it."

"What?" He almost forgot to whisper. "We can't hide in that!"

"Yes we can. And there's cover from the trees most of the way. Come on!" I started forward, and heard him following me. We were in familiar territory now; Lucius and I had played in every part of these woods, and I knew my way, day or night. We kept to the shadows, and then for just fifteen paces had to race across open ground, full in the low moonlight. Nobody saw us.

The building's wide entrance was in shadow, facing away from the moon. I pulled Quintus inside. "There's a kind of loft at the back. Like a big shelf for hay."

He looked up and saw the rough boards over our heads. "Is there a ladder?"

"Stone footholds in the wall."

Easier said than done, when you were no longer an agile child; as I struggled upwards, clinging to the tiny protruding stones, I realised how many years it was since I'd climbed them. Quintus gave me a push from below and I scrambled over the edge of the boards; then he followed me up. The old timbers creaked, but they held; we burrowed down in the hay, right against the wall of the byre, in deep shadow. As we lay back, a loud voice nearby shouted, "Try that round byre there!"

Footfalls sounded at the entrance, and we hardly dared breathe as three figures came into the byre below us. Despite the darkness I made out that two of them were helmeted warriors with pale faces, but the third had a dark skull for a face. So the Shadow of Death had come, to be in at the kill.

If they'd had torches we'd have been caught, but they hadn't. They stood bunched together at the entrance, peering into what must have looked like total darkness. We were invisible to them, as long as we kept still and they stayed where they were.

One of them shouted, "They've got to be in here. There's nowhere else they could have gone."

"It's as empty as a beggar's purse," another voice exclaimed. "By Taranis, we were so close! We can't lose them now!"

"Come on then, back outside. They won't have got far!" the first man yelled, and the three of them went out, making too much noise to hear our sighs of relief.

I lay back on the hay, feeling utterly exhausted. Quintus slid his arm round my shoulders and pulled me close, and for a little while we were still. We weren't waiting to see if our pursuers would return, or planning our next move, or anything else rational; we just wanted to be together, and not to have to move out of that hay-loft for a very long time.

"Quintus," I whispered. "If it had been Titch the Druids were sacrificing, would you have tried to get him out?"

After a long pause he murmured, "No."

"But I would. I'd have had to do something. One of our own boys. I know you think that's stupid."

His arm tightened around me. "I think it's stupid, and wonderful. And if you'd tried, of course I'd have tried too."

There were a series of wild yells not far away outside, and some Druid cursing started. The Oak Tree was being attacked again, and we had to go and help.

The most direct way would have been to cross the paddocks, but that only took us up to the new fence, and was in moonlight too. We chose the longer route, skirting the fields through trees, and came out on the main road near our turning and our new gate.

We stopped where we could see the gate and part of the fence, and as we watched, half-a-dozen warriors started battering at the fence with a tree-trunk as before, roughly at the point where they'd broken through last time. Of course it had been repaired and strengthened, so that got them nowhere, and it wasn't long before lighted hay-bundles thrown from inside drove them back. But there were a good forty or fifty men outside the fence by now; the senior fighters had come to join the new young warriors, and already they were dividing up their forces into several sizable groups, to attack from different directions. If they did that, it was the end. Even with the good light, our people inside were stretched to the limit.

The defenders were throwing out their fireballs and pouring boiling water, and yelling taunts and challenges back at the screaming warriors. I recognised their familiar voices—Taurus, Hippon, Brutus, and Albia and several of the other girls. She'd got absolutely everyone out and fighting. Only there weren't enough of them. Unless we could do something quickly, the natives would get inside the stockade by sheer force of numbers.

"What can we do?" I breathed.

"Create a diversion," Quintus whispered. "Draw them off into the woods."

"They'll catch us for sure."

"No they won't. We'll separate. It's easy to hide in woods at night. In a thicket, up a tree. If we split up and lure them away, we can take cover till it's safe, and then repeat the process. Keep them guessing."

"It's the craziest idea I've ever heard!"

"Have you got a better one?" he smiled at me.

"No. All right, let's do it."

"We'll start along the road, then you head away from the river, and I'll go towards it. Good luck!"

Before I had time to answer, he took a deep breath and called out in his parade-ground yell, "This way, men! We'll split up and surround them. Fabius, take your lot round the back. The rest of you follow me!"

It certainly made the attackers stop and look around. And sure enough, when Quintus yelled again, several of them turned and began to run up the track towards the main road. Someone called out, "It's the girl and the spy! This time we've got them!"

"It's working!" Quintus said. "Let's move."

We ran down the road side by side, in full view. The exultant yells behind us got closer. "Vanish!" he called, and I swerved to the left, and ran thankfully into the safe darkness of the trees, while he headed into the shadows to the right.

I forced a way through the blackness, tripping over roots, catching my cloak, but always moving. There were some noises of pursuit from the direction of the road, but not very close; if I kept my head, and if the gods were with me still, I'd stay free....

Then my blood froze. I caught the baying of dogs, distant at first, but coming nearer, and there were whoops and yells of hunters encouraging their hounds to the chase. The dogs could pick up my scent and follow my trail in among the trees. Or maybe they'd follow Quintus? Well, if they did, he could get down to the river and walk along it for a bit, to lose his scent in

the water. Whereas here in the woods, my only option was....
There wasn't an option.

Keep calm, Aurelia, and search for a tree to climb. If I can
only get up onto a high branch, they won't find me. Or will the
dogs lead them to the base of my tree, and then....Just keep on
searching. Concentrate now. There *must* be a tree....

But they were all too tall, without any convenient lower
branches to give me a start. I was sweating and out of breath,
still trying to run, and panicking more with every step. Suppose
I couldn't find a hiding place? Suppose they caught me....

The pursuit sounded near, or was that just my frightened
imagination? No, they were closing in. And still there was no
tree that offered me a chance of climbing. It was pitch black;
they'd have to be more or less on top of me before they actually saw me, but with the dogs that wouldn't take long. O holy
Diana, I prayed, you're a hunter. Please, help me now. Show
me where to hide.

I made myself stop and listen, trying to decide which direction to take. And then amidst the hideous howling and yelling, I
heard quite a different sound, so unexpected I almost called out.

Hoofbeats!

A group of horses were cantering up the road from the Oak
Bridges direction, five or six, I guessed. But were they friends or
foes? Most likely they were neither; just casual passers-by, riding
home late and wanting no trouble, so they'd canter straight past,
ignoring us, and get on their way as fast as they could.

But could they be, could they *possibly* be, friends who would
help us? From town? From Eburacum even? Cavalry?

No, of course not, Aurelia. You're tired, you're scared, and
you're imagining things. Those horses probably aren't there at
all, you're just dreaming and wishing. Or if they are there, they'll
soon be gone again.

And then above the pounding hooves came a stentorian
Roman voice, yelling: "Squadron, to the Oak Tree! *Charge!*"

Chapter XXVII

The fight was over by the time I reached the mansio. The warriors, taken completely by surprise, scattered to the four winds, leaving the battle-field to five mounted men, or to be exact four men and a skinny red-headed boy, who was yelling and whooping for sheer delight.

"Titch!" I called. "Where did you spring from? And who are your friends? And, oh, I'm glad to see you, you rascal!"

"I've brought me dad," the boy grinned. "I reckoned we needed reinforcements."

Quintus appeared then, raced towards us, and ignoring me, ran straight up to the leading horseman and grasped his hand. "Secundus! You're a sight for sore eyes! How in the name of Mars did you manage this?"

The rider smiled. "Blame this young tyke." He gestured at Titch. "My son Gaius. He said you needed an extra man or two. Looks like he was right. You always did like to cut things fine, Quintus Antonius."

The big gate to the mansio flew open, and Albia and the defenders streamed out. Miraculously, none of them had been seriously hurt; Hippon was rubbing a bruised shoulder, and Brutus' face was covered in blood, but he assured us it was just a nose-bleed. And, equally wonderful, no serious damage had been done.

After a short outburst of joyous confusion Secundus held up his hand and called, "Hold hard, everyone! Let's steady down. The game's not over yet!"

"You're right," Quintus nodded. "They may come back. Though not tonight, I think. You've spoiled the climax to their dedication ceremony."

"What a shame." Secundus swung down from his horse, and the rest of his party followed his example.

Quintus said, "Aurelia…Albia? I'd like to introduce our rescuers, Gaius Varius Secundus, ex-cavalryman, and his friends."

We shook hands, but I couldn't take it in at first, so they all took a hand explaining it to me.

"I've known Secundus a long time," Quintus began. "We served together in Germania."

Secundus grinned "He was my officer for a while, when he was a proper soldier, before he skived off and started playing at spies. But I hadn't set eyes on him for a couple of years, till two days ago in Eburacum."

"I told you I looked up a good friend in Eburacum? It was Secundus. I'd no idea he was Titch's father, though."

"He comes to me and says, 'Secundus, there's a couple of fools dressed as cavalry, following me about and wanting to kill me.' So I says, 'We'll sort them out then,' and he leads the two of them into the woods, and we finish them off."

"Nice tidy job," Quintus said.

Secundus gave a contemptuous snort. "I should hope so! They were just a couple of amateurs. Anyhow, when that's done I says goodbye to Quintus Antonius, thinking it'll be another two years till I get to see his ugly mug again, and then yesterday morning early comes young Gaius, starving hungry and filthy dirty and half dead, saying his friends at the Oak Tree have been attacked, and he's escaped to get reinforcements, and he got lost in the woods in the dark…."

"Only Dad wasn't at home yesterday," Titch put in. "He didn't get back till last night, and then he had to get hold of his mates….I thought I'd go mad, waiting and fretting!"

"So here we are," Secundus finished. "Me and three good mates, at your service. But," he added solemnly, "there's one thing I do need to know."

"What is it?" I asked.

"Why, the most important question of all. Any chance of a drink?"

"As much as you like! Come in and get it!" I led the way into the bar, and when we'd all got wine-mugs in our hands, I raised mine and said, "A toast, to our rescuers! Thank you with all my heart!"

We drank, and then Secundus turned to Quintus. "Well now, what's the plan? Those beggars may not come back this night, but they'll try again tomorrow, I'd bet any money."

"No." Quintus smiled, not a nice smile though. "By this time tomorrow, with your help, we'll have killed their leader and put an end to their campaign of terror. Now we know for sure that the Shadow of Death is Vitalis, all we've got to do is catch him."

"*All* we've got to do?" I repeated. "Capture a rebel leader surrounded by a band of dedicated killers? Oh well, I'm glad it's not something difficult!"

I led Secundus to my study, along with Quintus, Albia, Brutus and Hippon. We took a couple of jugs of wine with us, and sat down around my desk to hold a council of war.

"First of all," I said, "does anybody know a place called the house in the rock? Junius told us it's the rebel headquarters, but the name means nothing to me. Perhaps a cave of some kind…. Anybody heard of it?"

They were all shaking their heads, when there was a commotion in the passage outside. One of the riders from Eburacum came in with a torch in one hand and a drawn dagger in the other, shepherding a slightly built figure cloaked in brown homespun and followed by a huge dog. "This native," he said, "wants to see Mistress Aurelia."

"Hawk! Come in and join us. It's all right," I added for the guard's benefit. "This man is a very good friend and he's welcome to come and go whenever he likes."

As the tracker entered the brightly lit study I was shocked by his appearance. He was pale as death, his eyes staring, his face drawn as if he was in pain.

"Can I have a word, Aurelia? In private?" His voice was low and strained.

"Yes, of course, if you want to. But these are friends here…"

"In private. Please."

I picked up a lamp and led him to our sitting-room. Quintus followed uninvited, but Hawk didn't seem to mind.

His shoulders sagged and his head bowed, and he collapsed into a chair as if his legs had given way. The dog flopped down at his feet.

I said, "Gods, Hawk, what is it? Are you hurt?"

But Quintus went to him and put a hand on his shoulder. "Hawk, I think I know. And I'm so sorry. So terribly sorry. I wish there was something we could have done, but there wasn't."

"Wasn't there? Are you sure?" He raised his head and his black eyes looked first at Quintus, then at me, and his voice had an angry edge.

"Done?" I said. "I don't understand."

"The boy," Quintus said, "at the Druid ceremony. I thought there was something familiar. Now I know."

Hawk slumped down again. "Yes. Teilo. My son."

I felt all the elation drain out of me. The red-headed boy that I'd mistaken for Titch! I'd been upset enough, thinking they were killing a lad I'd known for a matter of days. Hawk had watched them murder his own son. "Hawk, how dreadful! You saw, what they did to him?"

"Yes. I watched it all. I couldn't think of any way to save him. But I kept hoping you might have managed something. There were two of you!"

Quintus said, "There were about two hundred of them. What could we have done?"

"Something. You could have done *something!* We all could— we shouldn't have just stood there and watched."

"It's horrible!" My words were so inadequate. There were no words.

Quintus was talking gently, still standing beside Hawk. "No, there was no way any of us could have saved him. It would have ended with us getting killed, and the lad would have died just the same. We didn't realise it was your boy. Only when I saw your face just now, then I knew."

"When did they catch him?" I asked.

"Some time this afternoon, I suppose." He rubbed a hand across his eyes. "I should have taken better care of him, not made him go out in the woods on his own."

"He wanted to look for Titch," I said. "You couldn't have stopped him, you know you couldn't. This is all so awful for you, Hawk. Don't make it even worse by thinking it was your fault. None of it was."

"It's all so pointless!" He almost shouted the words, and raised his head, staring at us, challenging, blaming, I don't know what. He was hurting and he was angry, and there was nothing I could think of to make the pain or the anger any less.

"May the gods witness," he growled, "I swear by Epona's holy name, I'll kill their Shadow of Death, if it's the last thing I do! And as many of his men as I can find! I swear it."

"Tomorrow we'll do it," Quintus told him. "And if we take Vitalis alive, he's yours to do as you like with."

"Good."

"We're having a war council now, to work out the details. Come and help us plan."

"No," he muttered. "I'll be with you tomorrow, but I can't sit still now and just talk. I need to be out doing something."

"Can you help us find their hideout?" I suggested. "Junius told us it's called 'the house in the rock.' But we don't know where it is."

"I know somewhere that would fit the description," he said slowly. "It would make an ideal place, big enough to conceal a whole war-band, and yet quite innocent-looking from outside. I'll take a look at it tonight."

"Is it near here?" Quintus demanded.

"About six miles, I think."

"But it's still dangerous," I said. "And in the dark....Why not wait till daylight, then we'll all be there with you."

"I'll be safe enough. I know every yard of these woods, and if you're going to strike tomorrow, we need to know the exact lie of the land. I'll meet you in the morning, at the holly-bush where that small track runs from the road to the Druids' clearing." He stood up, strong now and grim-faced. "And if there are any Shadow-men still loose in the woods, I can start to take a blood-price for my son."

As he turned to stalk out, Titch burst into the room, his face full of horror.

"Hawk! They're saying Teilo is dead, the Druids killed him. Is it true?"

Hawk nodded. "They caught him in the woods. He was out looking for you." He gazed at the stricken boy, hard-faced. He was a fair-minded man, I knew, and he was struggling not to blame Titch outright for Teilo's death.

Titch was fighting back tears. "Oh, I'm so sorry! I'd give anything for it not to have happened. If I'd known, I'd never have gone away, I'd have stayed here and let them catch me instead. We were blood brothers."

Hawk's eyes sharpened. "You took the oath?"

Titch held his left hand out under the lamplight. Across the palm was a livid red knife-scar, not fully healed yet.

"I didn't know," Hawk said.

"It was the day of the storm."

Hawk glanced down at his own left hand; perhaps there was a scar there, from his own boyhood, but only the eyes of memory could see it now. He looked up again at Titch.

"So that was why he was so set on finding you. He was honour bound."

"I'd have done the same for him, Hawk. I would!"

"I know, boy." Suddenly the tracker sank down on a couch, and putting his head in his hands, began to sob. Titch sat down close to him, and Hawk blindly reached out and put an arm around his shoulders. Quintus and I left them alone.

We rejoined the others, and to fight off the sadness that threatened us, we made ourselves very brisk and businesslike, getting on with our plans for catching Vitalis. It would all be fairly straightforward if Hawk could indeed pinpoint the Shadow-men's headquarters for us. We had enough men to capture Vitalis, given that we'd have the element of surprise on our side. But if the tracker didn't find the exact place, we'd have to spread ourselves out in groups, making enquiries about Vitalis and those of his followers we knew by name. That would take much longer, and require more men, in which case we would send Secundus to Eburacum with a letter from Quintus, asking the garrison again for help.

By about two hours after midnight we were all dropping with tiredness. We changed the sentries outside, and Quintus and Secundus threw dice for who was going to take first watch. Quintus lost, which meant I went to bed alone. I was too excited to sleep much, and glad enough to be up and about well before it was light.

Chapter XXVIII

By dawn the wind was blowing from the west, bringing low cloud and rain. Not the weather I'd normally choose for a woodland expedition; but the wet ground would show tracks to perfection, so I was in a buoyant mood as I helped Albia serve everyone with bread and cheese and watered wine, except Quintus, who was sleeping late after his watch.

Two couriers from Eburacum rode through early, bringing a tale of two more murders just outside Oak Bridges, but not the usual sort. The victims weren't Roman travellers, they were two armed natives in war-gear, and they'd each been stabbed through the neck and left in the middle of the road. Hawk's work, for sure; we all cheered the news.

I was on my way to wake Quintus so we could give everyone a final briefing, when Carina appeared.

"Mistress, good news. The army have finally got off their backsides. There's a centurion with six soldiers outside just arrived."

"At last!" I felt a surge of relief. "Help from Eburacum! I knew Lucius would send men to us soon. I'll come straight away."

I almost ran outside, and there in the drizzle was a smart centurion in good scale armour, and behind him stood six well-turned-out legionaries armed to the teeth. They looked so solidly reassuring, I could have hugged them. The officer saluted me. "Centurion Mallius Paulus, at your service. And you're Mistress Aurelia Marcella?"

"I am. And by the gods, you're a welcome sight! Have you come from Eburacum?"

"That's right. These are bad times. The commander reckons you can do with some protection around here."

"Excellent! Won't you and your men come inside out of the rain?"

He shook his head. "No such luck, I'm afraid. We've been sent here for two reasons, and both of them mean we're going to get soaked in the good old Brigantian weather. First, as I say, to protect you." He swung round to face his men. "Right lads—let's make the place secure. At the double!" The soldiers ran to take up positions all round our fence.

"You needn't worry any more," Mallius smiled. "I'm posting my men on guard around your compound, and closing all gates into the property." Even as he said it, one of the legionaries shut the big front gate with a bang.

There was something not right here. "We'll be extremely glad of extra guards at night," I said. "But during the day we're safe enough, and we've got to keep the mansio open for travellers."

"I'm afraid that's impossible," Mallius answered. "Because our other job here is to make sure you all stay safe inside the stockade today. There's a big military operation starting any time now, in the woods, rounding up the natives who've been causing all the trouble. We know who they are. We'll capture them for you. But it'll be dangerous for any civilians to be caught in the fighting—so we're keeping you here for now."

"You're putting us under curfew, in effect." My uneasiness grew. "Is that really necessary?"

"Hardly that! Just a bit of inconvenience for your own protection. It won't be for long. All right?"

Not all right at all! But by now both the gates were shut, and his men were posted round the fence. And too late, I'd seen what was happening. They'd taken us prisoner! In the blink of an eye we'd gone from being free agents, going about our business, in touch with the outside world, to being penned inside our stockade, isolated from our customers, our friends, and any possibility of outside help. And all achieved without a drawn weapon or a drop of spilt blood—without even a threat!

I could have kicked myself. How could I have let myself be trapped so easily? And how could I warn everyone what was happening? They'd realise what the situation was eventually, but we needed to do something fast, very fast, before more Shadow-men could turn up. Seven of them could not kill us all—but they could hold us here till reinforcements arrived. And then....

"Now," Mallius said cheerfully, "I'll accept your kind offer to get out of the rain. These lads can take care of things for a while. There have to be some privileges of rank, don't you think?"

Oh no you don't, sunshine—not yet. We need time to make some plans. Which means I've got to get a message to the others, and keep you outside for a bit, while they decide what to do. I looked round and spotted Titch across the forecourt, standing with the other horse-boys, staring round-eyed at the soldiers.

"I just need to send a message to my stable-master," I said, smiling at Mallius. "Victor! Come here, will you?"

Titch trotted over, looking at me keenly; I've never used his real name. To make it even clearer this was no ordinary message, I spoke to him slowly and clearly, as if to a child. "Listen carefully, Victor, I've got an errand for you. The black stallion is sick again."

The boy was quick; I was relying on it, and I was right. "Again, Mistress? Like the other day? What shall I do?" His look of puzzlement was convincing, to anyone who didn't know how sharp he was.

"I want you to find Albia for me," I said. "We're going to need some of her horse-medicine, the stuff that was recommended by the man from Arpinum. Got that?"

"The man from Arpinum," he repeated carefully. "Yes, I'll tell her."

"Good. And then go and tell Secundus and the lads we won't be able to let the animals outside today. Explain to him that we've got a detachment of soldiers looking after us, and they don't want anybody to go outside the stockade." I turned to Mallius. "That's right, isn't it?"

"That's right, yes."

"Off you go then, Victor." He ran off, whistling.

I turned back to Mallius. "I'd better do my rounds before I go inside. I always make a tour of the place to start the day off. The men will get worried if I don't stick to my routine, especially with one of the best horses sick. But you get out of the rain, by all means. My sister will find you something to keep the damp out."

Predictably, he said he'd come with me. Even though I'd apparently been taken in by his play-acting, he didn't want me wandering around talking to my men. Good—that should give Albia and Quintus a little time.

I gave Mallius the full guided tour of the outside of the mansio, slave quarters, gardens, and of course stables. I told him at great length all about our horses and my plans for breeding them. He was polite and interested to start with, but I saw him getting impatient as I spun the walk out. So eventually, with a mixture of relief and reluctance, I led him into the warm, dry bar-room.

Albia was there, with a jug of warm wine ready, and a big smile for the so-called centurion. "Welcome to the Oak Tree," she said. "Sit down and get dry. I've a good drop of warm wine here for you. Shall I send some out to your men?"

"Thank you, yes. They'd appreciate that."

I ushered him to a table, and hung up our wet cloaks.

"Everything going all right?" I asked Albia. "Titch gave you the message about the stallion?"

"Yes, he did. I've seen to all that. I'm afraid our cousin's no better though."

I put on a serious face. "No better? That's bad news." I sat down, and poured wine for all of us. Mallius took a large swig, and Albia barely wet her lips, so I only took a minute sip myself. Presumably she'd put something in it to make him sleepy.

"Still in bed," my sister continued dolefully, "and the rash is worse if anything. I made him drink some of my herb tonic, but he says he wants to talk to you, because you cheer him up. You know, Relia, I think he quite fancies you!" She gave an arch smile and a very obvious wink.

I heaved a great sigh and stood up. "Will you excuse me just for a while, Mallius? I'd better go and see what he wants. Albia will keep you company till I'm back, won't you, Albia?"

"A pleasure." She sat down far too close to Mallius, who smiled wolfishly and put an arm round her shoulders, while using the other hand to lift his mug. He was visibly relaxing, and from the look on his face, he thought it was his birthday. Sometimes it amazes me how easy men are.

I saw Albia quietly refill his beaker, as I strolled off, only hurrying when I was out of sight of the bar-room.

Quintus was sitting on his couch pulling on army boots. They were the final touches to his outfit; he was dressed in Junius' full parade uniform—polished armour, fancy sword and silver-trimmed belt.

"Very smart," I commented. "Going out to inspect the sentries?"

"Using my brains," he retorted, "in a situation which wouldn't have arisen if other people had done the same."

"I know. I'm sorry, Quintus. I should have seen it coming. After everything we've said about disguises, and obeying people in uniform! Only I was so sure they came from Lucius. But I did keep him outside a good long while, at the risk of catching my death of cold and getting seduced in the hay-store."

"Really?" He smiled. "Did you slap his face?"

"Wouldn't you like to know? Now, for the gods' sake, tell me what you're doing."

He stood up, flexing his shoulders. "Secundus and I are going out through the sentries, dressed as a tribune and a trooper. As long as you and Albia keep their so-called centurion occupied, we can do it. The other men won't be able to prevent us if I pull rank."

"Surely they can just stop you by force."

"That's the beauty of it, they won't dare. They can't harm us, while they're still keeping up this pretence of being legionary soldiers. Their leader might risk it, but the men won't. We'll play them at their own game." His purple eyes gleamed. "So you just distract his attention."

"He'll be fast asleep before long. Albia's put something strong in his wine."

"Good. Once we're out, we'll rendezvous with Hawk, and track down Vitalis. You keep things under control here, and dispose of the guards when you can."

"It's a reasonable plan. Only one thing wrong with it."

"And that is?"

"Secundus is needed here. To dispose of the guards, as you put it, and to make sure nothing similar happens later. You'll have to take someone else. So we'll find a disguise that will fit *me*."

I won't bore you with the ensuing argument; I won, eventually. I doubted if I could pass for a soldier though, so I dressed as a young male slave, in oldish clothes but with a military belt and boots, and a hooded cloak.

"It's quite convincing," Quintus conceded. "But you're too self-assured. Try to have more of a down-trodden look. And listen, Aurelia, before we go...."

"Yes, master?"

He leaned close and kissed me. "I love you. Now let's get moving."

Quintus strode through into the bar-room, and I marched a respectful distance behind. Mallius was sprawled on a bench near the fireplace, his arm around Albia and his head on her shoulder, almost asleep; he didn't stir as we walked past.

Quintus mimed drawing his sword, and looked at Albia enquiringly, but she shook her head, and motioned us to the door. She blew us each a kiss, and we gave her a wave as we left.

We went round to the stable yard and picked out a good horse for Quintus, and a mule for me. I mounted, having remembered to help my master mount first, and we rode straight up to the gate. The guard there looked at Quintus apathetically, until he snapped, "What's this? You men given up saluting officers?" and then he belatedly jumped to attention and saluted.

"Sorry, sir," he mumbled. "I didn't know—I mean Mallius didn't mention there were any other officers in the mansio."

"Mallius will have your guts for catapult springs, if you're not careful. I need to leave for Oak Bridges now. Unbar the gate for me."

"I'm afraid that's impossible, Tribune. I'm under orders not to let anybody out."

"I know what your orders are," Quintus rasped. "Mallius has explained them clearly enough to me, but not to you, it seems. Your orders are not to let any *Romans* out. They don't apply to me. Now jump to it."

"Then—then you're not...but I thought...."

"Well stop thinking and unbar the gate, soldier. *Now!*"

"Yes, sir." The man didn't look very happy, but as Quintus had guessed, he couldn't risk refusing to obey an order from someone of higher rank. So he opened the gate for us, and we rode out through the rain, and up to the main road.

They were presumably watching us, so we set a brisk pace and didn't speak until we were out of sight. And although I may have looked like a reluctant slave, inside I was bubbling with excitement. We'd escaped our captors, and now we were off to find the Shadow of Death. Whatever our fate was to be, this day would decide it.

And that's how it came about that the assault on the Shadowmen's headquarters was not made, as we'd planned it, by a well-armed band of soldiers and slaves, but by just three people: one spy, one tracker, and one innkeeper.

Chapter XXIX

Looking back, I can't remember much in detail about that journey through the woods. Small incidents stick in my mind, like disjointed scenes from a play, from which other connecting scenes have been missed out.

We had a long wait near the holly-bush in the rain, sitting on a log under the soaking trees, till Hawk arrived. And I remember the elation we felt when he told us he had found the Shadow-men's hideout, the house in the rock, and that he would take us there. But he didn't seem triumphant; he looked deadly serious, facing us as we stood up, ready to go.

"Before we start, I want to get a couple of things straight," he said quietly. "We're walking into danger, and we'll follow my rules, or we won't go at all. Tracking silently through woods is something you learn as a child, as I did, but if you don't learn it then, you never fully master it. You two do your best, but even when you think you're creeping like cats you still sound like elephants, and anybody with a good pair of ears can hear you half a mile away."

"The Shadow-men have good trackers in their band?" Quintus asked, quite unoffended by Hawk's bluntness.

"Oh yes. And some quite well-trained sentries in the woods. So once we leave the road, I'll scout ahead, and you'll stay put till I signal you to join me, and then you'll come up slowly and quietly. And no talking at any time. The trees have ears. And if

I do this," he raised his right hand— "it means freeze. If I do *that*—" he pointed his fingers to the earth— "it means drop to the ground and play dead. At once. Got it?"

"Got it," we agreed.

"Good. Let's get on then."

"One more thing," Quintus interrupted. "Your rules are fair and we accept them; here's our one rule, and you must accept it too. If we're in danger of getting caught, you escape, Hawk, and get back to the others for help. No nonsense about not deserting your friends; you won't be deserting us, you'll be our only hope. If they kill us, that's too bad, but my guess is they want us alive, to start with at any rate, and you might be able to organise a rescue. You'll be no use to us if you get captured too."

"Agreed. But maybe it won't come to that. I'd say our chances of getting through undetected are at least fifty-fifty."

"I don't like the cheery tone this conversation is taking," I said. "Let's go if we're going."

Hawk said we could walk alongside the road for a couple of hundred paces; it was quicker, and certainly pleasanter in the wet. He even let us talk softly.

"Where are we going?" I asked. "We're walking towards the Oak Bridges turning. I'd assumed we'd be heading up onto the wolds. Is their hideout in these woods somewhere?"

"We have to cut through the woods, but they aren't continuous to the north of us. There are clearings, and streams, and little steep valleys, and quite a few fields in among it all. There's one very steep, narrow valley that runs down from the wolds. The sides of it are almost like cliffs in places. That's where they have their base, built into the valley side. 'The house in the rock' is the right name for it. It's a stone house right up against the hill, which used to belong to a woodcutter years ago. Seen from outside it's not all that large, but there are caves leading from it under the hillside itself."

"Caves? Here? I've never heard of any," I said.

"They're man-made caves, not natural ones, and there are several, with underground passages connecting them. I couldn't get inside—they were too well guarded—but I overheard some of the Shadow-men talking about them last night."

"How about entrances and exits?" Quintus asked.

"Only one obvious one, through the old stone house. But…."

"You think there may be others?"

"One of the men made some reference to 'the guards at the back door.' I looked carefully, but I only saw them using one entrance."

"They must have some sort of emergency escape," I said. "On the principle of the Harpy's Cave, Quintus."

He laughed, and we explained to Hawk about that long-ago tavern.

Hawk said, "Yes, I'm sure you're right. The clever way they've used the old house shows that Vitalis or someone in his band has a brain in his head."

"Which way do we go?" I asked. "These woods all look the same, and there's no sun to give us direction."

Hawk smiled. "The most direct route would be to cross your little river behind the mansio, but I don't imagine you want to take the risk. We'll turn off the main road and work our way back through the trees, and then head north."

"Is Vitalis at the hideout now?" Quintus wanted to know.

"He was there last night. I saw him in his mask, but I couldn't get close. There are guards everywhere."

"But you can get us through them?" Quintus queried sharply.

"If you're careful." He looked doubtful. "But with only three of us….There must be forty or fifty warriors. We're not going to try to get into the place by ourselves, surely?"

"Probably not," Quintus answered. I'd have preferred that to be "Definitely not," myself. "First we'll have a close look. But if there's a chance to take Vitalis himself, dead or alive, then we must go for it."

Hawk motioned us to take cover in the trees, and we halted. "We'll head through the woods now. Stay quiet, and walk softly. It's not very easy going, especially in this weather, but you look as if you're dressed for it. If we keep walking north, we'll eventually cross the valley where the hideout is."

I remember the next couple of hours as a dreary mixture of discomfort and fear, as my first feelings of brave excitement melted away. We moved slowly and carefully, desperately anxious to be quiet, and it was pretty hard walking. I soon had soaking feet, and aching legs. Hawk as always slipped among the trees as gracefully as a deer, whereas I felt as if I was fighting through like a bull. Where the woods were old, moving between the huge trunks wasn't so bad, because the ground beneath was clear of undergrowth; but where the timber had been felled and started to grow again, there were whippy saplings that slapped our faces, and waist-high thorns that tore our clothes; and the lush plants hid slippery rocks and uneven roots. Three times I stumbled, and would have fallen but for Quintus' steadying hand.

We stopped and started countless times, following Hawk's signals as keenly as boy soldiers on their first training manoeuvres. Only twice did we have to lie flat, and that was twice too much in the clinging mud; once we heard footsteps quite near, but they passed us by, and the other time we two couldn't hear whatever it was that had alerted the tracker. Once we all three froze where we stood, as a deer crashed out of the undergrowth right across our path. But mostly it was just boring routine; Hawk moved on a few paces while we stayed motionless, then he beckoned us to follow; we caught him up, then he moved further on, and we remained as still as stones till he signalled us forward…over and over and over again.

It's always difficult to keep your sense of direction in dense woodland, especially if there's no sunlight, but we could feel that the ground was rising, and getting steeper. After going upwards for a while we turned at right angles to the slope, heading roughly north as Hawk had said. The ground got more uneven, and that was the cause of our final undoing. I stumbled over a particularly well-hidden root, went full-length into a bramble patch, felt a shattering pain in my ankle, and swore.

Hawk looked back from about twenty paces ahead, and I could feel his fury from where I lay. Quintus pulled me to my feet, and I clenched my teeth to keep from crying out at the pain in my right ankle. Whether it was sprained or broken I couldn't tell, but I knew I couldn't walk far.

Hawk motioned us to run, and I could hardly bear to put my weight on my injured foot; Quintus more or less carried me, but we were slow and, more to the point, making a noise like a cavalry charge. Then we heard a shout and the thump of running men. Hawk and Bran vanished, and we kept moving as fast as we could away from the enemy noises.

"Quintus," I whispered, "get out while you can. I can't go much further. Go and get help."

"No," he said softly.

"But you must, otherwise we'll both be caught. Go now! Please!" I was almost crying with the pain of it, and the frustration of knowing I was too slow to escape.

"I'm not leaving you."

We rounded a huge fallen tree into a small clearing, and found a tiny stream across our path. We splashed into it and followed it down the slope, because it made for easier going, and the cool water soothed the red-hot pain in my ankle. After a hundred paces the sounds of our pursuers had died down almost to nothing. We paused for a few heartbeats, trying to catch breath, and looking for a good hiding-place. If we waited quietly, Hawk would be sure to find us again, and my ankle could rest and recover; then we could carry on. We just had to be still for a while, just a very little while....I began to feel a faint stirring of hope. I'd endangered all of us by my clumsiness, but we were going to get away with it after all.

"Stand still, both of you!" a voice ahead of us said conversationally, and out from the willows that bordered the stream stepped a large native warrior, carrying a hunting bow with an arrow ready on the string. It was Segovax.

Quintus drew his sword, but Segovax called, "Drop that, or I'll shoot your girl-friend."

"He's bluffing," I muttered, but for answer Segovax shot his arrow, and I felt it glance off the top of my shoulder, ripping my cloak. "Next time I won't miss," he snarled. "Drop the sword!"

Quintus dropped the sword, and Segovax gave a shrill whistle, which caused two other warriors to appear almost at once; the woods must be teeming with them.

"We've been expecting you," Segovax said, "ever since we heard two people had escaped from the Oak Tree. It had to be you two. That fool Mallius wants his head cut off. Probably that's what he'll get, when the Chief sees him."

"Good riddance," I said. "I'll vote for cutting the head off every native who's playing at soldiers."

"We're not playing," Segovax snapped. "Haven't you got that into your stupid head yet? This isn't a game, it's war. And the Shadow of Death has won. He wants to see you." He turned to his two men. "Has someone gone after the tracker?"

"Yes, Segovax."

I sent a silent prayer to Diana, begging her to help Hawk escape, and then I remembered he usually prayed to Epona, so I asked her to help too.

"Tie them up," Segovax told his men, "and make a decent job of it. These two have slipped through our fingers before."

They made a very decent job of it; our wrists and ankles were bound with strong ropes, and we were gagged and blindfolded. More men came, it sounded like four or five, and we were half-carried and half-dragged through the woods for what felt like miles. I lost all sense of time and direction, and began to shiver with pain and fear. I prayed to Diana again, and to Jupiter too, the ruler of all the gods. I tried to console myself with an image of Hawk and Bran flitting through the trees, going to fetch help for us. But into my mind's eye another picture kept intruding, of a headless man and a dead dog, lying in a sodden thicket.

Our captors didn't utter a word, though there were occasional curses and grunts of extra effort as they hauled us none too gently over fallen branches, hidden logs, and at one place over some boggy ground where the slime sucked at our boots. I felt I was in a void, except for the sounds of our progress—the natives' footsteps squelching through the mud, the chink of their weapons, the dragging noise of our two bodies, the rain on the dripping leaves.

I knew we were getting near when we started to go steeply downwards; this must be the side of the valley where their hideout was. For me, it was the worst part of the journey. If you've never been dragged down a steep brambly hill with your ankle hurting so much you want to scream, don't try it.

Suddenly there was a shout quite close by, ordering us to halt. Segovax called back, "We've got the spy and the girl. Tell the Shadow of Death, will you?"

"I will." There was a short pause, and the other voice came again. "Bring them in. Then get back out and help find the tracker."

They dragged us the last few paces, through a narrow opening only just wide enough for two people. I could tell by the hard-packed earth under our feet and the echoes all around that we'd entered a building. It sounded big and the air smelled of smoke, and there were people inside it; I heard feet shuffling and quiet voices.

They carried us to the left, and dumped us against the wall. Our bodies weren't touching, but we were so close together, I could hear Quintus' breathing. We were tied up too tightly to move, and our gags prevented us from making more than inarticulate grunts. We exchanged grunts for a while though, until one of our captors came to stand over us and administered a kick every time one of us made a noise—a definite conversation stopper.

We must have lain like that for a couple of hours. I suppose it was a deliberate attempt to make us afraid, and it certainly was horribly frightening. But it was clear they wouldn't kill us before we'd seen Vitalis. So I lay there, cold and sore and scared; but I was also dead tired, and though it seems unbelievable, I dozed off for a while into an uneasy sleep, waking up occasionally to find I was colder and more sore and scared than before.

Once when I woke I heard voices, urgent but hushed, as if several men were discussing something they didn't want us to hear. I strained my ears and caught a few words. "The tracker.... no sign...all the men out searching....no luck....best not report." My heart gave a leap. They hadn't found Hawk, and what's more it wasn't our ears they were afraid would pick up the news, but their Chief's. They knew how serious Hawk's escape could be.

I drifted back to sleep, and woke when a shout rang out, raising echoes all around. "Get them up! The Shadow of Death wants them now."

Several warriors came over and untied us, and removed the gags and blindfolds. Then they stood us upright, but I couldn't stand properly because my ankle hurt so much and was very swollen now. When I collapsed to the floor two of the men picked me up, cursing me roundly, and held me steady while I tried to stay upright with all my weight on my left foot. They saw that I couldn't walk, and one of them laughed as he gave my swollen right ankle a spiteful kick; then they supported me as they marched us towards the back of the building.

Quintus and I exchanged glances, each relieved and reassured to see the other. Then as our captors pushed us forward I started to look round. We were being taken to the rear of quite a large stone house, lit by a smoky log fire in one corner and torches in brackets on two walls. The entrance was so narrow there was little natural light; the roof was high and the torchlight didn't reach it. I could see dim shapes of rough furniture: a big, square plank table, benches, and in a far corner a pile of blankets.

They urged us on towards a kind of passageway or tunnel. This must be the beginning of the caves; we were going under the mass of the hill. The walls were of rough light-coloured rock, closing in as the passage grew narrower, and at the far end shone a brighter light, as if there was a lamplit room there.

I suddenly felt a return of the excitement that had buoyed me up earlier. I suppose it sounds mad. We were in the hands of our enemies, probably about to be killed, yet my blood raced and my brain sang. In that brightly lit cave we would come face to face with the man behind the Campaign of Terror—the Shadow of Death.

But when we reached the lighted cave, it was empty. I felt a sting of disappointment; but the place itself was impressive enough. It wasn't large, only perhaps fifteen feet square, but richly decked out, more like a room in a villa than a hole in a hillside. Suspended by a metal ring in the roof was a huge bronze light fitting with three lamps hanging from it, making the centre of the room into an almost dazzling pool of radiance. The walls were in shadow, but I could see they were hung with rugs, woven in bright reds and purples. In the very middle stood a huge, ornate throne-like chair, with gilded arms and purple cushions, and a small citrus-wood table beside it.

He came slowly forward from the back of the cave, out of the shadows into the bright light, and sat down on the purple chair. His fair hair shone, and his handsome face wore a smile of triumph.

"Welcome, my dears," Felix said.

Chapter XXX

I stared in disbelief. The fair ringlets, the high forehead, the greenish-yellow eyes—they were all familiar, and yet I felt as if I'd never seen them before. And as for the purple cloak, the large gold torc and arm-bracelets, the golden head-dress....This couldn't be Felix, the clown, the dilettante, the cultivated Roman aristocrat! Felix couldn't be the arch-murderer, the Shadow of Death? Could he?

"Well say something, Aurelia dear," he said in his usual bantering way, "even if it's only that you're pleased to see me."

"I'm surprised, certainly," I admitted, trying to keep the tone light. "Actually I'm gobsmacked, if you'll pardon a vulgar expression. We were expecting someone else entirely."

"Sorry to disappoint," he smirked.

"Who says I'm disappointed?"

This was ridiculous, and certainly not the way I'd imagined my first conversation with the Shadow of Death. But then I'd been so sure it was Vitalis. And yet when I started to think about it, it fitted. It all fitted.

My mind began to race. Felix, the highly placed Roman, trusted intimate of a chief councillor, who knew every detail of our defence plans. Felix, with his network of contacts, his love of gossip, his regular visits to Eburacum. While he was in town, did he make contact with dissident soldiers? Did he borrow military disguises from them, and did they pass on military secrets?

And then Felix incriminating Balbus with the pale green paint, and the stories about his Brigantian friends; Felix coming to visit me each time I was attacked—to commiserate, or to gloat? Even Felix the flamboyant dresser, who liked to decorate his brightly coloured boots with gilded studs. And most telling of all, Felix with his grudge against Rome. "When love feels itself betrayed...."

I wasn't given long to ponder. "You didn't suspect then?" he asked gleefully, like a child who's performed a very good sleight-of-hand and wants the grown-ups to applaud. "You didn't have an inkling? Neither you nor your friend the all-knowing government investigator?" He shot a contemptuous glance at Quintus, then I got his full gloating smile again.

Quintus shook his head, and I said, "Not a clue. I'm still finding it hard to believe."

"I must see what I can do to convince you," he beamed. "Now, my dears, sit down, and let's be cosy for a while. Would you care for some refreshment?" It was like a mad dream. He was behaving as if we'd just called in at his villa for a drink and a gossip. He even helped me hobble to a stool, and Quintus sat down next to me.

"In due course," he went on, "I'll have to have you both killed, and probably rather publicly, to satisfy my native friends at the next Druid ceremony. You've learned too much, and I'm afraid they'll expect it. But meantime, we can enjoy a civilised hour and some decent wine."

He rang a tiny gold hand-bell, and his huge native servant came in, no longer in a Roman slave's tunic, but in full war gear. He brought a silver tray with a jug of white wine and three glasses. *Glasses!* It was the final bizarre touch. We were in a cave under a hill, being entertained by a murderer, and drinking wine from wonderful glasses, each one worth a consul's ransom! I'd drunk out of glasses a handful of times in my life, and if anyone had told me I'd encounter them in the Shadow of Death's lair, I'd simply have laughed. I wasn't laughing now.

Felix said to his servant, "Tell the musicians to play, will you. And pull the curtain as you go." The big man left, drawing a heavy red curtain across the entrance to the room.

"I find music very soothing," Felix remarked conversationally. "And a pleasant noise of drums and pipes stops anyone overhearing us. Caves are all very fine, but they do lack privacy, I find. Still—" he began to pour the wine— "I've done my best to make it comfortable here. Not bad, is it?"

"Very nice," I said inadequately. "Pretty weird," would have been a more honest comment, but that hardly seemed tactful.

He handed us each a wine-glass, as the sound of a drum and a couple of double-flutes floated in from the large outer building. He chuckled, and raised his glass. "A toast," he announced. "To your first meeting with the Shadow of Death."

He drank his wine in one long swallow and refilled the glass. After a small hesitation, Quintus and I drank too. Well, why not? We'd just been told, oh so politely, that we would soon be dead. We might as well enjoy the hospitality of the house till then. The wine was first class, and I was glad of its comforting warmth.

"I feel as if I'm dreaming," I said. "I'll wake up soon, and all this will never have happened."

"Oh, it's happened, never fear."

"You truly are the Chief? The Shadow of Death?"

"Ah, no, my dear."

"No? Then…then I'm confused."

"I am the Shadow of Death," he answered, "but I'm not the Chief. That, as you so rightly suspected, is someone else entirely. I'm sure even you can guess who." He laughed. "Good, isn't it?"

It was like emerging from a dark tunnel into brilliant sunlight. For a heartbeat the light dazzles you, and then it makes everything clear. "Vitalis is the Chief?" I exclaimed. "And you're the Shadow of Death? And we thought they were one and the same."

"Of course you did." Felix was enjoying himself. "You fell into the trap, just like everyone else. That's what makes the Shadowmen so outstanding, don't you see? Most war-bands have one leader; we have two."

"But why?"

"Why do you think? Because a rebel leader has to play two quite different roles, if you'll pardon the theatrical analogy. First he has to be a warrior chief. Well that's hardly my sort of thing, is it? Prancing about in armour, killing people and getting blood all over my clothes? No, I leave that to Vitalis. He's ideal for leading the young warriors, because he's one of them. Brave as lions, they are, and about as intelligent, on a good day. My part is to plan, to organise and direct them, get them information, and get them gold—so that their bravery is put to good use."

"The pay convoys," Quintus murmured.

"You heard about them, did you? I'm glad. It's such a pity when one's triumphs have to remain secret. I'm gratified to know that the news reached the famous Quintus Antonius Delfinus."

That was yet another shock. After all the trouble we'd gone to, the Shadow of Death knew Quintus' true identity. I glanced at Quintus; he was tense, but then made an effort to relax and smile.

"Ah," he said levelly. "So you know who I am."

"Of course, dear fellow. I've known for some time."

"You have?" Quintus sounded sceptical. "How?"

"Vitalis suspected something when he saw how efficiently you dealt with a couple of his drunken boys at the Oak Tree the other day. Actually he was quite impressed by the way you handled things, and he was sure you were a soldier. You said something about 'a couple of hours with a Roman drill instructor'…not the sort of language bridge surveyors usually go in for. And why would a soldier go around pretending to be a bridge surveyor? Because he's neither of those things, he's a spy. So I asked my friends at the Eburacum garrison to check, and back came the answer: yes, there's an investigator in the area calling himself Quintus Valerius Longinus, who is in reality a certain Quintus Antonius Delfinus, the scourge of all traitors. They said you have a formidable reputation. I can't think why."

Quintus merely shrugged. "It seems I've met my match," he answered.

Felix's cat-eyes glittered as he smiled his most mischievous smile. "Well, I'm glad you have the grace to admit it. And you didn't have even a tiny suspicion about what I was up to?"

I was beginning to get tired of this, but it was obviously giving him great pleasure, and when threatened by a murderer, it's only common sense to try to keep him sweet. I shook my head emphatically. "You've fooled us all, Felix, utterly and completely. That is, if this is real life, and not one of your silly jokes."

"A joke? Oh no, certainly not a joke!" Suddenly his smile was gone, and his face was angry. "That's where you've all been wrong, isn't it, Aurelia? You've always thought I was a joke. Good old Felix, forever clowning about, making everyone laugh. Well nobody will be laughing now. Will they?"

We said nothing.

"*Will they?*" he barked.

"No, they won't," Quintus answered. "They won't be laughing. They'll be sad, just as I'm sad, when I think of the way a Roman nobleman from an ancient family has turned into a traitor."

Felix leaned forward on his large throne. "Traitor," he repeated slowly, almost musingly. "Yes, I know that's how you think of it. A traitor to my ancestors. A traitor to the Empire. A traitor to the glorious future of Rome. Gods, I've had to listen to Silvanius banging on, day in and day out. 'We Romans must stand together'! Who stood by my family when we needed help, tell me that? When Rome was torn by civil war after Nero died, Romans lost the habit of standing together, didn't they? It was every man for himself, every clan for itself. Four different men grabbing at imperial power in the space of a year, like greedy babies reaching out for a bright toy! My family lost everything, and they didn't deserve to. Now I'm going to put matters right."

"But that's all history, Felix," I pointed out. "It's twenty-odd years since Nero died. You were treated badly, but what's done is done. How can you re-write twenty years of history?"

"I'm not re-writing history. I'm starting a fresh chapter, and I'm starting it here. Once we've driven out the Romans from Britannia, and we will, then this island will revert to its old freedom, ruled by tribal kings, but with one High King over them all, to hold them together and make sure they stay free." He sat up straight in his purple robe. "Vitalis will make a perfect High King. The tribes love him, and they'll follow him to battle and to death if he asks them to. He'll play the part of High King to perfection. But *I* shall be writing his lines for him."

"The High King on the throne," Quintus said, "and behind the throne, in the shadows, his trusted adviser, the Shadow of Death."

"Exactly so!" Felix crowed.

I had a clear image in my head of a native High King, dressed in ornate leather clothes and laden with gold jewellery, feasting in a timbered hall on joints of wild boar so massive he had to use two hands to lift them, throwing the bones on the earthen floor, and then swilling mead from a pewter mug. Night after smoky, noisy night, he'd be surrounded by boasting warriors and scheming Druids, while the bards sang stories of his greatness. I could picture Vitalis in that role, he was made for it.

But next to the High King, a shadow among the shadows, there was Felix, in his gaudy Roman tunic, reclining on a carved couch and eating dainty Roman dishes served on gold plates....

It would never work. Felix hadn't thought this through. It was one thing being the power behind the rebellion while it was in progress—he could still enjoy his luxurious Roman life from day to day, and only adopt the ways of the Britons when he chose. But if the rebellion succeeded and the Romans actually did disappear, he'd be forced into a barbarian way of life for good. The natives, with their hatred of all things Roman, wouldn't allow even the Shadow of Death to live in a modern villa and surround himself with well-trained slaves and elegant foreign luxuries. And as for the theatre...hadn't he realised that if he actually could drive out all Romans, he'd be saying goodbye to Greek and Roman art forever? The ludicrousness of all this hit me with such force that I laughed aloud.

"Be quiet!" Felix almost shrieked it, sending echoes rebounding through the cave. "Don't you laugh at me. Don't you *ever* laugh at me again, d'you hear? I've put up with you people not taking me seriously all these years, but now I don't have to. You'll treat me with respect! Understand?"

I stopped laughing.

"I said, do you understand?"

"I understand, Felix. And I apologise. I didn't mean to offend you."

"Well you have offended me, and you'd better learn not to do it again! Down on your knees, and ask my forgiveness." He reached behind his throne, and with a good dramatic flourish produced a sword. The lamplight glinted off goldwork in its hilt as he held it up.

This was too much, and my reply came out before I'd had time to think. "Oh, do be sensible, Felix. For one thing I can't kneel down because I've broken my ankle, and for another, your theatrical friends would say you're in serious danger of over-acting. If you're going to play the part of Caesar, then for the gods' sake play him as Gaius Julius, not Gaius Caligula."

I heard Quintus suppress a gasp; he clearly thought I'd gone too far, and perhaps I had, or perhaps I knew Felix better than most. Either way I didn't care; I'd nothing to lose, and I'd go down fighting, not kneeling to beg forgiveness.

The silence lasted somewhere between three heartbeats and three hours. Then, miraculously, Felix relaxed and laughed.

"Oh, Aurelia my dear, Publius is right. You always do talk such excellent common sense! I wish you'd taken up my repeated offers of marriage, you know. Ah well...I shall be quite sorry, when the time comes."

Very comforting, I'm sure, but I preferred not to pursue that line of thought. Let's get him back into his gloating, smug mood. "We've always been friends, Felix," I said. "And I thought I knew you, as a friend, quite well. I've always considered you to be one of the most thoroughly Roman men in the Empire. Now I find you're trying to drive all Romans out of Britannia."

"Trying and succeeding." He reached back and put the sword down behind his throne, and took another long swallow of his wine. "It can't be done overnight, but it will be done in a year or two. All Romans will be killed, if they don't depart. That's not an idle threat, it's a statement of fact. Including you, Aurelia dear, because you won't leave. Even after I came to see you in person to ask you nicely."

"I don't understand." My puzzlement pleased him.

"You didn't recognise me, of course. You thought I was an old and illegal Druid."

My surprise was genuine; I didn't need to ham it up for his benefit. "Jupiter's balls! That was *you?*"

"People are so unobservant. You didn't suspect a thing, did you?"

"No. I've never met a Druid before....Of course, you spoke to me in Latin; that ought to have told me something. But you're right, I never suspected him—I mean you."

"It was rather a good disguise. I had a little help from Dardanio."

"Your actor friend?"

"If you knew anything about the theatre, you'd know that Dardanio isn't just a fine actor, he's an expert in costume and make-up. A real artist. He gave me some useful lotions and potions. You noticed how my eyes looked black?"

"Yes. It was all very convincing. But if you were that Druid, then you know my answer to your threats and your campaign of terror. I'm not leaving the Oak Tree."

"It seems to me you've already left it," he said.

There was no answer to that. We sat in silence, sipping our wine.

"Aurelia dear," he went on. "For friendship's sake, I'll give you one more chance, although it's more than you deserve. Will you give me your word that you and all your household will leave the Oak Tree, and get out of Britannia? If you do, I'll give you *my* word that we'll let you go in peace."

"No thank you."

He sighed. He appeared genuinely sad. But by now I knew how deceptive appearances could be, where he was concerned.

"It puzzles me," he reflected, "why you put yourself through all this. You're actually prepared to lose your life defending your little parcel of land and your few buildings, and your right to be an innkeeper, waiting on drunks from morning till night?"

"Sneer all you like," I said, "but the Oak Tree is my home, and it's where I belong. I love Britannia, and I want to live here, as a Roman settler, part of the Roman Empire. And whatever may happen to me, there are thousands like me, hundreds of thousands probably by now. You and your killers won't ever succeed in driving us out."

He got up and began pacing about the cave, his purple cloak swishing and swirling. As he strode around he moved in and out of the pool of light, and his appearance changed from a bright familiar friend into a dark brooding threat, and back again. And I suddenly saw that this was how his whole life was. He had divided it into two separate compartments, each with its own personality, and he could switch from one to the other as easily as walking in or out of the shadows.

I've mentioned in this report that I've been scared on occasion. But the way Felix frightened me was quite unlike anything else. The idea of someone I knew, or thought I knew, turning from friend to foe in the blink of an eye was so terrifying it made my head spin. While he paced I felt fear seep through me, paralysing, numbing.

What could I do? What was the point of even trying? And yet we had to try. We had to do something, to keep him in his brightly lit persona, as Felix the civilised urbane Roman, the former friend. Because from the flashes of temper we'd already seen, when he stepped from light to dark and became the ruthless Shadow of Death, we were in mortal danger.

Quintus broke the silence, and his familiar voice, calm and half-amused, jolted me out of my panic. "Felix," he drawled lazily, as if making conversation at the dinner table. "Adviser to the High King of the Britons! Now I've heard everything! We underestimated you, all of us."

"If you want real power in politics, you don't need to be a Caesar or a tribal king," Felix answered. "You can achieve whatever you like as an adviser, as long as the king needs you. I'll be the ruler in all but name, because I can help the natives drive the Romans out, and keep their freedom afterwards. They need me, and they know it. The Shadow of Death needs the Chief—but equally, the Chief needs the Shadow of Death."

Felix sat down again and picked up the wine-jug. "Do have some more of this excellent wine, my dears. It's from near Pompeii—well near where Pompeii used to be. I thought, for our first meeting here, I'd provide something special. I hope you approve. Aurelia, tell me what you think, truthfully. You're a connoisseur of wines."

I told him it was very good, and again, as I complimented him and he refilled my glass, I had the strange feeling that we could be making small-talk at his villa. Except that the surroundings were richer, and darker, and very much scarier.

Quintus leaned forward, holding his glass between his hands and gazing at Felix with close attention. "Felix, there's something I've always wanted to know about the Shadow of Death and the way he operates."

"Indeed? The all-seeing, all-knowing investigator still has a teeny question unresolved?"

"About a hundred of them, actually," Quintus smiled. "You pulled the wool over my eyes, I'd be a fool to deny it."

"Ask away then." The smug look on Felix's face was sickening, but also encouraging. I listened as Quintus threw out more bait, like a fisherman on a river bank, waiting for his prey to swim in close.

"This business of the masked figure—or figures, I should say. Who helped you there?"

"Dardanio created the mask for me. I wear it as a symbol, like a legionary standard in a way. And of course it helps keep my identity secret. Only Vitalis and a few senior men have ever seen me without it."

"But you're cleverer than that," Quintus countered, almost teasingly. "There are times when the masked chief has been seen and yet it couldn't have been you. At the Druid ceremony, for instance. We saw you there in your Druid robes, and simultaneously we saw the Shadow of Death in his mask."

Felix said seriously, "It wasn't I in the Druid costume; that was a real Druid. True, I impersonated him when I came to the mansio to talk to Aurelia, but I wouldn't dare do that at one of their ceremonies. It would be blasphemy."

Blasphemy, indeed? Yet this was the man who had ordered two corpses to be placed in a sanctum dedicated to Jupiter and Juno!

Quintus was looking deeply impressed. "But there were other times—the masked figure has been seen often in this area, far oftener than you could have managed by yourself. Did Vitalis wear the mask sometimes too?"

Felix nodded. "We wanted to give the impression that the Shadow of Death could appear anywhere at any time. So sometimes he impersonated me, yes. But usually it was me. I was there the night you were attacked, Delfinus; and I was there when a certain message was painted on your stable wall, Aurelia dear. I even returned the cloak you'd so carelessly lost the night before. And of course I saw the attack on the Oak Tree. I wouldn't have missed that for anything."

"I'm surprised the Shadow-men didn't realise that the masked figure wasn't always the same person," I said. "But if you never spoke…and then, you and Vitalis are alike in build."

"Naturally," Felix agreed.

"I'm sorry?"

"Like father, like son."

I just sat staring. Had I heard him right? Had I understood what I'd heard correctly? I said at last, "You're telling us—that you are Vitalis' *father?*"

He gave a gleeful hoot of laughter. "I can't blame you for not knowing. It's been rather a closely guarded secret."

"But how…I mean when….All right, both stupid questions. But tell us what happened."

"Publius' wife and I had a bit of a fling shortly after I arrived in Britannia." He got up and started pacing about again. "Twenty-two years ago. I got to Oak Bridges the year that clod Vespasian became Caesar, after several other clods had tried and failed. She was a pretty little thing, but *very* provincial, whereas I was the Roman man of fashion, a courtier who'd lived with an emperor. Publius had always wanted a son, but they'd never had any children. However, she fell pregnant soon enough when I arrived on the scene! Poor Publius was mortified when he found out."

"You mean he *knows?*"

"Oh yes, he knows. If his wife had lived, it might have been difficult, but she died when Vitalis was born. So Publius and I agreed the boy should be brought up as his. One or two servants knew, inevitably—we sold them. Nobody else has any idea. Except Vitalis himself of course, now."

His pacing took him into a shadowed corner of the cave, and I looked at his dark figure, feeling a sudden stab of anger at the thought of how completely poor Silvanius had been betrayed.

"I hope you're proud of yourself," I said. "You've betrayed a man who thought of you as his best friend. Not content with stealing his wife, you've turned his son against him; and now you've given his enemies every last one of his secret plans."

He smiled. "Shocking, isn't it?"

"Actually, yes, it is," I snapped, anger making me incautious. "When I think of all of us at Clarus' meeting, believing we were among friends, taking our oath to keep our plans secret—and you broke your oath, and told everything to Vitalis and the natives."

He was still smiling. "My dear, you cut me to the quick! I broke no oath. I'm a Cornelius, and in the Cornelius family we don't break oaths. Especially when it isn't necessary."

Quintus said, "Then tell us how you got round it. You did take the oath of secrecy, didn't you? If you didn't betray the meeting, who did?"

"It's not so very hard to work out." His cat-eyes narrowed as he gazed at me. "You were there, Aurelia, after all."

I cast my mind back to the scene in Silvanius' sitting-room: the beautiful décor, the wall lined with scrolls, and all of us sitting round the fabulous citrus-wood table, solemnly planning how to defeat the Shadow of Death. We'd taken our oath of secrecy at the beginning of the meeting, we'd had our discussions, made our plans, then chosen our password.

"But we weren't overheard," I said. "We checked. Well, you did—you went and looked to see…oh, Jupiter's balls! You went to the sitting-room door, because you had someone listening just outside, didn't you? That bit of nonsense where you stuck your head into the corridor, you were actually making sure there *was* somebody there."

He nodded, and sat down again. "You see? I knew you could work it out."

"No, wait," I said, remembering, "Silvanius left the room after you'd looked outside, to fetch the statues from the shrine, before we took the oath. Why didn't he see your eavesdropper?"

"I expect he did. What he saw was one of Vitalis' slaves with a broom in his hand, in the act of sweeping the corridor floor."

There was a sharp tap on the cave wall, and Vitalis himself pushed through the heavy curtain. He was in his warrior gear. Behind him loomed Felix's giant slave.

"Vitalis," Felix smiled. "You've taken your time. Everything ready now?"

"Sorry, Father. Yes, all set now."

I noticed they were speaking in British; and I also saw that Quintus was looking puzzled, as if he couldn't understand what they said. Yet he spoke the British language fluently, despite an execrable accent.

"Good. Then I'm afraid, Antonius Delfinus, this is where we say good-bye for a while. Vitalis and his friends want to ask you a few questions. I advise you to answer them, otherwise they're likely to become rather insistent. They've got a good hot fire going, some pincers, a saw….What else, Vitalis?"

"Chains," Vitalis answered, looking Quintus up and down as if measuring him, "with spikes in them, hammers, nails...."

"So you see, you'll have to tell them what they want to know. Make it easy for yourself, I should."

There was a pause, and then Quintus said in Latin, "Sorry, I don't speak your barbarian grunt-and-spit talk. Would you mind repeating all that in a civilised language?"

Felix laughed, and said, still in British, "So the great investigator came to Britannia to find the Shadow of Death, and can't even understand the local language!" Then he switched to Latin. "Go with Vitalis, dear fellow. That's all you need to know. The rest will come as a lovely surprise."

But I couldn't just sit by. "No!" I cried out. "You'll get nothing out of him. He doesn't know anything worth passing on. Well, you've just seen why. Haven't you realised it yet, Felix? *I'm* the investigator here; I work with my brother Lucius, and I've sent him all the information he needs about the Shadow-men. So if we're considering answers to interesting questions, you'd better tell your savages to talk to *me*."

Felix sighed. "Isn't it romantic? A girl defending her lover. Almost like a play! Well better, because I'm the writer and the director of the show, so I can decide on the ending. Off you go, Vitalis."

"I'll see you soon, Aurelia," Quintus called, as Vitalis and the big slave began to march him out.

"Very soon. Love you!" I shouted after him.

I sat listening till their footsteps were lost in the flute music that was still incongruously filling the cave. Quintus was gone; I might never see him again. I've never felt so completely alone.

Chapter XXXI

What I did then is probably the hardest thing I've ever had to do. I smiled and made a joke.

"Alone at last! Is that how the next line goes in your play? Or is that too corny for you?"

He smiled in return. "Oh, the odd cliché never hurts. How about 'Now I've got you in my power'?"

"To which I answer, 'You surely know you can't get away with this.'"

"But I can, and I will." He stood up and walked towards me. "And that's quite enough bad dialogue for now."

He put his right hand on my shoulder; with his left he brushed back some locks of hair that had strayed over my face. "You're beautiful," he cooed in my ear. "So very beautiful. I want to touch you, to hold you, to...."

I'll leave out the rest of his wish list; some of it was quite flattering and some of it plain embarrassing. Eventually his tone became sad. "But you've always treated me as a joke, you've never even considered loving me. Now, I'm going to *make* you consider it." He kissed me. I wanted to pull away but he held me close until he'd finished.

My mind was whirling. Perhaps if I offered him what he wanted...if I went to him willingly....

"Well," I said, "there's more to you than meets the eye, Cornelius Felix Shadow-of-Death." And I stood up so that I could press my body against him. The pain of my ankle was excruciating; the hatefulness of what I was doing was even worse.

"I want you, Aurelia." He kissed me again. "Surely you know how I feel about you? Surely you've guessed?" He touched my cheek, and gazed into my eyes. It was disgusting, but I kept still, and let him kiss me again. He murmured, "Well, you're here now, and I shall have you."

So, I thought, it's time for the final throw of the dice. I leaned in close to him, and said softly, "I can't stop you. We both know you can do what you like. But I don't want to make love under duress. I want to enjoy it. And if I do, you'll enjoy it much more too. Won't you?" I kissed him hard, just for a heartbeat, then I pulled back.

He kissed my face and my neck, and I didn't stop his hands from exploring my breasts. I let my own hands do some exploring too. He said, "Now who's full of surprises?"

"That's just the start, as you'll find out if you put me in the right mood."

"But what about your handsome investigator? I thought he was the man to put you in the mood." There was more kissing, and his hands went lower.

I let him play awhile, then I said, "Forget about Quintus Antonius. You'll find he knows nothing worth knowing, so stop wasting your time on him. Just let him go, and once he's safely away, well, he'll be out of sight, out of mind, won't he?"

"You'd give yourself to me to save that oaf Antonius Delfinus?"

"There's an easy way to find out." I pressed my body hard against his.

He stepped back, and his sudden laughter rang out, peal after peal of it, and I knew I'd lost my final throw.

"My dear, you still haven't learnt to take me seriously, have you? Why in the gods' name should I release Antonius? I can have you in my own way, in my own time, as many times as I like. Perhaps I'll even let your precious Antonius watch us. That's after he's told us everything we need to know."

I moved away and sat down again. He came and stood over me, smiling, gloating. He didn't need to say anything; he'd won, and I'd lost. We'd both lost, Quintus and I. We were without hope, finished. I felt cast down and defeated. And then I thought of last night's sacrifice in the clearing, and I had a sharp memory of the Druid raising his dagger and killing a thin red-headed boy, and of Hawk's haunted look as he confronted us afterwards. The two visions made me angry, and anger gave me strength. Hawk was our only hope now. I wouldn't give up. I'd try, and I'd go on trying, to keep Felix talking, and reinforce his sense of security. If I was right and his men hadn't dared to tell him of Hawk's escape, then it might be a false sense of security.

I picked up my glass, which was empty, and held it out. Felix fetched the jug and refilled it automatically, and I took another drink. I said, "Can I ask you something?"

"Anything you like, dear heart." He sat down on the purple-covered throne, and took a drink himself. Good.

"I can see why the natives will follow you and Vitalis. They want to be free. But I'm puzzled how you got Marius to help you—a loyal Roman tribune. How did you manage it?"

He swirled the wine in his glass so the light made it sparkle. His insufferable smugness was back. "Yes, Marius was under my control for some time. Doing whatever I told him—and doing it well. I thought I'd get Junius too, but the fool fell in love with your precious sister. Love!" He sneered. "I ask you, *love!* They could have had power and wealth they'd never even dreamed of, those two. I told them, as Roman generals in our native army, they'd have been chiefs in our new free province, rich and powerful and…and Junius threw it all away for love! Ridiculous! And then he started trying to talk Marius out of helping us, making him doubt what he was doing. Sadly, I had to finish them both."

"Junius never believed the Shadow-men would succeed," I said. "I spoke to him, you know, when he was dying. It was thanks to him that we found your hideout here. Your native poisoners slipped up there, Felix. They didn't kill Junius outright."

Yes, I know, not the wisest of remarks. But the look of fury on his face, though it was alarming, was also wonderfully satisfying. He must have realised it, because he deliberately relaxed, and smiled.

"It makes no real difference," he said. "The Shadow-men and the other Brigantian war-bands are on the move now. We shall frighten the Romans out of this area, and when the tribes further south see how easy it is, they'll flock to join us. The rebellion will engulf the whole of Britannia, and in a year from now, two years at the most, we'll be free of Rome."

He sounded so sure, and just for a few heartbeats, I wondered if he could be right. "All Romans will be killed...." No, he was deluded, mad. But I'd gain nothing by arguing the point and making him angry. The trick was to get him boasting about his brilliance again.

"You still haven't told me why Marius helped you in the first place. Was it for money?"

"Not money, no. I doubt if he'd have done it for money. But sometimes information will serve where money won't."

"You blackmailed him?"

He nodded. "I discovered a nasty little scandal in the ranks of the Marius family."

"It must have been a ripe one."

He laughed. "It is—it was. Marius' father was in the army, a camp prefect in Gaul. He owed a lot of money to a local tradesman, a potter, and to avoid paying him, this Marius sent some army bully-boys along to smash up the pottery and make the potter move out....Yes, I see you've guessed the rest of the story."

"Balbus?"

"Balbus. Who left Gaul and moved to Oak Bridges, and settled and grew rich. But however rich he grew, he never forgot, and he swore he'd be revenged on the commandant, or on his family, if he ever met them again."

"So if he'd discovered who Marius' father was, he'd have killed him, after all this time? You really believe that?"

"Who knows? Marius believed it. Especially after I'd arranged some drastic alterations to Balbus' shop display. I could so easily have told Balbus that Marius had done it."

"You've just demonstrated a saying of my grandmother's," I remarked. "What people don't know, can't hurt them. It's what they do know, that isn't so."

Felix clapped his hands with delight. "How very profound! I'd no idea you had philosophers in your family. And it gives us a whole new game to play, doesn't it? You and me, just the two of us. What do we know, that turns out to be wrong? Let me see…." His smile took on its malicious twist again. "You think your brother Lucius will bring you help from Eburacum, because you know you've written to him begging him to come." He laughed shortly. "What you don't know is, I had all those letters intercepted. He hasn't heard from you at all for months! I even had the note that Antonius left for him in Eburacum quietly thrown away….Oh yes, I know all about his trip to Eburacum. I forged the letter that made him go there."

"But how could you get hold of my letters? You couldn't have known which couriers I'd use."

"No need. Our postal service is truly amazing, isn't it? You can send letters to any military base in the Empire, carried by trusty messengers galloping over mountains and through forests, and even braving the stormy seas. The letters will always reach their destination. That doesn't mean they'll ever get to the person they are intended for."

I remembered the army bases I'd lived in as a girl. "The camp's mail-clerk?" I said. "You bribed the clerk at Eburacum not to deliver mail for Lucius?"

"Persuaded, I'd call it," he smirked. "He's a very good friend of mine, young Tullius. A keen theatre-goer, never misses a performance. I introduce him to all the visiting actors, and they make a great fuss of him. In return for which…." He mimed tearing up a scroll, and sat back, looking for my reaction.

His words made me realise just how much I'd been counting on my brother's help coming sooner or later. But if Lucius hadn't had my letters, he might not realise how dangerously urgent our plight was. Disappointment crept around me like a cold fog. Desperately I tried to fight it off, to think of something bright and witty to say.

There was a rap on the rock wall behind me, and a slight breeze as the heavy red curtain was pushed aside. Vitalis strode in, excited and triumphant.

"Father, I've done it. Antonius is willing to talk."

"Excellent!" Felix said. "And almost disappointingly easy! I rather thought he'd give you more trouble than this. Bring him in, and let's hear what he has to say."

I felt numb with horror. To have Quintus tortured into revealing his secrets was bad enough; to be forced to watch it would be unbearable. Felix saw my expression and said, "Aurelia will enjoy the spectacle, I'm sure."

Vitalis shook his head. "He won't say anything in front of her. He wants to talk just to you, with nobody else there. Don't ask me why. He says if you come to the lower cave now, he'll spill the whole bag of beans."

I kept still, but it was an effort. Bag of *beans?* Quintus' password! It meant there was some hidden meaning to his message. But what was he trying to tell me? That he wasn't going to betray any secrets—or maybe just a few unimportant ones? I needed more information. I'd try to stir the pot a little.

"I'm not surprised he won't talk in my presence," I exclaimed. "He wouldn't get a word in because of all the abuse I'd be hurling at him! The lousy, cowardly…."

"He doesn't like you much either," Vitalis interrupted, grinning. "His exact words were, 'I'm not saying anything in front of that hard-hearted harpy. She can rot in her cave, for all I care.'"

I contented myself with an expression I'd learned from Father, though he'd have been shocked to hear me use it. But my heart was singing inside me. I'd got the message.

"So sad," Felix said, standing up, "when two young lovers fall out." Father and son left, laughing.

I jumped up, disregarding the pain in my ankle. Quintus was recalling the Harpy's Cave tavern in Pompeii, the one with the secret exit at the back. He must be telling me there was a hidden way out of the Shadow-men's lair. And he'd arranged matters so I'd be alone, with perhaps enough time to escape by the concealed exit. If I could find it....

There was only one place to look. Another cave led from this one; Felix had emerged from there when we first came in. Its entrance was dark, but as I entered I saw there were a couple of lamps on a table. This smaller cave appeared to be a more intimate version of the outer one. There were woven wall-rugs, and a bearskin on the floor, and it was furnished with a sleeping-couch and a couple of stools. And in one corner, surprise, surprise, was Felix's statue of Apollo, which had not, after all, been smashed to bits by the Shadow-men. So he'd fooled us yet again. We had never seen the remains of the Apollo, and never even thought to ask about them. I only wished I'd time to smash the thing up now.

I turned to examine the walls. Two of Felix's colourful Roman tunics were hanging up against one of them, and next to them there hung—holy Diana, a skull!

I stopped myself crying out, and told myself sternly not to be so foolish. It was the Shadow of Death's skull mask. It wasn't bone, but made of wood and plaster, and it would be a choice piece of evidence, if I ever escaped—no, *when* I escaped. I took it down from the wall, and looped its cord through my belt.

Though the light was dim, I could see clearly enough that there wasn't another doorway leading from this sleeping-cave. So if there was a way out, it had to be from here. Felix, like the cunning fox he was, must have made an escape route from his private quarters. But where?

I began to prowl round the walls, moving the heavy rugs, vainly searching for anything that could be a door, however small. Perhaps there was just a crack in the rock, indicating a false wall of some kind? I went and fetched a lamp and began to examine the surface carefully. If there was a way out, it must be a tunnel that led upwards to the hillside somewhere, and quite steeply too. So I must look up—to the tops of the walls, even to the ceiling.

I raised the lamp above my head; the ceiling was so low I could almost touch it, and it was uneven and marked, like most rough rock. But it was hard to see details. The wretched light was so small, and the stupid thing kept flickering....

Flickering? Yes, *flickering!*

There was a breeze making the flame flicker. A draught of air. It was blowing from the doorway, but—where was it blowing to? There were no more caves. The air must be escaping through an opening in the rock.

I licked two fingers of my left hand and held them up, feeling the slight but definite current of air. I followed it to the far wall, where the breeze was strongest, and pulled aside the heavy wall-hanging, raising the lamp high.

There was a vertical crack, running from the rock ceiling about two feet down the wall. It wasn't a wide crack but it was dead straight—much too straight to be natural. It must indicate an artificial bit of walling.

I could reach it with my finger-tips, but I needed more height. I ran and fetched a stool, and by standing on it I could easily touch the wall, and I began tapping at the rock. To the left of the crack it was depressingly solid, but—yes, there! The section to the right echoed with a hollow wooden sound.

I'd found it!

I pushed at the hollow wall, but nothing happened. I got a fingernail under the crack and pulled; slowly a whole section started moving towards me, like a door on a hinge, swinging outwards and almost knocking me off the stool. I felt a cold blast of air streaming in from a sizeable hole, and making the lamp flicker more than ever.

A rocky tunnel, big enough to crawl through, sloped steeply upwards. It was jet-black inside; no light at all penetrated from the open hillside above—if indeed that was where the tunnel led. Perhaps the other end was blocked by a rock, or a mound of earth? But no, if this was Felix's private exit, it must be ready for use at any time, so it couldn't be hard to get out of it at the far end. Well, I'd soon know.

I needed both hands to scramble into the opening, so reluctantly I put down the lamp, and hoisted myself up into the tunnel mouth. I hesitated a few heartbeats, suddenly frightened at the thought of crawling blindly into the pitch blackness. And then I heard a noise from the outer cave; it sounded like a shout. Oh gods, was it Quintus? Had they realised already that he wasn't going to be such an easy victim? What were they doing to him?

I thought: he's taken an enormous risk for me. I shan't waste it. And I began pulling myself through the tunnel, crawling upwards on hands and knees. The rock floor scraped my skin, but at least it wasn't slippery. The angle of the ascent steepened, and the tunnel twisted to the left, so now there was no light showing from below. I went slowly, blindly feeling the way ahead. But that cool wind was still blowing in my face, and I clung to the thought that if I kept going, I must reach the outside.

I stopped to listen. There was no sound at all now. Good. I started off again, and caught my knee on a point of rock, and realised the stabbing pain in my ankle was there in full force. I'd managed to ignore it while I was searching for the escape tunnel, but now it was excruciating. I crawled on, using both hands and only one knee, dragging the other leg uselessly behind me. But I kept moving. That was all I could do; keep moving.

And then I saw a faint glimmer of light above. The merest dim spot, but it was enough. Simultaneously there was a noise behind me. Not a voice this time; a scraping, scuffling sound—I felt it through the rock, as well as hearing it. Holy Diana! Someone else was climbing up this tunnel, presumably one of Felix's men pursuing me. And was another Shadow-man even now racing up the hill to block the exit?

I put on a last desperate spurt of speed. The light patch took shape as a roundish hole, silver-grey in colour, with some kind of tracery across it. Branches? Tree-roots? As I fought my way up to it, I realised it was only a few twigs, presumably put there for camouflage. I pushed through them, and was out.

I breathed in great gasps of the wonderful fresh air. I felt heavy rain cold on my skin as I hauled my body and my agonising leg into the open, and away from the tunnel. I was on a steep slope, in a patch of scrubby trees and undergrowth. With a final effort, I dragged myself to the nearest bush, and crawled under it, panting and utterly exhausted. I felt dizzy, and the ground swam; I was in danger of passing out, but with an effort of will I fought off the waves of darkness at the edges of my mind.

There was a scrambling sound at the tunnel mouth, and a shape emerged, a figure with fair hair and a purple cloak. The Shadow of Death! After all, I hadn't escaped him. But there was nothing more I could do about it: I was spent. If I keep still, I thought, maybe he won't see me. I held my breath and lay like a statue.

He stood up and glanced quickly around him, tilting his head as if listening to some sound. Then, to my amazement, he turned and ran down the hill, and disappeared among the trees. I couldn't believe my luck. Again the world spun round me, and this time it overwhelmed me, and everything went dark. As I slipped into blackness, I thought I heard a familiar voice calling my name.

Chapter XXXII

And now there are only a few more lines to add to my report. You'll probably pare it down to the bare bones before you pass it on to the Governor, but I hope you don't cut too much out. If you discard all the detail, he'll never understand properly how we were so completely deceived, or why the whole Campaign of Terror was so frightening.

I'm just glad it's all over. When I think back to that terrifying time in the Shadow of Death's cave, not even a month ago, it already feels remote. Soon it will seem as if it happened to somebody else, and I shall be free of the horror of it.

When I came back to a shaky consciousness, I didn't know where I was. I lay in a sort of dark cave, lit by a smoky fire, and I could hear sounds of men moving about. Then memory began to trickle back, and with it a cold dread. I was a captive. So was Quintus. We were prisoners of the Shadow of Death....

And then a voice close beside me exclaimed, "Aurelia! Thank the gods, you're awake!"

I knew that voice. It was Lucius.

Gradually, joyfully, I realised we were safe, and I began to piece together what had happened. Hawk had brought Lucius and his troop, and a contingent from the Oak Tree, to the house in the rock, and they'd simply stormed their way in. They'd killed Vitalis and Segovax and the few natives inside the caves, but most of the warriors were still out in the woods searching for Hawk, and these were being rounded up now. The rescue had come in time to save Quintus from serious injury; he'd had a severe beating, and they'd broken several ribs and two of his fingers. But he hadn't talked, and it could have been so much worse.

I remember lying beside him by the fire in the large outer room, both of us waiting till Lucius could organise stretchers to take us home. "I suppose one day I'll get the chance to see you without a lot of bumps and bruises," I said.

"If you wait long enough," he grinned, rather lop-sidedly because his lip was cut.

"I'll wait." I went to take his hand, remembered his injured fingers, and just touched his cheek instead. "You were brilliant, passing me that message. How did you know Felix had his own private exit?"

"After they first dragged us in here, I heard some of the warriors talking. About not daring to tell the Shadow of Death that Hawk had escaped. I think you were asleep...."

"I was, part of the time. I do remember bits of conversation, but nothing about a hidden way out."

"I heard someone say, 'Everyone is out searching. It leaves the tunnel unprotected, but it won't be for long.'"

"So you added two and two together. You took a horrible risk. I think it qualifies as the stupidest risk I've ever seen in my whole life."

He smiled. "I think you're right."

I managed to lean close enough to kiss him, and then Lucius bustled over, his green eyes gleaming. "All right now, break it up, you two!" He looked from one to the other of us. "You're a real pair of old wrecks! I'm afraid that's what you get for trying to take on the enemy all by yourselves."

He crouched down and held out a hand to each of us. "Good work, Sis. You too, Quintus. Thank you both! But you certainly like living dangerously."

"We didn't have much choice," I smiled back. "The cavalry turned up so late they almost missed the battle. Typical, of course, but...."

"There's gratitude! Quintus, don't let this sister of mine bully you the way she bullies me." He was suddenly serious. "You've done well. Both of you. I'll make sure the Governor gets to hear about it."

The others came crowding round, Secundus, Titch, and Taurus, who knelt down beside us, his face full of concern.

"Are you both all right?" he asked.

"Yes, we're both all right, Taurus," I assured him. "Or we will be, once we get home."

"Good. Now we've put an end to those bad men, home will be safe again." And for once I didn't feel like mocking his statement of the obvious. His few words were the best summing-up of all.

Secundus and Titch interrupted each other as they told how they'd managed to overpower the bogus legionaries, by creating a diversion, "just like the great Julius would have done...." They'd started a fire in one of the store-rooms and pretended it was out of control. They killed all seven guards, and had just armed everyone to set out and look for us, when Hawk appeared with the news that we'd been caught. As they were about to go with him to rescue us, Lucius and a troop of cavalry galloped down our track. At first Secundus thought this was yet another enemy trick and there was a nasty stand-off; but then Albia came out to see what all the noise was about, and ran straight into Lucius' arms to welcome him home.

Hawk stood aloof, silent amid all the chatter, and after a while I got up and hobbled my way over to him. "Thank you, Hawk. You've saved our lives. We won't forget this."

"I'm glad we were in time." He sighed. "But the Shadow of Death got away. So for me it's not over yet."

"Got away? But...oh yes, of course! I saw him come out of the tunnel. He had his escape route well planned."

"Oh, he was clever. But one thing about tracking, it teaches you patience. Every man leaves tracks, even clever men. And Felix's tracks will lead me to him in the end."

The Shadow of Death is the only one still at large, as you know. Despite a lot of searching, he has escaped us, the only blot on an otherwise shining papyrus. All the other Shadow-men, plus several Druids, were captured in the next few days; as convicted criminals they'll go to the arena. Whether they're devoured by wild animals, or nailed up on crosses to die, they'll deserve what they get.

Quintus and Lucius are confident they've destroyed the rebellion, despite Felix's escape. The Shadow-men were at the core of the revolt, and their destruction has knocked the heart out of other would-be rebels. This part of Brigantia will soon be safe and peaceful again. Perhaps I should say "is," not "will be," because the killings have stopped; but there's a lingering feeling of fear, and we Romans still take bodyguards with us when we travel the roads, and continue to guard our doors at nights. It'll be a month or two, or even a year or two, before we can put those habits aside.

Yesterday we held a large dinner at the Oak Tree, to celebrate our birthdays, and also to thank all the friends who'd helped us. We made it a truly spectacular affair. As our grandmother would have said, if you're pushing a boat out, make sure it's a huge quinquereme with a golden sail. Cook did us proud: the centrepiece of the meal was an enormous arrangement of geese, ducks, and swans on a blue board representing a lake—it took four slaves to carry it in. There were oysters, various sorts of sea-fish, wild sucking pig, and venison, with a host of summer vegetables and some delicious marinated asparagus; and finally peaches in wine, honey cakes, and apples with ginger, figs and grapes, and five kinds of cheese. And the wine was the best, Gaulish red and Campanian white. We hired in some entertainers from Eburacum too—musicians, dancers, and a fire-eater. It was quite a party, and it went on till nearly dawn.

Silvanius came to our celebration, bearing up well despite being clearly heartbroken over Felix's treachery and Vitalis' death. He told anybody who would listen how the Shadow of Death had led astray his "poor dear boy." If this cockeyed view of events comforts him, I suppose it can't do any harm now. He made a speech, only a short one, thank the gods, including a call for Romans to stand together; even betrayal by a close Roman friend could not shake Clarus' loyalty to the Empire. And to my delight, he presented us with a beautiful bronze statue of a horse, for our garden. "From the Oak Bridges Town Council," he declared, "as a token of our gratitude for your help in our time of trouble."

Balbus and Ennia were there too, and they've re-furbished and re-opened their shop. "The gods have given me justice," Balbus told me, "with the death of young Marius. And there's still a good living to be made in Brigantia."

"Besides," Ennia added gently, "we like it here. It's where our friends are."

Saturninus came along, newly appointed as aedile in succession to his father. Indeed most of the town council were there; I won't bore you with the names. And all their ladies too; but I won't bore you with the hairstyles.

Lucius and Quintus were the heroes of the night, and Secundus and his friends shared in the glory; Titch was allowed to join the party, on the one condition that he didn't utter the name of Julius Caesar throughout the celebration. I think he managed it, and the high spot for him was when Quintus presented him with a new bugle, engraved with his name.

And now I just want to get back to normal life, running a peaceful and efficient mansio. The future for the Oak Tree looks good. Lucius is taking some leave, so he'll be at home for another month or so. Uncle Titus is apparently very pleased with us all. He wrote a personal note to me and Albia, thanking us for our help, and promising to lend us some army builders next month, to repair the damage that the property has suffered, "and undertake any other necessary building work." Brilliant—with their help, we can rebuild the stable block in stone.

And the future for Quintus and me? Good too, I think; interesting, certainly. My life will never be boring while he's a part of it. How long he *will* be a part of it…well, who knows? Neither of us do, so we'll take things as they come. He'll stay with us for a while on leave, and he and I will have a proper chance to get to know each other, if one can ever really know a spy. I'll just have to try my best, and see how it goes.

But if that's any business of the Governor's, then I'm the Queen of Brigantia.

About the History

Looking at life in Roman Britannia is like standing in the dark outside a large house (a villa perhaps?) and trying to peer in through the windows to examine the many rooms inside. Some rooms are brightly lighted, some tantalisingly dim, and others completely black. So parts of the house are plainly visible in great detail, but not all, and the lighted rooms are scattered, not adjacent.

Similarly, we know only certain aspects of the history of Britannia in real depth. Our knowledge is growing all the time, but can never be complete. This is a pain or a challenge, depending on your standpoint. To me, a writer who cares about historical truth, it is both.

Nowadays we tend to think of Roman Britain as rich and fairly peaceful throughout its four centuries of history, judging it by the impressive remains at Bath, perhaps, or on Hadrian's wall. But in the first century AD it was a new province, frontier country, still not wholly pacified even by the 90s. That is especially true of the northern areas, like the old kingdom of Brigantia, where this book is set. While the conquest was going on, and for some years after it, life was much less settled and prosperous than it became later.

Aurelia, in 91 AD, would have known a good road system—indeed her livelihood at the mansio depended on it—and some towns, often rough but growing fast; and the first villas were being built in the countryside. But as an early settler in the province, she would have felt very much like colonists in any new outpost of Empire feel, by turns optimistic and insecure, but always determined to make a success of things. The Romans, like empire-builders through the ages, thought they had an absolute right to colonise wherever they chose, and were certain they were benefiting the peoples they conquered.

The natives they found in Britannia were Celts, but they did not think of themselves in any way as a single Celtic nation. They were divided into tribes, each with its own rulers and territory. Tribal attitudes to the Romans ranged from admiration to hatred. Aurelia would have encountered both, because the Oak Tree lies in the borderland territory between the Brigantes to the west, who were mainly anti-Roman, and the Parisi to the east, who welcomed the new conquerors. Tribal boundaries were vague and shifting even before the Romans came, but tribal identities were not wiped out by the conquest.

The geography of the book's setting is real. So were, and are, most of the places in it. Eburacum, in 91 AD a new but growing military town, is modern York—and Eburacum is how it was spelt at this date; the more familiar Eboracum came later. Derventio is modern Malton, though some historians are now associating the name with Stamford Bridge as well, or instead—an example of how difficult it is to see some aspects of the period clearly. I have stayed faithful to Malton.

The Oak Tree mansio is fictitious, but I have placed it at a real location—at the bottom of what we now call Garrowby Hill, on a road originally built by the Romans, which is still an important main road two thousand years later. The native town of Oak Bridges is fictitious too, but it is in an area that was well settled by Celts and Romans, from Italy and from other parts of the Empire.

I have taken the liberty of speculating about what went on behind some of those darkened windows of history, and my setting and characters are as real as my research and imagination can make them.